LAD IN THE
NEVER-NEVER LAND

Rosa Praed was born in Queensland in 1851 and lived on Curtis Island until 1876 when she and her husband settled in England. In a prolific career spanning the late nineteenth and early twentieth centuries, she published some fifty novels and stories. Writing in 1881, in her Preface to *Policy and Passion: A Novel of Australian Life*, she stated that only when Australia had become an independent nation and had 'formulated a social and political system adapted to the conditions of her development and growth' would the country 'possess a literature of her own as powerful and as original as might be prognosticated. But,' she added, 'the time for this is hardly yet ripe.'

Two of Rosa Praed's novels are currently available in Pandora as part of the Australian Women Writers: The Literary Heritage series: *The Bond of Wedlock* (1887), an example of her early work, and *Lady Bridget in the Never-Never Land* (1915) from a later phase in her career. *Outlaw and Lawmaker* (1893) will be published in Autumn 1987.

Pam Gilbert is a lecturer in education at James Cook University in Queensland. She has a particular interest in women's literature, and in the educational role of such literature within schools and universities. Her articles have appeared in various education journals in Australia.

PANDORA

AUSTRALIAN WOMEN WRITERS:
THE LITERARY HERITAGE

AUSTRALIAN WOMEN WRITERS
The Literary Heritage

General Editor: Dale Spender
Consultant: Elizabeth Webby

Pandora is reprinting a selection of nineteenth- and early twentieth-century novels written by Australian women. To accompany these finds from Australia's literary heritage there will be three brand-new non-fiction works, surveying Australian women writers past and present, including a handy bibliographical guide to fill in the background to the novels and their authors.

The first four novels in the series are:

A Marked Man: Some Episodes in His Life (1891) by Ada Cambridge
Introduced by Debra Adelaide

The Bond of Wedlock (1887) by Rosa Praed
Introduced by Lynne Spender

Lady Bridget in the Never-Never Land (1915) by Rosa Praed
Introduced by Pam Gilbert

The Incredible Journey (1923) by Catherine Martin
Introduced by Margaret Allen

And forthcoming in Autumn 1987:

Uncle Piper of Piper's Hill (1889) by Tasma

Outlaw and Lawmaker (1893) by Rosa Praed

An Australian Girl (1894) by Catherine Martin

Three companion books to this exciting new series will be published in 1987 and 1988:

Australian Women Writers: The First Two Hundred Years
by Dale Spender

A lively and provocative overview history of the literary scene and the position of women writers in Australia which shows that any image of the country as a cultural desert was not based on the achievement of Barbara Baynton, Ada Cambridge, Dymphna Cusack, Eleanor Dark, Katharine Susannah Prichard, Christina Stead and the many other women who have enjoyed tremendous international success.

Australian Women Writers: The Contemporary Scene
by Pam Gilbert

There are a number of outstanding contemporary women writers about whom relatively little is known. This book fills that gap with a comprehensive discussion of the work of Jean Bedford, Blanche d'Alpuget, Helen Garner, Beverley Farmer, Elizabeth Jolley, Olga Masters, Fay Zwicky, Patricia Wrightson and Jessica Anderson.

Australian Women Writers: A Bibliographical Guide
by Debra Adelaide

Covering over 200 Australian women writers, this invaluable sourcebook outlines their lives and works and puts rare manuscript collections throughout Australia on the literary map for the first time. A comprehensive guide to the articles and books written about these women is also included.

LADY BRIDGET
IN THE NEVER-NEVER LAND

A STORY OF AUSTRALIAN LIFE

ROSA PRAED

Introduced by Pam Gilbert

PANDORA

London, Sydney and New York

This edition first published in 1987
by Pandora Press
(Routledge & Kegan Paul Ltd)
11 New Fetter Lane, London EC4P 4EE

Publiished in Australia by
Routledge & Kegan Paul
c/o Methuen Law Book Co.
44 Waterloo Road, North Ryde, NSW 2113

Published in the USA by
Routledge & Kegan Paul Inc.
in association with Methuen Inc.
29 West 35th St, New York, NY 10001

Set in Ehrhardt 9 on 11$\frac{1}{2}$pt
by Columns of Reading
and printed in the British Isles
by The Guernsey Press Co. Ltd.
Guernsey, Channel Islands

British Library Cataloguing in Publication Data

Praed, Rosa
Lady Bridget in the Never-Never Land: a
story of Australian life.—(Australian
women writers)
I. Title II. Series
823[F] PR9619.2.P7

ISBN 0-86358-129-3

CONTENTS

———•———

INTRODUCTION

───────────●───────────

I must admit that I was at first intrigued by the name of this novel. A Lady Bridget? In the Never-Never Land? And the novel didn't disappoint me. It is a quite remarkable narrative, managing, on the one hand, to tell an interesting story of a woman's battle to build a positive and equal relationship with a man, whilst on the other, tackling what were, at the time, relatively controversial social issues such as marriage and the rights of women, unionisation of labour and the treatment of blacks in colonial Australia. To my delight, the novel's chief protagonists are women. Women who think, argue, make decisions for themselves, value independence and acquire it. The novel was first published in 1915, and whilst this predisposes its readers to expect a certain kind of narrative, it also predisposes us to expect a certain kind of feminine heroine. But Rosa Praed surprises us. Her female characters are an unusual group who challenge stereotypes at every turn.

The narrative's main strand is as the title suggests: the story of Lady Bridget O'Hara (an impulsive, intelligent, Irish aristocrat, who has a social conscience but little money) in the Never-Never Land (the western section of Leichhardt's Land – or Queensland, northern Australia). The Never-Never Land was originally the home of tribal Aboriginal people who had been disenfranchised by rifle-wielding whites, and had gained its name from the uncompromising nature of its climate and geography. Drought was common, but not predictable; communication with larger white settlements was difficult and hazardous; Aboriginal people had, in the past, waged successful guerilla attacks on their white enemies. Whilst there was always the chance of making good money from a few successful years in a row, or from a lucky mineral strike, the overwhelming isolation, uncertainty and unpleasantness of climate made life in the Never-Never Land very hard to tolerate. It was especially difficult for women, who were usually left behind at the head stations to care for the children, the vegetable gardens and the domestic animals, whilst the men were away working with the cattle or the runs. The loneliness, heat, fear, physical discomfort and sheer drudgery of such lives does not bear thinking on.

However, into this unlikely scenario comes Lady Bridget O'Hara, a woman approaching thirty, who is disenchanted with her current life, and keen for new experiences, particularly new men. She arrives in Leichhardt's Town – the coastal city capital of Leichardt's Land – hoping that in this new land she might find romantic adventure and 'savage freedom', and escape the restrictions of London society. She meets Colin McKeith, a tough Never-Never Land bushman who dreams of becoming an Empire-maker, Rhodes-style, and convinces herself that he represents the excitement that will give her life purpose. She seduces him, marries him and heads off to make a life with him on his property, Moongarr Station, in the upper reaches of the Leura River – the heart of the Never-Never Land. Fortunately, however, Rosa Praed refuses to succumb to a happy-ever-after romance in the Never-Never and instead we watch, with increasing dismay, the almost inevitable collapse of the O'Hara-McKeith union. Praed makes it obvious that her characters have to make a full journey through the trials of the Never-Never before she will bless their marriage.

Praed chooses to tell her story in three sections – each section or book being from the viewpoint of one of the major characters. It's an interesting technique, allowing her the option of giving her readers a much clearer understanding of why the characters act as they do. In the first section, the practical, sensible Joan Gildea – a journalist who is obviously happy and contented to live a life devoted to her career – introduces us to Leichhardt's Town and some of its people. Joan knows Bridget O'Hara and Colin McKeith, so when Bridget arrives in Leichhardt's Town with her old friends Sir Luke and Lady Rosamond Tallant (the new Governor and his wife), it is inevitable that Colin and Bridget will meet and that Joan's home will become the scene of their courtship. Joan tries in vain to make each see the dangers of a serious relationship between an Irish aristocrat and a Never-Never Land bushman. Her wise and careful counsel is ignored as the couple move closer and closer towards each other and the danger and excitement that they realise their relationship proposes. Significantly, the engagement occurs after Joan's departure on a commission to the south. Joan warns Biddie of the Never-Never Land struggles, of McKeith's intractability, of the extraordinary social changes that such a marriage would necessitate. And she warns Colin of Biddie's unsuitability for bushland living, of her tempestuousness and impetuosity, of her lack of understanding of bush poverty and loneliness. But the couple refuse counsel. Book One ends with the official announcement of the McKeith-O'Hara engagement, and with Joan Gildea's fears for the success of such a reckless venture.

The second book is purportedly Biddie O'Hara's view of the first year or so of her marriage, and of life in the Never-Never. All of Joan Gildea's prophecies come true of course. The Never-Never Land moves impassively towards severe drought, and as Moongarr faces serious threats, so too do Colin and Bridget. McKeith's stubborn arrogance sets the unions against him and they kill his bullocks and fire his paddocks, and Bridget's stubborn arrogance isolates her from the only other woman on Moongarr, and from any chance of female companionship. To complicate matters further, a former lover of Bridget's travels from Britain to Moongarr in an attempt to lure her back to civilisation. The marriage as well as Moongarr faces a serious drought. The couple fail to find common and comfortable ground to tread together, and an issue that they had long disagreed upon – the treatment of blacks in the Never-Never – re-emerges and causes a serious rift.

When McKeith is absent, Bridget insists on offering refuge to a fugitive black couple – Wombo and Oola – although she knows that McKeith refuses to allow blacks at Moongarr. McKeith returns and, in anger, whips Wombo off the property. Bridget is shocked at this cruelty and denial of her rights on Moongarr, and her indignation is fuelled by her visiting lover (Willoughby Maule), who shares her abhorrence of McKeith's actions, and pleads with her to leave Moongarr with him. Book Two ends with Bridget's rejection of McKeith's entreaties to her as his 'mate' but with her indecision about her future in the Never-Never.

Book Three is told 'from the point of view of Colin McKeith and others'. McKeith is consumed with jealousy after his wife's rejection of him and her continued interest in Maule, and after another incident involving the fugitive black couple of Book Two, he accepts information he hears from others that Bridget has been unfaithful to him, and assumes that she no longer wishes to be his wife. He believes he has failed to make her love him, and so encourages her to leave Moongarr. Bridget has, in the interim, received a telegram advising her she has inherited £50,000 from her Irish aunt, so she agrees to return to Ireland to sort out difficulties about the inheritance. The couple part – both unwilling to leave each other, but too proud to speak to each other and discover the truth about the incidents of the past months. The drought refuses to break, and McKeith has lost his best pastures through union firings. Moongarr is destroyed, as is the marriage. McKeith negotiates an 'honorable divorce' for Bridget, and all hope of recovery and reconciliation seems lost, until at the end of the novel McKeith learns of a potential gold discovery that could rescue him financially, and Bridget returns to Moongarr, apparently at peace with herself and her needs, and willing to negotiate the terms of a new and different marriage with Colin.

Whilst the narrative is very rich and full, undoubtedly the key issue in the novel is the way in which Bridget O'Hara and Colin McKeith struggle to reconcile ideals with reality: to build a relationship that restricts neither, and to make a good life together in the dreaded Never-Never. McKeith has a vision – of an aristocratic soul 'mate' who will share his spiritual passion for Nature and face all odds with a high-minded high-spirited dignity. A 'thoroughbred': a woman who will face up to the adversities of the Never-Never unflinchingly. The tempestuous Lady Bridget totally captivates him even before he meets her, and seems the answer to a dream. She has it all – blood, breeding, tradition and fiery independence. The Lady Bridget is herself looking for a man, although the term 'mate' is unfamiliar to her. She needs a man who will provide her with an escape from the aftermath of an unhappy romance, offer her protection from a society that would see her wed, and suggest the promise of a dangerous and exciting adventure to add zest to a rather dismal future. Bridget will not be tempted by offers of employment by women – she rejects Joan's offer to work on a book of illustrations and Rosamond's plea for assistance at Government House. She seeks a man for her future.

She seems fascinated by Colin McKeith's rawness and masculinity, his strength and size, his arrogance and determination, and his links with the romantic Never-Never. In a spur of the moment decision, she accepts his offer of marriage in a desperate bid to at last add meaning, challenge and excitement to her life. The couple share one idyllic marriage night of love under the stars in the pre-drought Never-Never, but from then on the relationship seems to become increasingly estranged. Praed describes the bride of a year and a quarter as 'a restless soul' who peered out through 'hungry eyes' (p. 142). Intellectual tensions between man and woman remained unresolved. Bridget had never agreed with Colin's harsh treatment of the blacks, or his arrogant rejection of unionised labour. Whilst he had assumed that Bridget would either accept his 'reality' once they were in the Never-Never, or his authority to determine such reality, he was mistaken. Bridget's refusal to forsake intellectual and emotional independence can only be admired. Her stand on the Wombo-Oola issue was a clear indication that the partnership with McKeith was to be on terms that she could find acceptable. She would not compromise herself.

When Bridget returns to the almost destroyed Moongarr at the end of the novel, she comes as an independent woman. She is now financially independent, thanks to her aunt's inheritance, and no longer needs a husband to provide for her or make settlements upon her. She is also emotionally independent, having had, and rejected, the opportunity to live with Willoughby Maule. This new woman can truly offer herself as a 'mate' to Colin McKeith, because for the first time she can stand beside him on equal terms.

Whilst this love affair dominates the novel, Praed quite clearly chooses to offer us more in *Lady Bridget in the Never-Never Land*. The questions of marriage and of the rights and expectations of women pervade the novel. Bridget tells McKeith that she doesn't like marriage – 'our system of marriage – a bargain in the sale shop. So much at such a price – birth, position, suitability, good looks – to be paid for at the market value,' (p. 88). And McKeith agrees. He, too, wants something else – the bush idea of a real mate, 'only closer, dearer – a thing you couldn't talk about even to your mate – unless your mate was your wife – a flower that blooms once in your life . . .' (p. 89) appeals to him. The couple's struggle to develop a marriage that values 'mateship' and rejects 'bargaining in the sale shop' dominates the novel. Praed stands firm on a woman's expectations of 'equality' in a marriage, tentatively resorting to the male term 'mateship' to develop her theme.

However, other women in the novel are shown to have eminently satisfying lives alone, without a 'mate'. Joan Gildea is an exceptionally interesting woman. Highly organised, efficient, productive and independent, Joan was *The Imperialist*'s Special Correspondent in Australia. Praed describes her at the outset as a widow and working journalist, 'shorn of most of her early illusions', and has Joan claim that she achieved independence through drudgery and being 'brought up with practical people' (p. 56)! The other widow in the story – Florrie Hensor, on Moongarr station – shows a similar strength. She works hard to make a life for herself and her young son in the unyielding Never-Never, and shows an impressive resilience and independence. Rosamond Tallant is also a clear-headed, intelligent woman, taking her role as the Governor's wife very seriously and properly, but showing a delightful sense of humour when with her friends. Even the unfortunate Oola shows courage and strength in Book Three when she manages to free Wombo from the police. In fact, rather than being secondary characters in the novel, the women are its chief protagonists. Whilst the focus is on Lady Bridget, the other female characters adequately underline the theme of female emancipation and independence.

Praed's attitude towards treatment of the blacks is less ambiguously presented than is her attitude towards other political issues. Lady Bridget becomes the 'radical' in the novel – the champion of the oppressed – and whilst she calls herself a socialist ('Why, I've always been a Socialist – in theory, you know. I've always rebelled against the established order of things.' (p. 49)), her political position is obviously half-hearted. Her socialist venture in London is treated by Joan as just another new craze in a life full of crazes, and Biddie's own actions are seldom political. She cares about the blacks and about Britain's poor record in dealing with other oppressed people, but is perfectly happy to 'play the lady' and treat poor whites arrogantly. Lady Bridget's attitudes to the unionisation of labour are assumed, but not stated, and Praed lets McKeith develop a case against union organisers, and supports it by obviously biased portraits of the unionists in the upper Leura. They are 'loafers at the bar', 'discontented bush rowdies', with 'narrow-lidded eyes', 'scowling foreheads' and 'sinister, foxy eyes' . . .! It seems as if support for the blacks is understandable, even admirable (in a woman of sensitivity such as Lady Bridget), but that the hard-headed Colin McKeith has every reason to be tough and uncompromising not only to the blacks, but to unionists who threaten the squatter's autocracy.

So, whilst *Lady Bridget in the Never-Never Land* will not be remembered as a left-wing tract, it does raise political questions of the day, and certainly gives colonial racism a decent hearing. Its implicit statements about women are probably its most significant feature, and it is for these – as well as for the rather good narrative it implants them in – that the novel is well worth reading. The adventures of Lady Bridget in the early twentieth-century Australian outback make for a very good read. The romantic story is interesting and unusual – the setting exciting and novel – and the characters larger than life in their passionate display of pride, determination and courage. It's good to have the past so vividly recreated for us – and it's wonderful to see some women to admire leading the field.

Pam Gilbert

BOOK I

From the Point of View of Mrs Gildea

CHAPTER 1

Mrs Gildea had settled early to her morning's work in what she called the veranda-study of her cottage in Leichardt's Town. It was a primitive cottage of the old style, standing in a garden and built on the cliff – the Emu Point side – overlooking the broad Leichardt River. The veranda, quite twelve feet wide, ran – Australian fashion – along the front of the cottage, except for the two closed-in ends forming, one a bathroom and the other a kind of store closet. Being raised a few feet above the ground, the veranda was enclosed by a wooden railing, and this and the supporting posts were twined with creepers that must have been planted at least thirty years. One of these, a stephanotis, showed masses of white bloom, which Joan Gildea casually reflected would have fetched a pretty sum in Covent Garden, and, joining in with a fine-growing asparagus fern, formed an arch over the entrance steps. The end of the veranda, where Mrs Gildea had established herself with her type-writer and paraphernalia of literary work, was screened by a thick-stemmed grape-vine, which made a dapple of shadow and sunshine upon the boarded floor. Some bunches of late grapes – it was the very beginning of March – hung upon the vine, and, at the other end of the veranda, grew a passion creeper, its great purple fruit looking like huge plums amidst its vivid green leaves.

The roof of the veranda was low, with projecting eaves, below which a bunch of yellowing bananas hung to ripen. In fact, the veranda and garden beyond would have been paradise to a fruitarian. Against the wall of the store-room, stood a large tin dish piled with melons, pine-apples and miscellaneous garden produce, while, between the veranda posts, could be seen a guava-tree, an elderly fig and a loquat all in full bearing. The garden seemed a tangle of all manner of vegetation – an oleander in bloom, a poinsettia, a yucca, lifting its spike of waxen white blossoms, a narrow flower-border in which the gardenias had become tall shrubs and the scented verbena shrubs almost trees. As for the blend of perfume, it was dreamily intoxicating. Two bamboos, guarding the side entrance gate, made a soft whispering that heightened the dream-sense. The bottom of the garden looked an inchoate mass of greenery topped by the upper boughs of tall straggling gum trees, growing outside where the ground fell gradually to the river.

From where Mrs Gildea sat, she had a view of almost the whole reach of the river where it circles Emu Point. For, as is known to all who know Leichardt's Town, the river winds in two great loops girdling two low points, so that, in striking a bee-line across the whole town, business and residential, one must cross the river three times. Mrs Gildea could see the plan of the main street in the Middle Point and the roofs of shops and offices. The busy wharves of the Leichardt's Land Steam Navigation Company – familiarly, the L.L.S.N. Co. – lay opposite on her right, while leftward, across the water, she could trace, as far as the grape-vine would allow, the boundary of the Botanical Gardens and get a sight of the white stone and grey slate end of the big Parliamentary Buildings.

The heat-haze over the town and the brilliant sun-sparkles on the river suggested a cruel glare outside the shady veranda and over-grown old garden.

A pleasant study, if a bit distracting from its plenitude of associations to Australian-born Joan Gildea, who, on her marriage, had been transplanted into English soil, as care-free as a rose cut from the parent stem, and who now, after nearly twenty years, had returned to the scene of her youth – a widow, a working journalist and shorn of most of her early illusions.

Her typewriter stood on a bamboo table before her. A pile of Australian Hansards for reference sat on a chair at convenient distance. A large table with a green cloth, at her elbow, had at one end a tray with the remains of her breakfast of tea, scones and fruit. The end nearest her was littered with sheaves of manuscript, newspaper-cuttings, photographs and sepia sketches – obviously for purposes of illustration: gum-bottle, stylographs and the rest, with, also, several note-books held open by bananas, recently plucked from the ripening bunch, to serve as paper-weights.

She had meant to be very busy that morning. There was her weekly letter for *The Imperialist* to send off by to-morrow's mail, and, moreover, she had to digest the reasons of that eminent journal for returning to her an article that had not met with the editor's approval – the great Gibbs: a potent newspaper-factor in the British policy of the day.

It had been an immense honour when Mr Gibbs had chosen Joan Gildea from amongst his staff for a roving commission to report upon the political, financial, economic and social aspects of Australia, and upon Imperial interests generally, as represented in various sideshows on her route.

But it happened that she was now suffering from a change at the last moment in that route – a substitution of the commplace P. & O. for the more exciting Canadian Pacific, Mr Gibbs having suddenly decided that Imperialism in Australia demanded his special correspondent's immediate attention.

For this story dates back to the time when Mr Joseph Chamberlain was in office; when Imperialism, Free Trade and Yellow Labour were the catch words of a party, and before the great Australian Commonwealth had become an historical fact.

The Imperialist's Special Correspondent looked worried. She was wondering whether the English mail expected to-day would bring her troublesome editorial instructions. She examined some of the photographs and drawings with a dissatisfied air. A running inarticulate commentary might have been put into words like this:

'No good . . . I can manage the letterpress all right once I get the hang of things. But when it comes to illustrations, I can't make even a gum-tree look as if it was growing . . . . And Gibbs hates having amateur snapshots to work up . . . . Hopeless to try for a local artist . . . . I wonder if Colin McKeith could give me an idea. . . . . Why to goodness didn't Biddy join me! . . . . If she'd only had the decency to let me know in time *why* she couldn't. . . . Money, I suppose – or a Man! . . . . Well, I'll write and tell her never to expect a literary leg-up from me again . . .'

Mrs Gildea pulled the sheet she had been typing out of the machine, inserted another, altered the notch to single spacing and rattled off at top speed till the page was covered. Then she appended her signature and wrote this address:

To the Lady Bridget O'Hara,
    Care of Eliza Countess of Gaverick,
        Upper Brook Street, London, W.

on an envelope, into which she slipped her letter – a letter never to be sent.

A snap of the gate between the bamboos added a metallic note to the tree's reedy whimperings, and the postman tramped along the short garden path and up the veranda steps.

'Morning, Mrs Gildea . . . a heavy mail for you!'

He planked down the usual editorial packet – two or three rolls of proofs, a collection of newspapers, a bulky parcel of private correspondence sent on by the porter of Mrs Gildea's London flat, some local letters and, finally, two square envelopes, with the remark, as he turned away on his round. 'My word! Mrs Gildea, those letters seem to have done a bit of globe-trotting on their own, don't they!'

For the envelopes were covered with directions, some in Japanese and Chinese hieroglyphics, some in official red ink from various postoffices, a few with the distinctive markings of British Legations and Government Houses where the Special Correspondent should have stayed, but did not – Only her own name showing through the obliterations, and a final re-addressing by the Bank of Leichardt's Land.

Mrs Gildea recognised the impulsive, untidy but characteristic handwriting of Lady Bridget O'Hara.

'From Biddy at last!' she exclaimed, tore the flap of number one letter, paused and laid it aside. 'Business first.'

So she went carefully through the editorial communication. Mr Gibbs was not quite so tiresome as she had feared he would be. After him, the packet from her London flat was inspected and its contents laid aside for future perusal. Next, she tackled the local letters. One was embossed with the Bank of Leichardt's Land stamp and contained a cablegram originally despatched from Rome, which had been received at Vancouver and, thence, had pursued her – first along the route originally designed, afterwards, with zigzagging, retrogression and much delay, along the one she had taken. That it had reached her at all, said a good deal for Mrs Gildea's fame as a freely paragraphed newspaper correspondent.

The telegram was phrased thus:

> *Sorry impossible no funds other reasons writing Biddy*

Mrs Gildea's illuminative 'H'm!' implied that her two inductions had been correct. No funds – and other reasons – meaning – a *Man*. She scented instantly another of Biddy's tempestuous love-affairs.

Had it been merely a question of lack of money with inclination goading, she felt pretty certain that Lady Bridget would have contrived to beg, borrow or steal – on a hazardous promissory note, after the happy-go-lucky financial morals of that section of society to which by birth she belonged. Or, failing these means, that she would have threatened some mad enterprise and so have frightened her aunt Eliza Countess of Gaverick into writing a cheque for three figures. Of course, less would have been of no account.

Mrs Gildea opened the two envelopes and sorted the pages in order of their dates. The first had the address of a house in South Belgravia, where lived Sir Luke Tallant of the Colonial Office and Rosamond his wife – distant connections of the Gavericks.

Lady Bridget's letters were type-written, most carelessly, with the mistakes corrected down the margin of the flimsy sheets in the manner of author's proof – the whole appearance of them suggesting literary 'copy.'

Likewise, the slapdash epistolary style of the MS., which had a certain vividness of its own.

CHAPTER 2

———————•———————

'Dearest Joan,
You'll have got my wire. Vancouver was right, I suppose. I sent it from Rome. Since then I have been at Montreux with Chris and Molly, and since I came back to England with them, I've been in too chaotic a state of mind to write letters. Really, Chris and Molly's atmosphere of struggling to keep in the swim on next to nothing a year and of eking out a precarious income by visits to second-rate country houses and cadging on their London friends gets on my nerves to such an extent that Luke and Rosamond's established "Colonial Office" sort of respectability is quite refreshing by contrast.

I should have loved the Australian trip. Your "Bush" sounds perfectly captivating, and, of course, I could do the illustrations you want. Besides, I'm stony-broke and, financially, the great god Gibbs appeals to me. I'd take my passage straight off – one would raise the money somehow – if it wasn't for – There! It's out. A *man* has come and upset the apple-cart.'

Mrs Gildea gave a funny little laugh. The letter answered her thought.

' "Oh, of course!" I can hear you sneer. "Just another of Biddy's emotional interests – bound to fizzle out before very long." But this is a good deal more than an emotional interest, and I don't think it will fizzle out so quickly. For one thing, *this* man is quite different from all the other men I've ever been interested in. The first moment I saw him, I had the queerest sort of *arrested* sensation. He's told me since, that he felt exactly the same about me. Kind of lived before – "*When I was a king in Babylon and you were a Christian Slave*" idea. Though I'm quite certain that if I ever was a slave it must have been a Pagan and not a Christian one. Joan, the experience was thrilling, positively electrifying – Glamour – personal magnetism. . . . You couldn't possibly understand unless you knew *him*. Descriptions are so hopeless. I'll leave him to your imagination.

By the way, Molly annoyed me horribly the other day. "You know, dear," she had the audacity to remark, "he's not of *our* class, and if you married him, you'd have to give up US! For could you suppose," she went on to say, "that Chris and Mama – to say nothing of Aunt Eliza – would tolerate an adventurer who tells tall stories about buried treasure and native rebellions and expects one to be amused!"

Our class! Oh, how I detest the label! And that unspeakably dreadful idea of social sheep and goats – and the unfathomable abyss between Suburbia and Belgravia! Though I frankly own that to me Suburbia represents the Absolutely Impossible. After all, one must go right into the Wilderness to escape the conditions of that state of life to which you happen to have been born.

Well, that speech of Molly's came out of a fascinating account my Soldier of Fortune gave us of how he stage-managed a revolution in South America, and of an expedition he'd made in the Andes on the strength of a local tradition about the Incas' hidden gold. I call him my Soldier of Fortune – though he's not in any known Army list, because it's what he called himself. Likewise a Champion of the Dispossessed. He has an intense sympathy with the indigenous populations, and thinks the British system of conquering and corrupting native races simply a disgrace to civilisation. With all of which sentiments I entirely agree. Luke has taken to him immensely, chiefly, I fancy, because he was once private secretary to some Administrating Rajah in an Eastern-Archipelago or Indian Island, and as Luke is hankering after a colonial governorship, he wants to scrape up all the information he can about such posts.

I answered Molly that one may have a violent attraction to a man without in the least wanting to marry him, and that relieved her mind a little.

As for *Him*, the attraction on his part seems equally violent. We do the most shockingly unconventional things together. He tells me that I carry him off his feet – that I've revolutionised his ideas about the "nice English Girl" (useless to protest that I'm not an English girl but a hybrid Celt). He says that I've wiped off his slate the scheme of life he'd been planning for his latter years. A comfortable existence in England – his doctor advises him to settle down in a temperate climate – an appointment on some City Board – rubber shares and that kind of thing – you know it all – a red brick house in South Kensington and perhaps a little place in the country. He did not fill in the picture – but I did for him – with the charmingly domesticated wife – well connected: the typical "nice English Girl," heiress of a comfortable fortune to supplement his own, which he candidly admitted needs supplementing.

Of course he's not a mere vulgar fortune-hunter. He must be genuinely in love with the nice English Girl. And that's where *I* upset *his* apple-cart.

In fact, we are both in an *impasse*. I'm not eligible for his post and I shouldn't want it if I were. To my mind marriage is only conceivable with a barbarian or a millionaire. From the sordid atmosphere of English conjugality upon an income of anything less than an assured £5,000 a year, good Lord deliver me! And you know my reasons for adding another clause to my litany. Good Lord deliver me also from further experience of the exciting vicissitudes of a stock-jobbing career!

Then again, apart from personal prejudices, I am appalled, quite simply, at the cold-blooded marriage traffic that I see going on in London. Any crime committed in the name of Love is forgivable, but to sell a girl – soul and body to the highest bidder is to my mind, the unpardonable sin against the Holy Ghost. Frankly, I'm petrified with amazement at the way in which mothers hurl their daughters at the head of any man who will make a good settlement. There's Molly's sister – she chases the game till she has corralled it, and once inside her walls the unfortunate prey hasn't swallowed his first cup of tea before she has wedded him in imagination to one of her girls – "How do you like Mr *Chose?*" "Like him? What is there to like? He's the same as all the rest of the men, and they're as like as a box of ninepins. . ."

"But what do you think of him. . . ?" "But really there's nothing to think." . . . "But don't you think he'd do for Hester?" etcetera, etcetera.

She has just married the one before Hester to what she calls the perfect type of an English country gentleman – meaning that he owns an historic castle in Scotland, a coal mine in Wales and a mansion in Park Lane. Heavens! I'd rather follow the fortunes of a Nihilist and be sent to Siberia, or drive wild cattle and fight wild blacks with one of your Bush cowboys, than I'd marry the perfect type of an English country gentleman! Give me something *real* – anything but the semi-detached indifference of most of the couples one knows. No. *My* man must be strong enough to carry *me* off my feet and to break down all the conventions of "*our class.*" Then, I'd cheerfully tramp through the forest beside him, if it came to that, or cook his dinner in front of our wigwam. Now, if my Soldier of Fortune were to ask me to climb the Andes with him in search of that buried treasure! But he won't: and – I confess it, Joan – I'm in mortal terror of his insisting upon my entering the sphere of stock-jobbing respectability instead, and of my being weak enough to consent. But we haven't got anywhere near that yet.

So far, I'm just – living – trying to make up my mind what it is that I want most. Do you know, that since my violent attraction to him – or whatever you like to call it – all sorts of odd bits of revelation have come to me as to the things that really matter!

For one thing, I'm pretty certain that the ultimate end of Being is Beauty and that Love means Beauty and Beauty means Love. The immediate result of this discovery is that I'm buying clothes with a reckless disregard of the state of my banking account.

I begin to understand and to sympathise with that pathetic striving after beauty which one sees in the tawdry finery and exaggerated hairdressing of a kitchenmaid – Rosamond Tallant has one who is wonderful to behold as she mounts the area steps on her Sundays out. Formerly I should have been horrified at that kitchenmaid. Now I have quite a fellow-feeling with her piteous attempts to make herself attractive to her young man, the grocer's boy or the under-footman I suppose. Am I not at this very moment sitting with complexion cream daubed on my face, in order that I may appear more attractive to *my* young man. I know now how Molly's maid – who is keeping company with Luke's butler – feels when we all dine early for a theatre and Josephine gets an evening out at the Earl's Court Exhibition with her gentleman.

Sounds beastly vulgar, doesn't it? But that's just what I'm making myself pretty for – dinner there this evening at the French Restaurant with *my* gentleman. It's quite proper: we are a party of four – the other two I may add are not in Rosamond's or Molly's set.

I've been interrupted – He has telephoned. The other pair have disappointed us. Will I defy conventions and dine with *Him* alone? Of course I will.'

CHAPTER 3

The particular sheet ended at this point. Mrs Gildea laid it down upon the earlier ones and took another from the little pile which she had spread in sequence for perusal. She smiled to herself in mournful amusement. For she scarcely questioned the probability that her friend would in due course become disillusioned of a very ordinary individual – he certainly sounded a little like an adventurer – who for some occult reason had been idealised by this great-souled, wayward and utterly foolish creature. How many shattered idols had not Lady Bridget picked up from beneath their over-turned pedestals and consigned to Memory's dust-bin! On how many pyres had not that oft-widowed soul committed suttee to be resurrected at the next freak of Destiny! And yet with it all, there was something strangely elusive, curiously virginal about Lady Bridget.

She had been in love so often: nevertheless, she had never loved. Joan Gildea perfectly realised the distinction. Biddy had been as much, and more in love with ideas as with persons. Art, Literature, Higher Thought, Nature, Philanthrophy, Mysticism – she spelled everything with a capital letter – Platonic Passion – the last most dangerous and most recurrent. As soon as one Emotional Interest burned out another rose from the ashes. And, while they lasted, she never counted the cost of these emotional interests.

But then she was an O'Hara: and all the O'Haras that had been were recklessly extravagant, squandering alike their feelings and their money. There wasn't a member of the house of Gaverick decently well to do, excepting indeed Eliza, Countess of Gaverick. She had been a Glasgow heiress and only belonged to the aristocracy by right of marriage with Bridget's uncle, the late Lord Gaverick, who on the death of his brother, about the time Bridget was grown up, had succeeded to the earldom, but not to the estate.

Gaverick Castle in the province of Connaught, which with the unproductive lands appertaining to it, had been in the possession of O'Haras from time immemorial, was sold by Bridget's father to pay his debts. His brother – the heiress' husband, who, unlike the traditional spendthrift O'Haras had accumulated a small fortune in business, was able by some lucky chance to buy back the Castle – partly with his wife's money – soon after his accession to the barren honours of the family. His widow inherited the place as well as the rest of her husband's property, and could do as she pleased with the whole. Thus the present holder of that ancient Irish title, young, charming and poor, stemming from a collateral branch, lived mainly upon his friends and upon the hope that Eliza, Countess of Gaverick, might at her death leave him the ancestral home and the wherewithal to maintain it.

As for Bridget's father, the last but one Earl of Gaverick, his career may be summed up as a series of dramatic episodes, matrimonial, social and financial.

His first wife had divorced him. His second wife – the mother of Lady Bridget – had deserted him for an operatic tenor and had died shortly afterwards. She herself had been an Italian singer.

Lord Gaverick did not marry again, and Mrs Gildea had gathered that the less said about his social adventures the better. Financially, he had subsisted precariously as a company promoter. There had come a final smash: and one morning the Earl of Gaverick had been found dead in his bed, an empty medicine bottle by his side. As he had been in the habit of taking chloral the Coroner's jury agreed upon the theory of an overdose.

Yes, Mrs Gildea could quite understand that apart from general views on the marriage question, Lady Bridget O'Hara might well shrink from further connection with City finance.

CHAPTER 4

———————————•———————————

A naughty little gust – herald of the sub-tropical afternoon breeze that comes up the Leichardt River from the sea, blew about the typed sheets on the table, and, among them, those of Lady Bridget's letter, as Mrs Gildea laid them down.

While she collected the various pages of manuscript that had been displaced and was bundling them together, with a banana on each sheaf to keep it safe, there came a second snap of the gate and a man's voice hailed her.

It was the voice of a man who sang baritone, and his accent was an odd combination of the Bush drawl grafted on to the mellifluous Gaelic, from which race he had originated.

'Any admittance, Mrs Gildea, except on business, during working hours?'

'Yes, it is working hours Colin, but you happen to be business because you're just the person I'm wanting to speak to, so come along.'

'Good for me, Joan,' and the man came along, clearing the rest of the garden path and the veranda steps in three strides.

He gripped Mrs Gildea's hand.

'You're nice and cool up here, and you get every bit of wind that's going along the river,' he said. 'It's a good thing you kept this humpey, Joan – a little nest for the bird to fly home to, eh?'

'Yes, I'm glad, though it seemed a silly piece of sentiment . . . and, as you say, I always *felt* the old bird might want to fly home for a bit some day. Well, *you* look cool enough, Colin.'

'This is temperate zone for me after the Leura. . . . But it's a hot March because we haven't had a proper rainy season, and I'll just stand here and catch the breeze for a minute or two before I sit down.'

He balanced himself on the veranda railing: took off his broad-brimmed Panama hat and mopped his forehead with a silk handkerchief. Mrs Gildea surveyed him with interested admiration.

A big man – large-limbed, bony – a typical Scotcher in that – with thin flanks, a well-set up back and massive shoulders. His face was browny-red all over except where the skin ran white under the hair and there was a ruddier ring round the upper part of the throat. His nose was thin between the eyes, broadening lower, high-bridged and with high cut nostrils, showing the sensitive red when he was enraged – as not infrequently happened. He had large honest blue eyes, intensely blue, of the fiery description with a trick of dropping the lids when he was in doubt or consideration. They were expressive eyes, as a rule keen and hard, but they could soften unexpectedly under the influence of emotion. At other times, according to the quality of the emotion, they glowed literally like blue flames. He was considered queer-tempered, rather sulky, and his face often took on a very unyielding expression.

He had thick reddish-yellow eyebrows at the base of a slightly receding forehead – wanting in benevolence, phrenologists would have said, and with the bump of self-esteem considerably developed. His hair was yellow, pure and simple – the colour of spun silk, only coarser, and it would have curled at the ends had he not worn it close-cropped. His moustache and beard were rather deeper yellow, the beard short, well-shaped – the cut of Colin McKeith's beard was almost his only vanity – there was one other, the 'millionare strut' in town – and he had the masculine habit of stroking and clasping his beard with his large open-fingered hand – spatulate tips to his digits, the practical hand – fairly well kept, though brown and hairy.

There were lines in his face and a way of setting his features – that a man gets when he has to front straight some cruel facts of human existence – to calculate at a glance the chances of death from a black's spear, a lost trail, an empty water-bag, the horns of a charging bullock or even worse things than these.

And such experiences had put a stamp on him, and distinguished him from the ordinary ruck of men – these and his undeniable manliness, and good looks.

He smiled as he glanced amusedly from the littered wind-blown papers on the table to his hostess' rather troubled face.

'Well you seem to have a pretty fair show here of what you call "copy,"' he said.

Mrs Gildea met his look with one of frank pleasure.

'That's what I want *you* for.'

'What's the job?' he asked. 'You ought to know that literary "copy" is not much in my line. Now if it had been yarding the fowls or cleaning up the garden, I'd feel more at home as a lady's help.'

'Colin, you take me back to Bungroopim – when it happened to be a slack day for you on the run, and when the married couple had levanted and I'd got an incompetent black-gin in the kitchen – or when the store wanted tidying and you and I had a good old spree amongst the rubbish.'

He laughed at a time-honoured joke.

'Sticky sugar-mats and weevilly flour-bins; and a breeding paddock of tarantulas and centipedes and white lizards to clear out. I *was* a bush hobbledehoy in those days, Joan. It's close on twenty years ago.'

Joan Gildea gave a little shudder.

'Don't remind me how old I am. There's the difference between a man and a woman. My life's behind me: yours in front of you.'

'I don't know about that, Joan. I've had my spell of roughing it – droving, mining, pioneering – humping bluey along the track – stoney-broke: sold up by the bank and only just beginning now to find out what Australia's worth.'

'That's what I said – you are just beginning. Roughing it has made a splendid man of you, Colin: and who would ever believe that you are four years older than I am. Colin, you ought to get married.'

'The Upper Leura is no place for the sort of wife I want,' he returned shortly.

'I don't see that. It isn't as if you were going to stop there always. When you're rich enough you can put on a manager. You've got an enormous piece of pretty good country, haven't you?'

'One thousand square miles – and a lot more to be got for the taking – mostly fair cattle pasture – now that we're going in for Artesian bores. But it means capital, sinking wells three thousand feet and more. It'll be three or four years at least before I can see a trip to Europe – doing the thing in the way I mean to do it.'

'Must you go to Europe for a wife? Aren't Australian girls good enough?'

'I've always meant to try for the best. You taught me that, Joan, I shall follow your example. You were an Australian girl.'

Mrs Gildea's face saddened. 'Well,' was all she said.

'You see,' he went on, and the eyes took their narrow concentrated look and suddenly blazed out as he straightened himself against the veranda post, 'I know something of what marriage in the back block means: and I've studied women – don't laugh – I mean theoretically – from books. I've read history – always managed a couple of volumes or so in my swag – nights and nights, by the light of a fat lamp and a camp fire. I've studied the women of great times – ancient and modern – they're always the same – and I've remarked the type of woman that's got grit – capacity for fine things – You understand all that as well as I do, Joan. Look at the women of the French Revolution for one instance – the aristocrats, you know – well, I've realised that it takes blood and breeding and tradition behind to carry a woman to the block with a sure step and a proud smile . . .' Suddenly, he became aware of Joan's gaze, half surprised, wholly interested. . . . He reddened and pulled himself up gruffly.

'Sentimental rot, d'ye call it?'

'No, Colin, I believe in all that and so do you.'

'Blood and breeding and tradition – all the grand stuff that's been grown in them on the *noblesse oblige* principle – self-respect, courage, dignity – the stuff that gives staying power as well as the fire for making good spunk. . . . Not that I'd put a pure-blood racer to haul up logs for an iron-bark fence: any more than I'd set out to plant an English lady of that sort to rough it on the Leura.'

'Well, why not? Do you want your wife to be like a canary in a cage?'

'You know I don't hold with gilded cages and spoiling a woman who is there to be your mate. But all the same, I shan't look out for *my* wife until I can afford to give her as good a show as she'd be likely to have if she stopped at home. You see, a real woman must be a sportsman in her way of taking life as much as a man, and I maintain as a general proposition that it's the English lady – even one of your sneered-at "Lady Clara Vere de Vere" lot who makes the best front against battle, murder and sudden death – if it has to come to that. . . . Just because,' he went on, 'though she might have been brought up in a castle and never have done a hand's turn that could be done for her, she's still got in her veins the blood of fighting ancestors – men who were ready to lay down their lives for God and King and country and their women's honour – and of women too who'd maybe held the stronghold that had been their husband's reward, and kept the flag flying, when to fail or flinch meant death or worse. . . . Why, look at your Lady Nithisdales and your Lady

Russells and your Maria Theresas. . . .'

'And your Joan of Arc – who was a peasant girl – and your Charlotte Corday. . . .'

'Oh, you beat me there. . . . And I wasn't intending to fire off a speech anyway. . . . And anyway, Joan, its awful cheek to think I could ever get the sort of wife I want, but if I can't, I won't have one at all. . . . I'll have my money's worth. Romance – Ideals – something more *lifting* than beef and mutton and cutting a bigger dash than your neighbour. . . . See?'

He broke off with a laugh, and the wonderfully vivid light that came into his blue eyes made him look like an ardent youth.

'And you a democrat!' jeered Mrs Gildea. 'You, a champion of the people's rights; you, an Imperialist in the broadest sense of the term! Oh, I really must put you into one of my articles as a certain type of modern Australian. In fact, Colin, that's what I wanted to talk to you about.'

'All right, fire away. We'll drop the marriage question.'

'To be resumed later.' A quizzical look passed over Mrs Gildea's mouth, and then, 'Oh, what a pity!' she muttered to herself.

'What's a pity?'

'Never mind! The English mail's in – as you may see. I'll show you what Mr Gibbs says. He didn't like my last letter. He says he wants bones and sinews, not an artist's lay figure dressed in stage bushman's clothes. There, Mr McKeith, among your other cogitations on the subject of women, you may try to realise that the mission of a lady special correspondent is not all' – she looked round for a metaphor – 'Muscat grapes and pineapple.'

'Or cooked-up information from heads of departments; or got-up shows of agricultural, mining and other industries. Or trips to the Bay to see the model island prison in which our weary criminals rehabilitate their enfeebled systems by cool sea-breezes and generous diet. Or ministerial picnics to experimental cotton and sugar plantations the size of your garden to prove that all tropical products can be raised to perfection without mentioning the difficulty in a White Australia of finding the labour to do it.'

'Oh, don't rub it in, Colin. I'm only a special reporter, and even special reporters can't know everything. Now, do just sit down and let me ask you questions. And first of all, do you want a whiskey peg or a cup of tea, or what? – I've had my late breakfast.'

'I'll have a smoke, please. Been swearing off store baccy now I'm

down from the Bush. I'm trying hard to smoke cigarettes like one of
your English toffs.'

He pulled out a copper cigarette case with some hieroglyphical
letters and numbers stamped on it, which he regarded with a
humorous smile.

'Only cost a shilling, but now I've my brand across, it looks fine.
You know that by the Brands Act you've got to have a number and
two letters on every head of stock – My brand's the Mark of the
Beast 666 C.K. See?'

He fixed his cigarette into a new amber mouthpiece, made a wry
face, and began to smoke.

'I don't think much of your quality of cigarettes,' said Mrs Gildea.
'On the whole, I prefer your tobacco.'

'All right. Give me my pipe any day –' And he pitched away the
cigarette and produced an ancient pipe, which he filled with tobacco
from an india-rubber pouch and lighted. 'Now, fire away.'

'Not for a little bit yet. You must read my rejected article and my
official instructions, and then you'll have some grasp of the subjects I
want information upon. Here they are – Mr Gibbs first.'

She handed him her editor's letters and pushed a small pile of
manuscript towards his elbow.

'There. It will take you about a quarter of an hour to digest all that;
and meanwhile, if you don't mind the noise, I shall go on typing
something I've got to send off by to-morrow's mail.'

She settled herself at the typewriter, her back partially turned to
him. The subject matter of what she was doing took all her attention.
She worked hard for about ten minutes, hearing sub-consciously the
rustle of papers under his hand and one or two faint ejaculations and
a queer little laugh he gave once or twice as he read.

Presently he said:

'I say, there's a mistake here. I've gone through your editor's
letters. He's sound; I think I can help you to get at what he wants.
But these other sheets have got mixed up with something else. I
thought at first it was a story you'd given me, and I went on reading
and got interested; and now I see it must have been written by some
young woman friend of yours' – if it's meant for a letter.'

Mrs Gildea turned with a dismayed exclamation.

'Good gracious! You don't mean to say that I've given you her
letter?'

'Is it really a letter? Do women type letters? It reads to me much more like what the heroine of a novel would be supposed to say than an ordinary everyday girl. If that's a flesh and blood woman I'd like to know her.'

Mrs Gildea took from him the three typed pages he had in his hand. They were certainly part of Lady Bridget's letter – almost the whole of it, for only the end and the beginning ones were missing. In her hurried rearrangement of the wind-scattered sheets she had put these into the wrong bundle. She ran her eye anxiously over the badly-typed slips, which, with their marginal corrections and smart, allusive jargon of a world entirely removed from Colin McKeith's experience, might easily have misled him into the belief that he was reading literary 'copy.' Of course he knew that Joan Gildea wrote novels as well as journalistic stuff.

He read her thoughts.

'You needn't worry. There isn't the least clue to her identity – I suppose that's what you're afraid of. Not a surname anywhere – I couldn't have imagined a woman would write like that – give herself away – as she does. But it's fine all the same. There'd be nothing small about that woman, Joan. Do you know how it ended?'

'I don't know yet. But I can guess.'

'Eh?' He blew out rings of smoke with less than his usual deliberation. 'D'ye think she'll marry the chap?'

'No – she never does.'

'She's a flirt, then?'

'Bid–' Mrs Gildrea swallowed the rest. '*She* would scorn such a commonplace suggestion. Do you remember that novel of Hardy's, *The Well-Beloved*? She's like the man there, who was always in love with the same Ideal – under different forms – until he found that he'd made a mistake, and then the game began all over again.'

McKeith ruminated. '*She's* like that, is she? . . . The fellow is what you'd call a bounder?' he exclaimed suddenly.

'So I imagine.'

'But she's in love with him – she must be, or she wouldn't write like that?'

'You don't know her. She can't do anything by halves – while she's doing it.'

'By Jove, that's what I like. There's a woman who'd never hang on the fence. And her ideas about love and all that: it's splendid.'

He brooded again a few moments, while Mrs Gildea sorted her papers afresh; then he exclaimed:

'It strikes me, she's one of the sort I was talking about just now.'

'Well, she *was* born in a castle.'

'I guessed it. . . . You won't tell me her name?'

'How could I – I ask you? After you'd read that!'

'No. All right. You can trust me not to find out.'

'Besides, she would never do for you.'

He laughed quizzically. 'Well, I'm a barbarian, and it's possible I may some day be a millionaire. But I'm not such a conceited cad as to imagine a woman like that would ever fall in love with *me*!' His voice sank almost to a reverential tone. 'The only thing I do know is that if I got the chance, I'd show her I was strong enough to carry her off to my wigwam and she could do what she pleased afterwards. I'd be her slave so long as she cared for me – and I'd never live with a woman who didn't.'

'My dear Colin, you're not likely to get the chance. Please forget that you ever read that letter.'

'No, I can't do that; but as she's in London and we're over here, it's not much odds anyway. Well, have you found the right sheets? Give them to me if you have and then we can come to business.'

CHAPTER 5

Colin McKeith had been gone some time and Mrs Gildea, primed with fresh ideas, had finished her article on the lines he suggested, before she again tackled Lady Bridget's love-affair.

The second letter (there is no need to reproduce the page of daring sentiment that closed the first) was dated from Castle Gaverick in South Connemara, and plunged straight into the tragic culmination.

'It's all over, Joan – was over soon after my last letter, but I've been too wretched ever since to write. If you had been in England you might have read in one of last week's "*Morning Post's*" that a marriage has been arranged and will shortly take place between Mr Willoughby Maule, formerly confidential adviser to His Highness the Rajah of Kasalpore – and Evelyn Mary, only daughter of the late John Bagallay, Esq, and the late Mrs Bagally of Bagallay Court, Birmingham.

Rosamond tells me that Luke told her that Evelyn Mary has been throwing herself at Will's head ever since they met last year on a P. & O. steamer between Singapore and Colombo. She and her chaperon went on a tour round the world, it seems, just before Evelyn Mary came of age. I wonder they did not get engaged then, and can only conclude – as there was no *me* then to upset the apple-cart – that he did not know how rich she was going to be. Anyway, I feel certain that it was Evelyn Mary who was at the back of his plan for settling down as a respectable stock-jobber. Molly Gaverick – who is a cat – said she knew for certain Willoughby Maule came to England with the fixed intention of marrying for birth and position or for money, and that he fancied, in me, he'd found both – she says that he took his impressions of us from the paragraphs in the Society papers and thought us much richer and bigger than we are, and that now he knows better he thinks it safer to drop birth and make sure of money.

The Bagallays made theirs in nails. Last year Evelyn Mary came into a fortune of a quarter of a million. I'm told that it's absolutely at her own disposal. She was an only child. A quarter of a million would be an immense temptation to a poor and ambitious man.

And yet, Joan, I *can't* believe that Will has been actuated by wholly sordid motives. He may be an adventurer, but he is not a mean one.

Rosamond Tallant thinks it much more likely that because I didn't introduce him to Aunt Eliza, and Chris and Molly never asked him to dinner, he got the idea that I considered him good enough to amuse myself with, but not good enough for serious consideration as a husband. And it's quite true that I always shirked that point when it was touched upon. If I must be perfectly honest with myself, I think I was afraid of his putting me at the cannon's mouth and telling me I must decide then and there to take him or leave him. Should I ever have had the strength to give him up? He's so frightfully dear to me, that I can't think of him now without a shudder at the thought of his belonging to another woman. I never really believed it would come to that. He once or twice hinted that there *was* a girl – the "nice English girl" that I had chaffed him about. I had an idea that it was his way of putting pressure on me.

The first time was the evening that I dined alone with him at the Exhibition., Heavens! I grow hot this moment thinking that he may have supposed I was in the *habit* of dining alone with men in French restaurants at popular Exhibitions. I don't know why I did for this man what I'd never done for any other, Partly, I fancy, because it never dawned upon me that he could misunderstand me. Rosamond says I idealised him too much, and that he's just the ordinary man and not the tiniest bit of the Bayard I imagined him. I daresay she's right, and that he may have laughed in his sleeve at my romantic rhapsodies.

All the same, I never can convince myself that he is a mere fortune-hunter. Perhaps the very fact that I didn't make the smallest effort to wrest him from Mademoiselle Crœsus when he tried to make me jealous seemed proof to him that he was no more to me than a caprice. So, when we made each other an atrocious scene and I told him to go off to her, he simply took me at my word.

The scene began with my telling him about my sort of engagement to Aubrey Blaine – whom as you know, I was really nearer to marrying than I have been to marrying anybody. And yet, as I tried to explain to Will, I didn't *want* to marry Aubrey. Only the mischief with me is always that I can't hold back with one hand and give with the other ... Will wasn't able to enter into my feelings about that affair in the very least or to understand how, when it came to the point, I realised that I *couldn't* sink to domesticity on seven hundred a year. Fancy taking a house in Pimlico or West Kensington, or one of those horrible places with a man to whom you have a violent attraction and consulting with your adored as to whether you could run to three maids and a Tweeny! The sordidness of it would be too disenchanting.

When I said something like that to Will, he flared up and we hurled nasty speeches at each other, and finally he walked off slamming the door – I used to hear that slam in my dreams sometimes – or it may have been Luke coming in late – the Tallants' hall door makes a particularly Kismetish bang. That was our real parting, though it wasn't the last. He wrote to me – a bitter sort of farewell. And I did a mad thing. I went to see him in his rooms. But when I got there, his manner – something he said which offended me – one can't explain the unexplainable – started the scene all over again. It was as if a mocking demon came up between us. That time it was *I* who left *him*. The next thing I heard was that he and Mademoiselle Crœsus were engaged.

I wrote to him – I know it wasn't the proper sort of letter – I daresay he saw through my pretended indifference. He sent me back my letters as I had asked him to do – wrote me in quite the right strain – said he was not worthy of me – that I'd shewn him I was far above him – that he might not presume to think I could be happy with a man of his inadequate means and position – that he could never forget me – and so on – but that it was best as it is.

And now I've got to get what consolation I can out of my own inner conviction – that it *is* best as it is, and that I ought to be thankful for being still Bridget O'Hara, mistress of my own fate, and free yet to sport about – sport! – oh, the irony of it – in what you call the stormy sea of my emotions.

I make over to you the copyright of my sufferings.'

The letter broke off abruptly. It was resumed on another sheet six weeks later at Gaverick Castle.

'Rosamond Tallant has just sent me a writing case I left at their house with these pages in it. I daren't read them over, but they'll give you an idea of my state of mind during those last dreadful weeks in London. My nerves are now in a little better condition. Since I came here, I've set myself resolutely *not* to think of Will – that is, not more than I can help; there are times when his ghost is extremely active. I'm putting out brain-feelers, for I know that I should go to pieces altogether if I didn't throw myself into some new interest. So that I'm trying a system for the development of one's higher faculties that was taught me by a queer old German professor I met at Caux last summer, who was interested in the odd little second-sight experiences I've had occasionally which I told him about. He made me do exercises in deep-breathing and meditation – you shut yourself up, darken your room and concentrate upon a subject – Beauty, Wisdom, Friendship, were some of the subjects he gave me – and you can't think how thrillingly absorbing it was. I worked frightfully hard at it for a bit, drinking only distilled water and living on vegetables – you *can* do that in Switzerland: you simply *can't* in civilised society – And then came Rome and the Willoughby Maule episode.

Episode! Has it come to that!

Ah Joan, I have a horrible suspicion that however much I may try to persuade myself I'm concentrating upon some abstract theme, I've really all the time been thinking of him.

Yesterday I took Friendship for my study in concentration. You, dear thing, came up, naturally, and your image actually kept Will away for a clear five seconds. I thought what a help it would be to be with you, and afterwards I made the suggestion of an Australian trip on literary business to Aunt Eliza, but it was no good. She is deeply engaged just now in driving batches of stuffy relatives in a stuffy brougham – luckily there's no room for me in it – to still stuffier garden parties. And, besides, I don't feel that I can take any desperate step of that kind until the Irrevocable has been written in Destiny's Book.

Will Maule is not married yet.

Well, anyhow, the meditation on Friendship was comparatively successful. Wisdom I found beyond me, and Beauty awakened painful memories. To-day I mean to concentrate on wealth – one of my Professor's theories is that if you concentrate regularly on a thing you are bound in the long run to get what you set your mind upon, and I do find my position of dependence upon Aunt Eliza too unspeakably galling. What a monstrous injustice it seems that I – who if I had been born a boy, must have been Earl of Gaverick, should be at the mercy of an ill-tempered, miserly, old woman who may leave the home of my forefathers to a crossing-sweeper if she pleases. I suppose it ought to go to Chris, but one doesn't feel called upon to arraign Fate on behalf of a distant cousin who by rights has no business to be Lord Gaverick at all.

I'm concentrating on Art too. Every day I do some inspirational painting by the sea shore. I've made some studies of Wave-fairies for the Children's Story Book we planned to do together. It's quite invigorating to sport about with them in imagination, in a grey-green stormy sea, out of reach of human banalities. I can feel the cold spray as I paint and the sense of power and rest in the elemental forces – an almost Wagnerian feeling of great Cosmic Realities.'

Again Mrs Gildea smiled to herself. How like Biddy O'Hara!

She couldn't be so utterly heart-broken if she was able to practise deep breathing and concentration – Wealth, Friendship, Art – a pretty comprehensive repertoire – and to prate on Cosmic Realities and the Wagnerian feeling!

But presently the tragic note shrieked again. Bridget went on:

'I am in a fever of suspense and misery wondering whether Will's marriage will come off or if, at the last moment, it will be broken. He has been obsessing me these last days. He too – I am certain of it – dreads the Irrevocable, and regrets the rupture between us. I dream of him continually – such restless, tantalising dreams. And yet my mood is so contradictory. If the marriage *were* broken off and he stood before me, free, and offered himself! –

Could I bring myself to face our future together with all its depoeticising influences, its almost certainty of friction? No. Something deep down inside me says – has always said – "It would be a mistake; this is not the real thing: we are not suited to each other; the attraction might even turn to repulsion." Imagine the agony of that!

Life goes on here, all dribble, waste and fret – I cannot concentrate, I cannot paint – the Wave-fairies won't play – Your Bush gobies appeal more to my present humour. I feel a sort of nostalgia for the wild – though my nostalgia is mental, and not from any former association. Do not be surprised if some day you get a telegram saying that I am coming.'

Another sheet.

'Will was married yesterday. I have just read the account of the ceremony – I can see it all – the usual semi-smart opulent wedding – palms lining the aisle, Orange blossom galore. The bride "beautiful in cream satin and old lace" – Evelyn Mary is simply a *Lump* – Pages in white velvet – The fussy overdressed Bagallay crowd of friends – I hear there are no "in-laws," And the bridegroom's face – dark, cynical – I know the sort of miserable smile and the queer glitter in his eyes. – "*I Willoughby take thee Evelyn Mary . . . for better and for worse . . . till death us do part*" . . . There! I'm a blithering idiot to mind . . . I ought to be dancing with joy at my escape. Let us end the chapter. The incident is closed, I'm going for a long tramp by the sea and shall post this on my way.

Your BIDDY.'

CHAPTER 6

Mrs Gildea was too busy in the next two or three weeks to trouble herself unduly over Lady Bridget O'Hara's tragic love-affair. She had to report on the small holders of property in Leichardt's Land and made a trip for that purpose among the free-selectors in her own old district. The *Twenty Years After* letter she wrote about this expedition for *The Imperialist* was one of her best, and for that she was greatly indebted to Colin McKeith's commentaries.

Old associations with him had been vividly reawakened by this visit to the home of her youth. She remembered, as if it had been yesterday, how McKeith, a raw youth of eighteen with a horrible tragedy at the back of his young life, had been picked up by her father and brought to Bungroopim to learn the work of a cattle-station .... hitherto his experience, such as it was, had been with sheep in the, then, unsettled north. Joan was herself a girl in short frocks, three or four years younger than Colin McKeith, and with no apparent prospect of ever crossing the 'big fella Water,' as the Ubi Blacks called it, or of joining the band of Bohemian scribblers in London.

She remembered how quickly Colin had learned his work – remembered how the shy self-contained lad, with always that grim memory of his boyhood shaping a vengeful purpose in his mind and making him old for his years, had developed the flair of the Bush in his hardy Scotch constitution. She was compelled to own that he had developed, too, some of the worst as well as the best of those Scotch qualities inherited from his parents, expatriated though they had been, and from the staunch clansmen behind them. He had the Scotch loyalty; likewise, the Scotch tenacity of character which never forgot and very seldom forgave; the Scotch obstinacy of purpose and opinion; the Scotch acquisitiveness; a tendency too to 'nearness' in matters of small expenditure which combined oddly with a generosity amounting almost to recklessness in large enterprise. It was on the whole not a bad outfit for a pioneer who meant to get on in his world.

The beginnings were small, but indicative of the trend of his career. He contrived, even when he was earning no salary but working only for his 'tucker,' to get together a horse or two, a cow or two, a specially good cattle-dog or two, which last he made the nucleus of a profitable breed. The cows and bullocks he left at Bungroopim when the time came for him to push out, reclaiming them after they had increased and multiplied in those pleasant pastures like Jacob's herds in the fields of Laban.

Not that there was any seven years matrimonial question. There had been no Leah. Or if Joan Gildea had ever played the part of Rachel in Colin McKeith's sentimental dreams, those boyish dreams had left no serious mark upon him. He had gone north to a newly-formed station and had there out-bushed the bushman in his knowledge of the idiosyncrasies of cattle and sheep and his amazing faculty for spotting country suitable for either. Here no doubt his descent from generations of herdsmen had stood him in good stead.

He sold his knowledge to rich squatters in the settled districts who employed him to take up new country for them and to manage the hundreds of square miles and the thousands of stock from which they derived the best part of their wealth. But he only managed for other men until he had made enough money of his own to take up and stock new country for himself.

In a few years he had acquired a moderate-sized herd and established himself with it on the almost unexplored reaches of the Upper Leura. Life on that river never lacked dangerous adventure. McKeith's father had owned a station on the Lower Leura – the bank took it in payment of their mortgage after the catastrophe occurred. That station had been the scene of one of the most horrible native outrages in the history of Australia. The tragedy had set its mark on Colin McKeith. Left a penniless boy after having worked his way to independent manhood he had made it his purpose to pursue the wild black with relentless animosity.

All along the Upper Leura to the fastnesses at the river's head where his new station stood on the boundaries of civilisation he had gone, mercilessly punishing native depredations.

He had been put on trial by a humanitarian Government for so-called manslaughter of natives, and had been acquitted under an administration immediately succeeding it. Afterwards he had at the peril of his life, made an exploring trip across the base of the northern peninsula of the colony with the intention, as he phrased it, of 'shaking round a bit.' He 'shook round' to some purpose, penetrated to the Big Bight, and got on the tracks of a famous lost explorer. Colin McKeith solved the mystery of that explorer's fate and had his revenge on the Government which had impeached him by pocketing the reward which it had offered any adventurous pioneer following on the lost explorer's steps.

Later, McKeith was given a mission to explore and develop a certain tract of fertile country between the heads of the Leura and the Big Bight – the particular Premier instigating the mission being a far-sighted politician who realised that a Japanese invasion of the northern coast might eventually interfere very radically with the plan for a White Australia.

Colin McKeith threw into his own scheme of life a trip to Japan, by way of India and China. He volunteered, too, for the Boer War, and did a short term of service with the Australian Contingent in South Africa.

He dreamed more and more of becoming an Empire-maker – a sort of Australian Cecil Rhodes. But he was wise enough to realise that all Empire-making cannot be on the Rhodesian scale.

He realised that his personal fortune must first be secured. Without money one can do nothing. Cecil Rhodes had had the natural wealth of Rhodesia at his back. McKeith had set himself the task of opening up the fine country out West, which he knew only needed a system of irrigation by Artesian Bores to defy drought, the squatters curse. That object once accomplished – he gave himself with luck and good seasons five or six years – there would be nothing to stop his becoming a patriot and a millionaire.

But Colin went slowly and cannily – and that was why the Leichardt's Land Government believed in him. He had the reputation of never spending a penny on his private or public ambitions where a halfpenny would serve his purpose, and he was known to be a man of deep counsels and sparing of speech. Thus, no one knew exactly what was his business down south at this time. Only the general remark was that Colin McKeith had his head screwed on the right way and that some day he would come out on top.

But that there was deep down a spring of romance beneath that hard Bushman's exterior, Joan Gildea, herself a romance writer, guessed easily. And her intuition told her that a little thin bore had been made in the direction of that vital spring of romance by his inadvertent reading of Lady Bridget O'Hara's letter.

CHAPTER 7

———————•———————

Joan saw that McKeith was extremely anxious to know more about the writer of that letter and the progress of that love-affair, though he had given his word of honour that he would not try to find out her identity. But he put subtle questions to Joan about her friends in England and her acquaintance with the higher circles of society in London. Once, he asked her straight out whether she had heard again from her typewriting correspondent, and if the Soldier of Fortune had proved himself a Bounder, as they had suspected?

'Yes,' Joan answered unguardedly. 'I'm thankful to say that he is married to his heiress.'

The eager light which suddenly shone in McKeith's eyes startled Mrs Gildea.

'You don't mean to say that you're thinking of her like that?' she exclaimed. 'It's no use, Colin.'

'Probably not,' he answered composedly. 'Tell me, how does she take it?'

'Deadly seriously. She's practising Deep-breathing and Concentration to try and drive the man from her thoughts.'

'What! Oh, you mean Theosophy and that kind of thing. I went to hear Mrs Annie Besant lecture once, and I couldn't make head or tail of it.'

'No. You wouldn't. But it was a German Professor who taught B—— No. I will *not* tell you her name.'

'Anyway, I know that it begins with a "B." And I know that she's got one relation called Molly, and another called Chris, and a friend whose name is Rosamond – likewise that Rosamond is the wife of Luke. . . . By Jove!' He stopped short and looked at Mrs Gildea with sharp enlightenment.

They were in the veranda of her cottage, and he was seated on the steps smoking, his long legs stretched out against one veranda post, his broad back against another. 'Seen the paper this morning?' he asked.

'No. If you pass the *Chronicle* Office, I wish you'd lodge a complaint for me against the vagaries of their distribution department. Twice lately I haven't had the paper till the afternoon.'

He pulled it from his pocket, and, leaning across, handed it to her.

'Read the English Telegrams,' he said.

Joan stopped cleaning her typewriter and examined the column of latest intelligence.

'Good gracious! So they've appointed Sir Luke Tallant new Governor of Leichardt's Land!'

'Luke! – A coincidence you'll say. No good telling me that. *She* wrote that "Luke" was hankering after a colonial governorship.'

'Well, he's got it,' replied Mrs Gildea noncommittally.

'And if you read the leading article you'll see that the *Chronicle* is justly outraged at so important a post as that of Governor of Leichardt's Land being given to an unknown man who has never served outside the Colonial Office in London and who doesn't even belong to the noble army of Peers.'

'That's all nonsense. Luke Tallant's a friend of Chamberlain's, a thorough Imperialist and a very good man for the post.'

'You know him then?'

'I know *of* him.'

'From *her?*'

'*Her!* Has it come to *Her!* Colin, if anyone had told me that you would ever be fool enough to fall in love with a woman you've never seen, I should have laughed outright. You don't even know what she's like.'

'I can see her in my mind's eye, as I used to see the women I read about by my camp fire. You'd never believe either what a queer idealistic chap I can be when I'm mooning about the Bush. Don't you know, Joan' – and his voice got suddenly grave and deep-toned – 'you ought to, for you were a bush girl and you've had men-kind out in the Back Blocks – Don't you know that when a man has got to go on day after day, week after week, year after year, fighting devils of loneliness and worse – with nothing to look at except miles and miles of stark staring gum trees and black, smelling *gidgee*[1] and dead-finish

---

[1] Gidgee – Colloquial pronunciation of gidia, an Australian tree.

scrub – and never the glimpse of a woman – not counting black gins – to remind him he once had a mother and might have a wife. Well, can't you see that his only chance of not growing into a rotten *hatter*[1] is to start picturing in his imagination all the beautiful things he's ever seen or read about – the sort of lady-wife he hopes to have some day and in making such a companion of her that she seems to him as real as the stars and far more real than the gum trees. So as he'll keep saying to her always in his thoughts: "I'll keep myself sound and wholesome for your sake. I'll never forget that I'm a gentleman, so as *you* won't shrink away from me in horror if ever I've the luck to come across *you* down here on this Earth." '

He stopped, fitted another cigarette from the copper case into the holder and, before beginning upon it, said without looking at Mrs Gildea:

'I wouldn't spout like that to anybody but you, Joan. My word! Though I see by your writing that you've a fair notion of how this cursed, grim, glorious old Bush can play the deuce with a chap – body and brain and soul – if he doesn't wear the right kind of talisman to safeguard himself.'

'Yes – I understand. And your talisman, Colin? What was your picture of the lady-wife? Describe your Ideal and I'll tell you if *She* is the least bit like it.'

McKeith smoked ruminatively for a few moments, his eyes narrowed. The lines in his forehead and round his mouth showed plainly. He was gazing out into space, far beyond the sun-flecked Leichardt River and the Botanical Gardens, and the glaring city and the range of distant hills on the horizon.

'Well,' he said at last, slowly, 'you can laugh at me if you like, but I'll tell you how I see *Her*. She is tall – got a presence, so that if *She's* there, you'd know it and everybody else would know it, no matter how many other women there might be in the place. Most big men take to their opposites. Now, though I'm a big man I've never fancied a snippet of a girl. Five foot seven of height is my measure of a woman, and a good ten stone in the saddle – What are you laughing at, Joan? I'm out there, I suppose?'

Mrs Gildea controlled her muscles.

'No, no, not in the least. In fact, your description fits the Ideal Wife perfectly. Go on, Colin. Five foot seven and a good ten stone.

[1] Hatter – A white man who prefers the Society of Blacks.

How is the rest of *Her*? Fair or dark – her hair now – and her eyes?'

'Her hair – oh, it isn't fair – not yellow or noticeable in colour – like those dyed beauties you see about. Her hair is dark, soft and cloudy looking. And she's got a small head set like – like a lily on its stem – and her hair is parted in the middle and coiled smoothly each side and into a sort of Greek knot. . . .'

'In short, she's a cross between the Venus of Milo and the Madonna.'

Mrs Gildea was smiling amusedly.

'Perhaps. . . . Something of that sort. Dignity and sweetness, you know – those are what I admire in a woman. But not too much of the goddess or of the angel either. I shouldn't want always to have to load up with a pedestal when we shifted camp, and the only shrine I'd keep going for her would be in my heart. It's a Mate I'm wanting, as well as an Ideal. . . . Now you're laughing again.'

'No, I'm not. I agree with you entirely – and so would *She*.'

'There! You needn't tell me. I shouldn't wonder if I'd got the second sight where *She's* concerned.'

Again Mrs Gildea smiled enigmatically.

'I shouldn't wonder, Colin. But you haven't finished your personal description. What about the colour of her eyes?'

'Now I don't believe I could say exactly the colour of her eyes any more than of her hair. They're the kind, to me, that have no colour. Soft and melting and sort of mysterious – Deep and clear and with a light far down in them like starlight reflected in a still lagoon. . . . I say, Joan, you remember the old Eight Mile Water-hole on Dingo Flat – middle of the patch of flooded gum and she-oak – that the Blacks used to say had no bottom to it? *Her* eyes seemed to me a bit like that water-hole – No bottom to her possibilities.'

'That's true enough,' assented Mrs Gildea. 'There's no bottom to *Her* possibilities.'

'I could tell it from her letter. She seemed to write flippantly about things – but that was just because she hates insincerity and flummery, and the world she lives in doesn't satisfy her. Why, it was as if I read slick through to her soul. That woman would go through anything for a man she really loved.'

He had a way of lowering his voice when he spoke of love – as if he felt it a sacred subject; and this in him surprised Joan. She was discovering a new Colin McKeith. She answered softly.

'Yes. I think she would – *if* she really loved him.'

'What I haven't been able to make out is whether she did care – does care – for that chap. You see, that would make a difference.'

'A difference! How? What do you mean?'

'I mean that I don't believe I should feel about her as I do if I wasn't going to meet her. Look here, Joan, you've as good as told me – and if you hadn't, I'd be pretty thick-headed not to have put two and two together – that the Luke of her letters is Sir Luke Tallant, our new Governor. Well, if she was staying with him in London, and his wife is a friend of hers, why shouldn't she come and stay with them out here?'

The idea had already presented itself to Mrs Gildea, but she tried not to show that it had, or that there had ever been any question of the sort in Bridget's mind. Colin had not read the opening sheet of her letter.

'I suppose more unlikely things than that have happened,' Joan said neutrally. 'But really, Colin,' she went on with strenuous emphasis, 'I can't understand this phase of you. You – a hard-headed Bushman, to be dreaming romantic dreams and falling all of a sudden over head and ears in love with – with a figment of your imagination – just because you happen to have read by mistake some sentimental outpourings of a woman you know nothing about and who would never forgive me if she knew I'd let you see her letter.'

'She won't know – You have my word of honour that I'll never give you away over that letter – not under *any* circumstances, so you can set your mind at rest on that score, Joan. And as to my falling in love with – a figment of my own imagination' – he spat the words out savagely – 'we'll see how far your remark is justified when She does come out and I recognise her – as I am convinced I shall do directly I set eyes on Her.'

Mrs Gildea burst into rather hysterical laughter, which manifestly offended Colin McKeith.

'We'll drop the subject, please,' he said stiffly. 'And now, Mrs Gildea, I'm quite at your service for any information you desire about the Big Bight country and the probability of a Japanese invasion so soon as our future Commonwealth comes to crucial loggerheads with the Eastern Powers on the question of a strictly White Australia.'

After that Colin pointedly abstained from allusion to the Ideal Wife and to Joan Gildea's Typewriting-Correspondent, as he had called her. He was very busy himself at this time in connection with a threatened labour strike that was agitating sheep and cattle owners of the Leura District. Likewise with a report he had been asked to furnish of a projected telegraph line for the opening of his 'Big Bight Country'. Colin McKeith appeared to be deep in the confidence of the Leichardt's Land Executive Council and to have taken up his abode for the winter session in the Seat of Government, though he seemed to regard his recent election for a Northern constituency as an unimportant episode in a career ultimately consecrated to the elucidation of far-reaching Imperial problems.

Joan Gildea found him excellent 'copy,' and the great Gibbs cablegrammed, in code, approval of her lately-tapped source of information.

She almost forgot Bridget O'Hara in her absorption in colonial topics. But three weeks before the expected arrival of the new Governor of Leichardt's Land a cablegram was shot at her from Colombo which made her feel that there was no use in setting oneself against Destiny. This was the wire:

Expect me with Tallants Biddy.

She said nothing to Colin McKeith about the message – partly because his movements were erratic and he was a good deal away from Leichardt's town just then. Thus Mrs Gildea did not know whether or not he had read the flowery description telegraphed by a Melbourne correspondent who interviewed Sir Luke Tallant and his party at that city and wired an ecstatic paragraph about the beautiful Lady Bridget O'Hara who was accompanying her friend and distant relative, the Honourable Lady Tallant.

Anyway, McKeith made no references to the newspaper correspondent's rhapsodies when he paid Mrs Gildea a short visit two or three days before the landing of the new Governor. But his very reticence and something in his expression made Joan suspect that he was puzzled and excited, and would have been glad had she volunteered any information about Lady Tallant's companion. Joan, however, kept perverse silence. In truth, she felt considerably nervous over the prospect. What was going to happen when Colin McKeith set eyes on Bridget?

Joan Gildea was a simple woman though circumstances had made her a shrewd one, and she had all the elementary feminine instincts. She believed in love and in strange affinities and in hidden threads of destiny – all of which ideas fitted beautifully on to Bridget O'Hara's personality, but not at all on to that of Colin McKeith.

CHAPTER 8

The first dinner-party given by Sir Luke and Lady Tallant at Government House included Mrs Gildea and Colin McKeith.

These two met in the vestibule as they emerged respectively from the ladies' and gentlemen's cloak-room. Both held back to allow certain Members of the Ministry to enter the drawing-room before them, which gave opportunity for an interchange of greetings.

'Well!' both said at once, and the tones in which the monosyllable was uttered and the glances accompanying it held volumes of hidden meaning. 'I haven't seen you since the Governor arrived,' Joan went on. 'Where have you been all these three weeks?'

'At Alexandra City, close on the desert, where they bored for water and struck ready-made gas – the whole place now is lighted with it. If you like, I'll give you material for a first-rate article upon an uncommon phenomenon of Nature.'

'Thank you. I shall be grateful. Colin' – hesitatingly, 'I did think you'd have come and looked after an old friend at the big Show in the Botanical Gardens when the Governor made his State Entry.'

'State Entry! Good Lord! Sir Luke Tallant has got a bit too much red tape and too many airs about him to suit the Leichardt'stonians.'

'You *were* there, then?'

'Started for Alexandra City that afternoon.'

'But you saw – Colin did you see – the Tallants and – their party?'

His face changed: it looked positively angry, and his jaw under the neatly trimmed, sandy beard, protruded determinedly. But at that moment a footman came towards them, and Mrs Gildea was handed on to an imposing butler and ushered through a wide palm-screened doorway into the large inner hall which had a gallery round it and the big staircase at one end. Joan saw that the room, formerly stiffly furnished and used chiefly as a ballroom, had been transmogrified with comfortable lounge chairs and sofas, beautiful embroideries, screens, a spinet and many flowers and books into a delightful general sitting-room. It seemed quite full – mostly of official Leichardt'stonians. Joan looked for the new Governor and his wife, or at least for Lady Biddy, but none of them had yet put in an appearance. A handsome, fair-moustachioed young aide-de-camp, looking very smart in his evening uniform with white lapels, was fluttering round, his dinner list in his hand, and introducing people who already knew each other. He looked distinctly worried, so did the private secretary – sallow-faced, of a clerkish type, and obviously without social qualifications – who was also wandering round and trying ineffectively to do the right thing. The aide-de-camp rushed forward to shake hands with Joan, exclaiming in a relieved undertone:

'Oh, Mrs Gildea, do help me. I believe I've made an awful hash of it all. People out here,' he murmured, 'ain't used to viceregal etiquette as she is interpreted in Ceylon – that was my last post you know. They seem to think his Excellency ought to have been standing at the door to receive *them*, instead of their waiting to receive *him*.'

Clearly, the aide-de-camp had failed to please, though he looked spruced and his manners were beautiful. The Premier of Leichardt's Land, a red-faced gentleman of blunt speech, was grumbling audibly to the Attorney-General. Mrs Gildea caught snatches of discontent as she passed from one to another.

'Damned impertinence, I call it. A salaried official, no better than any of us, giving himself royal airs. . . . May do in India . . . won't go down in a free country like this.'

The *aide* finished pairing his couples.

'Mrs Gildea, you're to go in with the Warden of the University. Of course you know Dr Plumtree? Literature and learning is an obvious combination, but' (in a confidential aside) 'if you *knew* the job I've had to find out the right order of precedence. Mr McKeith, the Governor will be so glad to meet you. Will you take in Lady Bridget O'Hara? She's not down yet. You see,' he explained again to Mrs Gildea, 'we're strictly official to-night and Debrett's out of it.'

'So am I,' put in Colin McKeith. 'I guess that Lady Bridget would be better pleased if she wasn't handed over to a rough bushman.'

'Now, there you *are* quite out of it,' laughed the aide-de-camp. 'Lady Bridget asked specially to be sent in with you,' and at Mrs Gildea's enquiring smile, he explained once more: 'Sir Luke was speaking about Mr McKeith, said his name had been mentioned at a meeting of the Executive yesterday. Oh! you're top hole, Mr McKeith, I assure you.'

The *aide* broke off suddenly.

There was a rustle of silk on the grand staircase – the slam of a door above, the sound of a laugh and the patter of little high-heeled shoes on the parquet floor of the gallery. The *aide* darted to the foot of the staircase and all eyes turned upward.

The new Governor and his wife came down in slow and stately fashion, arm-in-arm, Sir Luke looking very impressive with the Ribbon and Order of St Michael and St George. He was a handsome man, clean-shaven but for a heavy dark moustache, and carried his dignities with perhaps a little too conscious an air – 'Representative of the Throne' seemed written all over him and no greater contrast could be imagined than the new Governor presented to his predecessor, an elderly, impoverished marquis who had the brain of a diplomatist and the manners of a British farmer, and who with his homely wife had been immensely popular in Leichardt's Land.

Nor a greater contrast than the new Governor's wife to the fat, kindly, old marchioness. Lady Tallant was a London woman, of about forty-five. She had been excessively pretty, but had rather lost her looks after a bad illness, and her worst affliction was now a tendency to scragginess, cleverly concealed where the chest was no longer visible. Obviously artificial outside, at any rate Lady Tallant was, as Mrs Gildea had reason to believe, a genuine sort underneath. She had a thin, high-nosed face of the conventional English aristocratic type, a good deal rouged to-night, but with natural shadows under the eyes and below the arch of the brows which were toned to correspond with the evidently dyed hair. Her dress, a Paris creation of pale satin and glistening embroidery, was draped to hide her thinness, and her neck and throat were almost covered with strings of pearls and clusters of clear-set diamonds. Judging from the way in which the Leichardt'stonians stared at her as she came down the stairs, it seemed probable that none of them had ever before seen anyone quite like Lady Tallant.

Joan Gildea's eyes passed quickly from Sir Luke and Lady Tallant to a third figure behind them, on the half-landing, but first she realised in a flashing glance that Colin McKeith's gaze had been all the while riveted upon that figure. Not in astonishment – a proof to Joan that he had seen it before – but in a kind of unwilling fascination, most upsetting to Mrs Gildea's sense of responsibility in the matter.

The Visionary Woman of the camp-fire! And she had let Colin McKeith believe that Bridget O'Hara was the embodiment of his Ideal – height five foot seven at the least: weight ten stone or more: smooth-parted, Greek-coiled hair: a cross between a goddess and a Madonna – that was Colin's Ideal – Good Heavens! What did he now behold? A very little woman. One of the snippets he despised. Not an ounce of the traditional dignity about her. Lady Bridget gave the impression of an old-fashioned, precocious child, dressed up in a picture frock of soft shining white stuff, hanging on a straight slender form and gathered into a girdle at the waist, with a wisp of old lace flung carelessly over the slight shoulders. She stood for a moment or two on the half landing, then, as the aide-de-camp murmured in the Governor's ear at the foot of the stairs, she came close to the bannisters and looked down amusedly at the party in the hall. Her face was a little poked forward – a small oval face, pale except for the redness of a rather thin-lipped mouth – the upper lip like a scarlet bow – and the brilliance of the eyes, deep-set under finely-drawn brows and with thick lashes, golden-brown, and curling up at the tips. Peculiar eyes: Mrs Gildea, who knew them well, never could decide their exact colour. The nose was a delicate aquiline, the chin pointed. An untidy mass of wavy chestnut hair stuck out in uneven puffs and insubordinate curls, all round the small head. At this moment Mrs Gildea remembered a suggestive charm sent to Lady Bridget by her cousin, Chris Gaverick, one Christmas, of a miniature gold curry-comb.

It was a vivid brief impression, for the girl moved on immediately, but Joan noticed that Colin McKeith had arrested Lady Bridget's wandering gaze. That was not surprising, for his great height and the distinctiveness of his appearance, made him more likely than anyone else present to attract her attention. Then, as she caught sight of Joan, the interested, startled look changed to one of bright recognition, the red lips smiled, showing dimples at their sensitive corners.

'His Excellency and Lady Tallant,' said the aide-de-camp, and Bridget seemed hardly able to keep herself in the background while Sir Luke and his wife advanced to greet the assembled guests. This, Lady Tallant did with quite enchanting courtesy, making an apt apology for having kept them waiting, which almost mollified the irate

Premier. Bridget came with a swift gliding movement to the side of her friend, squeezed her hand and held it, while she talked in a soft rapid monotone.

'How cool you look. I've never been so hot in my life. And the mosquitoes! Rosamond is in despair. She says she really can't afford to lose more flesh. Do you see how she has had to make herself up to hide the mosquito bites? Luckily, I've got a skin that insects don't find palatable. . . .'

They had of course met since the Landing. Joan had paid her formal visit, had lunched at Government House, and was now on intimate terms with the new people. Also, Lady Bridget had found her way to the cottage on Emu Point.

She looked round at the different groups and gave a cynical little shrug.

'Why! it's like everything one had left behind! I might be at a party to the Colonial Delegates in London for all the difference there is. Where's your barbarism, Joan? . . . I'm pining for a savage existence. . . . That's an excessively good-looking man' – her eyebrows indicated Colin McKeith – 'I do hope he is the man I asked for to take me in to dinner – I told Vereker Wells that I wanted a new sensation – that man looks as if he might give it to me – No, don't tell me: there's excitement in uncertainty.'

She went on in eager monologue, giving no time for replies.

'It seems we've put the official backs up. Vereker Wells was determined to follow Indian vice-regal precedents – so ridiculous – as I told him: and as for Luke, he's got it on the brain that his mission is to uphold the dignity of the British Throne. Like a *nouveau riche* – terribly afraid of doing the wrong thing and showing every moment that he's new to the great Panjandrum part. . . . Ah so!' . . . an ejaculatory trick of Bridget's. 'He *is* my fate!'

Captain Vereker Wells brought up Colin who was holding himself stiffly, limping just a little, as he did when he was nervous, and looking very big and strong and masterful – likewise extraordinarily well-groomed and tailored.

'Lady Bridget O'Hara, let me present Mr Colin McKeith.'

Lady Biddy looked up at Colin and he looked down at her.

'Do you think I can *possibly* reach your arm?' as he held his elbow crooked to about the level of her shoulder. 'You know I asked to be sent in with you – it was rather bold of me, wasn't it? But if I had known how *very* tall you are!'

Mr McKeith lowered his arm, stooping over her, and Mrs Gildea heard him say in a voice that sounded different somehow from his ordinary deep drawl:

'I wonder why I was chosen for this honour?'

And Bridget's reply:

'I'd been told that you were an explorer – that you're a kind of Bush Cecil Rhodes – I don't know Mr Cecil Rhodes, but I have an adoration for him – I wanted to talk to a real Bushman – I always felt that I should like Australian Bushmen from Joan Gildea's description of them. . . . And you. . . .'

The rest was lost, as the groups converged and the long line of couples went forward.

CHAPTER 9

———————•———————

It was not an altogether successful party. The dinner had portentous suggestiveness; the Leidchardt'stonians were at first rather difficult. Sir Luke a little too conscious of his responsibilities towards the British Throne: Lady Tallant so brilliant as to be bewildering. But except as it concerns Lady Bridget and McKeith, the Tallant's first dinner-party at Government House is not of special importance in this story. Mrs Gildea, very well occupied with Dr Plumtree, only caught diagonal gimpses of her two friends a little lower down on the opposite side of the table, and, in occasional lulls of conversation, the musical ring of Lady Bridget's rapid chatter. Colin did not seem to be talking much, but every time Mrs Gildea glanced at him, he appeared absorbed in contemplation of the small pointed face and the farouche, golden-brown eyes turned up to him from under the top heavy mass of chestnut hair. Lady Bridget, at any rate, had a great deal to say for herself, and Mrs Gildea wondered what was going to come of it all.

Conversation became more general as champagne flowed and the courses proceeded.

Sir Luke, discreetly on the prowl for information, attacked Antipodean questions – the Blacks for instance. He had observed the small company of natives theatrically got up in the war-paint of former times, which, grouped round the dais on which he had been received at the State Landing, had furnished an effective bit of local colour to the pageant. Up to what degree of latitude might these semi-civilised, and he feared demoralised beings, be taken as a survival of the indigenous population of Leichardt's Land? Did wild and dangerous Blacks still exist up north and in the interior of the Colony?

'You'd better ask McKeith about that, your Excellency,' said the Premier. 'He knows more about the Blacks up north than any of us.'

The Governor enquired as to the amenability of the Australian native to missionary methods of civilisation, and one of the other Ministers broke in with a laugh.

'Bible in one hand and baccy in the other! No, Sir, the Exeter Hall and General Gordon principles aren't workable with our Blacks. Kindness doesn't do. The early pioneers soon found that out.'

Lady Bridget had stopped suddenly in her talk with Colin, and was listening, her eyes glowering at her companion.

'Why didn't kindness do?' she asked sharply.

'Yes; Mr McKeith, tell us why the early pioneers abandoned the gentle method,' said the Governor.

McKeith's face changed: it became dark and a dangerous fire blazed in his blue eyes.

'Because they found that the Blacks repaid kindness with ingratitude – treachery – foul murder –' He pulled himself up as though afraid of losing command of himself if he pursued the subject: his voice thrilled with some deep-seated feeling. Mrs Gildea, who understood the personal application, broke in across the table with an apposite remark about her own early experiences of the Blacks. Lady Bridget impatiently addressed McKeith.

'Go on. What do the Blacks do now to you people to make you treat them unkindly?'

'What do they do now – to us squatters you mean?' Colin had recovered himself. 'Why they begin by spearing our cattle and then they take to spearing ourselves.'

'Did they ever spear you?' she asked.

Colin smiled at her grimly.

'Well, you wouldn't have noticed, of course, that I've got just a touch of a limp – it's only if I'm not in my best form that it shows. I owe that to a spear through my thigh one night that the Blacks rushed my camp when I was asleep. And I'd given their gins rations that very morning.'

'And then?' Lady Bridget's voice was tense.

'Oh then – after they'd murdered a white man or two, the rest of us whites – there wasn't more than a handful of us at that time up on the Leura – banded together and drove them off into the back country. We had a dangerous job with those Blacks until King Mograbar was shot down.'

'King Mograbar! How cruelly unjust. It was his country you were *stealing*.' She accentuated the last word with bitter scorn.

'Well! If you come to that, I suppose Captain Cook was stealing when he hoisted the British flag in Botany Bay,' said McKeith.

'And if he hadn't, what about the glorious British record, and the March of Civilisation?' put in Vereker Wells.

Bridget shot a scathing glance at the aide-de-camp.

'I don't admire your glorious British record, I think it's nothing but a record of robbery, murder and cruelty, beginning with Ireland and ending with South Africa.'

'Oh! my dear! – I warn you,' said Lady Tallant, bending from her end of the table and addressing the Leichardt'stonians generally. 'Lady Bridget is a little Englander, a pro-Boer, a champion of the poor oppressed native. If she had been alive then she'd have wanted to hand India back to the Indians after the Mutiny, and now when she has made Cecil Rhodes Emperor of Rhodesia, she'll give over all the rest again to the Dutch.'

Bridget responded calmly to the indictment.

'Yes, I would – if Cecil Rhodes were to decline the Emperorship of all South Africa – which I should make his job. . . . But you'd better add on that I'm a Socialist too, Rosamond, because I've become one, as you know. I think the working man is in a shamefully unjust position, and that the capitalists are no better than slave-drivers.'

'Oh, not out here, my word!' exclaimed a Leichardt'stonian who happened to be one of the old squattocracy. 'The landowners and the capitalists are not slave-drivers, they are slave-driven. We've got to pay what the Trades' Union organisers tell us – or else go without stockmen or shearers. Fact is, our Labour War is only just beginning; and I can tell you, Sir, that before a year is out the so-called bloated capitalist and the sheep and cattle station owner will sing either pretty big or very small.'

'I don't think it will be very small – on *my* station,' murmured McKeith. 'But it's quite true about the Labour War. They're organising, as they call it, already all along the Leura.'

The Governor asked to have the Labour situation explained from the squatters' point of view; and for a few minutes McKeith forgot to look at lady Bridget. He was on his own ground and knew what he was talking about.

'It's this way,' he began. 'You see, though, I'm cattle – and I'm the furthest squatter out my way. But there are a few sheep stations down the river, and there isn't an unlimited supply of either cattle-hands or shearers, so we've got to look sharp about hiring them. Now, last year, we – of course I'm classing myself with the sheep-owners, for we all stand together – hired our shearers for seventeen shillings and sixpence a day. Then, up come the Union organisers, form a Union of the men and say to them: "You've got to pay ten shillings down to the Union and sign a contract that you won't shear under twenty shillings a day." The Organiser pockets the ten shillings, and makes three pounds a week and his expenses besides, so it pays *him* pretty well. Well then, the shearers go to the squatters. "All right," say they, "we'll shear your sheep, but it's going to be twenty shillings instead of seventeen and six." The squatters grumble, but they've got to have their sheep shorn, and they pay the twenty shillings. Next year, I'm told, the word is to go round that it's to be twenty-two and sixpence. Well sir, we're to see what's to happen then!'

The Labour talk lacked local picturesqueness. Sir Luke preferred the Blacks, and started the question of danger to white men in the out-districts. How far had officialdom penetrated into the back blocks? He understood that Mr McKeith had explored for the laying of a telegraph-line to the Big Bight. Could Mr McKeith give him any information about all that?

McKeith explained again. He had stopped a week, he said, at the last outpost of Leichardt's land civilisation. The telegraph master there lived in a hut made of sheets of corrugated zinc, raised on piles twenty feet high and fortified against the Blacks. The entrance to it was masked, spear-proof and had two men always on guard – there were four men at the post. McKeith told a gruesome story of an assault by the natives, and of rifles at work through gun-holes in the zinc tower.

Lady Bridget listened in silence. Now and then, she looked up at McKeith, and, though her eyes gave forth ominous red-brown sparks, they had in them something of the same unwilling fascination Joan Gildea had noticed in the eyes of Colin McKeith.

CHAPTER 10

In the drawing room, before the men came in, Bridget talked to Joan Gildea. They hadn't yet had, as Biddy reminded her, a regular outpouring. The outpouring it should be stated, was always mostly on Bridget's side.

'When did you start Socialism?' Mrs Gildea asked. 'That's something new, isn't it?'

Biddy gave one of her slow smiles in which lips, eyes, brows, what could be seen of them under her towzle of hair – all seemed to light up together.

'Why, I've always been a Socialist – in theory, you know. I've *always* rebelled against the established order of things.'

'But latterly,' said Joan, 'I haven't heard anything about your doings – not since you wrote from Castle Gaverick after – after Mr Willoughby Maule's marriage?'

The light died out of Bridget's face. 'Ah, I'll tell you – Do you know, Rosamond saw them – the Willoughby Maules before we all left. She met them at Shoolbred's – buying furniture. Rosamond said *she* was dragging after him looking – a bundle – and cross and ill; and that he seemed intensely bored. Poor Will!'

There was silence, Bridget's thoughts seemed far away.

'But about the Socialism?' prompted Mrs Gildea.

'Oh well, Aunt Eliza made up her mind suddenly to consult her new doctor – Aunt Eliza's chief excitement is changing her doctors, and she grows quite youthful in the process. They say that love and religion are the chief emotional interests of unattached women. I should add on doctors when a woman is growing old. Don't you think, Joan, that in that case, all three come invariably to the same thing?'

'Love, religion and doctors! As emotional interests, do they come to the same thing for elderly women?' repeated Mrs Gildea, as if she were propounding a syllogism. 'No, certainly not, when the elderly woman happens to be a hard-working journalist.'

'Oh, there you have the pull – I suggested the idea to Rosamond the other day and she gave a true Rosamondian answer. "They don't come at all to the same thing," she said, "because usually you have to pay your doctor and *sometimes* your lover pays you." Rather smart, wasn't it?'

'Yes, but I think you'd better warn Lady Tallant that the Leichardt'stonian ladies are a bit Puritanical in their ideas of repartee.'

'Oh, Rosamond is clever enough to have found that out already for herself;' and the two glanced at Lady Tallant, who seemed to be playing up quite satisfactorily to the female representatives of the Ministerial circle.

'I suppose you made friends with some Socialists when you were in London?' went on Mrs Gildea.

'My dear, I would have made friends with Beelzebub just then, if he would have helped me to escape from myself.'

Bridget sighed and paused.

'But you *are* getting over it, Biddy – the disappointment about Mr Maule? You *are* growing not to care?'

'I don't want to grow not to care – though, of course, now I should prefer to care about someone or something that isn't Willoughby Maule, I feel inside me that my salvation lies in caring – in caring intensely. . . . But you wouldn't understand, Joan. You weren't built that way.'

'No,' assented Mrs Gildea doubtfully.

'But,' went on Biddy brightly, 'I think sometimes that if one could get to the pitch of feeling nothing matters, it would be a way of reaching the "letting go" stage which one *must* arrive at before one can even *begin* to live in the Eternal.'

There seemed something a little comic in the notion of Bridget O'Hara living in the Eternal, and yet Mrs Gildea realised that there really was a certain stable quality underneath the flashing, ever changing temperamental sheath, which might perhaps form a base for the Verities to rest upon.

'Beelzebub didn't teach you that,' she said.

'No, quite the contrary. It all came out of my concentration studies and the Higher Thought Centre where I met some most original dears – Christian Scientists and Spiritualists – and then these Socialists – not a bit on the lines of the old Fabians and Bernard Shavians and the rest who used to believe only in Matter – specially landed property matter – and in parcelling that out among themselves. My friends are for parcelling out what they call the Divine Intelligence, which they say will bring them everything they need for the good of others and, incidentally, themselves. Of course none of them have a penny. But they do contrive to get what they want for other people – it was a soup kitchen this winter where they fed 11,000 starving poor. Only, when they begin, they never have the smallest idea of *how* it's going to be done.'

Lady Bridget was so absorbed in her subject that she did not notice the entrance of the men; but Mrs Gildea saw that Colin McKeith was making straight towards them. He halted behind Bridget's chair. Biddy went on in reply to a question from her friend.

'You see, they argue this way, "We don't know," they say, "the *how* of the simplest things in life, we don't know the *how* of our actual existence – how we move or think – not even the *how* of the most ordinary fact in science. We only know that there must be an Intelligence who does know and who has forces at command and the power to set them in motion." '

'And how do we know that?' asked Colin McKeith.

Bridget turned with a start and looked at him solemnly for a second or two.

'You paralyse me: you are too big. I can't speak to you when you are standing up. Please sit down.'

He went to fetch a chair. At the moment, Lady Tallant came up.

'Biddy, will you sing. Do for Heaven's sake make a sensation. Help me out! You know how!'

Lady Bridget had a funny inscrutable little smile and a gleam in her eyes which crinkled up when she was going to say or do something rather naughty.

'I'll do my best, Rosamond. But you don't think it would be a dangerous experiment, do you?'

Lady Tallant laughed, and told Captain Vereker Wells to take her to the piano.

'*You* know that Biddy does a lot of mischief when she sings,' said the Governor's wife, sitting down in Lady Bridget's vacant place beside Mrs Gildea. Colin McKeith, still on the outskirts with his chair, stood leaning upon it, watching the performer.

The piano was in such a position that Lady Bridget faced him.

A vain man might have fancied that she was singing at him, and that the by-play of her song – the sudden eye-brightenings, the little twists of her mouth, the head gestures, were for his particular benefit.

She was singing one of the Neapolitan folk-songs which one hears along the shores of the Mediterranean beyond Marseilles – a love song.

Most people know that particular love-song. Lady Bridget gave it with all the tricks and all the verve and whimsical audacity of a born Italian singer. Well, she was Italian – on one side at least, and had inherited the tricks and a certain quality of voice, irresistibly catching. And she looked captivating as she sang – the small pointed face within its frame of reddish-brown hair, the strange eyes, the expressive red lips, alive with coquetry. The men – even the old politicians, listened and stared, quite fascinated.

Some of the Leichardt's Town ladies – good, homely wives and mothers who, in their early married days of struggle, had toiled and cooked and sewed, with no time to imagine an aspect of the Eternal Feminine of which they had never had any experience, were perhaps a little shocked, perhaps a little regretful. One or two others, younger, with budding aspirations, but provincial in their ideals, were filled with wonder and vague envy.

A few of them had made the usual trip 'Home,' landing at Naples and journeying to London, via Monte Carlo and Paris, and these felt they had missed something in that journey which Lady Bridget was now revealing to them. Joan Gildea, whose profession it was to realise vividly such modes of life as came within her purview, felt herself once more in the blue lands girdling the Sea of Story – It all came back upon her – moonlight nights in Naples; on the Chiaja; looking down from her windows on sunny gardens on the Riviera, and the strolling minstrels in front of the hotel. . . .

As for Colin McKeith who had never been in the Blue Land and knew little even of the British Isles except for London – chiefly around St Paul's School, Hammersmith – and the Scotch Manse where he had occasionally spent his holidays – even he was transported from the Government House drawing-room. Where? . . . . Not to the realm of visions such as he had seen in the smoke of his camp fire. Oh no. He had never dreamed of this kind of enchantment.

A fresh impulse seized the singer. She struck a few chords. A familiar lilt sounded. Her face and manner changed. She burst into the famous song of *Carmen*. She *was Carmen*. One could almost see the swaying form, the seductive flirt of fan. There could be no doubt that had the voice been more powerful, Lady Bridget might have done well on the operatic stage.

Yet it had a *timbre*, a peculiar, devil-may-care passion which produced a very thrilling effect upon her audience. She got up when she had finished in a dead silence and was half-way across the room before the applause burst out. There was a little rush of men towards her.

'Beats Zélie de Lussan and runs Calvé hard,' said the Premier who had made more than one trip to England and considered himself an authority in the matter.

Bridget skimmed through the groups of admirers, stopping to murmur something to Lady Tallant who had met her half way; then stopped with hands before her like a meek schoolgirl, in front of Mrs Gildea and Colin McKeith – he almost the only man who had made no movement towards her. Bridget sank into her former seat.

'The last time I sang that was at a Factory Girls' entertainment at Poplar,' she said. . . 'You should have seen them, Joan: they stood up and tried to sing in chorus and some of them came on to the platform and danced. . . . Mr McKeith you look at me as if I had been doing something desperately improper. Don't you like the music of *Carmen*?'

Colin was staring at her dazedly.

'It seemed to me a kind of witchcraft,' he said. . . . 'I should think you might go on the stage and make a fortune like Melba.'

She laughed. 'Why my voice is a very poor thing. And besides, I could never depend upon it.'

'Everything just how you feel at the time, eh?' he said. 'You wouldn't care what you did if you had a mind to do it.'

'No,' she answered. 'I shouldn't care in the least what I did if I had a mind to do it.'

There was the faintest mimicry of his half Scotch, half Australian accent in her voice – a little husky, with now and then unsuspected modulations. She looked at him and the gleam in her eyes and her strange smile made him stare at her in a sort of fascination. Joan knew those tricks of hers and knew that they boded mischief. She got up at the moment saying that people were going and that she must bid Lady Tallant good-night.

Then the Premier's wife came up shyly; she wanted to thank Lady Bridget for her singing. It had been as good as the Opera – They sometimes had good opera companies in Leichardt's Town, etcetera, etcetera.

Lady Bridget made the prettiest curtsey, which bewildered the Premier's wife and gave her food for speculation as to the manners and customs of the British aristocracy. She had always understood you only curtsied to Royalty. But she took it as a great compliment and never said anything but kind words about Bridget ever after.

Colin McKeith escorted Mrs Gildea to her cab and as they waited in the vestibule, obtained from her a few more particulars of Lady Bridget O'Hara's parentage and conditions. But he said not a word implying that he had discovered her identity with the author of the typed letter.

'I'll come along to-morrow morning if I can manage it, and tell you about Alexandra City and the Gas-Bore,' he said carelessly as she shut the fly door. Joan wondered whether he had caught Lady Biddy's parting words in the drawing room.

'If Rosamond doesn't insist on my doing some stuffy exploration with her, I'll bring my sketches some time in the morning, Joan, and you can see whether any of them would do for the great god Gibbs.'

CHAPTER 11

———————•———————

And what are you going to do, Biddy? How long are you going to stay with the Tallants?'

'Until Rosamond gets tired of me – or I feel no further need of the moral support of the British Throne,' answered Lady Bridget lightly. 'I'm not sure whether I shall be able to stand Luke's Jingo attitude in regard to Labour and the Indigenous Population – all the Colonial problems in capitals, observe. He does take his position so strenuously; it's no good my reminding him that even the Queen is obliged to respect a Constitutional government.'

Bridget took a cigarette from a gold case with her initials in tiny precious stones across it, and handed the case to Mrs Gildea who shook her head.

'Still too old-fashioned to smoke! I should have thought you'd have been driven to it here to keep the mosquitoes at a distance. . . .

'Do you like my case, Joan? Willoughby Maule gave it to me,' she asked.

'You didn't return it then?'

'Why should I have hurt his feelings? We weren't engaged.' A meditative pause and then suddenly, 'Evelyn Mary doesn't smoke. Nice girls don't!'

'Biddy, I shall be sorry for Evelyn Mary if the Maules are to live in London and you go back there again – which I suppose you will do.'

'You needn't suppose for certain that I shall go back.' She savoured her cigarette slowly. 'I can't go on with that old life, the sort of life one has to lead with Aunt Eliza and the Gavericks and their set. I can't go on pushing and striving and rushing here and there in order to be seen at the right houses and join the hunt after fleeing eligibles.'

She gave a bitter little laugh, and then her tone changed to that ripple of frivolity in which nevertheless Mrs Gildea discerned the under-beat of tragedy.

'Besides, even so, it's incongruous – impossible. I've come to the conclusion that the only things which make London – as I've known it – endurable are unlimited credit at a good dressmaker – Oh, and one of the beautiful new motor-cars. You don't mind travelling from Dan to Beersheba if you can do it in five minutes. But when you've got to catch omnibuses or take the Tube, dressed in garden-party finery – well it's all too disproportionate and tiresome.'

Mrs Gildea laughed. 'You must remember that I am out of all your fine social business – except when I go as a reporter or look on from the upper boxes.'

'It's abominable: it's stifling,' exclaimed Lady Biddy, 'it kills all the best part of one. You know I've tried time after time to strike out on my own individual self, but I've always been brought back again by my hopeless, hopeless lack of practical knowledge of how to earn a livelihood. The one gift I'd inherited wasn't good enough to be of any use – If my mother had only left me the whole of her voice, I'd have been an opera-singer. But I don't think I could have stood the drudgery – and I should have hated the publicity of it all. . . . Joan, how did you ever manage to make yourself independent?'

'By drudging,' said Mrs Gildea dryly. 'Besides, I was born differently. And I was brought up with practical people.'

'Mr McKeith, for instance. He told me about his having been what he called a "cattle new-chum" on your father's station.'

'He wasn't exactly a "new-chum." His father had owned a sheep-station up in the unsettled districts. There was a tragedy – the place was sold up when Colin was a boy. He wanted to learn how we did things further south – and besides, he was left without a penny – that's how he came to be with us.'

'Oh! . . . anyway, he's practical. But it isn't that side of him that appeals to me. He believes in Missions – in a sort of way.'

Mrs Gildea laughed uneasily. 'So you have discovered the streak of idealism in Colin. But' – she veered off hastily, 'I didn't want to talk about Colin McKeith. What I want is to hear about your own state of mind.'

'My state of mind! That's chaotic. The fact is, I feel in a horrible sort of transition state. . . . It's just as if one were trying to wind a skein backwards – taking up one end and finding a confusion of knots; then, taking up another and after forcing a few of the knots, giving the thing up in despair. One knows the right end is there, but how to find it through all that hopeless, woolly tangle!'

'Still, you must have learned something about how to wind your skein while you've been working through your various enterprises,' said Mrs Gildea. She took up one of Bridget's sketches which were on the table and looked at it thoughtfully.

'This is quite charming, Biddy – if only it wasn't too fine for reproduction. The block would cost more than the thing is worth.'

Biddy made a *moue*. 'Oh I know. Like me isn't it? Impracticable. But I *could* do you some illustrations. I drew Rosamond entertaining the Ministerial Circle last night and showed it to Vereker Wells while we were waiting for breakfast. He nearly died with laughing. I couldn't have dared to let Luke see it.'

'That I can believe. And I should be murdered by the Leichardt'stonians if I allowed it to be published. But if you'd come with me through the Blue Mountains and caricature yourself exploring the Jenolan Caves – like the "Lady of Quality" in the Dolomite Country I could do something with that.'

Mrs Gildea alluded to their first and only collaboration as author and artist.

'Yes, I might. We'll think about it. And if I did perhaps I could make money enough to keep me out here for a year or two travelling about.'

Joan Gildea looked up in a startled way from the drawing she had been studying, and asked with some eagerness:

'Biddy, do you really mean that you are thinking of stopping out here for a year or two?'

'I do. I want to shake myself free from the old clogs. I want to be honest with myself and with – with the people who *are* honest with themselves. I've always envied you, Joan. Your life is real at least. You can put your finger on vital pulse beats. I should like to do as you are doing, study and learn from a country that has no traditions, but is making itself. I want to breathe Nature unadulterated – if I could only reach the reality of her. Joan, I have the feeling that if one could go right up to the Bush – far away from the Government House atmosphere and Luke Tallant's red-tapism and the stupid imitation of our English social shams – well, I think one might touch a more vital set of heart-beats than the heart-beats of civilization.'

'You are off civilization, Biddy?'

'Yes I am, I've had a horrible time. I was quite reckless and spent far too much on clothes and things – but that's not what matters – it's the effect on one's inner self that matters. And now I'm going through the pangs of revulsion, and just wondering where I can find anything that's true and satisfying. I believe it may be a kind of birth into a new life – coming out here you know and all the rest.'

She stopped, her long golden brown eyes fixed Sphinx-like on Joan, who returned the gaze, but did not answer in words. Biddy went on: '*Your* work is practical – not idealistic. I believe the truth of it all is that the idealists haven't built up on a practical basis. There's too much *pose*. Joan, I do think it's only the pinch of starvation that knocks down the ridiculous *pose* of people.'

'True enough. Your cranks don't get much beyond *pose*. – They think they do, but they don't.'

'Even the ones who believe in themselves – and who are in their way truly sincere. Joan, do you know, there were moments at the meetings I went to of those people – Christian Scientists, and my Spiritual Socialists, and all those philo-factory-girls and tramps, and philo-beasts, and philo-blacks and the rest of it – Moments when a ghastly wonder would come over me whether, if we were all stranded on a desert island with a shortage of food and water, it wouldn't be a case of fighting for bare existence and of Nature red of tooth and claw.'

'True for you, Lady Bridget. I like the way that's put,' broke in a voice from the other side of the veranda railing.

Lady Bridget started and looked round, a sudden flush rushing upon the ivory paleness of her face. If she had not had her back turned to the garden; if she had not left the gate open behind her, and if the wind in the bamboos had not then made a noisy rustling, she would have seen the visitor or heard his steps on the gravel path. Or if she had not been so absorbed in her subject and her cigarette she might have noticed that Mrs Gildea had looked up quickly a minute before and given a mute signal to the intruder not to interrupt the conversation untowardly.

CHAPTER 12

———•———

Lady Bridget recovered herself as Colin McKeith mounted the steps and made the two ladies a rather self-conscious salute.

'I suppose you know that's a quotation,' she said.

'Weren't you a bit out?' he answered, and repeated the phrase. 'Excuse my correcting you.'

Bridget shrugged.

'Thank you. But I always thought men of action weren't great readers. How did you do your reading?'

'Some day –if you care to hear – I'll tell you.'

She looked at him interestedly. 'Yes, I should care to hear.'

'Not now,' put in Mrs Gildea. 'You've come this morning to tell us about the Gas-Bore at Alexandra City, and, as it's got to go into my next letter, I shall take some notes. Do look for a comfortable chair, Colin, and you may smoke if you want to.'

'This is good enough,' and he settled himself after his own fashion at Lady Bridget's feet with his back against the veranda post and his long legs sprawling over the steps.

Lady Bridget leaned out of the depths of her deep canvas chair and offered him her cigarette case.

He eyed it in amused criticism – the dull gold of the case, and the initials in diamonds, sapphires and rubies set diagonally across it.

'*Your* writing?'

Again the faint pink rose in her paleness.

'No, it's the writing of the person who gave it to me.'

'Was it a man?' he asked bluntly.

Bridget looked at him with slight haughtiness.

'Really, Mr McKeith, I think you are – inquisitive.'

'Yes, I am. And I've Bush manners – not up to your form. Please excuse my impertinence.'

'I don't mind Bush manners. They're – rather refreshing sometimes. . . . But' – again extending and then half-withdrawing her offering hand. 'You'd despise my cigarettes?'

He made an eager movement.

'No I shouldn't. Choose me one, won't you – two – if I may have one to keep.'

'Why to keep?' She selected two of the dainty gold-tipped cigarettes, and he received them almost as if they had been sacred symbols. One he placed carefully, notwithstanding her laughing protest, in a letter-case which he carried in an inner pocket. She tilted her face forward for him to light the other cigarette at hers, and he did so, always with that suggestion of reverence which sat so oddly upon him. Mrs Gildea watching the pair was immensely struck by it.

He smoked in silence for a few moments, his eyes still apparently fascinated by the glittering initials on the case which now Bridget attached to her chatelaine chain. She threw away the end of her cigarette.

'Well, so you've become the Governor's unconstitutional adviser?' she said. 'Joan, do you know that Luke Tallant kept Mr McKeith talking and smoking in the loggia just below my bedroom for hours last night after every one had gone – I know, because I couldn't get to sleep.'

McKeith was all compunction, 'I'm downright sorry for that, Lady Bridget. I'd have gone away if I'd only guessed your room was up above.'

'Oh, it didn't matter. I'd lots to think about – my own shortcomings and Luke's responsibilities.'

'He takes them – hard,' hazarded McKeith.

'I hope you gave him good advice,' put in Mrs Gildea.

McKeith's lips twisted into a humorous smile.

'Well, I told Sir Luke that I didn't think he need bother himself just yet awhile over that northern tour of inspection he's talking about.'

'He wants to make a kind of royal progress, Joan, through the Back-Blocks,' said Lady Biddy.

'It'll mean a bit of stiff riding,' said McKeith, 'but I've offered to show him round the Upper Leura anyway, and to find him a quiet hack.'

'Rosamond flatly declines the Royal Progress,' said Bridget. 'I'm coming instead of her.'

'Can you ride?' he asked.

'*Can* I ride – Can any O'Hara ride! You needn't find *me* a quiet hack.'

'All right,' said McKeith. 'But I wouldn't make sure of that by putting you on a buckjumper. It's a bargain then, Lady Bridget.'

'A bargain – what?'

'You promise to pay me a visit when the Governor makes his trip north – when he carries out his notion of establishing military patrols and a Maxim gun or two to put down Trades-Unionism and native outrages in the Back-Blocks?'

Lady Bridget looked at him thoughtfully. He had pulled out his tobacco pouch and was filling a well-worn pipe. 'You won't mind my pipe, will you – as you're a smoker yourself. Mrs Gildea likes it best – And so do I.'

Lady Bridget sniffed his raw tobacco and made a tiny moue. 'Well, if you prefer that – No, of course I don't mind. I see,' she went on, 'that you favour the Maxim gun idea, Mr McKeith. I understand that you're one of the Oppressors; and you and I wouldn't agree on that point.'

Mr McKeith returned her look, all the hardness in his face softening to an expression of almost tender indulgence.

'We'd see about that. I might convert you – but in the Back-Blocks.'

'Or *I* might convert *you*.'

He shook his head, and then laughed in a shy, boyish way.

'There's no knowing what might happen – but in the Back-Blocks.'

Lady Bridget leaned forward. 'Tell me about them – Tell me about your life in the Bush and what makes you hate the Blacks.'

'What makes me hate the Blacks?' he repeated slowly and the soft look in his face changed now to one very dour and grim.

'You do hate them, don't you? Mr McKeith, the Premier told me something about you last night, which simply filled me with horror. If I believed it – or unless I knew that what you did had been in honourable warfare, I don't think I could bear to speak to you again. Now, I'm going to ask you if it's true.'

'If what is true? Lady Bridget, I'll tell you the truth if you ask me for it, about anything I've done. But – I warn you – ugly things happen – in the Back-Blocks.'

'The Premier said that you were the terror of the natives. He told me about a gun you have with a great many notches on the barrel of it, and he said that each notch represented a black-fellow that you had killed.'

'I never killed a black-fellow except in fair fight, or under lawful provocation. Many a time one of them has sneaked a spear at me from behind a gum tree; and I'd have been done for if I hadn't been keeping a sharp look-out.'

'But you were taking their land,' Lady Bridget exclaimed impetuously, 'you had come, an invader, into their territory. What right had you to do that? you were the aggressor. And you can't judge them by the moral laws of civilised humanity. They fought in the only way they understood.'

'Lady Bridget, there are moral laws, which all humanity – civilised or savage understands. I'm not saying that no white man in the Bush has ever violated these laws, I'm not saying that the Blacks hadn't something on their side. I'm only saying that in my experience – it was the black man and not the white man who was the aggressor. And when you ask me what made me hate the Blacks – well – it isn't a pretty story – but, if you like, I'll tell it to you some time.'

'Tell me now,' she exclaimed, 'Oh, Joan . . . Won't your notes keep?'

Mrs Gildea had got up, a sheaf of pencils and a reporter's note book in her hand.

'Yes, for a few minutes. But I've just remembered something I've got to refer to in one of Mr Gibbs' letters. Don't mind me; I'll be back presently.'

McKeith seemed to take no heed of her departure; his eyes were fixed on Lady Bridget; there was in them a light of inward excitement.

'Please go on,' she said, 'I want so much to hear.'

He thought for a few moments, shook the ashes from his pipe and then plunged into his story.

'I've got to go back to when I was quite a youngster – taken from school – I went to St Paul's in the Hammersmith Road – just before I was seventeen. You see before that my father had scraped together his little bit of money and we'd been living in West Kensington waiting while he made out what we were all going to do. He wasn't any great shakes, my father, in the way of birth, and fortune. I daresay, you guessed that, Lady Bridget?'

She tossed her head back impatiently. 'Oh what *does* that matter! Go on, please.'

'He'd been a farmer, Glasgow way' – McKeith still pronounced it 'Glesca,' 'and my mother was a minister's daughter, as good a woman and as true a lady as ever breathed. But that's neither here nor there in what turned out a bad business. Well, we all emigrated out here, and, after a while, my old dad bought a station on the Lower Leura – taken in he was, of course, over the deal, and not realising that it was unsettled country in those days. So the whole family of us started up from the coast to it. . . . He drove my mother and my two sisters just grown up, and a woman servant – Marty – in a double buggy, and Jerry the bullock driver and me in the dray with him and taught me to drive bullocks. There were stock-boys, two of them riding along side.

'It took us three and a half weeks, to reach the station, averaging about thirty miles a day and camping out each night.

'I'd like you to camp out in the Bush sometime, Lady Bridget, right away from everything – it'ud be an experience that 'ud live with you all your life – My word! It's like nothing else – lying straight under the Southern Cross and watching its pointers, and, one by one, the stars coming up above the gum trees – and the queer wild smell of the gums and the loneliness of it all – not a sound until the birds begin at dawn but the *hop-hop* of the Wallabies, and the funny noises of opossums, and the crying of the curlews and native dogs – dingoes we call 'em. . . . Well, there! I won't bother you with all that – though, truly, I tell you, it's the nearest touch with the Infinite *I've* ever known. . . . Lord! I remember the first night I camped right in the Bush – me rolled in my blanket on one side of the fire, and Leura-Jim the black-boy on the other. And the wonder of it all coming over me as I lay broad awake thinking of the contrast between London and its teeming millions – and the awful solitude of the Bush. . . . I wonder if your blood would have run cold as mine did when the grass rustled under stealthy footsteps and me thinking it was the blacks sneaking us – and the relief of hearing three dismal howls and knowing it was dingoes and not blacks.'

'I'd have loved it,' murmured Bridget tensely. 'Go on, please.'

'Well, I've got to come to the tragedy. It began this way through an act of kindness on our journey up. We were going through the bunya-bunya country not far from our station, when out of the Bush there came a black gin with two half-caste girls, she ran up and stopped the buggy and implored my mother's protection for her girls because the Blacks wanted to kill and eat them.'

'O . . . oh!' Biddy made a shuddering exclamation.

'Didn't I say the Blacks hadn't everything on their side – I ought to explain though that in our district were large forests of a kind of pine – there's one in this garden,' and he pointed to a pyramidal fir tree with spreading branches of small pointed leaves spiked at the ends, and with a cone of nuts about the size of a big man's head, hanging from one of the branches.

'That's the bunya-bunya, and the nuts are splendid roasted in the ashes – if ever that one gets properly ripe – it has to be yellow, you know – I'll ask Joan Gildea to let me roast it for you. Only it wouldn't be the same thing at all as when it's done in a fire of gum logs, the nuts covered with red ashes, and then peeled and washed down with quartpot tea. . . .'

'Quartpot tea! What a lot you'll have to show me if – if I ever come to your station in the Back-Blocks.'

'Different from your London Life, eh? . . . Your balls and dinners and big shows and coaching meets in Hyde Park, and all the rest of the flummery! Different, too, from your kid-glove fox-hunts over grass fields and trimmed hedges and puddles of ditches – the sort of thing you've been accustomed to, Lady Bridget, when you've gone out from your castle for a sporting spree!'

'A sporting spree!' She laughed with a child's merriment, and he joined in the laugh. 'It's clear to me, Mr McKeith, that *you've* never hunted in Ireland. And how did you know, by the way, that I'd lived in a castle?'

'I was led to believe that a good many of your kind owned historic castles which your forefathers had won and defended with the sword,' he answered, a little embarrassed.

'That's true enough. . . . But if you could see Castle Gaverick! My old Aunt is always talking of restoring it, but she never will, and if my cousin Chris Gaverick ever does come into it, he'd rather spend his money in doing something else. . . . But never mind that. . . . I want to hear about the black gin and the half-caste girls, and if your mother saved them from the cannibals . . . and why the blacks wanted to eat their own kind. Dog doesn't eat dog – at least, so they tell one.'

'It's this way. Our blacks weren't regular cannibals, but in the bunya season they'd all collect in the scrubs and feed on the nuts and nothing else for months. Then after a bit they'd get meat-hungry, and there not being many wild animals in Australia and only a few cattle in those outlying districts, they'd satisfy their cravings by killing and eating some of themselves – lubras – young girls – by preference, and, naturally, half-castes, as having no particular tribal status, for choice.'

'Half-castes!' She repeated, a little puzzled.

'These ones had Chinky blood in them – daughters of a Chinaman fossicker. . . . We're not partial to the Chinese in Australia – only we don't eat them, we expel them – methods just a bit dissimilar, but the principle the same, you see. . . . Anyway, of course we took on the gin and her girls, and for about a year didn't have any particular trouble at the station with the blacks – though there was a shepherd speared in one of the out-huts. . . . That was his fault, however, poor devil – the old story – but it don't matter. The trouble came to a head with a black boy, called Leura-Jimmy, that Jerry the bullock-driver brought up with him and left at the station when he went down to the township for store supplies – He took me with him – I told you I was learning bullock-driving. . . .'

McKeith paused, and the dark look came upon his face.

'And Leura-Jimmy?' put in Bridget.

'Oh, he was a fine, big fellow – plausible, too, and could speak pidgin English – he was never weaned from his tribe, and he was a treacherous scoundrel at heart. . . . As a precautionary measure, my father forbade the blacks to come up to the head-station. But Jimmy fell in love with the eldest of the half-caste girls. She encouraged him at first, then took up with one of the stock-boys. . . .

'It was the bunya season again, and the girls' old tribe, under their King Mograbar – a devil incarnate in a brute – I sent him to Hell afterwards with my own hand and never did a better deed' – McKeith's brown fists clenched and the fury in his eyes blazed so that he himself looked almost devilish for a moment. His face remained very grim and dour as he proceeded.

'Jimmy had got to know through the half-caste girl about our ways and doings, and he made a diabolic plot with King Mograbar to get the blacks into the house. . . . Every living soul was murdered . . . surprised in their sleep. . . . My father . . . my mother . . . my sisters. . . . God! . . . I can't speak of it. . . .'

He got up abruptly, jerking his long legs, and went to the further end of the veranda, where he stood with set features and brows like a red bar, below which staring eyes were fixed vacantly upon the avenue of bunya trees in the long walk of the Botanical Gardens across the river. But they did not see those bunya trees. What they saw was a row of mutilated bodies, lying stark along the veranda of that head-station on the Leura.

Bridget was leaning forward in her squatter's chair, her fingers grasping the arms of it, her face very white and her eyes staring too, as though they also beheld the scene of horror.

Presently McKeith came back, pale too, but quite composed.

'I beg your pardon,' he said stiffly. 'Perhaps I should not have told you.'

'It's – horrible. But I'm glad to know. Thank you for telling me.'

He looked at her wistfully. There was silence for a moment or two.

'And you . . . you . . . where were you?' she stammered.

'Me! I was with the drays, you know. We got back about noon that day. . . . If we'd been twelve hours sooner! Well, I suppose I should have been murdered with the rest. . . . The blacks had gone off with their loot. . . . We . . . we buried our dead. . . . And then we ran up our best horses and never drew rein for forty miles till we'd got to where a band of the Native Police were camped. . . . And then . . . we took what vengeance we could. . . . It wasn't complete till a long time afterwards.'

He was standing behind Bridget's chair, his eyes still gazing beyond the river. He did not notice that she leaned back suddenly, that her hands fell nervelessly to her lap. He felt a touch on his arm. It was Mrs Gildea, who had come out to the veranda again. 'Colin,' she said, 'I want you to go and bring me my typewriter from the parlour. And then you've got to dictate "copy," about the Alexandra City Gas-Bore. Please go at once.'

He obeyed. Mrs Gildea bent over Lady Bridget.

'Biddy! . . . You're not faint, are you?'

Lady Bridget roused herself and looked up at her friend rather wildly. . . . 'No. . . . What do you take me for? . . . I said I wanted real things, Joan . . . And I've got them.'

She laughed a little hysterically.

'All right! But we shall give you a taste of real Australia that isn't quite so gruesome. That some of tragedy belongs to the pioneer days. . . . I could tell you things myself that my father has told me. . . . But I won't. . . . Mind, Colin McKeith is no more of a hero than a dozen bush boys I knew when I first knew him. Yes, put it there, Colin, please. . . . And now, if Biddy doesn't mind, we'll proceed to business, which is my *Imperialist* Letter. I suppose you haven't brought back any snapshots of Alexandra City and your wonderful Gas-Bore that Mr Gibbs could get worked up for his paper?'

CHAPTER 13

————————●————————

That was not the only time Lady Bridget and McKeith met on Mrs Gildea's veranda. In fact, Biddy, reminiscent of wild sea-excursions along the shore by Castle Gaverick, developed a passion for what she called tame boating on the Leichardt River. She found a suitable skiff in the boat-house – the Government House grounds sloped to the water's edge, and would row herself up and down the river reaches. It was easy to round the point, skirt the Botanical Gardens, and, crossing above the ferry, land below Mrs Gildea's cottage, then climb up the bank and enter by a lower gate to the garden. Thus she would often turn up unexpectedly of mornings for a chat with her friend in the veranda study.

At this time, Colin McKeith contracted a similar habit. He showed a still greater interest in Mrs Gildea's journalistic work and professed a strong desire to enlighten British statesmen, through the medium of Mr Gibbs' admirable paper, on certain Imperial questions affecting Australia – the danger of a Japanese invasion in the northern waters – the establishment of a naval base by Germany in New Guinea – the Yellow Labour Problem and so forth. He would intersperse his political dissertation with racy bits of description of life in the Bush, and would give the points of view of pearl fishers, miners, loafers, officials in out-of-the-way townships, Labour reformers, sheep and cattle owners – all of which vastly amused Lady Bridget, and was valuable 'copy,' typed unscrupulously by Mrs Gildea. In fact, she owed to it much of the success which, later, attended her journalistic venture. Mrs Gildea thought at first that the 'copy' would be more easily obtainable in the intervals before and after Lady Bridget's arrival, or on the days when she failed to come. But, finding that Colin was distinctly at his best as a narrator with Biddy for an audience, she artfully arranged to take her notes under those conditions. This lasted two or three weeks, during which period Sir Luke and Lady Tallant conscientiously improved their acquaintance with the new sphere of their labours. They visited hospitals, inspected public buildings, inaugurated social schemes, and, to the strains of 'God Save the Queen,' performed many other insignificant public functions, from which, as often as not, their guest, Lady Bridget, basely cried off.

On one such occasion, Joan, arrayed in her best, had patriotically gone forth on a steaming March day to support their Excellencies, fondly expecting that, as arranged, Lady Bridget and Colin would meet her. But Lady Tallant, looking distinctly cross, accompanied the Governor alone. Bridget, it appeared, had come down, just as the carriage drove up, in her morning frock and garden hat, saying that she had a bad headache and meant to spend the afternoon in a hammock by the river bank. As for Colin, there was no sign of him.

But when Mrs Gildea got home very tired and hot she was made extremely angry by hearing the voices of Lady Bridget and McKeith in the veranda where they were drinking tea and, it seemed, holding a confidential conversation. Mrs Gildea's gorge rose higher. She had to stop a minute to try and recover her temper. Here was Biddy disburdening herself to Colin of her family troubles and short-comings, showing herself and them in the worst light, singing small to a man with whom it was highly desirable she should maintain her dignity. Instead of that, she was deliberately pulling down the barrier of rank and social position which should exist between Lady Bridget O'Hara and the Factor's son, the Out-Back squatter – Colin McKeith.

Biddy was saying: 'Oh, but you're as bad as that sort of person who can't be made to realise that the oldest peerage in Ireland counts for nothing in comparison with an oil-king's millions and being able to entertain the right set. . . . And besides, really Mr McKeith, there's no difference at all between us. You talk such a lot about *your* grandfather having been a Scotch peasant. Why! *my* mother's father was an Italian beggar – Ugh! haven't you seen them with their crutches and things on the steps of the churches? – And my mother sang in the streets of Naples until a kind musician heard her and had her trained to be an opera singer.'

'Your mother?'

'My mother! That's where my *Carmen* comes from – only that my voice, I'm told, isn't to be compared with what hers was. . . . But that's not the worst about my mother. Not that I blame her. I think that a woman has a perfect right to leave her husband if she has ceased to care for him, and that it's far more moral to live with a man you love and can't marry, than with a husband you hate.'

Mrs Gildea cut short Lady Bridget's exposition of her views on morality before McKeith had time to answer. Her voice was sharp as she went up the steps and arraigned the pair.

'Really, Biddy, I do call this too bad of you. May I ask how you and Mr McKeith come to be drinking tea together in my veranda?'

'Sure, and it's by accident intoirely,' answered Biddy, with a whimsical look and the touch of the brogue she sometimes put on when a situation became embarrassing.

'A prearranged accident!'

'No it wasn't, Joan. As a matter-of-fact, we were the last persons either of us expected to meet.'

'Honour bright,' put in McKeith. 'I'd forgotten all about the Pineapple Products Exhibition, and I just dropped in at Government House to pay my respects after a pleasant dinner two nights ago – What you'd call a visit of digestion.'

'And since when, Colin, have you become an observer of social obligations?' jeered Mrs Gildea.

He grinned. 'Ah! you have me there. Anyway, I asked for Lady Bridget, and found her down by the boat-shed.'

'And we thought it would be cooler on the water, so he rowed me round the point. It was the most natural thing in the world that we should discover we were thirsty, and that we should come up the garden and ask your old woman to give us some tea. Don't be a cat, Joan. You never used to be grudging of your hospitality.'

Mrs Gildea quickly recovered her usual genial demeanour. She poured herself out a cup of tea, and remarked that it was refreshing after the pine-apple syrups and other concoctions she had, as in duty bound, sampled at the Show. Lady Bridget rattled along with questions about the Function and the behaviour of the Government House party. Had Sir Luke been too over-poweringly pompous? Was Lady Tallant really cross? and had Vereker Wells made any more blunders? and so forth. But she did not enlighten Mrs Gildea much about her doings with Colin McKeith, and presently said she must go and make her peace with Rosamond. McKeith accompanied her – naturally, since he had to row her back to the Government House landing. There was something in the manner of the pair that Mrs Gildea could not understand. Of course, Colin was in love – that she knew already. But was Biddy merely playing with the big primitive-souled bushman – or was it possible that she, too, could be in love?

CHAPTER 14

The next time Biddy came, Joan tackled matters boldly.

'Biddy, I've had my marching orders. Mr Gibbs friends Leichardt's Land a bit stale. I take train to Sydney next week and tour the Riverina, the Blue Mountains and the country along the railway line to Melbourne. Are you coming with me?'

Bridget gave a deprecatory laugh. 'I don't know what Rosamond would say.'

'She'd recognise the necessities of the situation. Besides, you could come back again.'

'I haven't been here a month. And I don't find Leichardt's Land stale. On the contrary, I find it extremely stimulating. No, I think the Riverina and the Blue Mountains will keep, as far as I'm concerned.'

'But *I* won't keep. Mr Gibbs, and the drawings for *The Imperialist* won't keep. The question is whether you want to make some money or not?'

'It's the one thing I've *wanted* to do all my life, and have never yet succeeded in doing except when we collaborated in "The Lady of Quality." '

'Here's your chance for a continuation series, "The Lady of Quality in the Bush." How does that sound?'

'Rather clumsy and long, don't you think? "Lady Bridget in the Bush" would be more alliterative and catching. Only I should be giving myself away.'

'I think you're doing that already,' said Mrs Gildea.

'How do you mean, Joan? I don't see it.'

'Yes, you do. Look here, Biddy. Colin McKeith isn't Mr Willoughby Maule.'

'He's a hundred times better man, Joan.'

'That you needn't tell me; and I'm glad you recognise the fact. But from the point of view of "The Lady of Quality," would he be a better husband?'

'You forget, my dear, that I'm not the genuine article. I'm nothing but a pinchbeck imitation of the real "Lady of Quality." If *his* grandfather was a peasant, remember that my maternal grandparents were peasants too. I told him so yesterday.'

'Has it come to that? You go fast, Biddy. But I warn you – Colin McKeith isn't the man to be trifled with. He knows his own mind. The question is whether you know yours.'

Biddy nodded her head like a Chinese Mandarin.

'Two months ago you were wildly in love – or, at least, from your letters one might have judged so – with another man,' said Mrs Gildea.

'No – no – don't call that love.'

'Call it a violent attraction, then. I suspect the man could have made you marry him if he had chosen. So far as I can understand, you quarrelled because neither of you would face matrimony on what you considered an inadequate income.'

'Middle-class respectability – living in Pimlico or further Kensington,' scoffed Biddy. 'Ordering sprats and plaice for dinner and pretending they're soles and whitebait. Perambulators stuffing up the hall; paying your own books and having your gown made at home! No, thank you. 'Possum skins and a black's gunya – that's Australese for a wigwam, isn't it? – appeal to me infinitely more.'

Mrs Gildea threw up her hands.

'Biddy, you haven't the faintest notion how dull and uncomfortable – how utterly unpoetic – how sordid the life of a struggling bushman can be.'

'No! You know, Joan, I think that it might be perfectly fascinating – if one really cared for the bushman.'

'Really cared! Have you *ever* really cared for any man? *Could* you ever really care?'

'That's what I've been asking myself. It would have to be someone quite different from all the other men I've liked – something altogether above the ordinary man, to make me *really* care.'

'You said that Mr Willoughby Maule was different from any man you'd ever met. Each man you've ever fancied yourself in love with has been different from all the rest.'

Lady Bridget laughed rather uneasily.

'How tiresomely exact you are, Joan! Of course, they were different. Everybody is different from everybody else. And I attract marked types. Will was more marked and more attractive – as well as attracted – that's all.'

'His attraction doesn't seem to have been as strong as self-interest, any way,' said Joan, with deliberate terseness.

The girl's small, pale face flushed to deep crimson for a moment.

'Joan, you are cruel! You know that was the sting! And it wouldn't have stung so if I hadn't cared. Sometimes I feel the maddest desire to hurt him – to pay him out. I never felt like that about any of the others – the ones I really did *almost* want to marry. And then – at other times I'd give *anything* just to have him again as he used to be.'

'I'm certain you weren't really in love with him,' exclaimed Mrs Gildea.

Bridget seemed to be considering. 'Wasn't I? – I'm not so sure of that. No –' she went on impetuously, 'I was not *really* in love with him. He had a magnetic influence over me as I told you. Perhaps I might get a little under it again if he were to appear suddenly without his wife – it turns me sick to think of a married man having a magnetic influence over me. . . . Even if there was no wife – now. So, when you've idealised a person and can't idealise him any more: *C'est fini*. There's nothing but a ghost to come and make you uncomfortable sometimes – and that *can't* last. . . . Besides, I've been breathing the strong clear air of your gum trees lately. It's a case of pull devil – pull bushman. Do you see?'

'I see, my dear, that you're idealising Colin McKeith, and let me tell you that a bushman is very far removed from the super-man. Oh, Colin is a fine enough specimen of a pioneer in a rough country. But his rough life, his bush surroundings, and all the rest – why, he'd jar upon you in a hundred ways if you were alone with him in them. Then – he's not of your order – though I hate the phrase and I hate the kind of man. All the same, Biddy, you may pretend to despise the men of your own class, but I fancy that, after a spell of roughing it with Colin on the Upper Leura, you'd hanker after something in them that Colin hasn't and never will have. . . . And then,' Joan's swift imagination carried her on with a rush, 'you don't know in the least the type of man he is. You'd have to give in to him: he'd never give in to you. He's domineering, jealous, vindictive and reserved. Before a month was out you'd quarrel, and there would be no chance of your ever making it up again.'

'I must say, Joan, that for a friend of his you're not an enthusiastic advocate.'

'It's because I'm so fond of Colin that I hate the thought of your making him miserable. Anyway, however, you're bound to do that.'

'I don't see why.'

'If you flirt with him and then drop him, he'll suffer, though he'll be too proud to show it. And as for the alternative, it's out of the question. you must see that it would be sheer folly.'

'I've committed a great many follies,' said Bridget wistfully.

'But, so far, none that are quite irrevocable.'

'Well, he hasn't asked me yet to commit this one.'

'You're leading him on to it. Biddy, it is abominable of you to encourage him as you do – coming here with him that day. . . . And you let him take you riding. . . .'

'Yes, he knows now that I *can* ride.'

'And he's at Government House nearly every day – I can't think what Lady Tallant is about to ask him so often to dinner.'

'She likes him because he takes Luke off her hands. You know we've nick-named him the Unconstitutional Adviser.'

'That's rubbish. You sing to him.'

'What harm is there in my singing to Colin McKeith?'

'As if you didn't know well enough that you're perfectly irresistible when you look at a man while you're singing those Neapolitan things. Biddy, it won't do. Give it up.'

'I can't do that, Joan.' She spoke with a strange earnestness. 'Don't you see that it's giving me a chance.'

'Of forgetting Mr Willoughby Maule!'

'Yes. . . . But it's more than that.'

'More than that. . . . Do you mean . . . can you mean that you could love Colin McKeith – for himself?'

'Love is a big word, Joan. I've never said to any man – "I love you." ' She spoke the words now as if she were uttering a sacred formula. Her voice reminded Mrs Gildea of something – the same note in the voice of Colin McKeith when he, too, had spoken of love. Yet what she had said was true. Bridget had talked often enough of falling 'in love'– which she had always been at pains to define as a mere transitory condition – not by any means the 'real thing,' and she had freely confessed to violent attractions and even adorations. But, as she had sometimes solemnly stated, she had never 'loved.'

'I can't explain,' she went on. 'I know you think me a heartless, emotional flirt. Yes, I am. I admit it. But there's a locked door in the inner chamber – a shrine that no one has desecrated. The Goddess is there, waiting – waiting to reveal herself.'

'And so – all the rest have been – experiments?'

'No, The Quest of the Ideal through the Forest of Illusion. I've often thought, Joan, there was a lot in the motive of that novel of Thomas Hardy's *The Well Beloved*. But I seem to be mixing up my metaphor, and it's time I went back to Government House.' She got up and began putting on her gloves.

Mrs Gildea laughed hysterically. Somehow, she could not imagine Colin McKeith producing the golden key and masterfully taking possession of Lady Bridget's locked shrine. She could only think of him as tricked, deceived and suffering hideously at the end. She stammered out her fear, beseeching Biddy to be merciful, but Biddy's mood had changed, and she only smiled her Sphinx smile.

'I think he's quite able to look after himself,' she said. 'And if he isn't, sure, he must take the consequences.'

CHAPTER 15

Mrs Gildea could get nothing more out of Lady Bridget. She attacked McKeith in a more tentative manner, but Colin was doggedly reticent. He was taking the thing hardly. His way of facing a serious situation was by setting his teeth and saying nothing. After these unsuccessful attempts, Joan made opportunity, before leaving, for a private word on the subject with Lady Tallant. But Rosamond Tallant treated the matter, at first, very lightly.

'Dear Mrs Gildea, you needn't worry, it's only Biddy's way. She must have some excitement to keep her going. If it isn't one thing, it's another. In London, I tried to interest her in Society, or Politics, and the Opera – and now Luke is trying to interest her in Colonial questions – but she always drifts back to – Men. She can't help it. And the funny thing is, I don't believe that in her heart she is capable of a serious attachment.'

'I'm not so sure of that,' answered Mrs Gildea.

'If so, she has had plenty of opportunities of proving it. But I wasn't ever afraid even of Willoughby Maule. I was certain that would fizzle out before real harm could come of it. And mercifully it did. He's married a woman with a quarter of a million and the right to dispose of it absolutely as she pleases. I heard that she signed a will on her wedding day, leaving it all to him in the event of her death. Too great a temptation, wasn't it? Though I do think if Biddy had chosen she might have kept him in spite of Miss Baggalay and her money. As it is, Colin McKeith, or else the novelty of it all out here – has driven him out of her head. I felt sure of that when I asked her to come. You needn't worry about her.'

'It's not so much about Biddy that I'm worrying as about my old

friend, Colin McKeith,' said Mrs Gildea. 'It isn't fair that he should
be made a victim.'

'Oh, well, it isn't altogether Biddy's fault that she attracts all types
of men.' And then Lady Tallant made exactly the same remark as
Lady Bridget. 'I think Mr McKeith is quite able to look after himself.
I don't pity him in the least. Didn't somebody say of Lady Something
or Other that to love her was a liberal education?'

'Steele said it of Lady Elizabeth Hastings.'

'I call it a liberal education for Colin McKeith to love Lady Bridget
O'Hara,' laughed Lady Tallant.

Mrs Gildea changed her tactics and voiced her other fear – a more
insistent fear.

'Has it ever occurred to you that Lady Bridget O'Hara might fall in
love with Colin McKeith?'

'Why, my dear, she's wildly in love with him already,' rejoined
Lady Tallant, to Joan Gildea's surprise.

'You've seen it?'

'I'm not blind, and I know Biddy. But I've seen that she's taking
this affair differently from the others, and that's what makes me think
it has gone deeper. A very good thing for Biddy.'

'You can't mean that it would be a good thing for Biddy to marry
Colin McKeith?'

Lady Tallant's social manner was rather full of affectations.
Underneath it, however, lay commonsense and sympathy. She
became suddenly simple and direct.

'Well, now, Mrs Gildea, let us look at the matter without
prejudice. You are fond of Biddy and so am I, but we know her
drawbacks. Naturally, it wouldn't be a good thing under ordinary
conditions, but *is* she likely to do much better?'

'She has had plenty of chances.'

'And thrown them all away. And though she looks so young, she is
close on thirty. Of course, with her looks and her fascination she
ought to have married well. I'm sure her friends have tried hard
enough for her. But what can you do with a girl who throws herself at
the heads of ineligibles, and when one trots out an unexceptionable
parti and does one's best to bring them together, goes off at a tangent
and lets the whole thing drop through. You know how it was
with. . . .' Lady Tallant enumerated names.

Mrs Gildea acquiesced mournfully. Lady Tallant continued:

'The truth is, Biddy has tired out the patience of her relatives and friends. Molly and Chris Gaverick got the hump over Willoughby Maule – who would have done well enough if he had only had more money. Old Eliza' – so Lady Tallant irreverently styled the Dowager Countess of Gaverick – 'told me herself that she was going to wash her hands of Biddy. I shouldn't wonder if she didn't leave her a penny. And, after all, it was her own fortune, and she has a horde of needy relatives. She will consider that she has done her duty to the Gavericks if she lets Chris have the Castle. When all's said and done, I don't see that it would be such a bad thing for Biddy to marry a rich Australian squatter.'

'Colin McKeith is not rich.'

'Oh, he will be. Sir Luke has been hearing all about him.'

'He's not her equal. His father was just a land bailiff, and his grandfather a crofter.'

'Oh, what *does* that matter! In these days any of us would marry the roughest of rough diamonds, provided he was decently well off. Biddy has always been mad after adventure and an open-air life. She's an original, and everything would be in keeping.' Lady Tallant went on briskly. 'She would enjoy living among the blacks, provided they did not murder her, and I suppose one could trust Mr McKeith for that.'

'Oh, there's no danger from the blacks now,' put in Mrs Gildea.

'And then she needn't be buried for ever in the Bush. Luke tells me that Colin McKeith is certain to come to the fore in politics – I daresay he will be Premier of Leichardt's Land before long. Biddy would like bossing the show and airing her philanthropic crazes.'

Mrs Gildea shook her head doubtfully.

'Colin wouldn't agree with them. Besides, she would be expatriated.'

'Oh no. The big men over here are always taking trips to England, being fêted and made much of in Downing Street – Imperialist Policy and that sort of thing – I can see Biddy at it.'

Mrs Gildea was silent. She scarcely knew Lady Tallant in this downright mood.

'There's no use blinking matters,' said that lady. 'At home, Biddy has been a failure. That was why I persuaded her to come out with us. I knew she wanted a fresh start badly.'

It was quite true. Mrs Gildea remembered Bridget's confidences to herself. She could not help feeling that Lady Tallant was right in the main, and put forward no more objections. But she explained her own plans and the necessity for her immediate departure from Leichardt's Land – how she had hoped, too, to take Biddy with her and interest her once more in literary and artistic work.

'Biddy won't go, she told me so, and I don't mean to let her,' said Lady Tallant decidedly. 'We're short-handed till the new Private Secretary gets here, and she helps me with my notes and things generally. And if it wasn't for Biddy's singing, our dinners would be too deadly dull for words.'

Joan gave up in despair. She suspected that Lady Tallant's affectionate candour was not unadulterated with selfishness. Finally, Rosamond promised that she would interest and amuse Lady Bridget to such an extent as would deter her from rash love-making for want of counter excitement. Then, Joan reflected, Colin was pre-eminently a prudent business man, and, as he had told her some time before, would have to go back to the Upper Leura before the strenuous work of the Session came on. This was always supposing that the present Ministry kept in without going to the country upon certain Labour measures unacceptable to the large land-owners, in which case it was just possible McKeith might be thrown out of his seat.

Events lay in the lap of the gods. Mrs Gildea wound up matters at the Cottage and took train south, where she was soon wholly occupied in describing the wonder of the Jenolan Caves and the wild gorges and primæval gum forests in the Blue Mountains. She was really too busy in the interests of the *Imperialist* to worry over her friend's love affairs. In fact, she gleaned most of her information as to the Leichardt's Town Government House Party from the newspapers she happened upon at bush hotels. For Lady Bridget was evidently in a reactionary mood as regards letter-writing and Colin McKeith never put pen to paper, if he could avoid doing so, except on business.

It was at Mossvale that she read a florid paragraph in the Ladies' Page of a Sydney Journal, telling of the engagement of 'that intrepid Pioneer and future Empire-builder, Mr Colin McKeith, to the Lady Bridget O'Hara, niece of the late, and cousin of the present, Earl of Gaverick'.

Next post brought her three brief and characteristic letters. She opened Lady Tallant's first:

'Government House,
Leichardt's Town.

'DEAR MRS GILDEA,

I do hope this may catch you before the newspapers, which I find announced the engagement rather prematurely last week. I am still of opinion that Biddy might do much worse than marry Colin McKeith, though, *entre nous*, the settlements – or rather want of them – for Mr McKeith tells us that he needs all his capital for making wells and buying cattle, and he won't injure his prospects and Biddy's by tying it up – does not at all please Sir Luke, who, before he would countenance the marriage, insisted upon a cablegram being sent to the Dowager Lady Gaverick. Her answer: "Not my business, must do as she pleases," only confirms what I said to you, and I am afraid Biddy's chances are worth nothing in that quarter.

The wedding is to be early in May, from Government House, of course, and I need scarcely say how much we all hope you will come back for it.

Always sincerely,
ROSAMOND TALLANT.

P.S. – No doubt, Biddy is giving you full details.'

But Biddy did not indulge either in details or rhapsodies. She began:

'They say hanging and wiving go by destiny, and clearly my destiny is to become the wife of Colin McKeith. I've always felt that the only thing which could reconcile me to marriage would be marrying a MAN; and at last I've found one. I want to tell you, Joan, that we've made an agreement to ask each other no questions about our respective Pasts. The black-fellows he has slain – the one jarring note between us – are never to be resuscitated. The men whose hearts I have broken and *vice versa* are henceforth dead and buried on the other side of the Equator, under a monument of inviolable silence. Such are the terms of the marriage contract: and you in especial must respect them. I need say no more, except this: Have no fears for the happiness of

Your BIDDY.'

From Colin in telegraphic conciseness:

'Tremendously happy. She's absolutely my Ideal – in everything but size.'

All very satisfactory and conclusive. But – Mrs Gildea could not escape from a vague misgiving. She was not afraid of the ghost of Mr Willoughby Maule: indeed, she argued favourably from the baldness of Bridget's letter in comparison with the reams of sentiment she had written upon the previous occasion. Nor did she feel uneasy on the score of any others of Lady Bridget's bygone passions. But had this complex, fastidious, physically-refined creature the least comprehension of what life on the Upper Leura might mean? And how about an Ideal dethroned from her pedestal and plumped down amid the crude realities of the nethermost Bush?

Mrs Gildea did not get to the wedding. She was ordered to report on the mines of Western Australia, and was on the other side of the continent when the marriage took place. In fact, it seemed doubtful whether she would again meet Lady Bridget before her mission as Special Correspondent ended. But the McKeiths were to spend their honeymoon in travelling to his station on the Upper Leura, a distance of some hundreds of miles from the nearest port, and quite out of *The Imperialist* programme.

She read, however, circumstantial accounts of the wedding, and there were portraits of the pair – in which Colin looked grumpy and Lady Bridget whimsically amused – snap shots, too, of the wedding cortège, in which Sir Luke Tallant, fathering the Bride, appeared a pompous figure in full uniform; and Lady Tallant in splendid panoply, most stately and gracious. A long account followed of the bride's family connections, in which the biographer touched upon the accident of sex that had deprived her of the hereditary honours; the ancient descent of the Gavericks, with a picture of the old Irish castle where Lady Bridget had been brought up – and so forth, and so forth. Mrs Gildea sighed as she read, and pictured in her imagination the wild wastes of the Never-Never Land and the rough head-station which was to be Lady Bridget's home.

BOOK II

From the Point of View of Lady Bridget O'Hara

CHAPTER 1

———————•———————

It was the way of the O'Haras to do things first and to consider afterwards whether it were well or ill that they should be done. Many a ruined O'Hara might have fared differently in life's battle had he thought before he acted.

Lady Bridget was no exception to the rule of her family. She had accepted Colin McKeith in a blind impulse of escape from the old hedged-in existence of her order, of which she was quite tired and where-in she had proved herself a failure. She had been attracted by the idea that he represented, of wide spaces and primitive adventures. She had always longed to travel in untrodden ways, and had loved stories of romantic barbarism. And then, too, some queer glamour of the man had got hold of her. She was intensely susceptible to personal influence – his bigness, his simplicity, his strength and daring, and the feeling that he was quite capable of mastering her, not only by brute force – which always appeals to a certain type of woman – but by power of will, by a tenacity of passion which she recognised even through the shy reserve with which McKeith tried to cloak his adoration. For she was goddess to him, as well as lady-love – and that she realised plainly. A look from her would make him go white and his large hands tremble; an unexpected grace from her would fill him with reverent ecstasy.

The thing happened one soft moonlit evening after dinner at Government House, when she had strolled out alone to a secluded part of the terrace, and he had followed her after the men left the dining-room. She was in a mood of tempestuous raging against her ordained lot. Letters had come from England that day which had irritated her and made her wonder how she could endure any longer her galling state of dependence. Eliza Countess of Gaverick had sent her a meagre cheque, accompanied by a scathing rebuke of her extravagance. Some cutting little sarcasms of Molly Gaverick's had likewise annoyed her, and she fretted under the miserable sense of her inadequacy to the demands of a world she despised and yet hankered after. Then Sir Luke had been tiresomely pertinacious over some small dereliction on Bridget's part from the canons of Government House etiquette, which he had requested should not be repeated. Rosamond Tallant had been tiresome also and had made her feel that even here she was no more than a dependent who must conform to the wills of her official superiors. Joan Gildea might have served as a safety-valve, but Joan was away in or near the Jenolan Caves, and could not be got at unless Bridget chose to throw up other things and go to her, which Bridget was not inclined to do.

The whole thing was a tangle. If only it were possible to find a way out that would not prove still more painfully complicated.

At the moment the ting-tang of a steamer bell bound outward to the northern coast, borne to her on the river-breeze, intensified her desire for escape from conventional limitations. Oh! to find herself under totally new conditions! The heavy fragrance of magnolia and gardenia blossoms seemed freighted with exotic suggestion. The tropical odours blended with the perfume of autumn roses, which made a trellis over her head and overran the balustrades. The subtle mingling of perfumes that float in the clear air of an Australian garden, when the fierce heats of summer are gone, gave her a sense of almost intoxication.

In fact, Bridget was in the mood for any desperate leap into the Unknown. Such was her unconscious thought as she crunched a spray of verbena in her fingers and inhaled the scent which had always a faintly heady effect upon her imagination. She was leaning on the stone kerb of the balustrade, vague emotions stirring her, when she heard McKeith's step on the gravel. Presently he stood beside her, his tall form, in the well-cut evening suit which always became him best, towering head and shoulders above her small stature. It was always a satisfaction to Lady Bridget, fastidious in such masculine details, that he was particular about his tailoring, and to-night he exhaled the scent of one of Sir Luke Tallant's excellent cigars. There used to be a good deal of chaff between them about one of his personal predilections which jarred a little upon Bridget – his pipe and, particularly, the quality of his tobacco. But he did not change it in spite of her chaff. She was beginning to find a certain mule-like obstinacy about him in unimportant details.

'If you object to this, what *would* you say to the store tobacco I smoke when I'm in the Bush?' he said. And then he had explained that, when camping out with the stockmen on their expeditions after cattle, he always smoked the same tobacco that he supplied to his hands. That was according to *his* rule of social equality by the camp fire, he said. . . . And where was all Lady Bridget's vaunted socialism if she jibbed at such a simple illustration of the first principles of socialism? Of course, Bridget had taken his banter in good part, and with a pretty grimace had told him she would get out a consignment of the stuff her Aunt Eliza gave at Christmas to the old men in their Irish village and present him with it.

He threw away the butt end of Sir Luke's cigar when he joined her. For several moments he stood watching her – the picturesque little figure in its dainty frock, the grace of the small head with its crop of untidy hair, the pale pointed face – chin resting in the cup of one flower-like hand, red lips – the upper one like Cupid's bow – slightly parted, strange deep eyes gazing across the dark expanse of river to the scattered lights on the high land opposite. Above, the Southern Cross, set diagonally, in the dark clear sky gemmed with its myriad stars.

There could be no doubt that Colin McKeith was in the grip of an infatuation such as he had never known before in his life. It staggered him. His breath caught in his throat and ended in an uncertain laugh. He stuttered in sheer awkwardness.

'I – I say . . . you seem to be up in the clouds. You've been awfully down in the mouth – all through dinner. Won't you tell me? Is anything the matter?'

Bridget turned and looked at him. Her eyes were softly glistening, her lips trembled. He thought of her as of a child seeking sympathy in a strange land, where nobody understood her and somebody had been unkind. He was intensely stirred by her impulsive appeal.

'Oh! I'm worried. I'm so alone in the world. Nobody wants me – here or in England either. I was just wondering if I couldn't go off and join Joan Gildea. . . . But she wouldn't want me either, perhaps.'

He went closer, stooping over the balustrade. Magnetic threads seemed to be drawing them to each other. He wanted to say, '*I* want you,' but dared not. He blurted forth instead?

'What is it? I'd cut off my right hand if that would be of any use to you. Good Lord! That does sound cheek! Only – you know – I'm big enough to bully the whole of Leichardt's Land from the Governor down – and I'd do it if you wanted me to. Just tell me what's worrying you?'

'It's everything – the whole set of conditions from the day I was born into them.'

'Conditions are easy enough things to break, if you're determined to do it. Look here – talk it out. . . . You can trust me.'

Then she recklessly set the flood gates open – laughed with tears in the laughter; drew a tragically amusing picture of her life – her anomalous position, her dependence, her hatred of the pretences, the shifts, the sordid bravado by means of which her impoverished Gaverick relatives clung on to their social birthright, the toadying of the Dowager, the worldly admonitions of Rosamond Tallant and her set – she used some of the phrases he had himself read in that letter. Had he been in any doubt as to its authorship that doubt must now be at rest. But he would never tell her of that episode. For one thing, his promise to Joan bound him. Like a stab came the remembrance of that man of whom Biddy had written – the man towards whom she had confessed a violent attraction – and who had behaved as a cad and a fortune-hunter would naturally behave. That he could have weighed money in the balance with *this*! She could not have cared for the fellow, or he *must* have thrown over everything else for her. Was it possible that she had cared – that she still cared?

'Tell me,' he asked hoarsely. 'Is it that you are fretting after somebody over there who – someone you can't marry? There must have been a lot of men in your life. Perhaps there was one who – whom you – loved.'

His voice dropped, as it had a way of doing when he touched the sacred subject.

'There have been a lot of men,' she admitted frankly. 'But there has never been one true Man among them. I've never really in my heart wanted to marry any of them, if that's what you mean – I don't like marriage – *our* system of marriage – a bargain in the sale shop. So much at such a price – birth, position, suitability, good looks – to be paid for at the market value. Or else it's just because the man happens to have taken a fancy to one, and while the fancy lasts doesn't think whether or not it's a fair bargain – on either side. I've seen people fall madly in love and marry like that. Then before very long the love turns to hate and it's a case for the Divorce Court.'

'Nothing of that is – love – not as I – and you – understand it.'

She gave him one of her inscrutable looks and then turned again to the stars. There was silence; Colin thought she must hear his heart thumping, but she seemed lost in her dreams. He put out his big hand and timidly, reverently, took hers, crushed verbena and all, as it lay on the balustrade. It rested like a prisoned bird within his; he could feel the nervous twitch of the little fingers.

'There's another system of marriage – a better one, I think – where the man doesn't ask for anything but the right to love until – until he has compelled the woman's love in return.'

'Compelled! I like that word. I could yield to my master. But he would have to prove himself my master.'

'Will you let me try?' McKeith said boldly. He grasped her hand tightly as he spoke; she gave a little cry, for he had hurt her. He was all compunction and gentleness in a moment.

'Oh, you are strong!' she said. 'I almost think you could make me do anything you chose.'

'No – that isn't what I meant.' He seemed trying to steady himself. 'I'm damned if I'd ever give up my free-will to anybody, and I wouldn't like even the woman who was my mate to do it either. But love – that's a different thing. . . .'

'Your mate!' she repeated.

'You don't know the Bush idea of a real mate – shoulder to shoulder, back to back – no getting behind one or the other – giving up your life for your mate, if it came to a pinch.'

'And that's your idea of – love?'

'Something like it, only closer, dearer – a thing you couldn't talk about even to your mate – unless your mate was your wife – a flower that blooms once in your life, and that would never – if it were cut off – come to bloom again. Look here,' he said fiercely, 'have you ever felt for any one of the lot of men you spoke about just like that?'

'N – no,' she answered slowly.

'If you told me you had, I'd walk away now down those steps –' he pointed to the flight of stone steps leading from the terrace to the drive – 'and you wouldn't see me any more. . . . But I'm not going to leave you now, I mean to stick on for all I'm worth, so long as I see the faintest chance of your giving me what I've set my heart on.'

'Yes – well?' She stared at him in a fascinated manner.

'Well – Bridget – I can't milady you. We're man and woman and nothing else to-night. . . .'

She interrupted. 'I like you to say that. I feel now that *we*, at least, are real – not social shams.'

'Bridget – you said you'd never found yet a Real Man to love you. Here's one.' He patted his broad chest with his open palm. 'I'm a rough Bushy and there's not a frill about me, but I'm bed-rock if you come to Reality. I'm a lode you've never struck in your life before. There's payable gold here, if you choose to work me,'

She laughed nervously, considering him.

'Mr McKeith, I'm sure that you're a perfect Mount Morgan, and you certainly have a most original way of putting things. Do you happen to own a gold mine, by the way?'

He drew in his breath slowly, as if he were considering the check, then he took her cue.

'Oh, well! I have pegged out a good many claims in my time and never got much more than my tucker out of any of them – though there was a show I came on once up the Gulf way that I've always been a bit sorry I didn't stop and look into. But rations were short and the Blacks bad. . . . However, that's neither here nor there, now. Gold mine or not, I'm positive that I shall be a rich man before many years have passed – all the richer for a true mate to stand by me.'

'Yes, of course,' she said hastily – 'I wasn't thinking of that – whether you were rich or not, I mean.'

'I know you weren't. All the same, I suppose your grand relations would consider me a presumptuous boor for daring to lift my eyes to you. And yet, if I could make you love me, it wouldn't count for a blade of grass that your father was born in a castle and mine in a crofter's cabin. . . . Only – you know too –' he became timid and hesitant again – 'you know it isn't that I don't feel you as far above me, almost, as those stars in the sky. . . .'

'Oh don't, don't, Mr McKeith. It isn't true, you know. I've told you how I despise all that – all the life I've led.'

'Yes, I know. There's not such a difference between us when we stand as we are now, right on the bed rock. You're like me in having a strain of working-folk's blood in you. It's Nature you're hankering after – God's sweet air and the breath of the gum trees and freedom for your soul.'

'Freedom for my soul! How strange that you should understand.'

'I understand better than you might think. You want more than freedom to make you content. You want a kind of bondage that is the truest freedom – Love – a strong man's love, a strong man's worship.

And that's what I'd give you, Bridget. Are you angry with me for saying it?'

'No.' She turned her face straight to him without any shadow of embarrassment. 'Mr McKeith, I'm too honest to pretend that I didn't half expect this. I felt you were beginning to care for me, and I was wondering whether I ought to let you go on.'

'Whether you ought to let me! As if you would be able to hinder it! Why, you couldn't stop me loving you. You might as well try to dam up the river Leichardt with this little hand I'm holding.'

She would have withdrawn it, but could not.

'No, no. It isn't strong enough – this tiny, trembling hand, which I could break to bits in mine if I wanted to. And could you prevent me from taking you in my arms – you wee great lady – and carrying you right away – away, out into the Bush where I'm on my own ground and where not one of your swell men folk would have a chance to find you.'

'I don't think any one of them would want to.' She laughed again tremulously. 'If it comes to that though, I fancy you'd have some trouble in disposing of me against my will.'

'Do you think I'd ever want you against your will! No. I'd sooner cut the whole show, and let you scorn me at a distance as much as you pleased.'

'I – scorn you! . . . I wouldn't scorn you.'

'And even your scorn wouldn't kill my love,' he said, in that moved voice that was so unlike his ordinary utterance – 'because there's nothing in the Universe, so far as I know it, that would be able to do that. Why, it seems to me that my feeling for you is as much a part of myself as the very blood in my heart. I knew you were the only woman in the world for me the moment I saw you – so slim and small and strange, the very contrary of what I'd always thought would be the kind of woman I'd be in love with – that day when you came walking along that gangway behind Lady Tallant. It was just a revelation, and then I bolted straight off to Alexandra City.'

'Which seems rather odd, doesn't it, in the circumstances?'

'No, it's this way. I had to take a few days for getting over the shock – for rubbing in the fact that what I wanted more than anything on God's earth, now I'd seen it, was utterly beyond my reach.'

'One might think I was an enchanted princess – a sort of Brunhilda guarded by a fiery dragon.'

'That's a good bit of how I looked on you – though I've never

made much out of Wagner – he isn't human enough for me. . . . And
how could I have dreamed then that you'd ever let me come as near
you as I am this evening!'

'I must say, Mr McKeith, you haven't shown such extreme
diffidence in approaching me.'

'Ah! Because you soon showed that Brunhilda's dragon was only
pasteboard and blue fire after all – one of the shams you despise. I'm
not afraid of him now. . . . Oh, it's wonderful. . . . It's beautiful. . . .'

He took her other hand and held the two covered over by his own
as he said with an odd solemnity:

'Lady Bridget O'Hara will you come away with me to the Bush,
leaving everything else behind you?'

She stood very slender and erect, her eyes shining in the moonlight
out of her small pale face and fixed upon him thoughtfully as if she
were weighing his proposition. After a few minutes, she answered
deliberately.

'Yes, Mr Colin McKeith, I will go away with you into the Bush,
leaving everything else behind me – the old "Lady Bridget O'Hara"
included.'

He gave an indescribable ejaculation – joy, surprise, triumph – all
were in the utterance. Dropping her hands, he stooped to her and his
arm went round her.

'Oh! Biddy . . . darling.'

She knew he wanted to kiss her, and that he scarcely dared so
greatly. . . . As his beard brushed her cheek, she shrank and moved a
step from him. He, too, shrank, hurt by her rebuff.

'You mustn't be – ardent,' she said. 'You must give me time to get
accustomed to – the fate I've chosen. You know the dragon isn't
altogether a sham. He's got a few kicks in him – yet.'

CHAPTER 2

On other occasions also Lady Bridget made McKeith feel that she preferred good fellowship to love-making. She was perfectly charming, always excellent company, and she had a sense of humour which delighted him, but she did not encourage effusiveness. She seemed to want to hear about the Bush a great deal more than she wanted to hear about his feelings towards herself, and appeared anxious to show him that she meant to be a thorough-going 'mate.' The phrase had taken her fancy.

There was not much opportunity, however, for exchanging sentimental confidences. Everything was rush and hurry during the few weeks between the engagement and the marriage. It was plain that Lady Tallant wished to get the wedding over before she and the Governor started upon a tour of the important stations in the settled districts round Leichardt's Town, officially contemplated. Bridget had a shrewd suspicion, which she confided to Colin, that Lady Tallant was getting tired of her. Perhaps Bridget did not keep herself sufficiently in the background to please the lady of Government House. Her unpunctuality too often annoyed Sir Luke.

Another reason for not delaying the marriage was that the Leichardt's Land government was expected to go out of office on a Labour Bill, and that an appeal to the country would certainly follow its defeat. In that case McKeith's re-election would have to be considered, and an electioneering honeymoon in one of the out-back districts was an inspiring prospect to Lady Bridget. Then the preparation of a Bush trousseau needed thought and discussion. She had not much money, either, to buy her trousseau with. Bridget would have none of Sir Luke's suggestions of conciliatory letters and cablegrams to Eliza Lady Gaverick on the subject of settlements. She said she did not intend to cadge any longer upon her rich relative, and that she preferred to marry without settlements. Sir Luke was not satisfied with McKeith's views upon the financial question, and had some difficulty in getting him to tie up even the insignificant sum of three thousand pounds in settlement upon his wife. Colin pointed out that his capital was all invested in cattle, and that though things would be all right as long as there were good seasons, a bad one would cripple him, and he would need money to recoup his losses and buy fresh stock. Bridget took his view and Sir Luke frowned, but did what he considered his duty so far as the paltry settlement went. At all events, it was a satisfaction to Colin McKeith's shrewd Scotch mind that nobody insisted upon getting the better of him in the matter. He knew that Bridget never gave it a second thought. She was much more interested in the social and racial problems of this new country of her adoption, and especially in the blacks. What time she could spare from her trousseau she spent in reading books about them, which some of her official friends got her from the Parliamentary Library, and had already learned to think of herself as a 'bujeri[1] White Mary,' whose mission it might be to compose the racial feud between blackman and white.

To Colin, knowing now the tragedy of his youth, she did not speak much on this subject. The time went with startling rapidity. The two were borne on the tide of Colin's wild elation and Bridget's more impersonal enthusiasms. They were like travellers steaming through strange seas, not knowing what they were going to find at the end of the voyage and too excited to care.

That was the way of Bridget O'Hara, but it was not the way of Colin McKeith.

Yet his closest intimates would scarcely have known him at this period. He was as a man bewitched, with intervals only of his ordinary commonsense. In these intervals the consciousness of glamour made him vaguely uneasy.

Had Joan Gildea been there she would have seen all this and would have observed signs of over-strain in Bridget – something faintly apprehensive yet obstinately determined. And Joan would have understood that when an O'Hara woman gets the bit between her teeth, she will not stop to look back or to consider whither she is

[1] Bujeri – Black's term of commendation.

galloping. Bridget kept herself continually on the go. Latterly, even Colin was warned by her nervous restlessness. When they were alone together, which was not long, nor often, her body seemed never still, her tongue rarely at rest. Sometimes her talk was brilliantly allusive; at others it was frothy chatter. One day it really irritated him. She had been fluttering about the sitting-room opening on to the terrace, which Lady Tallant had made over to her guest. An English mail had come in. She read him bits of a letter from Molly Gaverick and made explanatory, satiric comments upon those impecunious, aristocratic relatives who were on the fringe of the London smart set of which Bridget herself had lately formed a yet more outside part.

'Chris Gaverick has gone into the wine business, and they've taken a tiny house in Davies Street, Berkeley Square, and the Eaton Place house pays its rent.... You don't understand? ... No.... Molly and I talked it out when they were married. Of course, it seemed madness, with their means to take a house in Eaton Place. They ought to have had one in Bayswater. But it has answered splendidly. You see, they put their wedding presents into it and let it for the season, and managed to live rent free and have the use of other people's motors and all the going about they wanted without paying even for their food ... and no expense of entertaining .outside a dinner or two at Hurlingham.... Cadging! ... In London Society everybody cadges except the millionaires – and they're cadged upon... You see, as Molly said, you can't entertain in Bayswater, or know the right people, and go about to the right houses, which is the most important thing for a poor couple who want to keep their heads up. Now the result is that Chris is able to bring in quantities of clients and gets a commission on all the wine he sells.... What's the matter, Colin? You look quite fierce.'

'And that,' commented McKeith, 'is an English belted Earl!'

'Irish – there's a difference. And are they belted – really? Isn't it a figure of speech?'

'I don't know, and I don't care.'

'But wouldn't you care to hear Molly's account of their visit to the Duke and Duchess of Brockenhurst to meet the King and Queen of Hartenburg? Molly is very sorry I wasn't there. She says that it would have made everything so much nicer for her and Chris, and that the King might have ordered some wine from his firm.'

She was teasing. He knew it, and it infuriated him.

'Oh, no doubt you're sorry too that you weren't there with the

Duke and Duchess, and the King and Queen, and your cousins, the Earl and Countess,' he flung at her.

'They'll be your cousins too – by marriage. And if you ever become a very rich man and take me back to England, you'll have to "Chris and Molly" them, and to give him a big order for wine. . . .'

That mollified McKeith.

'And if I wasn't a rich man, and didn't give a big order, they wouldn't care a twopenny damn for me.'

'Molly mightn't – unless by chance you were taken up in high quarters and made the fashion – like Cecil Rhodes and "Doctor Jim," or some new edition of Buffalo Bill. Then she'd call you "one of nature's uncrowned kings." But Chris Gaverick isn't a bad sort, if his wife would let him be natural. . . . They hadn't got my cablegram about you, Colin, when this was written,' she went on. 'I wish I could have told the Queen myself. I'm sure she would have been sympathetic. And now I don't suppose I shall ever meet her again.'

He rejoined with clumsy sarcasm.

'I see. The Queen of Hartenburg was an intimate friend of yours – the sort of chum who'd have been likely to drop in any day for a yarn and a cup of tea!'

'She often did when she hunted with our hounds in Ireland, and it *is* true that the Queen of Hartenburg was quite an intimate friend of mine – for two winters, anyhow. But I assure you, it hasn't made me proud, and if the Queen of Hartenburg bores you, let us talk of something else.'

She gave another glance at the last sheet of Lady Gaverick's letter and thrust it into a pigeon-hole of the writing-table, then came back to the long settee on which he sat. All the time, his gaze had never left her. She saw that he was disturbed.

'What is the matter?' she asked again, and sat down, a little way from him, on the settee. He turned sideways to her, bending forward, one large hand twisting his fair beard. There was a hungry look in his eyes, but his passing ill-humour had melted into a deep, adoring tenderness.

'Biddy – my mate – will you answer me a question – truthfully?'

'I believe I can say honestly, that truth is one of my strong points,' she parried lightly.

'I want you to be serious. I mean it seriously. I want you to tell me what determined you on marrying a rough chap like me? That letter – thinking of you among those grandees, you talking a language that's worse than Greek to me, brings the wonder of it home. As I look at you, the thing seems just incredible.'

'I can't understand why it should seem so surprising.'

'*Why!* You know what I mean. It's not only that your birth and bringing up are so superior to mine, and that you had a right to look for a husband in a very different sort of position – I can see plainly that is what Sir Luke thinks. . . .'

'I don't care – a twopenny d-a-m-n – as you said – for what Sir Luke thinks. I've got my own ideas as to the kind of husband most likely to suit me.'

'There's the marvel of it. For you must have had dozens of men wanting you. You are so beautiful.'

'Oh, Colin, I've told you what I feel about the English marriage system. And, *par parenthèse*, I'm not beautiful. I don't come up in the least to the artist's standard. My measurements are wrong. I'm too small.'

'That's rot. There's a fascination about you no man can resist – or woman either. I see it in the people who come here.'

'If I happen to have drawn them into what Rosamond used to call my mysterious sphere of influence – which I seem to do without knowing it. I'm not sure, though, that either Rosamond or Luke approve of my drawing the Leichardt's Town people into my mysterious sphere of influence.'

'I think, if you ask me, that Lady Tallant is a bit of a cat, and Sir Luke more than a bit of a prig.'

'No. You mustn't say a word against them.' It was not in Bridget to be disloyal. 'They've given me the time of my life.'

'When you smile like that, you remind me of a photograph of a picture I've seen – a woman, I don't remember her name.'

'Mona Lisa – La Gioconda. I know – I've been told that before.'

'Yes, that's it. Mona Lisa. People have written about her.'

'Reams. Some day I'll read you what Pater says of her, unless you've read him already – by your camp fire.'

For he had talked to her, as he had talked to Joan Gildea, about his readings and his dreamings under the stars in the Bush.

'Eh! you shall teach me about these new writing chaps. I don't understand your up-to-date theories. I've aways gone in for plain facts – standard reading – history – great thoughts of great minds – old books brought out in people's editions. I'm up a tree – downright bushed when you begin upon your queer ideas – all those newfangled religions and notions – Theosophy, spooks – about the earth being alive, and thoughts making a sort of wireless telegraph system – I do believe in that, though – to a certain extent. And your Brotherhood of Man! Bosh! We're all like a lot of potatoes thrown into a sack and shaken about by circumstance. And the big ones come to the top, and the little ones – because they're little – sink to the bottom. I've always wanted to be one of the big potatoes, and I mean to be.'

Bridget laughed. She had a ringing laugh when she was amused.

'Oh! go on, Colin. I grant that you're a very big potato and I'm a very little one.'

'You know I didn't mean it that way. You're the biggest potato in the whole bag as far as mind goes, and you make me feel the smallest. You're so wonderful that the marvel of your being contented to marry me is a bit staggering. And that brings me back to my question, which you haven't answered.'

'How have I brought myself to the incredible enterprise of marrying an Australian bushman? Do you know?' – she became suddenly serious – 'I have asked myself that question once or twice, and I haven't been able to answer it.'

The light of adoration in his eyes faded a little.

'I've been afraid of that,' he said slowly, 'I've been afraid that you might be rushing into the business without reasoning it out – weighing all the sides of it.'

'If I were, it would only be the way of the O'Haras.'

His blue eyes became more troubled.

'I've been afraid of that,' he repeated. 'Bridget – suppose – my dear, suppose it was to turn out a mistake.'

'Well, I've made so many mistakes in my life and lived through them that one more wouldn't matter,' she rejoined lightly.

'This one would matter – because it would be irretrievable. Suppose that you were to find that you couldn't put up with the Bush life – I've told you that you are letting your imagination and your enthusiasm run a bit away with you, and that there may be hardships you don't reckon on. For though it all looks to me plain sailing now, and I hope it will only be a year or two before I can put on a manager, and give you the home and the climate that are more suited to you, one can't tell in Australia that there may not be a drought or that a cattle boom may not turn to a slump – do you see?'

'I shan't mind in the least, Colin – that is, I shall mind immensely, but if there comes a drought it will be quite exciting helping you to drag out the poor, thirsty beasts, when they get bogged into the waterholes as you were describing the other day.'

He laughed.

'*You* – helping to drag out bogged beasts! Why! they'd drag you in.'

'Well, there are other things. Riding! I could help you to break in horses. All the O'Haras are good on horseback' – at which he laughed immoderately and told her that when she had seen one, Zack Duppo, on a buckjumper, she would not be keen to try that game. But it might amuse her to help cut out a few tame bullocks on a drafting camp if she had a good old station mount that knew its work.

She shuddered. 'I love horses, but I should run away from the first bullock that looked at me. I'm frightened of beasts, and, on second thoughts, I should not want to pull out bogged ones. And I loathe cooking – domestic work – in a house. It would be different out of doors. You've promised to teach me the first time we camp out how to make – what do you call them – johnny-cakes?'

'Ah! The first time we camp out together. If you knew how I've dreamed of that. Biddy, I've got plans in my mind for that –' He caught her two hands in a fierce grasp, and as he looked at her, his eyes full of love, he would – greatly daring – have held her close to his breast and kissed the provocative lips, as yet almost virgin to his. But she made a shrinking movement, and he, acutely sensitive, dropped her hands, and the love that had flamed in his eyes gave place to the dour look she did not know so well.

'Why do you always keep me at a distance?' he said, and drew abruptly away from her.

'Dear man, you mustn't be importunate. It – it's constitutional with me. I've always hated love-making at close quarters.'

'Always! Does that mean that you've been in the habit of letting men kiss you?'

'Colin, you are rude – brutal.'

'D'ye think so? It seems to me that I'm only as Nature made me. Biddy – if you feel like that now – how will it be when you're my wife?'

She flushed a little, but as her way was, evaded him.

'Perhaps I shall have grown more used to it all by that time.'

'The time is not so long – only a fortnight from now. And when you hold me off from the touch of your hand – the feel of your lips – well, it makes me wonder. . . .'

She gave a little alarmed shiver.

'Don't wonder, Colin. Don't worry.... And oh! before every-thing, don't drive me – it isn't safe with an O'Hara woman. I can see that you don't understand women – of a certain type.'

'Oh! I grant you women haven't stood for a great deal in my life, and the few I've known well have been of the humble, human sort. But I do know this, Bridget – his face softened – 'I do know that a proud, sensitive woman – which is what you are and what I love you for being – is like a thoroughbred mare, out the first time in harness. You must keep your hands tight on her and let her go her own pace. I can tell you, too, the cart-horse kind that has to be driven with a whip and a "gee-up" all the time wouldn't be the type for me.'

She laughed gain, but shakily. There was an appeal in her voice.

'Colin, you've told me a lot about breaking in young horses, and how patient one has to be with them. Be patient with me.... Now, I'll try and answer your question – truthfully. I only know in a very confused sort of way *why* I want to marry you.... I think you must understand what a lonely sort of life I've led, really – and what a dreadful muddle I've made of it – Well, I've told you how I hated everything. And though I can laugh, and be interested, too, in Molly Gaverick's way of looking at things, and in her determination not "to be out of the swim" – *I* was just as determined myself, when I had the mood to be in it – and though one side of me hankers after the push and the struggle and the worldliness – yet the other side of me revolts against it, and longs to be washed clean of all the sordid social grime. There! I've felt about marrying you that it would be a new baptism into a bigger, fresher, purer life – do you see?'

'Yes – I see.' His tone was doubtful. 'You've tried it before – that idea of bigger interests – a different kind of life – in other ways, Biddy, haven't you?'

'Oh! in ever so many ways. Of course, that wasn't only in the sense of love – hero worship, you know. It was the schemes, ideas, plans for living in the higher part of one. Tolstoy, Prentice Mulford – that kind of thing.... Colin, you blame me for not *giving*; yet, all my life, I've been blamed for giving too freely.'

'For giving too freely!' He repeated sharply.

'You mustn't misunderstand me. I said it hadn't only to do with men making love to me – my ideas about a different life. It was my general attitude – expecting to meet something great and being disappointed.... Of course, I've suffered – suffered horribly – in my heart – in my pride. And I've often found that my attitude towards things brought me into difficulties. The average person, if it's a man – supposes that because one has such ideas one must be a kind of abandoned creature. And, if it's a woman, that one has some mean, ulterior motive. I've always seemed to be looking for largeness and finding only what was small. You attracted me because you're like nature – big, simple, elemental.'

'Now, what the deuce do you mean by elemental?'

'Primal, unadulterated – closer to the heart of life and nature. It's a sort of cosmic quality. You are large – your surroundings are large.'

He laughed, only half comprehending, gauche in the expression of his deep-hearted satisfaction.

'One thousand square miles, two thirds of it fair grazing country in good seasons, and will be first-rate when I've worked out my artesian bore system. Plenty of space there for a woman to swing her petticoats, in – your riding skirt it'll have to be.'

'There! You see!' she cried. '*Could* one be mean or small in such conditions? It's glorious, the thought of riding over one thousand square miles – and tapping Mother Earth for your water supply! It will be just what I said – a new baptism – a washing in Jordan. But you will be patient, Colin; promise me that you will be good to me, and not ask too much – at first.'

There came a note into her voice which intoxicated the man with hope and joy. But he restrained himself. He would not frighten her again.

'Good to you! Biddy – you know you're sacred to me – I'll do everything – I'll be as patient as you could wish until you get so used to me that everything comes naturally. You understand? So long as you'll trust me and open your heart to me, I'm not afraid that you won't love me, my dear, in the end.'

'I *want* to love you, Colin.'

She moved a little closer to him and put her hand up, timidly, to his shoulder. His breath came quickly, but he did not lose his self-control. He knew that he must go gently with her. She drew her hand down his coat sleeve and let it rest like a snowflake on his – a contrast in its smallness and whiteness to the great brown hand beneath. She looked at that, smiling whimsically, and he saw her smile, and reddened. But he did not know that she found a pleasure in the sight of his hand – scrupulously kept, the nails as well trimmed as a bushman's nails can be, while showing the traces of manual labour.

'How ridiculous they are together!' she said softly 'But I like your hand, Colin. It's like you – different from the other men's hands.'

He was glad she said 'the other men's,' and not 'the other man's'. Through all the gusts of passionate tenderness that went out to her, there was always rankling the thought of 'that other man.'

CHAPTER 3

———————•———————

They had only one more talk, in the real sense, before their marriage, and that was an unpremeditated but natural outrush of the vague jealousy which slumbered at the core of McKeith's love. It was on the last evening, and it made an ineffaceable impression upon him.

They were standing, after dinner, close together by the balustrade of the terrace.

It was a clear night, with a young moon, and the stars set deep in blue so dark that the sky gave an impression of solidity. The air was full of scents and of a soft balminess, with the faint nip of an early May in the Southern hemisphere.

He had folded her light scarf round the child-like shoulders. The touch of his big hand stirred her – it had not often done so in that peculiar way. It roused something in her that she had thought dead or drugged to sleep, and took her back for an emotional moment to a certain late summer evening at Hurlingham, when she and Willoughby Maule had stood in the garden together under the stars. There came to her an almost fierce reaction against that moment. She felt a distinct emotion now, but it was different – less tumultuous, and bringing her a soft sense of enfoldment.

She slipped her hand gently into McKeith's, and they remained thus for nearly a n.inute without speaking. He was the first to break the silence.

'Bridget,' he said impetuously, 'we're going to be husband and wife to-morrow. It makes me tremble, darling – with happiness and hope, and with fear, too. What have I done, a rough Bushy like me – to win a woman like you? Well you know how I think about that. And I don't believe in a man belittling himself to the woman he loves, though it's just because he loves her so that he feels himself unworthy of her. And then it comes again over me – badly sometimes – how little I really know of you, and of your life, and of your feelings towards the other men you must have had to do with – one other man in especial, may be, that you've loved, or may have thought you loved. That's what I want to know about, my dear.'

Her face was turned from his as she answered:

'Where's the good of your knowing, Colin? Whatever there was is past.'

'But *is* it past. Over and over again I've started to ask you and have pulled back. Now it's got like a festering sore in my heart, and I'm afraid it will go on festering unless I'm satisfied. There *was* somebody in especial – a man you cared for and might have married if he had been a finer sort of chap than he turned out to be?'

She looked at him sharply.

'How do you know? Has Rosamond Tallant been telling you?'

'No,' he said, with complete candour. 'There wasn't a word of that sort passed between us – and I wouldn't have heeded it if there had.'

'Joan, then? No, I'm sure Joan Gildea wouldn't have talked behind my back.'

'You may bet your life on that. Joan hasn't said anything about whatever love-affairs you may have had.'

'Every girl has had love-affairs. I'm no exception to the rule. There's been no real harm in them. Let them lie – buried in oblivion. They're not worth resurrecting.'

'No, but,' – he persisted – thinking all the while of that letter – 'Bridget, I must ask you this one thing. Is there any man in the world you care for more than you care for me? I know,' he added sadly, 'that you don't love in the way I love you – in the way I'd like to be loved by you. I know that's too much to expect – yet.'

The melancholy note in his speech touched her.

'I told you that I do *want* to love you, Colin – only I can't help being what I am,' she said softly. She looked up at him in the pale brightness of thin moon and myriad stars. He stood with the faint illumination from the open windows of Government House upon his fine head and his neat fair beard. It intensified the gleam in his earnest blue eyes, while it softened his angularities and bush roughnesses, and as she looked up at him, she could not help feeling what a splendid fellow he was! What a *man!* So much finer than that other man to whom she had so nearly given herself! Ah, she had had an escape! Under all his show of romantic adventure, his ardent protestations, his magnetic charm, that other man had been utterly sophisticated, worldly, self-interested. He had shown this in his money-grabbing, in his disloyalty both to the woman he had professed to love, and to the woman he had married for her fortune. Thinking of him in this way, Lady Bridget felt that in time she might come to care a great deal more for Colin McKeith.

He caught up her last words.

'Yes, I know that you *want* to love me Biddy, and I hope with all my heart and soul that you will – or else – or else –' he broke off, his face darkening.

'Or else – what?'

'I don't know. It would be hell. I can't think such a thing at this moment. If it comes – well, I'll face it as I've had to face other ugly things. Don't let us speak of the possibility!'

She sensed some quality in him that she had not realised before.

'You frighten me a little, Colin. It's as if I might any day come up against something I wasn't prepared for; and yet – I rather like it.'

He smiled at her.

'I'm glad you like it, anyway. You seem to me such a child, Biddy, though you are always telling me you are such an old soul. I can't for the life of me make out what you mean by that.'

'Oh! a soul that has come back and back, and has lived a great many – perhaps naughty – lives.'

'H'm! Yes! Well, one life is good enough for me, and as we can't prove the other thing, what does it matter anyhow? I wouldn't want you in another life if you were going to be quite a different person. I want you as you are in this one. And so I reckon would every man who has ever been in love with you. Let us go back now to what I was asking you. Biddy, there *was* a man – one man that you did care for? You've admitted as much.'

'Yes – I suppose there was.'

'And not so long before you came out here?'

'I suppose that's true too.'

Bridget! – do you know what's been festering in my mind – the thought that you might be marrying me in a fit of pique – a sort of reaction. Biddy – tell me honestly, my dear, if it's anything of that sort?'

She seemed to be considering.

'I don't quite know how to answer you, Colin – if I'm to be

absolutely honest. And I'd always rather tell you the truth.'

'Thank God for that. Let there be truth between us – truth at any cost.'

'You see,' she said slowly. 'My whole coming out here – everything I've done lately, has been done in reaction against all I've done and felt before.'

'Would you have married that man – if everything had been on the square?'

'What do you mean by "on the square"? I've done nothing to be properly ashamed of!'

'No – no – I was thinking only of him, Biddy, did you love that man? – really love him?'

'I'm not sure yet whether I'm capable of what you'd call loving really. I had a violent attraction to him,' – he remembered the phrase – 'I confess I did feel it dreadfully when he married someone else. Now it doesn't hurt me. And of course, he has gone out of my life altogether. I'm glad he has, and I hope he will keep on the other side of the world.'

'Well, let it stop at that.' He drew a breath of relief. 'I don't believe you really cared for him. If you had, you couldn't take it as you do. I'll never bother you again about that man. And oh, my dear – my dear – it doesn't seem to me possible that you shouldn't come to love me, when I love you as I do – with my whole heart and soul – I worship you, Biddy. And I'll not say again that I'm unworthy of you – a man who loves a woman like that *can't* be wholly unworthy.'

He took her in his arms and kissed her. And this time she did not resist the caress.

They were married with much flourish of trumpets and local paraphernalia. Never before in the annals of Leichardt's Land had a wedding taken place from Government House. This one was regarded as quite an official event. The Executive Council – at that moment about to undergo the pangs of dissolution – attended in a body. There were a great many members of parliament present also. It became even a question whether the official uniforms worn at Sir Luke's 'Swearing In' should not lend éclat to the occasion. But Colin McKeith vetoed that proposition.

The bridal party drove straight from the Church to that same extemporized wharf by the Botanical Gardens which had been put up for the Governor's State Landing. It had been re-constructed and redecorated for to-day's event. Thus the embarcation of the bride and bridegroom, of the viceregal party and the wedding guests, in the Government yacht, which was to take the new-made pair to the big mail boat in the Bay, was almost as imposing a ceremony as the Governor's Entry into his new kingdom. The day was glorious – an early Australian winter's day, when the camellia trees are in bud, and the autumn bulbs shedding perfumes, and garlands of late roses, honeysuckle and jasmine are still hanging on trellis and tree.

As the bridal party came down the avenue of bunyas, and the band played the Wedding Chorus from *Lohengrin* a feeling of dream-like incongruity came over Bridget. She laughed hysterically.

'What a pity Joan Gildea isn't here!' she said. 'Think of the "copy" she might have made out of this!'

Lady Tallant had conceived the original idea of having the wedding breakfast on the deck of the Government yacht, while it steamed down the forty miles between Leichardt's Town and the river bar, beyond which, in those days, large vessels could not pass. There, the repast was laid on tables decorated with white blossoms and maidenhair fern, under an awning festooned with flowers and exotic creepers, and supported apparently, by palm trees and tree ferns which had been taken from the Government Gardens.

The bride looked small, pale and quaint in her white satin dress and lace veil, now thrown back and partly confining the untidily curling hair. Some of the reports described her as being like an old picture; others as a vision from Fairyland. She came barely up to her husband's shoulder as they stood together, and the adoring pride of his downward gaze at her, stirred all the women's hearts and roused a sympathetic thrill in the men's breasts. Colin made a good show in the regulation bridegroom's frock coat, and with a sprig of orange blossom in his buttonhole. There was no doubt that he was extremely happy. He gave a short manly speech in response to Sir Luke's rather academic oration proposing the health of the wedded pair. The Premier too made a speech and so did the Attorney-General, who was best man. Bridget's bridesmaids had been selected from the daughters of the Executive with as much attention to precedence as though she had been a royal princess. All this had delighted the Leichardstonians, and when Sir Luke read out congratulatory cablegrams received that morning from the Earl and Countess of Gaverick, Eliza, Countess of Gaverick, and one or two other members of the British aristocracy, the enthusiasm was great.

The speeches were over; the wedding cake had been cut; the river-bar and the liner were in sight, when Lady Bridget went below and changed into sea-going blue serge. The mail-boat, beflagged in honour of the occasion, dipped a salute. The Governor led the bride along the gangway, introduced the Captain of the mail-boat, and there were more congratulatory speeches, and still more of official ceremony as the bride passed by a line of inquisitive and admiring passengers – fortunately there were not many – and down to the state-room prepared for her. Then the curtain seemed to fall that divided her from her past, and when the Governor stepped again on to the Leichardt's Land yacht, and the last farewell had been waved, Lady Bridget felt thankfully that she had become a private individual at last. Only just Bridget, wife of Colin McKeith, Bushman, now starting upon her voyage towards the Wild.

She could not get away from the bewildering sense of unreality. It dominated every other feeling. She did not even reflect that there was no going back; that her fate was sealed, and that the Bush was henceforth to be her prison or her paradise.

All the way up the river, Rosamond Tallant congratulated herself upon having done the best that was possible for poor Biddy the failure. It was all entirely satisfactory. She wove a halo of romance round Colin McKeith, and, after reading her laudation of him, and her description of Bridget's send off, old Lady Gaverick and the impecunious Chris and his wife declared to each other that Biddy had done as well for herself as the family had any reason to expect.

Eliza, Lady Gaverick, was highly pleased, though she would not for the world have let her niece by marriage know it. Being Scotch herself she approved of the Scotch bridegroom, and began now to think seriously of the alteration she subsequently made in her will.

It was a four days' passage to Leuraville the port at which the McKeith's were to be dropped. Not being a good sailor Lady Bridget retired to her berth when the steamer got into a choppy sea.

Of course she had no maid. Colin unpacked the cabin trunk and dressing bag and arranged things so far as he could understand his wife's dainty toilet equipments, and his mistakes made them laugh and got them over the first awkwardness of close quarters.

Then he said:

'Now I'm going to stow away my own traps. My cabin is just facing this and you've only got to call out if you want anything. Eh, but my word! Biddy, it's a fine thing to be marrying from Government House. The Company has done us both proud.'

CHAPTER 4

———•———

They were landed at Leuraville on the evening of the fourth day. A tender took them off with the mails – as it happened, they were the only passengers for that small sea-township. Ordinary business folk going north, preferred the smaller coasting steamers which put in at every port. The postmaster, the portmaster, the police magistrate, and a few local notabilities were waiting to receive them at the wharf. McKeith greeted them all heartily and rather shyly introduced them to his bride. The local men were shy also. They mostly addressed her as Mrs McKeith. The Police magistrate – Captain Halliwell, lean, dark, sallow, with a rather weak mouth, but more carefully dressed than the others, and with an English voice, called her Lady Bridget. He was a retired officer of the *Royal Engineers*. She had been told and now remembered that men in the *Royal Engineers* were popularly said either to be religious or cranks. This man was a Christian Scientist which he announced when apologising for not offering the hospitality of his house, a new baby having arrived the day previously, ushered into the world, he explained, by prayer and faith and without benefit of medical skill.

Bridget knew something about Christian Scientists. She plunged at once into faith-healing ethics with the police-magistrate, while Colin saw about getting the trunks off the tender. How odd it seemed to be talking about London and Christian science in a place like this!

Leuraville too seemed part of a dream. But her face soon lost its bewildered look. She became interested in her surroundings, although there was no suggestion here of savage freedom or romantic adventure.

Leuraville showed low and hot and ugly. A red sun near its dropping, drew up the miasmic vapours from mangrove-fringed reaches stretching on either side of the wharf. Some light crafts were

moored about. A schooner was loading up with cattle – wretched
diseased beasts. Bridget watched them with shuddering repulsion –
being hoisted up and slung aboard with ropes. The men at their task
swore so abominably that the police-magistrate stepped up to them
and remonstrated on the plea of a lady's presence. Bridget had never
heard such swear-words. She was used to the ordinary 'damn,' but
these oaths were so horribly coarse. Colin, who was asking local
questions of the other men appeared to take it all as a matter of
course. The men stopped their work to stare at Lady Bridget. They
wore dirty corduroys hitched up with a strap over flannel shirts that
were open at the neck and left their brawny breasts exposed. There
were other loafers in flannel shirts, hitched up trousers and greasy
felt or cabbage-tree hats, and there were two or three blacks – the
demoralised type seen in coast townships. Now, one of the bullocks
got loose and rushed blindly down the wharf, and Bridget shrieked
and clung wildly to her husband's arm until it was headed back again.

Colin laughed at her terror.

'It's all right, Biddy. But how's that for a Bushman's wife. You'll
see lots of cattle up at Moongarr.'

Moongarr was the name of his station which was to be her future
home.

'I hate cows. Once I was charged by a wild cow and I've been
afraid of them ever since.'

'That isn't a cow. It's Mickey Field's poley-tailed bullock being
shunted off to the Boiling-down Works on Shark Island,' said a local
man.

The police-magistrate found his opportunity.

'You wouldn't be afraid, Lady Bridget, if you realised that cow as
an expression of the Divine mind.'

Bridget laughed. Her sense of the queerness of it all was almost
hysterical. She had the Irish wit to make the men grin at her prompt
answer, which when it became bruited up and down the Leura,
earned her the reputation of being sharp at repartee.

'But do you think,' said she confidingly, 'that the cow would be
after realising *me* as an expression of the Divine Mind?'

'Eh, you needn't think you're going to knock spots off my wife, any
of you,' cried Colin delighted at the sally. And now he walked and
talked like a man on his own soil again, as more of the townsfolk
came about – extraordinary people, Bridget thought. Loose-limbed
bush-riders, really trim, some of them, in clean breeches and with a

scarlet handkerchief doing duty for a belt, unkempt old men, a Unionist Labour organiser addressing a knot of station-hands out of work – even a Chinaman – a Chinky, McKeith called him, who, it appeared kept a nondescript store. That was in the days before the Commonwealth and the battle cry of 'White Australia.'

All of them showed the deepest interest in the small, pale, picturesque woman walking by Colin's side.

It seemed incredible to Biddy that she should be walking like that beside the big Bushman, in this sort of town, and that he should be her lawful protector.

The street they walked up began from the wharf with two-storied respectable buildings – the Bank, the Post-Office, the police-magistrate's residence, some dwelling houses, within palings enclosing gardens – clumps of bananas, pawpaw apple trees, a few flower beds, bushes of flaunting red poinsettia, and so forth. There were stores, public houses, meaner shanties straggling along a dusty road that lost itself in vistas of lank gum trees.

The Postmaster hoped that Mr McKeith's lady would not find the hotel too rowdy. It was one of the two-storied buildings, and had a bar giving on to the street, and a veranda round both lower and upper storey. A number of Bushmen and loafers were drinking in the bar, and others were on the edge of the veranda dangling their legs over it into the street. All of them stopped their talk and their drink to stare at Lady Bridget. The landlady – a big, florid Irish-woman in black silk, with a gold chain round her neck came out on to the veranda and greeted McKeith as an old friend, holding out her hand to Lady Bridget. She took the husband and wife up to their rooms, a parlour opening on the balcony, a bedroom over the bar and a little room at the back of it.

'It's a rough sort of shop, Biddy,' said Colin, when the woman had departed. 'But it will do for a shake-down for to-night. If the steamer had come in earlier I'd have taken you straight up to Fig Tree Mount, where the buggy will be waiting for us; and after that we'll begin our camping out, and you'll be in the real Bush. But we've lost the train, and must wait till daylight to-morrow. You'll be tired my dear – and you must be feeling strange,' he added kindly. 'I'll go and have your traps brought up and leave you to fix yourself. I want to see one or two chaps and find out whether my drays are down as far as Fig Tree for stores and what's going on up along the Leura.'

Bridget noticed that the change in McKeith seemed yet more

accentuated. His manner was more curt and decided – rougher than before. He appeared to have taken on the tone of the Back-Blocks. Yet she admired him. She did not dislike the roughness.

But she felt a womanish aggrievement at his having left her to undo her own things. And the rooms were horrible – the meagre appliances – the coarse cotton sheets, the awful Reckitt's-blue colouring of the painted walls. And then the dreadful noise of men drinking below in the bar! If this was the Bush! But Colin had said it was not the Bush.

He left her again after dinner which was horrible likewise – burned up steak, messy fried potatoes and cabbage, an uneatable rice pudding. He did not seem to mind. The result of his enquiries had left him grim and preoccupied. Yes, he had taken on the Bushman, and had more or less dropped the lover. The practical Scotch side of him was uppermost, and he appeared more disturbed over station affairs than at her want of appetite. She resented this unreasonably. She had not wanted him to play the lover in these surroundings, they would have been fatal to romance, but she had not bargained for his glumness. He was angry at the non-arrival of his draymen and the probability that they were drinking at a grog-shanty on the road. He would certainly sack them, he said if that were the case. And he had disquieting news from Moongarr. Pleuro had broken out among the cattle. What was Pleuro? Lady Bridget wondered, but she was not sufficiently interested in cattle to ask the question. And the Unionist labour men were making themselves a nuisance – going round the stations burning the grass of squatters who employed non-Union stockmen and shearers – in one instance, threatening to burn a wool-shed. And there hadn't been any rain on the Leura for a month past, and weather prophets were predicting a drought.

It was dreadfully prosaic and boring. After he had gone out again to transact further business, Lady Bridget went to bed and squirmed between the cotton sheets, remembering ruefully the luxuries of Government House. Never in all her life had she slept between cotton sheets or washed herself in an enamelled tin basin. The noise in the bar became intolerable. She could hear the swear-words quite distinctly. They were disgusting. She tried to stop her ears. . . . Oh what a dreadful life was this into which she had plunged so recklessly!

Her thoughts went back to the old-world – to the luxurious veneer covering the younger Gavericks' petty economies – stealing the notepaper at country-houses for the sake of the address – cadging for motors and dinners – 'keeping in' with the people likely to be of use; pulling strings in a manner which Bridget knew would have been too utterly galling to Colin McKeith's self-respect. And she thought of her father and his financial unscrupulousness! But none of these could have conceived of life without certain appurtenances of that position to which they and she had been born. The only one who was self-respecting among the lot was old 'Eliza Countess' as they designated her. It struck Bridget that Eliza Countess and Colin McKeith had points of character in common – it was true they both came from Glasgow. She thought of the parsimonious rectitude – which had of course included linen sheets and fine porcelain and shining silver – of old Lady Gaverick's establishment, of its stuffy conventionality – though that had been soothing sometimes after a dose of Upper Bohemia; and Bridget wept, feeling rather like a wilful child who had strayed out of the nursery among a horde of savages.

At last she could bear it no longer. They were singing now – a terrible thing with a refrain of oaths and *Gee-ups*, and whistling noises like the cracking of whips – a bullock drivers' camp ditty. Bridget shudderingly decided that a row in Whitechapel could be nothing to this in the matter of bad language. She got up and paced the sitting-room in her dressing-gown, wondering when her husband would come and rescue her from these beasts. Watching for him she could see through the uncurtained French windows the starry brilliance of the night, and the moon now in its middle quarter. And down below, the houses and shanties along the opposite side of the street, the fantastic tufts of the pawpaws, the long white road stretching away into the ragged blur of gum-forest.

Presently a firm step sounded on the veranda and came up the stairs.

When Colin opened the door, he saw standing by the table, which had a kerosene lamp on the red cloth, and, even at this time of the year, winged insects buzzing round, and sticking to its greasy bowl – a small white figure like an apparition from another world, in its wonderful draperies of lace and filmy white, the little pale face framed in a cloud of shining hair, and the strange eyes wide, scared, and with tears glistening on the reddened lids.

She cried out at him.

'How could you have left me here alone with those horrible drunken men down there making such a noise that I thought every

minute they would break in on me? And swearing! I've never
dreamed of such dreadful language; and I can't stand it – I won't
stand it a minute longer.'

'You shan't. It's abominable, I've been a thoughtless beast.'

He swooped out through the open door, down the wooden stairs
which creaked under his wrathful steps. Bridget heard him call the
landlady, 'Mrs Maloney! Come here!' in a voice of sharp command.
Presently she heard him speaking to the men in the bar, not
abusively, indeed almost good humoured tone, but imperatively.

'Look here, mates.' The uproar stopped suddenly. 'You're decent
blokes I know, and you've all had mothers if you haven't had wives.
Well, there's a lady up there – she's my wife, and she's never heard
bullock-drivers swear before, and you've scared her a bit. Just you
stop it. Shut up and be off like good chaps.'

Some dissentient voices arose; an attempt at drunken ribaldry,
strident hisses, 'Sh! Sh!' Cries of 'Shame.' 'Chuck it!' Then again,
McKeith's voice, this time like thunder. 'Stop that I say – one more
word and out you go, whether you like it or not.'

On that, came the noise of a scuffle and the fall of a heavy body
across the veranda. And of McKeith, once more breathing satisfaction:

'All right! I haven't killed him – only given him a lesson. . . . But
just you understand I'm not taking any of your bluff. You've *got to go.*
If you don't, it'll be a case of the lock-up for some of you. And if you
do – quietly mind, there'll be a shout all round for the lot of you to-
morrow. Drink my health and my wife's, d'ye see? Here
Mrs Maloney, chalk it down.'

In five minutes he was back in the sitting-room, looking rather
dishevelled, and with his coat awry. But there was silence below
except for the putting up of shutters, the sound of shuffling feet along
the road and snatches of the bullock drivers' chorus which gradually
died away in the night.

McKeith went up to his wife who was still standing by the corner
of the table, and put his arm round the little trembling form.

'Oh! Biddy – my darling. I've been a brute. I'm not fit to take care
of you. I ought to have thought of all that. But one gets used to such
goings-on in the Bush, and they aren't bad chaps – the bullockys, and
you've got to discount their lurid language a bit. I don't know
whether it is that bullocks are more profane than most animals, but
it's certain sure that you can't get them to move without swearing at
them.'

Then, as she said, half crying, half laughing, 'I see. So this is my baptism into the Bush! You should have taught me the vocabulary, Colin, first.'

'Don't be hard on me. You won't have this kind of thing at Moongarr. That's the worst of these cursed coast townships. I shouldn't have left you alone, but if I hadn't, we couldn't have got off properly to-morrow, and I'd set my heart on having things ship-shape for our first camping out. Everything's fixed up now – I've been wiring like mad up the line. . . . The buggy's at the Terminus all right, and I've got the black-boys there, and the tent and all that. It's going to be an experience you'll never forget. *That's* to be your baptism into the Bush, my dear . . . if only there's water enough left in the Creek yet. . . . But if there isn't we can dig for it. Oh, Biddy, think of it – a night like this – moonlight and starlight – *my* starlight – *my* star, that I used to look up at and wonder about, come down to earth. No, no, I won't maunder, I won't be a romantic zany – not till to-morrow night – I know the very spot for our camp. . . .'

He began to describe it – a pocket by the river bed – pasturage for the horses – then pulled himself short. No! He wanted it all to be a surprise. . . . She was to have just the very thing she had often said to him she would like best. . . . And now it was getting late and they must be up in good time to-morrow. Would she go to bed and try to sleep. . . .

He took her to the door of her room. . . . Was she as comfortable as she could be here, anyhow? . . . . He knew it must seem cruelly rough to her; but it wouldn't be his fault in the future if she didn't have things as she liked them – so far as conditions would permit. . . . And after all, there were women who had enjoyed a wild life with their husbands. There was Lady Burton – and scores of other women – Biddy had asked him to have patience – and he meant to be patient – he worshipped her too much not to be patient. Well, she must be patient too with him, and with this queer old Bush which she would get to feel as much at home in as he did himself – in time.

He left her at her bedroom door, kissing her hand with the native chivalry that sat well upon him, and went back to his pipe and the waking dreams of an ardent but self-restrained lover who had practical as well as romantic considerations to weigh. Bridget went to sleep with the smell of his tobacco – and yet did not seem to mind it in the least – coming in whiffs through the door cracks and filling her nostrils. She too dreamed – a vivid dream, but by some law of contrariety, not of any idyllic camping ground in the Never-Never Land. She dreamed that she was seeing the Carnival at Nice – a medley of dancing waves, azure sky, palms, gold-laden orange trees and white green-shuttered houses – flowers, *confetti*, masks, grotesque pageantry, the merry music of the South. And though he had never been with her at Nice, Willoughby Maule came into her dream. They were doing impossible things – dancing together in the Carnival crowd, flinging confetti, bobbing and grimacing before the comic masks. Then the carnival scene seemed to turn flat, and to become a painted picture on the drop curtain of a stage, and she started up at the sound of knocks such as one hears before the curtain rises in a French theatre.

CHAPTER 5

───────────●───────────

Her husband was at her door calling her in the grey of dawn. He had everything ready he said. She dressed fumblingly as if she were still in her dream, and they walked to the station-shed whither the baggage had already gone. The sun was only a little way above the horizon when they took their places in the bush train that was to bear her on the second stage of her journey into the Unknown. Such a wheezy, shaky little train, and such funny, ugly country! Sandy flats sparsely grown, mostly with gum trees, where there were no houses and gardens. Near the township there were a good many of these wooden dwellings with corrugated iron roofs – some of the more aged ones of slab – and with a huge chimney at one end. They were set in fenced patches of millet and Indian corn or gardens that wanted watering and with children perched on the top rail of the fences who cheered the train as it passed. Sometimes the train puffed between lines of grey slab fencing in which were armies of white skeleton trees that had been 'rung' for extermination, or with bleached stumps sticking up in a chaos of felled trunks, while in some there had sprung up sickly iron-bark saplings.

Now and then, they would stop at a deserted-looking station, round which stood a few shanties, and the inevitable public house. Maybe it had formerly been a sheepfold, abandoned when the scab had destroyed the flocks; and there were enormous rusty iron boiling-pots to which a fetid odour still clung, and where the dust that blew up, had the grittiness and faint smell of sun-dried sheeps' droppings.

At one of the more important stopping places, they had early lunch of more fried steak, with sweet potatoes and heavy bread and butter and peach jam. Most of the other passengers got out for lunch also.

There was a fifth-rate theatrical company cracking jokes among themselves, drinking brandy and soda at extortionate prices, and staring hard at Lady Bridget. Colin pointed out to her a lucky digger and his family – two daughters in blue serge trimmed with gold braid, and a fat red-faced Mamma, very fine in a feathered hat, black brocade, a diamond brooch, and with many rings and jangling bangles. There were some battered, bearded bushmen who seemed to be friends of Colin's, though he did not introduce them to his wife, and who talked on topical subjects in a vernacular which Lady Bridget thought to herself she would never be able to master. There was a professional horse-breaker whom McKeith hailed as Zack Duppo, and to whom he had a good deal to say also. There were some gangs of shearers or stockmen or what not, who appeared to be the following of two or three rakish, aggressive looking males upon whom the bushmen scowled. Union delegates, Strike Organisers, McKeith explained.

After that station, marks of civilisation diminished. The Noah's Ark humpeys in their clearings became few and far between, and the long lines of grey two-railed fences melted into gum forest. Now and then, they saw herds of cattle and horses. Once, a company of kangaroos sitting up with fore paws drooping and a baby marsupial poking its head out of the pouch of one of the does. Then, taking fright in a second, all leaped up, long back legs stretched, tails in air, and, in a few ungainly bounds they were lost to sight among the gum trees. Early in the afternoon the train reached the temporary Terminus, for the line was being carried on by degrees through the Leura district. This was a mining town called Fig Tree Mount – why, nobody could tell, for there were no fig trees, and not a sign of a hill as far as the level horizon – except for the heaps of refuse mullock that showed where shafts had been sunk. A good many years ago, Bridget was told, there had been a rush to the place, but the gold field turned out not so good as had been expected, and it was only lately that the discovery of a payable reef had brought the digging population back again. From one direction came the whirr of machinery, and there was in the same quarter a collection of white tents and roughly put up humpeys. Otherwise, the township consisted of a long dusty street cutting the sandy plain and, out of the two score or so of zinc-roofed buildings, twenty were public houses.

Lady Bridget had been very silent all day. To Colin's anxious enquiries she answered that it was enough to take in so many new impressions without talking about them. Through the crude blur of these impressions her husband stood out definitely, a dominant influence. She seemed to be only now beginning to feel his dominance. Yet all the time, she could not get away from the sense of living in some fantastic dream – an Edward Lear nonsense dream. The sight of the kangaroos in the Bush brought a particular rhyme of her childhood to her mind. She half said, half sang it to an improvised tune:

> 'Said the Duck to the Kangaroo,
>   "Good gracious! how you hop!
> Over the fields and water too,
>   As if you never would stop!" '

She caught her husband looking at her in a fascinated, puzzled way, and paused and gave him her funny little smile.

'That's a very pretty song,' he said. 'But I can't make out what it means. What is it about a duck or a kangaroo? They're nonsense words, aren't they?'

'Nonsense – oh yes, frightful nonsense. Only it struck me that there's sometimes a lot of truth in nonsense. Listen now,' and she went on:

> '"My life is a bore in this nasty pond,
> And I long to go out in the world beyond.
> I wish I could hop like you!"
> Said the Duck to the Kangaroo.'

He still looked puzzled – but adoring.

'You've got no sense of humour,' she said, 'Don't you see that you and I are as incongruous as the duck and the kangaroo?'

'That is so,' he answered gravely. 'But I'll be a kangaroo with pleasure if it makes the Bush more attractive to you.'

She fell suddenly silent again, and sat gloomy and staring at the endless procession of gum trees as the train lumbered on through that fantastic forest, which made her think of all kinds of ridiculous things. And she was conscious all the time of his furtive watching from the corner opposite, and of his readiness to spring forward at the least indication of her wanting anything. It bewildered her – the strangeness of being alone with, entirely dependent upon this big man of the Bush, who had the right to look after her, and yet of whom she knew so little.

He did look after her with sedulous care. He had natty bush dodges for minimising the discomfort of the hot, dusty train journey. He manufactured a windsail outside the carriage window, which brought in a little breeze during the airless heat of mid-day. He contrived to get cool drinks and improvised for her head a cushion out of his rolled up poncho, a silk handkerchief and a large cold cabbage leaf against which she leaned her hot forehead. In all his actions she watched him with a curious blend of feelings. There was a satisfaction in his largeness, his commonsense, his breeziness. She liked hearing his quaint Bush colloquialisms, when he leaned out of the window at the small stations and exchanged greetings with whomsoever happened to be there —· officials, navvies, miners, even Chinamen — most of whom saluted him with a 'Glad to see you back, sir!' . . . or a 'Good-day, Boss. Good luck to you,' as if they all knew the significance of this wedding journey — which no doubt they all did.

Bridget kept in the background and smiled enigmatically at it all. She was interested in her husband both in the personal and abstract sense, and was a little surprised at herself for being pleased when he paid her any attention or sat down beside her. At moments, she even hankered after the touch of his fingers, and had a perverse desire to break down the restraint he was so manifestly putting upon himself. Once, when he had been sitting very still in the further corner, thinking she was asleep, she had looked at him suddenly, and had found his eyes fixed on her in a gaze so concentrated, so full of intense longing, that she felt as if he were trying to hypnotise her into loving hm. She knew that if he were, it must be unconscious hypnotism on his part. There were no subtleties of that kind in Colin McKeith. No, it was the primal element in him that appealed to her, dominated her. For she was startled by a sudden realization of that dominant quality in him as applied to herself. In their courtship it had been she who dominated him.

He reddened guiltily when he caught her eyes. His long upper lip went down in obstinate resistance to impulse. But if he had kissed her then, she would not have rebelled.

'Colin, what are you thinking of?' she said, and he answered in a tone, husky with pent emotion.

'I was thinking of our camp to-night — of how we should be alone together in the starlight. . . . And of how I want to make you happy and of how wonderful it all is — like some impossible dream.'

'Yes. I've been feeling too that it is like a dream,' she replied gravely.

'A bit of nightmare so far, I'm afraid, for you, Biddy,' he said shaking himself free from sentiment. 'But this part of it will soon be over.'

He got up, pulled the blind down behind her, and readjusted the cabbage leaf under her head. Just then, the train pulled up at a station where there were selectors' holdings, and a German woman was lugging along a crate of garden produce. He jumped out and bought another cabbage from which he shredded a fresh cool leaf for her pillow. And at that they laughed and he relapsed into normal commonplace.

When she got out at Fig Tree Mount, he took her across the sandy street to the nearest and largest of the public houses which had 'Station Hotel' printed on it in big blue letters – a glaring, crude, zinc-roofed box with a dirty veranda that seemed a receptacle for rubbish and a lounge for kangaroo dogs, to say nothing of drunken men. The dogs took no notice of the male loungers, but started a vigorous barking at the sight of a lady. There was the usual bar at one end, the usual noise going on inside, and the usual groups of bush loafers outside. Several riding horses were hitched up to the palings at a right angle with the Bar, and a bullock dray loaded with wool-bales – on the top of which a whole family appeared to reside under a canvas tilt – was drawn up in the road. The beasts were a repulsive sight, with whip-weals on their panting sides, their great heads bowed under the yoke and their slavering tongues protruding. Bridget looked at everything with a wide detached gaze, as she followed her husband along the hotel veranda. McKeith, motioning to his wife to proceed, stopped to peer at the faces of two men lying in a drunken sleep on the boards.

'Not my men, anyway,' he said, rejoining her. 'But that will keep.' The place seemed deserted and in disorder. There were glimpses through the open windows of unmade beds within, and, on the veranda, lay some red blankets bundled together. Colin took his wife into a parlour, where flies buzzed round the remains of a meal and some empty whisky bottles and glasses. After considerable shouting and knocking at doors along the passage, he succeeded in arousing the landlady, who came in, buttoning her blouse. Her obviously dyed yellow hair was in a dishevelled state, her eyes were heavy and her face sodden. She had evidently been sleeping off the effects of drink.

'Had a night of it, I suppose, Mrs Hurst?' observed McKeith glumly. 'This is a nice sort of place to show a lady into.'

The woman burst out on the defensive, but McKeith silenced her.

'That'll do. Clear away all that mess and let us have a clean cloth and some tea. And I say, if you have got a decent room for my wife to wash the dust off and take a bit of a rest in, I'll be obliged.'

The landlady blinked her puffed eyelids, muttered an uncourteous rejoinder and went off with some of the debris from the table. Bridget laughed blankly. She looked so small and flower like, so absolutely incongruous with her surroundings, that the humour of it all struck McKeith tragically.

'Good Lord! I wonder what your opinion is of this show! Here is the beginning of what is called the Never-Never Country, my dear. Do you want to go back again to Government House?'

'No, I don't,' and she touched him to the heart's core by putting her little hand in his.

'That's my Mate,' said he, his blue eyes glistening. 'But I'll tell you what I think of your splendid pluck when we're quit of these beastly townships, and have gone straight into Nature. Now, I've got to go and see after the buggy and find my boys, and I shall have all my work cut out to be ready in an hour. You just make the best of things, and if the bedroom is impossible spread out my poncho and take a rest on that sofa there, and don't be frightened if you hear any rowdiness going on.'

The bedroom *was* impossible, and the sofa seemed equally so. Bridget drank the coarse bush tea which the landlady brought in, and was glad that the woman seemed too sulky to want to talk. Then she sat down at the window and watched the life of the township – the diggers slouching in for drinks, the riders from the bush who hung up their horses and went into the bar, the teams of bullocks coming slowly down the road and drawing up here or at some other of the nineteen public houses 'to wet the wool,' in bush vernacular. She counted as many as twenty-four bullocks in one of the teams, and watched with interest the family life that went on in the narrow space between the wool bales and the canvas roof above. There were women up there and little children. She saw bedding spread and a baby's clothes fluttering out to dry, and tin pannikins and chunks of salt beef slung to the ropes that bound the wool bales together. Then, when the wool was wetted, or when some other teams behind disputed the right of way in lurid terms which Lady Bridget was now beginning to accept as inevitably concomitant with bullocks, the first dray would proceed, all the cattle bells jingling and making, in the distance, not unpleasant music.

It was the horses that interested Lady Bridget most, for, like all the O'Haras, she was a born horsewoman. Though she was moved almost to tears by the spur scars on the lean sides of some of them – spirited creatures in which she recognised the marks of breeding – and by the unkempt condition of some that were just from grass, she decided within herself that there could never be a lack of interest and excitement in a land where such horseflesh abounded.

Presently she had her first sight of the typical stockman got up in 'township rig.' Spotless moleskins, new Crimean shirt, regulation silk handkerchief, red, of course, and brand new, tied in a sailor's knot at the neck, leather belt with pouches of every shape and size slung from it, tobacco pouch, watch pouch, knife pouch and what not. Cabbage tree hat of intricate plait pushed back to the back of the head and held firm by a thin strap coming down to the upper lip and caught in two gaps on either side of the prominent front teeth – there are very few stockmen who have kept all their front teeth. Stockwhip, out of commission for the present, with an elaborately carved and beautifully polished sandal-wood handle hanging down behind, a long snake-like lash coiled in three loops over the left shoulder.

Lady Bridget knew most of the types of men who have to do with horses – huntsmen, trainers, jockeys, riding masters and the rest, but the Australian bush-rider is a product by itself. She liked this son of the gum forest-tanned face, taut nerves, alert eyes piercing long distances – a man, vital, shrewd, simple as a child, cunning as an animal. And the way he sat in his saddle, the poise of the lean, lanky muscular frame! No wonder the first stockman seemed to the wild blacks a new sort of beast with four legs and two bodies. And the clean-limbed mettlesome creature under him! Man and beast seemed truly a part of each other. Lady Bridget O'Hara's soul warmed to that stockman and to his steed.

He was looking at the windows of the bar-parlour. As soon as he saw the lady, the cabbage tree hat was raised in a flourish, the horse was reined in, the man off his saddle and the bridle hitched to a post.

Now the stockman stepped on to the veranda.

'Mrs McKeith – or is it Lady McKeith I should say – I haven't got the hang of the name if you'll pardon me – Mr McKeith sent me on to say that he'll be here with the buggy in a minute or two. . . . I'm

Moongarr Bill. . . . Glad to welcome you up the Leura, ma'am, though I expect things seem a bit rough to you straight out from England and not knowing the Bush.'

Lady Bridget won Moongarr Bill's good favour instantly by the look in her eyes and the smile with which she answered him.

'I'm from Ireland, Moongarr Bill, and if we Irish know anything we know a good horse, and that's a beauty you're riding.

'Out of a Pitsford mare by a Royallieu colt, and there's not a finer breed in the Never-Never. My word! you've struck it there, ma'am, and no mistake,' responded the stockman enthusiastically. 'I bought 'im out of the yard at Breeza Downs – that's Windeatt's run about sixty miles from Moongarr, and I will say that though it's a sheep-run they've beat us in the breed of their 'osses. . . . Got 'im cheap because he'd bucked young Windeatt off and nearly kicked his brains out, and there wasn't a man along the Leura that he'd let stop on his back except me and Zack Duppo – the horse-breaker who first put the tackling on 'im.'

After the interchange of one or two remarks, Lady Bridget had no doubt of being friends with Moongarr Bill, and Moongarr Bill decided that for a dashed new-chum woman, Lady Bridget had a remarkable knowledge of horseflesh.

The quick *clop-clop* of a four horse team and a clatter of tin billys and pannikins – as Lady Bridget presently discovered slung upon the back rail of an American buggy – sounded up the street.

'There's the Boss,' said Moongarr Bill. 'Look alive, with that packhorse, Wombo.'

Lady Bridget now perceived behind the stockman a black boy on a young colt, leading a sturdy flea-bitten grey, laden with a pack bag on either side. He jumped off as lightly as Moongarr Bill and hitched his horses also to the veranda posts. Except that he was black as a coal, save for the whites of his eyes and his gleaming teeth, he seemed a grotesque understudy of the stockman – moleskins, not too clean and rubbed and frayed in places, fastened up with a strap; faded Crimean shirt exposing a wealed and tattooed breast; old felt hat – not a cabbage tree – with a pipe stuck in its greasy band; an ancient red silk handkerchief with ragged edges, where whip crackers had been torn off, round his neck, and a short axe slipped among a few old pouches into the strap at his waist. He jumped on to the veranda, clicked his teeth in an admiring ejaculation as he gazed at Lady Bridget.

'My word! *Bujeri* feller White Mary you! . . . new feller Mithsis belonging to Boss. My word!' Then as McKeith drew up his horses in front of the hotel, Wombo and Moongarr Bill sprang to the heads of wheelers and leaders.

It seemed to Bridget that there was a change in her husband even since he had left her. He looked more determined, more practical, wholly absorbed in the unsentimental business of the moment. He had changed into looser, more workmanlike rig – was belted, pouched, carried his whip grandly, handled his reins with a royal air of command, as if he were now thoroughly at home in his own dominions, had already asserted his authority – which she found presently to be the case – and intended the rest of the world to knock under to him. There flashed on Lady Bridget an absurd idea of having been married by proxy – like the little princesses of history – and of being now received into her lord's country by the monarch in person. Her face was rippling all over with laughter when he joined her in the veranda.

'What! Another delicious black boy! He looks like a Christy Minstrel. I thought you hated blacks, Colin.'

'So I do. You've got to have 'em though for stock boys, and I keep my heel on the lot at Moongarr. Wombo and Cudgee aren't bad chaps so long as they are kept clear of their tribe. How do you like the new buggy, my lady? A dandy go-cart, eh?'

He looked as pleased as a child with a new toy carriage. The buggy was quite a smart bush turn-out – comfortable seats in front – a varnished cover, now lying back; a well behind, filled with luggage; a narrow back seat whence Cudgee – a smaller edition of Wombo – sprang down. Cudgee, too, stared at Lady Bridget and clicked his teeth in admiration, exclaiming:

'Hullo! New feller Mithsis.'

Afterwards, Lady Bridget remembered the greetings and wondered why the black boys had said: 'New feller Mithsis!' Who had been the old feller Mithsis? she asked herself.

McKeith sternly quashed the black boys' ebullition and told them to mind their own business. Bridget agreed that the buggy was first rate and became enthusiastic over the horses, four fairly matched and powerful roans.

'Oh! what beauties! I'd like to go and make friends with them.'

He was delighted. 'Good 'uns, ain't they? But wait and make friends when you're behind 'em. We've twenty-five miles to do before sundown. Got your traps fixed up? That's right. Here, Bill, take her ladyship's bag and stow it safely at the back of the buggy. Handle it gingerly – it's full of silver and glass fallals – not what we're much used to on the Leura.'

The stockman grinned and carried the dressing-bag – one of Sir Luke's and Lady Tallant's wedding presents – as if it were dynamite. Colin seemed anxious to impress his wife's dignity upon her new subjects. She felt still more like a queen of comic opera. He helped her into her dust cloak, paid the bill, cut short the landlady's sulky apologies – she had done her hair and recovered herself a little. Then he settled Lady Bridget into the buggy after the manner of a bush courtier – her feet on a footstool, the rug over her knees, a cushion at her back. His whole air seemed to say:

'This is the Queen, and I, the King, expect that proper homage be paid her.'

CHAPTER 6

————————•————————

The loafers at the bar all came out to see the start. The family on the top of the bullock-dray peered forth from under the tilt. The bar-keeper shouted, 'Good luck to you and your lady, Mr McKeith.' The drunken reprobates, awakened from their slumber on the boards, called out, too, 'Goo-luksh!' There was an attempt at a cheer, but before McKeith had got out his answering, 'Thank ye – Good day, mates,' a shower of opprobrious epithets rained upon him from a little band of discontented bush rowdies – the advance guard of that same Union delegate who had come up with them in the train from Leuraville.

Three of these men lurched on to the bar veranda, and, so to speak, took the stage. In front was a stumpily-built bullock driver with a red, truculent face, a ragged carrotty beard and inflamed narrow-lidded eyes. A little to the rear stood a lanky, muscular bushman in very dirty moleskins, with a smooth loose-lipped face, no eyelashes, and a scowling forehead, who was evidently the worse for drink; next to him, a shorter man of the drover type, older, eagle-beaked and with sinister, foxy eyes. This one hailed McKeith.

'Yah! Look at him and his spanking team! What price honest labour, you blamed scab of a squatter? Just you wait a bit. It'll be our turn soon to burn all you blanked capitalists off the Leura.'

The lanky bushman took up the jeering note.

'Pretty flash turn-out, ain't it! My word, you think yourself a bloated fine gentleman now you've married into the British hairystocracy, don't you, Mister Colin McKeith? You can take it from us, boys, he's the meanest cuss that ever downed a harmless nigger. . . . Ask him what the twenty-five notches on his gun stand for?'

'And *I* tell you *what* it is; Steve Baines. There'll be another notch on my gun, and it won't be for a nigger, if you give me any more of your insolence,' said McKeith coolly. 'Get out of the way, men. Let the horses go, Cudgee. Ready, Biddy?'

But Cudgee, out of malice or stupidity, did not let the roans go or else someone else put a restraining hand on the reins. The man with the ragged beard roared out.

'Ho, you think you're going to ride over us! – you and your fine ladyship! Wot do we care about the British hairystocracy. What we're asking for is the rights of labour, and we mean to have 'em. Do you want to know what he's done to us boys? Fired us out straight away cos we was 'avin' a bit of a spell and a drink to keep the life in us after we'd close up killed ourselves lifting that there ladyship's blanked hundred-ton weight of pianner on to the dray. . . .'

Moongarr Bill's chivalrous instinct flamed to a counter attack. He had just mounted, but swung down from his saddle and made a rush at the speaker. McKeith's stern voice stopped him.

'Don't be a fool, Bill. Let the brutes alone and push on with the pack. This is not the time for a row. As for you, Jim Steadbolt – you know me, and you know that if this was any other sort of occasion, you'd pay on the nail for your infernal cheek. . . . Leave go of those reins. D'ye hear'; for the man of the ragged beard was jerking the near leader's bit and putting the mettlesome animal on its haunches.

'Damn you! Let go.'

He leaned forward to strike at Steadbolt with his riding whip, but the lash had caught round the pole-bar of the buggy, and he could not extricate it. Bridget tried to help him. He turned to her for an instant, a soft gleam of tenderness shining through the steely anger on his face.

'No. Keep still, my dear. Don't be frightened.'

'*I* frightened!' She gave a little laugh. Her form stiffened. The small pale face poked forward between the folds of her motor veil, and all the O'Hara spirit flashed as she spoke to the group of malcontents.

'How dare you! Stand back. I thought Australian men *were* men, and that they didn't insult women.'

There was an uproar in the veranda, and more cries of 'Shame, Steadbolt, you! . . . You just git, Gumsucker Steve. We ain't got no use for you, Micky Phayle. . . . Can't you see a lady as is a lady?' sounded from the bar and parlour. It was the landlady who asked the last question. The two reprobates who had been asleep, lunged off the veranda, and made a feeble assault on Steadbolt, who still clung to the reins. The man, lashed to fury by the scorn ringing in Lady Bridget's voice, made a last envenomed attack.

'It ain't us *genuine* Australians that insults you. . . . Takes a mongrel Scotchy for that. . . . Say, Ladyship, just you ask your husband what a sort of an insult he's got ready for *you* up at his Bachelor's Quarters at Moongarr.'

The words had not left his mouth when McKeith's driving whip whizzed in the air and raised blood on the speaker's cheek. Steadbolt dropped his hold of the roan leader's bridle and fell back screaming imprecations. At a touch, the buggy-horses bounded forward.

'Sit tight, Biddy,' said her husband. 'Up you get, Cudgee,' he shouted. The black boy leaped to the back-seat, and in a moment the buggy swerved by the bullock-dray that was drawn up a little further down the road, and the excited horses galloped past the nineteen public houses and the zinc-roofed shanties, past the new quarter of tents and whirring machinery, past the deserted shafts and desolate mullock heaps, then way out along the sandy wheel-track into the unpopulated Bush.

For the first mile scarcely a word was exchanged between husband and wife. The horses were fresh and McKeith had enough to do to keep them from bolting. Moreover, even in emotional phases, he was always silent while chewing the cud of his reflections. Bridget was thinking, too. She had an uneasy sense of startlement, without exactly knowing why she felt startled in that inward way. It was as though some great obscene bird of flight had brushed her with its wings, and brought vaguely to her consciousness unpleasant possibilities. But presently she became interested in watching Colin's handling of the team. She had often sat behind such a team, but never beside such a splendid whip. Impulsively she made some such remark, and he looked down at her, the hard face breaking into a smile.

'That's good. . . . Wait a bit, my dear, until they've steadied down again. . . . Y'see they take a lot of driving, and I don't want to lay an accident on top of that unholy shindy. . . .' He spoke in jerks. The roans were inclined to 'show nasty' as Moongarr Bill came abreast of them, and Wombo's pack jingled behind. McKeith gave Moongarr Bill directions about the camp in Bush lingo, which again turned Bridget's thoughts. The black boy and the stockman spurred on as the roans slackened pace. McKeith was able to relax the strain.

'My word! we scooted pretty quick out of that piece of scenery,' he said. 'I felt downright mad at your being let in for such a disgraceful bit of business. I hadn't time to tell you that I'd sacked those men half an hour before. Found them in the lowest of the grog shanties, their horses not looked after, dray only half loaded, and the three of them – Gumsucker Steve was to have come and taken off our leaders when we got into broken country – thick with the Union delegates and sticking for higher wages. I paid them off and filled their places on the spot with two chaps off a wool-drive. . . . So I left the brutes vowing vengeance, and I suppose they thought they'd lose no time in giving me a taste of it. . . . Well, they're no loss.' He had been explaining things in jerks while he brought the team to an harmonious jog-trot along a piece of uneven road. 'That fellow Steadbolt is a wrong 'un – not good even at his own job of wood and water joey – which means, my dear, the odd cart-driving on a place – and not to be trusted within ten miles of a public house.'

Lady Bridget asked suddenly:

'I want to know, Colin – what did that man mean by saying you had an insult ready for me at your Bachelor's Quarters? What insult?'

It seemed as though blue fire leaped from McKeith's eyes.

'Insult! Good God! Biddy you can't hold me responsible for the foul insinuations of a beast like that. Insult *you!* my wife!'

The passionate tenderness thrilling his voice, the honest wrath and bewilderment in his face must have silenced any doubt, had doubt existed in Lady Bridget's mind.

'I don't know, Colin. I don't even know what Bachelors' Quarters mean. Have you an army of Bachelors at Moongarr, and what do they do when they're at home?'

He laughed. 'It's a shanty I put up for the new-chums when I've got any – and for the gentlemen-sun-downers that come along, and visitors that I don't want to be bothered with at the House. There's a woman up there. . . .' He stopped suddenly and his face grew grim again. 'That's it, I suppose – I'm sorry I didn't sling the whip harder and cut the fellow's cheek open. I would if I'd thought. . . . !'

He stopped again.

'What woman? Have I a rival? This is becoming dramatic!' Lady Bridget's voice was amusedly ironic, but she carried her head erect. 'Tell me about the woman at the Bachelors' Quarters, Colin.'

'There's nothing to tell, except that's she's the widow of a man who went up with me on my last Big Bight expedition, and was killed

– partly through his own, and partly through my, fault. That's why I've made a point of looking after her, and I built my Bachelor's Quarters chiefly to give her a job. I thought she was too young and too good looking to be drawing grog for diggers at Fig Tree Mount – which was what she set out doing.'

'I see. . . . So she's young – and handsome.'

'Oh, in a coarse sort of way. . . . No, I wouldn't say that; she's rather refined for her upbringing. Anyway, Steadbolt – as well as a lot of other men fell in love with her – Steadbolt was pretty well off his head over it. She wouldn't have him at any price – naturally – and I had to give the fellow work outside the head-station to keep him away from her. That was before I went south. Very likely he's been trying it on again, and knew I should have to get rid of him as soon as I came back.'

'Why doesn't the woman marry again?'

McKeith shrugged. 'Too jolly comfortable perhaps – or perhaps the right man hasn't turned up. Florrie Hensor is several cuts above a malingering lout like Steadbolt. Well there, poor devil! Maybe, it's not unnatural that I should feel a sneaking sympathy for an unsuccessful lover. That abominable lie was a bit too strong though – and before *you*! The man must have been downright mad from drink and fury and bitterness. It – it's all funny – isn't it? One of the queer sides of the Bush. Good old Bush! I am glad to be back in it again, Biddy.'

He lifted his head and seemed to draw in the strong odour of the gum trees and the pure vitality of the westering sun. His anger appeared to have left only compunction behind it. And again he begged her to forgive him for having subjected her to an experience so disagreeable. They were on a stretch of clear road now, and the roans trotted pleasantly along. Lady Bridget took up his words.

'Yes, it's all funny – that kind of thing – in this setting. . . . I never supposed that I should be howled at by a revolutionary mob in the Australian Bush. . . . *A bas les aristocrats*. It's quite exciting. I think I should have enjoyed the Reign of Terror.'

'Eh! You're only frightened of four-footed beasts. If you'd lived then, you'd have gone up to the block with that smile on your lips, and the proud turn of your little head – just as I used to dream of you. . .'

'Of *me!*'

'You don't know – I'll tell you some day. I remember talking to

Joan Gildea once. . . . It's queer. . . . But never mind now. D'ye like this, Biddy?'

'I love it. I wish we could drive on through the forest all day and all night – a dream drive. I think I might be able to place myself at the end of it.'

'To place yourself!'

'I've never been able to find my true pivot inside. All my life I've been howling in my soul and haven't known what I was howling for. I thought to-day that you might teach me.'

'Is it only to-day that you have thought that?' he said wistfully. 'Well, anyway, I'm glad of it.'

'Colin,' she said abruptly, 'wasn't it funking a little bit, don't you think – running away?'

'No – not with *you* beside me. You'll have other opportunities for seeing whether I've got much of the funker in me. No doubt those brutes will give trouble some time.'

'What can they do?'

'Fire my run – spoil my cattle sales – get hold of my stockmen. . . . But I'm not so badly off as my "sheep" neighbours at Breeza Downs. They've got to have their shearing done. . . . Though I've had a lot of bother to-day,' his face became gloomy, 'and I foresee more ahead.'

She asked what other sort of trouble.

'Why! there's been no rain at Moongarr since I left it five months ago. And Pleuro means innoculation and short sales. . . . Ah well! . . .'

He flicked the wheelers gently. 'Shake it up, Alexander! Look alive, Roxalana. . . . I named 'em when I was reading *Rollin's Ancient History*, my dear . . . my dear!' He looked down at the little woman by his side with deep tenderness in his blue eyes and a smile that banished the shade from his face. 'Oh, my dear, there ain't going to be any bush worries for us this blessed afternoon and evening. It's the poetry and romance' – he pronounced it rōmance – 'of the bush that's got hold of me now. I'm just longing for us to strike the camping place – and then – just you and me together – just man and woman – alone with Nature!'

He put his hand on hers and she pressed it in return. The Woman in her thrilled to the Man in him.

Cudgee, on the hind seat with his back to them, broke the spell.

'My word, Massa! You look out, Mithsis – big feller goanner sit down along a tree.' And for the first time in her existence, Lady Bridget beheld a monster iguana dragging its huge lizard tail and turning its stately, brown crocodile head round at her from the safe vantage place of a thick gum branch.

After that, the way led off the main road, on by a less used track through wilder country. Here Wombo, the black boy, was waiting – Moongarr Bill having gone on with the pack horse to the camping place – and helped to unharness the two leaders which he drove before him ahead. The trees thickened, the buggy wheels caught on stumps. Cudgee had to get down at intervals and, with his axe, lop and clear fallen timber. Every mile the progress grew slower and the forest more lonely. No sign now of a selector's clearing, or of any human occupation. . . . But there was a pack of emus hustling and shaking their big bunches of feathers like startled ballet girls.

'I feel as if part of the Zoo had been let loose,' said Lady Bridget when again there bounded along in the near distance a pair of kangaroos with a little Joey kangaroo taking a lesson in locomotion behind its parents.

They were still in the gum forest, but now and then came a belt of gidia scrub – mournful trees with stiff black trunks and grey green foliage and a pale sort of wattle flower smelling like dead cattle when rain is about, as McKeith explained. But there was no rain about now, and, in truth, he would have welcomed the unpleasant odour. Perhaps it was that which made the ground so stark and bare beneath these trees where no grass will grow. The sun was lowering when they left the gidia. Out in the gum forest again, the birds were chattering before retiring to rest. All life is still in the bush at mid-day, but now there were curious scutterings among the grass tussocks, and the whirr of its insect population sounded all round. The country got prettier – swelling pastures and stony pinches and a distant outline of hills. They could see the green line of a water course.

'Plenty water sit down along a creek?' McKeith asked the black boy. But Cudgee shook his woolly head.

'Ba'al[1] mine think it, Massa. No rain plenty long time.'

McKeith sighed. The dark shadow of coming drought is a fearsome spectre on the Never-Never Land.

---

[1] Ba'al – the Aboriginal negative.

CHAPTER 7

————————●————————

A *Coo-ee* sounded long, clear, vibrant. Moongarr Bill and Wombo, who had gone on ahead, were fixing camp. Lady Bridget's musical voice caught up the note. She answered it with another *Coo-ee*, to Cudgee's delight.

'My word! Ba'al newchum, that feller white Mary,' said he.

They had rounded a knoll abutting on the green line of ti-trees and swamp oak. It was a barren hump; upon its crest, and alone in barbaric majesty, stood a row of grass trees silhouetted against the sunset sky. Weird sentinels of the bridal camp they seemed – tall, thick black trunks like palm-stems, from each of which spread an enormous tuft of gigantic grass blades green and upright in the middle, grey and jaggled and drooping where they hung over at the bottom. Out of each green heart sprang a great black spear many feet in height.

The stony knoll dropped sheer like a wall. On the other side of it was a space the size of an amphitheatre, a large part of it spread with soft green grass, like a carpet, and the rest of the floor scattered with low shrubs and big tussocks. Amongst them was a herb giving out a fragrance, when the feet crushed it, like that of wild thyme. The whole air seemed filled with a blend of aromatic perfumes.

Here was a roofless room, open on one side where a break in the ti-trees showed the sandy bed of the creek, which, at first, to Lady Bridget's fancy, had the appearance of a broad shallow stream. On this side, low rocks with ferns growing in their crannies, edged the stream. On the opposite shore, one giant eucalyptus stood by itself and cast its shadow across. Beyond, lay the gum-peopled immensity of the bush. The stony walls of the knoll, curving inward and sheltering a thick growth of ferns and scrubby vegetation, closed in the bridal chamber. Creepers festooned the rocky ledges and crevices. Here and there, a young sapling slanted forward to greet the morning sun when it should rise behind the hummock.

Moongarr Bill had undone the pack-bags and was building a fire between two large stones. The flames leaped up, the dead twigs crackled. Long years after, Lady Bridget could recall vividly the smell of the dry burning gum leaves – her first experience of a bush campfire.

Close to the fire, under the flank of the rocky knoll the tent was pitched, a roll of blankets and oilskin thrown just within it.

Presently, from the hummock above came the sound of Cudgee's axe. He had felled the youngest of the grass-trees, and was now chopping off its green tuft. Soon he appeared, carrying a huge bunch of the coarse blades of foliage, which he brought to the tent. With an odd mixture of emotions, Lady Bridget watched her husband take the grass tops from the black boy and spread them carefully on the floor of the tent, heaping up and smoothing the mass into a bed, upon which he laid the oilskin and then one of the blankets – they were new white blankets, fresh from the store. After that, he set the cushions from the buggy, covering them with the rug, at the head of the couch, making a bolster, and, over that, the one she had had at her back.

'No down pillows or linen sheets allowed in a bush camp-out, my lady Biddy,' he said with a laugh, a half timorous glance at his wife, but her answering smile reassured him.

'You'll never sleep on a sweeter bed,' he said, sniffing the resinous fragrance of the grass-tree tops. He would not let her help him with the upper blankets when she wished to lend a hand.

'No, this camp is my own show. Go and look at the scenery until I've got our wigwam in order.'

And she submissively obeyed.

Against the other side of the rock wall, the black boys had built a second fire. The horses were hobbled and grazing along the green border of the creek. The buggy propped up, was covered with a tarpaulin. The pack-bags had disgorged their contents. A miscellaneous heap of camp properties lay on the ground. And now, Cudgee's axe was at work again, stripping a section of bark from a gum tree, for what purpose Lady Bridget did not divine.

She walked down to the creek and stood among the rocks at its edge. She had expected a rippling stream, and, to her disappointment, saw only a broad strip of dry sand, along which Moongarr Bill was mooching, a spade in his hand.

'What are we going to do for water?' she exclaimed.

'Dig for it, my ladyship,' answered Moongarr Bill. 'That's one of the upside-down things in 'Stralia. Here's two of them – mighty queer, come to think of it – the rivers that run underground and the cherries that grow with their stones outside.'

Lady Bridget observed that she was already acquainted with that oft-quoted botanical phenomenon. In her rides around Leichardt's Town she had been shown and had tasted the disagreeable little orange berry which has a hard green knob at the end of it and is, for some ironical reason, called a cherry. She also told Moongarr Bill that in England she had seen a dowser searching for hidden springs by means of a forked hazel twig carried in front of him which pointed downwards where there was water and asked why Australians didn't adopt a similar method. At which Moongarr Bill laughed derisively, and said he did not hold with any such hanky-panky.

'Bad luck, Biddy,' McKeith said behind her. 'If there had been the proper amount of rain in these last three or four months, we'd have had the one thing that's wanting now to make this the ideal camp I've had on the top of my fancy – a running creek of pure water. But never mind – the water's there, though you can't see it. . . . That's got it, Bill!'

For already the sand was darkening and moisture was oozing in the hole Moongarr Bill had been digging, and which he widened gradually into a respectable pool of water. When it had settled down, all the billies were filled and the horses driven to it, whinnying for a drink.

Lady Bridget watched the evening meal being prepared between the two fires – only watched, for she was sternly forbidden to set hand to it.

'No canned goods, nor cooked food,' McKeith said, were allowed at this lay-out. Moongarr Bill was first-class at frying steak. He himself was going to boil the quart-pot tea and would give Biddy a demonstration in johnny-cakes, made bush fashion at their own camp fire. The sheet of bark had been cut into sections – one sub-divided into small squares to serve as plates. The inside looked clean as paint, and smelled of Mother Nature's still-room. Colin mixed the flour and water upon the larger sheet and worked up a stiff dough. He kneaded it, slapped it between his broad palms, cut it and baked the cakes in the ashes; then, butter being the only luxury permitted, he split them and buttered them; and Lady Bridget found in due time that not even the lightest Scotch scones taste better than bush johnny-cakes.

Quart pot tea, likewise – made also in true bush fashion. First the boiling of the billy – Colin's own particular billy, battered and blackened from much usage – half the battle, he explained, in brewing bush tea. Then, regulation handfuls of tea and brown store sugar thrown in at the precise boiling moment. Now the stirring of the frothing liquid with a fresh gum-twig. Then the blending and the cooling of it – pouring the beverage from one quart pot into another, and finally into the pannikins ready for the drinking.

Proudly, round the rock-flank of the hummock, Moongarr Bill brought fried steak and potatoes steaming in a clean tin dish and done to a turn, then went to cook more for himself at his own camp. They ate off the bark plates. Salt, sugar and mustard came out of small ration bags. McKeith produced black-handled knives and forks – the last a concession. And good to taste were the fizzling johnny-cakes and the strong, sweet, milkless tea.

Such was Lady Bridget's real marriage feast.

They were hungry, yet they dallied over the repast. It was the most delicious food she had ever tasted, Bridget said. They made little jokes. He was entranced by her happiness. Joyously she compared this banquet with others she had eaten in great houses and European restaurants, which were the last word in luxury. Oh! how she loved the dramatic contrast of it. Nature was supreme, glorious. . . . Oh no, no! never could she hanker after that which she had left behind – for ever. Because, if ever she were to go back again to the old life, she would be an ugly dried-up old woman for whom the smart world would have no further use. . . .

Then suddenly she became quiet, and busied herself in the tent, while McKeith took out his pipe and smoked in ruminative bliss. When she came back she had no more talk of contrasts or of her old life, no more fantastic outbursts. Indeed, there seemed to have come over her a mood of sweet sobriety, of blushing, womanly shyness.

'Mayn't I be your squaw and help you to wash up?' she said, when he collected the tin pots and pannikins and proceeded to get the camp shipshape. No, she was not to stir a finger towards the dirty work. It was *his* job to-night. Another camping-out time she might play the squaw if she liked. She was not on in this act.

He amused her greatly by his tidy bush methods. The billies were refilled, the ration-bags laid ready for the morning.

Now darkness had fallen. He put more logs on the fire, and the flames blazed up. Then he made up a little pile of johnny-cakes that he had not buttered, and covered it with the bark plates. 'We shall have to make an early start, and there'll be no time to bake fresh ones – and no more use for these things,' he said. The square of bark on which he had mixed the dough was in his hands and he was about the fling it among the bushes, but she stopped him.

'No – don't throw it away. . . . I – I want it for a keepsake, Colin.'

He stared at her in surprise. The red flames threw a strange glow on her face, and made her eyes look very bright.

'My dearest! A sheet of bark!' Then a great light broke on him. The strip of bark dropped from his hands. His arms went out and enfolded the small woman, lifting her almost from the ground as he crushed her against his breast and kissed her lips with the first passionate lover's kisses he had ever given her. . . . 'Oh, my dear – my sweetheart!' He gave a big, tremulous laugh. . . . 'There was never any woman in the world like you. . . . To think of your caring about just a sheet of bark!'

'You made me my first johnny-cakes upon it. . . . And to-night is the beginning of our married life – and oh, Colin, it is the first time I have felt really married to you, and I want a bit of the bush to remember it by.'

He kissed her again. . . . The miracle was accomplished. He seemed to have no words in which to say all that filled his heart.

The night sounds of the bush stirred the vast silence. For the first time, Lady Bridget heard the wail of the curlew – a long note, weirdly melancholy. It startled her out of her husband's arms. There were uncanny swishings of wings in the great gum tree on the other side of the creek. And now the clanking of the horses' hobbles which had been dilatory, intermittent, became sharply recurrent. A shout from Moongarr Bill cut short the monotonous corroboree tune which the two black boys had been singing at their camp some little distance away.

'My word, I believe *yarraman*[1] break him hobble!'

At which the boys scampered off through the grass, and presently

---

[1] Yarraman – Horse.

came the cracking of a stock whip among the trees.

'It's all right, Moongarr Bill's after them,' said McKeith, as his bride released herself from his arms. 'But if you don't mind darling. I'd better just see if anything has started the beasts.'

Lady Bridget watched him disappear round the knoll. The curlews went on wailing, and as if in answer a night owl sent forth his portentous *Hoot – hoot!* . . . Apparently nothing was much amiss with the horses; they had quieted down again. Lady Bridget picked up the strip of bark and carried it in her arms into the tent, laughing to herself as she did so.

'Only a sheet of bark! What a fool I am – But it's quite appropriate, anyway.'

She put it beside her dressing-bag, and then went out once more into the night. Through the interlacing gum branches she saw a great coppery disk, and the moon rose slowly to be a lamp in her bridal chamber. How wonderful the stars were! . . . There was the Southern Cross with its pointers, and the Pleiades. And that bright star above the tops of the trees, which seemed to throw a distinct ray of light, must be Venus. . . . The moon was high enough to cast shadows – black – distorted. The low clumps of shrubs beyond the carpet of grass looked like strange couched beasts. . . .

As she stood by the rocks at the creek edge, she heard her husband speaking to Moongarr Bill, who seemed to be walking down along the sandy bed.

'Horses all right, Bill?'

'Oh, ay – just a possum up a tree gev Julius Cæsar a start. . . . Been digging a decent bath-hole for the ladyship in the morning, boss. There's plenty there.'

'I wish it was as near the surface at Moongarr, Bill. We shall have our work cut out making new bores, if the dry weather lasts.'

'My word, it's no joke going down three thousand feet. Amazing queer the amount of water running underground on this dried-up old earth.'

'But we can always strike it, Bill; no matter how dried up the outside looks, there's the living spring waiting to be tapped. And how's that in human nature too, Bill. Same idea, eh?'

Moongarr Bill emitted a harsh grunt.

'My best girl chucked me a month back, boss, and as for your darned sentiment and poetry, and sech-like – well, I ain't takin' any just at present.'

'Bad luck, Bill! Struck a dead-head that time, eh? . . . Well, good-night.'

'Good-night, boss – and good luck to you. I reckon your spring ain't a dead-head, anyway. . . . Say, Mr McKeith, me and the boys are shifting our fire over to the other side of the creek. . . . Keep the 'osses from hevin' any more of their blessed starts. . . . Handier for gettin' them up in the morning.'

CHAPTER 8

Lady Bridget McKeith had been married about a year and a quarter. Winter was now merging into spring. But it was not a bounteous spring. That drear spectre of drought hung over the Never-Never Land.

Lady Bridget stood by the railing of the veranda at Moongarr, looking out for two expected arrivals at the head-station – that of her husband, who had been camping out after cattle – and of the mail-man – colloquially, Harry the Blower – who this week was to bring an English mail.

Perhaps the last arrival seemed to her at the moment most important of the two. The bush wife had long since begun to feel a sort of home sickness for English news. Yet, had you asked her, she would have told you that barbarism still had a greater hold than civilisation.

There did not, however, appear to be much of the barbarian about Lady Bridget. She still looked like an old picture in the high-waisted tea-gown of limp yellow silk that she had put on early for dinner, and she still trailed wisps of old lace round her slender shoulders. There was the same touzle of curly hair, like yellow-brown spun glass or filaments of burnished copper, which was shining now in the westering sun. The finely-modelled brows and shadowy eyes were as beautiful as when Colin McKeith had first beheld his goddess stepping on to Australian earth.

But for all that, a change had taken place in her – a different one from the indefinable yet significant change which is felt in almost every woman after marriage. There is usually in the young wife's face an expression of fulfilment, of deepened experience – a certain settled, satisfied look. And this was what was lacking in Lady

Bridget's face. The restless soul within seemed to be peering out through hungry eyes.

She could see nothing human from the veranda except the blue-smocked figure of Fo Wung, the Chinaman, at work in his vegetable garden by the lagoon. There was one large water-hole and a succession of small ones, connected by water-courses, now dry, and meandering from a gully, which on the eastern side broke the hill against which Moongarr head-station was built. The straggling gum forest, interspersed with patches of sandal-wood and mulga, that backed the head-station, stopped short at the gully, and beyond, stretched wolds of melancholy gidia scrub. Looking up from the end of the veranda, Lady Bridget could see an irregular line of grey-brown boulders, jagged and evidently of volcanic origin, marking the line of gully. These gave a touch of romantic wildness to the otherwise peaceful scene.

Lady Bridget's gaze went along a track skirting the gidia scrub, and crossing the lower end of the gully near the lagoon, to the great plain which spread in front of the head-station. Except for some green trees by the lagoon, a few ragged belts of gum and sandal-wood or single isolated trees dotted about, the plain was unwooded to the horizon. There were also silhouetted upon the sky the grotesque-looking sails of one or two windmill-pumps. In the foreground the plain was intersected by lines of grey fencing, within which browsed straggling herds of lean cattle, mostly along the curve of the lagoon.

Neither plain nor lagoon formed altogether pleasing objects of contemplation just now, for they spoke eloquently of the threatened drought. When Lady Bridget had come up a bride, the plain had been fairly green. The sandal-wood blossoms were out and wild flowers plentiful. The lagoon was then flush with the grass, and its water, on which white, pink and blue lilies floated, had reflected the vegetation at its edge. Now the lagoon had shrunk and the water in the gully was in places a mere trickle. Of course, the trees were there – ti-tree, flooded gum, and so forth – but they looked brown and ragged. One standing by itself, a giant white cedar, which in spring was a mass of white and mauve bloom and in winter of scarlet berries, had a wide strip of brown mud between it and the water that had formerly laved its roots.

Lady Bridget had thought that the rocky gully, the lagoon and the vast plain made as pretty a landscape as she had ever seen, when she had first looked upon it in the early morn after her homecoming.

Now, as she paced up and down the veranda – for she was in a restless mood – her mind went back to that bridal homecoming. They had not arrived at the head-station till after dusk, but it had been visible from the plain a long way off, and she had examined it with ardent curiosity through her field-glasses in the clear light of sunset.

She had seen a collection of rough buildings backed by the forest, and from different points of view, as they drew nearer, had made out that the three principal ones formed three sides of a square. Two of these – the side wings – were old and of primitive construction – slab walls, bark roofs, and low verandas, overgrown with creepers. Colin explained that these were the Old Humpey – as he called the original dwelling house – and the kitchen and store building opposite. Lately, the New House had been put up at right angles with the old buildings, and fronting the plain. It had been begun before his trip south and practically finished during his absence. Colin was very proud of the New House.

It was made of sawn wood and had a high-pitched roof of corrugated zinc, turned to gold by the sunset rays upon it. There was a deep veranda all round the New House, and it was much taller than the wings, being raised on blood-wood piles, that had been tarred to keep off white ants, and with a flight of wooden steps leading up to the veranda.

The details of Moongarr head-station became familiar enough later to its new mistress. Besides the dwelling houses were various huts and outbuildings. The stock-yards lay on a piece of level ground behind at the side of the gully, and between the yards and the House stood a small slab and bark cottage – the Bachelors' Quarters.

Even though glorified by the sunset, it had given Lady Bridget a little shock to see how crude and – architecturally speaking – unlovely was her new home. But her Celtic imagination was stirred by the weirdness of the grey-green gum forest, and of the mournful gidia scrub, framing the picture.

Then, as dusk crept closer, and the great plain, along which the tired horses plodded, became one illimitable shadow out of which rose strange sounds of beasts and eerie night cries of birds, the spell of the wilderness renewed itself and she felt herself enveloped in world-old mystery.

She remembered how the lights of the head-station against the forest blackness had looked like welcoming torches and how she had roused herself out of her weariness at the last spurt of the equally weary buggy horses. Then the jolt in the dark over the sliprails, the slow strain of the wheels up the hill, the cracking of Moongarr Bill's stock-whip, and the sound of long drawn *coo-ēes*. Also of dogs barking, of men running forward. Then how Colin had lifted her down and half carried her into the parlour. She remembered her dazed glance round and the rushing thought of how she could soften its ugliness. Yet it had looked welcoming. A log fire blazing, the table spread, a Chinese cook in baggy blue garments – pigtail flowing; a Malay boy; her bewildered question – was there no woman in the establishment? Then Colin's strident call from the veranda – 'Mrs Hensor. Where's Mrs Hensor!' And the appearance presently of Florrie Hensor – youngish, tall, a full figure; black hair, frizzed and puffed, a showy face, red cheeks, redder lips, rather sullen, flashing dark eyes – who had received Lady Bridget almost as if she had been her equal, and of whom the bride had at once made an enemy by her frigidly haughty response. From the first moment, Lady Bridget had disliked Mrs Hensor. But she had felt a vague attraction towards the little yellow-headed, blue-eyed boy clinging to Mrs Hensor's skirts. As for any uneasiness on the score of Steadbolt's insolent insinuations, she had absolutely dismissed that from her mind.

Yes – that bridal homecoming – how strange it had seemed! How rough everything was! How impossible the whole thing would have appeared to her had any fortune-teller in Bond Street prophesied the end of her marriage journey!

And how, in the first moment of settling down, she had laughed with Colin at the thought of what Chris and Molly Gaverick, and 'Eliza Countess' would have said! But with what dauntless energy she had worked in transforming her new abode and in making it reflect her own personality. She had felt really grateful, she said, to the Union delegates for having enticed away the builders before the inside furnishings were complete. Soon they got hold of a bush carpenter, and she was provided with occupation for a good many months.

Lady Bridget had been very happy in those early days. Colin had seemed so thoroughly in the picture – strong, chivalrous, adoring – like a Viking worshipping his conquered bride. The romance of it all appealed tremendously to the Celtic blood in Bridget. It was her nature, when she gave, to give generously. She had become genuinely in love with her bush husband during that wonderful honeymoon journey.

Ah, that journey! What an experience! If she could have written it down as a new adventure of 'The Lady of Quality,' how the great Gibbs would have jumped at her 'copy!' Well, she had practically done so in her letters to Joan Gildea – now back in her London flat. But the true inwardness of the adventure was a thing never to be put into words.

No sign yet of the men. Lady Bridget ceased her restless pacing and swung herself slowly to and fro in a hammock at the end of the veranda. As she swung she traversed over again in her imagination the stages of that honeymoon journey.

Two hundred and twenty-five miles of it, after the first camp out. Many more nights under the stars. Then out of the gum forests they had gone through the great western plains, covering ground fairly easily, for McKeith had arranged to have fresh horses on the road, and they always drove a spare pair ahead of the buggy. Occasionally they stopped at a head-station. Once at night they pulled up at a bush house, and a strange old man had put his head out of a window and shouted to them in the darkness. 'If ye've come to see me, I'm drunk,' he had said, 'and if you've come to drink, the rum-keg's empty, but ye'll find a pint pot outside and a little water in the tank.' And then he had shut the window again and refused further parley.

They had camped, hungry, in the paddock – for provisions had run out, and on that account, and because the horses had strayed in the night, they had to go again to the house. The old man, sober and ashamed, captivated likewise by Lady Bridget's beauty and charm, apologised almost on his knees – he made Biddy think of Thackeray's picture of Sir Pitt Crawley proposing to Becky Sharp. Old Mr Duppo, it was – the father of Zack Duppo, the horse-breaker, who had recently been breaking in colts at Moongarr.

They stayed till the horses were found. Mr Duppo had a housekeeper – now if Mrs Hensor had been like that housekeeper there could have been no cause for jealous scandal. An aged dame, long, bony – dressed in a short green petticoat and tartan jacket with a little checked shawl over her head and pinned under a bearded chin. She poured tea out of a tin teapot and leaned over her master's chair at meal times to carve the salt beef.

Lady Bridget sketched the pair. The old man roared over the sketch, but the housekeeper bore her a grudge for it, and afterwards had not a good word for the 'Ladyship' who had slipped out of her proper sphere into the Never-Never country.

There were plenty of other small adventures which would have made the hair of Lady Gaverick and her friends stand on end. A dream-drive indeed, full of sort of 'Alice in Wonderland' episodes. Bush life Out Back – a jumble of odd characters and situations. Fencers' camps, cattle-drivers' camps, bullock-dray camps. There had been a baby born unexpectedly under the tilt of a bullock-dray, on one occasion, the night before McKeith's party appeared on the scene, and Lady Bridget had a trunk down from the buggy, and there in the road tore up some of her fine-laced smocks and petticoats to provide swaddling clothes for the poor little scrap of mortality. And there were tramps 'humping bluey' on the track likewise, and diggers carrying their picks. Bridget liked seeing Colin hail-fellow-well-met with them all – sharing tucker and quart-pot tea. She wished that her socialistic friends of the old played-out civilisation could see this shrewd, practical humanitarian of the Bush.

They came very close to each other in those long days of the dream-drive. He talked to her as he had never talked before, and as he talked rarely afterwards. He drew aside curtains from recesses of his real nature, the existence of which she had not suspected, and, in truth, at a later time, doubted. Then, if in broad sunlight the shy, rough exterior of the man would close suddenly over those secret chambers, when evening came, it would seem as though the camp fire illuminated them once more.

After the first time or two, he allowed her to boss the camp 'lay-out.' It was she who spread the blankets on Wombo's beds of grass-tree tops and dry herbage. Wombo and the 'big feller White Mary' (the adjective used metaphorically as expressive of distinction) made great friends in those days – out of which friendship sprang, alas! in due time, certain tragic happenings. It was Lady Bridget who would set the billy boiling and who, after one or two failures, succeeded in making excellent johnny-cakes. She remembered her first perform-ance in that line under the eyes of a small group of admiring spectators – her husband 'just waiting to see how the new-chum cook shaped,' and, as he said the words, she, glancing up from the sheet of bark and the dough she was kneading, caught a look in his face which was something she could never in all her life forget. And Moongarr Bill with the horses' reins over his arm, and the two black-boys agape, beady eyes twinkling, white teeth glistening, emitting their queer guttural clicks of approbation, and an occasional 'My word! Būjeri you, Lathy-chap,' the nearest they could get to Moongarr

Bill's accepted form of address. There was joy, glory to Lady Bridget in this playing of the squaw and fending for her man, ceasing to be the goddess and becoming the primal woman.

And the sports, and songs, and stories by the camp fire! Moongarr Bill's yarns, Colin's exploring tales, Wombo's and Cudgee's dances and corroboree-tunes – strange, weird music that had a fascination for Lady Bridget. She, too, would get up and sing *Carmen's* famous air, and the Neapolitan peasant songs of her mother's youth. Never, for sure, had the gaunt gum trees echoed back such strains as these.

But time came when all the romance of barbarism seemed to have fizzled out and only cruel realities remained – when work and worry turned McKeith from the worshipping lover into the rough-tongued, irritable bushman – when his 'hands' deserted him, his cattle died and things generally went wrong, and when he showed himself something of the hard-headed, parsimonious, ill-conditioned Scotch mongrel that Steadbolt had called him. When, indeed, he seemed to have forgotten that Lady Bridget O'Hara had graciously permitted him to worship her, but had not bargained for being treated – well, as many another out-back squatter – treats his help-mate. Then Bridget would tell herself bitterly that it might have been better had she married a civilised gentleman. There would sometimes be scenes and sometimes sulks, and those times no doubt accounted for the hungry look in Lady Bridget's eyes and the slight hardening of her mouth.

She was loyal though, in spite of her many faults, and 'game' in her own way – and when Colin came out of his dour moods, she was generally ready to meet him half way.

For, through all, the memory of the dream-drive honeymoon lingered. And the bit of bark, sapless, brown, curled up by the heat into almost a tube, and partially eaten by white ants – before the desecrating assault had been discovered and the termites' nest destroyed with boiling water – was still cherished as a sacred symbol.

While she swung in the hammock the memory pictures came and went like a cinematograph show – the dream-drive presently merging into an electioneering trip through McKeith's constituency a few weeks after her bridal homecoming.

The 'Lady of Quality' might, had she been so minded, have also made spicy capital out of the humours of that political contest – in which, unhappily, the Labour Party had triumphed. Steadbolt had had his say on the occasion, and there had been a free fight – Lady Bridget was not present, and only heard darkly of the occurrence –

when Steadbolt had got the worst of it in an encounter with his late employer.

But all that was but a small side-show, and not likely to affect in any great measure Lady Bridget's life. Except that the loss of McKeith's seat in the Legislative Assembly made it no longer necessary for him to spend at least part of the winter session in Leichardt's Town. Nor would Lady Bridget have the opportunity to resume her old intimacy at Government House. In any case, however, she was not destined to see more of her old friend in Australia. A few months previously, Lady Tallant had developed symptoms of grave disease – it was said that the Leichardt's Land climate did not agree with her, and she had gone back to England, leaving Sir Luke to perform his duties without her help.

CHAPTER 9

———•———

At last, Lady Bridget heard the unmistakable sound of cattle in the distance – the low, multitudinous roar of lowing beasts and tramping hoofs and the reverberating crack of stock-whips. It came from the gidia scrub. She knew that they had been mustering *scrubbers* – otherwise, wild cattle from the broken country at the foot of Moongarr Range.

She left the hammock and went again to the veranda railing. Looking along a side path from the Chinaman's garden she saw that Mrs Hensor and her boy – the yellow-headed urchin of about six – were hastening towards the Bachelors' Quarters. The woman carried a basket of vegetables, the boy hugged a big pawpaw fruit which he held up proudly as his mother responded in her free-and-easy, rather sulky fashion to Lady Bridget's stiff nod.

'It's for the House,' cried the child. 'Fo Wung said I was to bring it up.'

Lady Bridget made a wry face – she did not like pawpaws.

'Very well, Tommy, and if you're good you can have what's left to-morrow.'

'That's all right,' responded Tommy in bush formula.

'Have you seen anything of your master – or the postman?' asked Lady Bridget of Mrs Hensor.

'I believe Mr McKeith is coming on ahead with Harry the Blower,' said Mrs Hensor. 'Look sharp, Tommy, the cattle will be at the yard directly, and I've got my dinner to cook for the whole lot of them, seeing that some visitors aren't good enough for the house.'

The woman pointed her last sentence by a malicious glance at the mistress of Moongarr.

'I suppose that is what your master keeps you here for – to cook for the visitors at the Quarters, Mrs Hensor,' said Lady Bridget, with incisive sweetness.

Mrs Hensor flushed scarlet, but she checked an impudent reply. Pulling Tommy angrily along, she hurried up to the four-roomed, zinc-roofed humpey and its lean-to kitchen, protected by a bough shade, which lay between the head-station and the gully, with the stockyard close to it, and which constituted her domain. It annoyed Mrs Hensor to hear McKeith called her master. She always spoke of her late husband as having been the Boss-mate on that – to him – fatal exploring expedition. Also, she resented having all the bachelors 'dumped down' – as she phrased it – on her, while the 'Ladyship's swell staff' was spared the trouble. At present the Bachelors' Quarters was fairly full. Mr Ninnis, store-keeper and overseer in the owner's absence, abode there permanently, and just now, there were Zack Duppo, the horse-breaker, and a young man from Breeza Downs – a combined cattle and sheep station about fifty miles distant – who had come to help in the mustering and to collect any beasts strayed from the Breeza Downs' herd.

The gully crossing lay below the boulders of rock at the head of the lagoon. Presently, two horsemen appeared on the rise. One was McKeith; the other Harry the Mailman – otherwise the Blower – a foxy, browny-red little man on a raw-boned chestnut, carrying his mail-bags strapped in front and at the side of his saddle.

Lady Bridget supposed they had met at the turn-off track just above the crossing. McKeith was carrying a leather mail-bag, from which he appeared to have extracted a bundle of letters, with one hand. He held his bridle and coiled stock-whip in the other. He was listening to the mailman, who seemed to be talking animatedly. As they neared the house, he gave the usual *Coo-ee*, that set all the dogs barking, and put the Chinaman-cook and black-boys on the alert.

The riders passed by the end of the veranda where Lady Bridget stood. McKeith looked up at her. He seemed preoccupied and angry, and merely nodded to his wife, but did not take off his hat as he had done in earlier days – and, somehow, to-day she noticed the omission.

'All right, eh, Biddy?' he called out casually. 'Here's your mail – I've taken out mine,' and he pitched the leather bag, with the string cut and the official red seal broken, on to the veranda at her feet. 'I say – you might bring the whisky out to the back veranda. I daresay you could do with a nip, eh, Harry?'

'That I can, Mr McKeith. Riding along these plains is dry work. Good day, Ladyship. I'm a bit behind time, but I lost an hour looking for a hole to fill my water bag at – And then I could not drink out of it – for a derned old pleuro bullock had got there first and died in it. My word, Boss, you'll be in a fix if it don't rain before long.'

McKeith made an angry gesture. He spoke sharply to the horses. The two men rode round the kitchen-wing and dismounted at the paling fence, which made the fourth side of the little square. The back veranda of the new house, with steps ascending to it, in the middle, the Old Humpey, with its veranda, along one side, the kitchen and store building along the other, and a rough slab and bark outhouse beyond it. Native-cucumber vines and other creepers partially closed in the older verandas. In the centre of the square was a small flower bed with a flowering shrub in the middle.

Lady Bridget brought the whisky decanter from the dining room to the back veranda, and McKeith mounted the steps, the mailman remaining beside them. A canvas water-bag, oozing moisture, hung from the rafters, and there were tumblers on a table beneath it. McKeith took the decanter from his wife's hand, too preoccupied, it seemed, even to notice the little satirical smile on her lips. She was thinking how funny it seemed that she should be playing Hebe to Harry the Blower. She soon realised, however, that serious things had happened. As McKeith mixed a liberal allowance of whisky with water from the water-bag and handed it to the mailman, he asked curtly:

'This isn't one of your blowing yarns, Harry? You're positive about the fact?'

'Saw the thing with my own eyes, Boss. As fine a team as ever I'd wish to own, lying with their throats cut, and the trees black with crows all round. There was the dray-load all turned over, and two cases prized open. I bet that the rum-kegs and spirits that couldn't be carried off, are buried in some handy dry water-hole close by. I saw two or three empty brandy bottles with the heads of 'em smashed to show that the rascals had wet the wool before starting off.'

McKeith cursed in his throat. 'No sign of my men?'

'Scooted clean out of the scenery – the whole lot. I reckon that's what they shook hands on with the Union chaps, and that the natural consequences of absorbing your grog will be another woolshed or two burned down before long. Here's your health, Boss, and the Ladyship's.' And the mailman gulped down his 'nobbler' and turned to remount the lean chestnut, which was standing hitched to the palings, observing cheerfully:

'Well, so long, Sir. Go'day, Ma'am. This sort of argufying ain't going to carry my mail-bags along the river.'

'Go up to the Quarters and ask Mrs Hensor for a feed,' called McKeith. 'And look here, Harry, you can tell them at the Myall Creek out-station as you go by, to have two good horses ready in the yard for me. I'm off to Tunumburra to put the police on to those devils straight away.'

'All right, Boss. You'll find it will take some tall calculatin' though. Them Unionists are getting too strong for the police to tackle. Windeatt up at Breeza Downs is in a mortal funk, and sending word everywhere for a squad of Specials to protect his woolshed.'

'It seems,' said Lady Biddy to her husband, when the mailman had gone, 'that there might be some use after all for Luke Tallant's Maxims.'

'It seems that Jim Steadbolt has been taking his revenge,' he answered, 'and that I must be in the saddle in an hour's time. Mix me a drink, Biddy, and order in some grub, while I go and have a bath.'

He looked as if he needed one. The dust of the drafting camp was caked upon his face and clothes. His was the appearance of a man who had been riding hard after stock and sleeping, between his blankets only, under the stars.

Lady Bridget mixed him his drink and went to see Chen Sing in the kitchen. When she came back, Colin was in the front veranda. He had tumbled the rest of the letters and papers out of the mail-bag, and was hastily and eagerly scanning the last *Leichardt's Town Chronicle*.

'Any news, Colin?'

'I don't know, I was looking to see if the Government were going to act against the strikers – I see they are sending troops.'

'And is Luke Tallant coming at the head of them, in official uniform, to read the Riot Act? – if there is a Riot Act in Australia. I'd like to see Luke maintaining the supremacy of the British Crown on the Leura.'

He looked up at her in vague rebuke of her levity, and there was suppressed tenderness in his eyes, notwithstanding his preoccupation with his own troubles.

'No, no. But there's something in the paper about Lady Tallant being ill and having an operation. Poor chap! He wouldn't have been bothering much about strikes in the Never-Never and the supremacy of the British Crown, any more than I should in similar circumstances. . . . Well, there! I must go and bogey.[1]

Sudden compunction overswept Bridget.

'Oh, Colin! You would care . . . really . . . even though they had cut the throats of your four best dray-horses?' But he had disappeared into a little veranda room, against which a corrugated iron tank backed conveniently, and in a minute she heard the splash of water.

She picked up the paper and looked at the English Intelligence before examining her own letters. It was quite true. There was a paragraph stating that Lady Tallant's health had not improved since her arrival in England, and hinting at the likelihood of an operation being advisable. Bridget reflected, however, that Sir Luke would probably have received a cablegram by this time, one way or other – which would have put him out of suspense, and, presumably, there had been no later bad news.

A letter from Molly Gaverick confirmed that item of the English Intelligence. Rosamond Tallant's condition was certainly far from satisfactory. Molly, however, seemed much more taken up with a recent illness of Eliza Countess of Gaverick than with that of Lady Tallant. Being a tactless and absolutely frank young person, she had no scruple in proclaiming her hope that 'old Eliza' would make Lord Gaverick her heir. This was the more likely, wrote young Lady Gaverick, because the old lady had lately quarrelled with her own relatives, and never now asked any of her stuffy provincial cousins to share the dulness of Castle Gaverick and of the house in Brook Street. If she did not leave her money to Chris Gaverick, there was not, conceivably, anyone else to whom she would leave it.

'By the way,' Molly continued, as if it had been an afterthought – 'Old Eliza is immensely interested in you and your cow-boy husband – ranch-owner is what, I suppose, I ought to call him. She asked Mrs Gildea so many questions about you both that Joan read her your account of your honeymoon journey through the Bush, and all the rest of it. How you can endure such a life is incomprehensible to me – but Aunt Eliza says it shows you've got some grit in you, and that evidently your husband has cured you of

[1] Bogey – In Black's language, 'bathe out of doors.'

a lot of ridiculous nonsense – I am quoting her, so don't be offended, and you needn't show this to Nature's gentleman, which is what Aunt Eliza calls him. I can't help feeling though, that it's rather a pity you didn't wait a bit before taking the Irrevocable Step. I don't know whether you ever heard about Mrs Willougby Maule's death – eleven months after their marriage.'

No, Bridget had not heard. Molly Gaverick was an uncertain correspondent, and, no doubt, Joan Gildea and Rosamond Tallant, if they had known of the event, had thought is wiser, in writing to her, to suppress the news. For a moment, Lady Bridget sat meditating, and all the blood seemed to rush from her brain to her heart – she could almost hear her heart pounding. Then she went on again with Lady Gaverick's letter.

'It was a motor accident – nothing serious at the time, but the baby was born prematurely, and she lingered a week or two, and then died. I must do him the justice to say that he seemed to feel her death very much. It looked as though, after all, the marriage had been quite a success. Her money gave him a lift and they were going out a good deal in the political set. She left her quarter of a million to him, *absolutely*. I heard that some remote Bagallys were going to contest the will, but they found that they hadn't a leg to stand upon. I wish now that we hadn't been so sniffy about W.M. As Chris observed with unconscious cynicism, there's a good deal of difference between a penniless adventurer and the possessor of quarter of a million. Unattached men with money can be so useful. As soon as Rosamond Tallant gets better – if she does – I'll make her ask him to meet us. I know he used to be a great friend of Luke's. . . .'

CHAPTER 10

Lady Bridget had read so far when the door of the bathroom opened and McKeith came out, clean again in fresh riding gear, and with a valise ready packed and strapped in his hand.

The noise of the cattle became much louder, though the mob was not yet in sight.

'I wish I hadn't got to go off before the branding,' he said. 'These Breeza Downs people always want to claim every cleanskin.[1] You might tell Ninnis and Moongarr Bill, Biddy, to keep a sharp look-out. And now let me have my grub – I'm sorry, dear, to have you hurry up your dinner.' He strode along to the dining-room, too absorbed in his own annoyances to notice his wife's face or to ask any questions about her letters.

Lady Bridget gathered them up and followed him. The Malay boy waited at table with the assistance of a servant girl from Leuraville, the only female domestic – with the exception of Mrs Hensor – on the head-station.

McKeith swallowed his soup and ate the savoury stew prepared by the Chinese cook with the appetite of a man who had been all day in the saddle. Lady Bridget, who was an extraordinarily rapid eater, as well as a fastidious one, had finished long before he was half-way through. She sat silent at first, while he growled over the outrage upon the horses. Then suddenly visualising the poor beasts lying stiff in congealed blood, and the mailman's exaggerated description of trees black with crows, she flamed out in wrathful horror, and was as anxious as her husband that the perpetrators of the crime should be

---

[1] Cleanskin – Unbranded calf.

brought to justice. He seemed pleased, and a little surprised at the ebullition.

'I thought you weren't taking it quite in, Biddy. I am glad you think like me, though I expect yours is the humanitarian view and mine's the practical one. This touches my pocket, you see. Well, anyway, you won't be so keen now on defending the Unionists.'

'I think they've got as much right to fight for their principles as we have for ours, but I don't think they've the right to torture horses,' she rejoined. Her sympathy with oppressed shearers and dispossessed natives struck always a jarring note between them. His long upper lip closed tightly on the lower one, and he hunched his great shoulders.

'Well, that sort of argufying won't muster the cattle,' he observed drily, plagiarising Harry the Blower. She changed the subject.

'Did you have a good muster?'

'Oh, fair! Between three and four hundred head. The water is running still up in the range. We should have done better if that skunk Wombo hadn't bolted.'

Lady Bridget leaned forward with interest.

'Oh! Then he *has* gone after the black-gin. Brave Wombo!'

'I wouldn't care a cuss whether he went after the black-gin or not; she's a half-caste, by the way, and all the worse for that. And he might stop with her, if it wasn't that he knows the country, and can spot the gullies where the cattle hide. I've no use for sentiment – especially black sentiment – when it's a case of a forced sale to keep me going. My heavens! there's only one thing, Biddy, that could break me, and it's drought. I believe we're in for a long one, and unless I can make sales quickly and get money to sink new bores on the run, things will go hardly with me. Harry the Blower spoke naked truth for once in his life.'

'Oh! but there's sure to be rain soon. It looked so like it last night,' she answered lightly.

'*Looked* so like it! Yes, and ended in wind and dust. Sure sign of drought! I must be off. . . . Here, give me the *Leichardt Land Chronicle*, and don't expect me till you see me. . . . And by the way, Biddy, I hear there's a Unionist Organiser going the round of the stations and pretending to parley with the masters. Don't you be philanthropic enough to let him open his jaws – I've told Ninnis he's to be hounded off before he has time to get off his saddle.'

'Colin, you are unjust all round. You were very unjust to Wombo. Why shouldn't the poor black-boy marry as well as you or anyone else?'

McKeith gave a hard laugh.

'I'm not preventing him from marrying. I only said I wasn't going to have his gin on my station.'

'You wouldn't listen when he told you that he didn't dare go back to his tribe – because his gin's husband threatened to kill him.'

'My sympathies are with the gin's husband. What business has Wombo to steal another man's wife?'

'The husband broke her head with a nulla-nulla, and she loves Wombo and Wombo loves her. I consider that any woman, whether she's black or white, who lives with her husband while she loves another man is committing a sin,' said Lady Bridget hotly.

McKeith stopped in the act of filling his tobacco pouch from a jar on the mantelpiece and looked sharply at his wife.

'You think that, Biddy. I remember long ago you said something of that sort to me. It isn't my idea of morality or of justice. But I'm one with you this far. If I'd ever reason to believe that you loved another man and wanted to go off with him – you might go – I wouldn't put out a hand to stop you. And then. . . .'

'And then?' She had grown very white.

'Well, I think I'd make another notch in my gun first – and it would be a previous one – for myself that time.'

'No, you wouldn't, Colin. Because you know I shouldn't be worth it – and you are not the man to funk.'

'I'm not. But where *you* come in – Good Lord! Mate! What would there be left for me to live for?'

Her heart thrilled to the old term of endearment, to which in their early honeymoon days she had attached a sentimental value. Of late it had fallen into disuse, and when she had heard him on occasions greet the foreman, may be of some stray party of drivers or surveyors with the bush formula: 'Good day, mate!' she had felt with deep aggrievement that she no longer desired the appellative. She had not yet realised that while the word 'mate' in Australese, like the verb *aimer* in French, may be used as a mere colloquial term, it implies in the deeper sense a sanctity of relation upon which hangs the whole code of Bush chivalry.

'Oh, Colin!' Her eyes glistened with tears. She felt ashamed of her

neurotic fancies and her resentment of his lacks in the matter of
conventional courtesies – of his outward hardness, his want of
sympathy with her ideals.

He came to her, taking her two hands while keeping his pipe in
one of his own so that the whiff of the coarse 'Store-cut' tobacco
made her wrinkle her nose and stemmed the tide of emotion. But he
did not seem to notice this.

'No, you're not going to put that theory into practice, Mate. . . .
I'm not afraid. So we'll leave it at that. And now what's this about the
black-boy to do with my being unjust to that Organiser? There's no
beastly sentiment in his case. He's out to make money, that's all.'

'You won't hear what he's got to put forward on his side any more
than you would listen to poor Wombo.'

'No, I won't. I'm not taking any – either in gins or in organisers.
Let 'em show their faces here, and they'll pretty soon become aware
of the fact.'

Lady Bridget took away her hands and moved to the veranda.
Outside, McKeith's horse was waiting. He strapped on his valise,
finished ramming the tobacco into his pipe, then going behind his
wife, bent downward and hastily kissed her cheek. She did not turn
her head.

'Good-bye, Biddy. Don't you go worrying over the blacks or the
Unionists. And if you're dull and want a job there'll be a spice of
excitement in helping to tail that mob of scrubbers. I had to hire two
stray chaps, we're so short-handed.' He went down the steps to the
outer paling. Still she made no response, though now she turned and
watched him vault into the saddle. She also saw his face lighten at
sight of Mrs Hensor's boy with the great pawpaw apple. Tommy
Hensor was a favourite with the Boss.

'Bless you, boy, it's as big as yourself. Take it back to the Quarters
and tell your mother to give you a slice, or perhaps her ladyship will
cut it for you.'

He trotted off in the direction of the gully and of the roar of cattle.
Lady Bridget could see the heaving backs of the mob, and could hear
the shouts of the stockmen as they rounded the beasts to the
crossing. Tommy Hensor looked up pleadingly to her, holding out
the pawpaw apple. His yellow hair flamed to gold in the sunset, his
blue eyes were as bright almost as Colin's. Lady Bridget shook her
head.

'No, I don't want you this evening, Tommy. Take that back to your mother.'

She settled herself in the hammock and read Molly Gaverick's letter over again. Then she read one from Joan Gildea. Joan was in the full swing of London journalism again. She gave Bridget rather fuller news of Eliza Countess of Gaverick, and dwelt at some length upon the old lady's interest in Bridget's wild life and in Bridget's husband.

'You may be sure,' wrote Joan, 'that I had nothing but good to say of Colin, and oh! Biddy, dearest, how rejoiced I am to know that he is making you so happy. I could read between the lines of all your amusing descriptions and sketches of "the Dream-drive." I had my doubts and my fears, as I never concealed from you, but I believe that you have found the true, well-beloved at last.'

There was a good deal, too, in the letter about Rosamond Tallant, who was in cheerful spirits, it seemed, in spite of the impending operation, and would not hear of Sir Luke's asking for leave to be with her – and so on – and so on. Not a word about Willoughby Maule and his bereavement – which, after all, could not be so very recent. Why had Joan never mentioned it? Was she afraid of rousing regret and of awakening painful memories.

CHAPTER 11

McKeith's absence was longer than he had expected. Lady Bridget heard from Harry the Blower on his return round with the down-going mails that the little bush township of Tunumburra had become the scene of a convocation of Pastoralists called to concert measures against the threatened strike. The mailman reported that the district was now in a state of great commotion, and the strikers, gathering silently in armed force, prepared to defend their rights against a number of free labourers whom the sheep-owners were importing from the South. The men who had killed McKeith's horses were, according to the mailman, entrenched in the Range, awaiting developments. It was thought that nothing would happen on a large scale until the arrival of the free labourers and the troops, which it was said the Government was sending. Harry the Blower talked darkly of marauding bands, ambushed foes and perilous encounters on his road, all of which waxed in number and blood-thirstiness after the manner of Falstaff's men in buckram. But nobody ever took Harry the Blower's yarns very seriously.

It would have been natural for Lady Bridget to work herself up into a state of humanitarian excitement – the O'Hara's had always espoused unpopular causes – but since the arrival of the English mail a curious dreaminess had come upon her. She spent idle hours in the hammock on the veranda, and would only rouse herself spasmodically to some trivial burst of energy – perhaps a boiling water skirmish against white ants, or a sudden fit of gardening – planting seeds, training the wild cucumber vines upon the veranda posts, or watering the shrubs and flowers within the rough paling fence that enclosed the house and garden. A new-made garden, for ornament rather than for use, for the staple produce was grown in the Chinaman's garden by the lagoon. Young passion-fruit vines barely concealing the fences' nakedness, a mango, a few small orange trees now in flower. A Brazilian cherry, two or three flat-stone peach trees and loquets – all looking thirsty for rain – that was all. The Old Humpey, as it was called, had creepers overgrowing its roof, a nesting-place for frogs, lizards, snakes – and Lady Bridget, brave enough for doughty deeds, could never overcome her terror of horned beasts and reptiles. McKeith's office, where he entered branding tallies and posted the station log, was in the Old Humpey, and two or three bachelor bedrooms opposite the wing with kitchen and store. But Lady Bridget lived chiefly in the new house – less picturesque with its zinc roofing and deficiency of green drapings, but, being built on sawn lengths of saplings, more or less fortified against snakes. In front there was a great vacant space between the ground and the floor of the house – pleasant enough in summer, when a gentle draught could find its way through the cracks between the boards, but cold in winter, though the northern winters were not sharp enough or long enough for this to be a serious discomfort.

Nor, when Lady Bridget slept alone in the new house, did she mind much the dogs and harmless animals that couched under the boards, they gave her a sense of companionship. But there was a herd of goats – some of them old and with big tough horns – which McKeith had started in his bachelor days to provide milk when, as sometimes happened, the milch cows failed; also to furnish savoury messes of kid's flesh – a pleasant change from the eternal salt beef varied with wild duck. Occasionally it happened, especially in mustering times, that nobody remembered to pen the goats in their yard by the lagoon, and on these occasions they would get under the house, and the noise of their horns knocking against the floor of her bedroom would so effectively destroy Lady Bridget's chances of sleep that she would rise in the night and drive them into their fold. These were incidents which added variety to the monotony of her life in the Bush.

The head-station was very quiet one afternoon, most of the hands being out with the tailing mob; and Lady Bridget, in a restless mood, went for a roam through the bush. She walked past the Chinamen's garden and Fo Wung, carrying up buckets of water to his young cabbages, stopped to smile blandly and report on his produce. But she was in no mood for the interchange of remarks in pidgin English.

It was lonelier at the head of the lagoon. She could hear the trumpeter geese tuning up in shrill cornet-like notes and the discordant shriek of native-companions, as the long-legged grey birds stalked consequentially at the water's edge. She disturbed a flock of parrots in the white cedar tree, and a covey of duck rose with a whirring of pinions and a mighty quacking, shaking the drips off their plumage so that they glittered like diamonds in the sun. From the limbs of the dead gum tree hung flying foxes, their bat-like wings extended limply, and a gigantic crane stood in melancholy reflection upon one leg.

Lady Bridget crossed the gully and roamed the borders of the gidia scrub. Here, in an occasional open patch, were wattles breaking into yellow bloom, and sandalwood trees already in blossom, scenting the air faintly and making bright splashes upon the grey and black background of the mournful gidia. She filled her arms with flowers and wandered on, long past the stockyards, into the fastnesses of the gully, where lay dark pools almost empty now and where grey, volcanic looking rocks seemed to make a rampart between the scrub and the head-station.

She was sitting there, her back against a boulder, the forest behind her, so motionless that inquisitive bower-birds and leather-heads came quite close to her feet, her small pointed chin poked forward, her eyes shadowy and mysterious as the still waterpools below. She was visioning in space that man who had once undoubtedly cast a strong spell upon her. The spell had been broken by his own infidelity – if it *were* infidelity of the real man. For she could never believe that he had not truly loved her. Broken, secondly, by the counteracting influence of her husband. But now it seemed that the news of him in Lady Gaverick's letter had started the old vibrations afresh. It was as if an iron wall between them had suddenly been knocked down and he had gained access to her inner self. For months she had scarcely thought of him. Last night she had seen him in a dream, and he had spoken to her. He had said, 'Of course, I loved you. I never loved anyone better, but I felt that you were not of an accommodating disposition – that I could not give you anything you really wanted, and that we should not be happy together.' That was all of the dream she had brought back. But she *knew* that there had been a great deal more. The impression had been so vivid that she could not rid herself of the fancy that he was within actual reach of her. It was impossible to imagine him fourteen thousand miles distant.

She did not try now to fight against this haunting, but yielded herself to the power of the dream. When she heard a footstep in the forest behind her, she started and turned and stared into the dim aisles of the gidia, as though she expected to see his ghost.

'Mithsis – mithsis – me Wombo – plenty my been look out for you. Plenty mine frightened to go along a head-station.'

Lady Bridget laughed hysterically. What a contrast between the romantic hero of her dreams and the figure of the black-boy before her. Wombo had been in the wars. Very little was left of the trim understudy of Moongarr Bill. He was hatless; his Crimean shirt was torn into ribbons; his moleskin breeches were covered with blood and dirt; the strap belt, with its sheath-knife and various pouches, was gone, and this, judging from the state of his legs and feet, had been forcibly removed.

A gash from a tomahawk disfigured his head; the woolly hair was matted with blood. But there remained still something of the *preux chevalier* about Wombo.

'Mine bring it gin belonging to me,' he announced with dignity, making an introductory gesture towards what appeared almost an excrescence upon the black trunk of a gidia tree except for an old red blanket slung round one shoulder, which only half covered a woman's dusky form.

'That Oola. Mine want 'im marry Oola. Black feller belonging to that feller plenty *coolla*. My been sneak camp. Me catch 'em Oola. Black feller look out, throw 'im tomahawk, *nulla-nulla*. My word! big feller fight. Me *yan* plenty quick. Oola *yan* plenty quick. Black feller come after – throw 'im spear – close up *mumkull*. *Ba'al* can pull out spear, Oola plenty cry.'

Oola joined in with the black's plaintive wail.

'*Yūcke!* Poor fellow, Oola!'

Wombo pulled her forward. A comely half-caste who, as a child, had been partially civilised by a stockman's wife on one of the Leura out-stations, but who had, later, gone back to her tribe and married a Myall, as the wild blacks are called. She was very young, soft and

Coolla – in Blacks language, meaning Angry.
Nulla-nulla – A black's weapon.
Yan – To go away.
Mumkull – To kill.
Ba'al – No – Not.

Yucke! – Alas!
Bujeri – Very good.
Murra make haste – To run quickly.
Pho-pho – To shoot.
Yowi – Yes.

round of outline, with hair straighter and more glossy than is usual among her kind, and large black eyes now raining tears. She wiped them away with a sooty hand, pink in the palm. Her left arm hung limp by her side.

Lady Bridget jumped to her feet, all concern.

'Oh, you poor thing! You poor, poor thing,' she cried. For Wombo, tweaking aside the concealing blanket, showed the smooth shaft of a spear transfixed in the quivering flesh of Oola's arm, above the elbow. He had broken off the long end of the spear to expedite their flight – so he explained in his queer lingo – but Oola had cried so much that he had not been able to draw out the rest of the shaft.

'*Bujeri you*, white Mary!' pleaded Oola in the native formula. 'You gib it medsin. . . . You gib it one old fellow skirt. . . . *Ba'al*, Oola got 'im clothes . . . *ba'al* got 'im ration . . . plenty sick this feller. . . .' And she beat her breast with the arm that was unhurt.

'Of course, I'll give you medicine – and food, and I'll look out something for you to put on. Only for heaven's sake, stop crying,' said Lady Bridget. 'Come along. You must have that spear pulled out and your arm seen to. Come with me to the Humpey. Quick – *murra* make haste.'

But Wombo drew back, casting an affrighted glance down the gully towards the crossing.

'Ba'al me go long-a Humpey – I believe Boss *pho-pho*, Oola,' he said.

'Wombo, you are foolish. What for Boss shoot Oola?'

'*Yowi* – I believe when Boss say *pho-pho*, my word! that one *pho-pho*. Plenty black feller frightened.'

Bridget pushed the unhappy gin along the track.

'You needn't be frightened. Boss has gone away.'

'Boss no sit down long-a Humpey?' Wombo looked relieved, and while Bridget reassured him, the three moved on towards the crossing. In answer to Lady Bridget's questioning the black-boy told his story as they went. She already knew of Wombo's passion for the young gin, who was within the prohibited degree of relationship, therefore *tabu* to him, and who, moreover, was already legitimately wedded to a warrior of the tribe. She knew also that McKeith had forbidden the black-boy, under pain of severe penalty, to seek the coveted bride. Of course, it was all nonsense about his shooting the poor creature, though no doubt, in ordinary circumstances, he would have sent them off the station. But hard as he was – and Lady

Bridget had learned that her husband could be very hard, he would never be inhuman, and, naturally, Oola's wound must be dressed.

Lady Bridget hurried them over the crossing and up the hill. The white men were all out with the cattle. She needed assistance, and seeing Mrs Hensor at the kitchen window of the Bachelors' Quarters, called to her.

'Please come out at once, I want you.'

The woman's face became sullen on the instant.

'I can't come now. I'm in the middle of my baking.'

'But don't you see? The thing is important. This poor gin has a spear through her arm – it must be attended to immediately. Wombo is hurt too. The wounds must be washed and dressed. . . . Look at the poor creatures.'

Mrs Hensor contemptuously surveyed Wombo and his erring partner.

'Serve them right. He's stolen her from her husband and the Blacks have given them what for. They don't need any fussing over, these niggers. They are used to being knocked about.'

Lady Bridget's eyes blazed, but her tone was icy.

'I suppose you understand that I've given you my orders to attend to a wounded fellow-creature.'

'Well, I don't call Blacks fellow-creatures. Do you suppose we should not all be having spears thrown at us if the niggers weren't afraid of Mr McKeith's gun?'

'You have my orders,' repeated Lady Bridget sharply, her wrath at white heat.

'I take no orders from anybody but the Boss, and his orders were that if Wombo brought the gin here, they'd got to be driven off,' retorted Mrs Hensor.

'They will not be driven off. You will answer to your master for this disobedience!' said Lady Bridget.

Mrs Hensor laughed insolently.

'Oh, I'm not afraid of Mr McKeith finding fault with *me*,' and she withdrew out of sight into the kitchen.

CHAPTER 12

Lady Bridget made as dignified a retreat as was possible in the circumstances. She could have slain Mrs Hensor at that moment. She took the blacks to the veranda of the old Humpey and went to look in the office for antiseptics, lint and bandages. Chen Sing, the Chinese cook, came at her call, and rendered assistance with the bland phlegm of his race. The spear had been pulled out of Oola's arm by the time Lady Bridget came back with the dressings. In her spasms of East End philanthropy she had learned the first principles of surgical aid. When Oola's arm and Wombo's gashed head had been washed and bandaged, the trouble was to know what to do with the pair.

Now that they were comfortable and out of pain, fed and given tobacco to smoke and a tot of rum apiece, they had time to remember superstitious fears kept at bay while they had been running for their life. Both were afraid to show themselves in the open. On one hand, there was the terror of McKeith; on the other, of Oola's husband. Lady Bridget gathered that Oola's husband was a medicine man, and that he had 'pointed a bone at his faithless wife and her lover.' To 'point a bone' at an enemy – the bone having first been smeared with human blood, and subjected to magical incantations – is the worst spell that one aboriginal can cast upon another. It means death or the direst misfortune. All that the afflicted one can do is to fly – to hide himself beyond the sorcerer's ken and the reach of pursuit. For this reason, Wombo and Oola had fled back to Moongarr. No outside black dared venture within range of McKeith's gun. Now Wombo and Oola besought Bridget to hide them from the vengeful furies. There was that slab and bark hut at the end of the kitchen and store wing. Nobody was likely at present to want to go into it. The door had a padlock, and it was used as a store-house for the hides of beasts that had been killed for the sake of the skins when in the last stage of pleuro. The key was always kept hung up in McKeith's office.

Here Lady Bridget installed Wombo and Oola. She brought them cooked meat, bread and a ration of tea and sugar, provided them with a pair of blankets, and found for Wombo some old moleskins, a shirt, and a pair of boots, while Oola almost forgot the medicine man's evil spell in her puzzled delight over a lacey undergarment and a discarded kimono dressing-grown, which had been part of Lady Bridget's trousseau. That excitement over, the lonely mistress of Moongarr went back to her own habitation. She ate her solitary dinner and paced the veranda till darkness fell and the haunted loneliness became an almost unbearable oppression. Vast plains, distant ranges, gidia scrub and the far horizon melted into an illimitable shadow. The world seemed boundless as the starry sky – and yet she was in prison! She had longed for the freedom of the wild, and her life was more circumscribed than ever. A phrase in an Australian poem, that had struck her when she had read it not long ago came back upon her with poignant meaning. 'Eucalyptic cloisterdom' – that was the phrase, and it was this to which she had condemned herself. The gum trees enclosed for her one immense cell and she had become utterly weary of her mental and her spiritual incarceration. Oh! for the sting of love's strong emotion to break the monotony. The most sordid sights and sounds of London streets, the most inane babble of a fashionable crowd would be more stimulating to her brain, sweeter in her ears than the arid expanse, the weird bush noises – howl of dingoes, wail of curlews, lowing of cattle – that a year ago had seemed so eerily fascinating.

Even her marriage! The romance of it had faded, as it were, into the dull drab of withered gum leaves. The charm of primal conditions had been overpowered by their discomfort. Nature had never intended her for the wife of a backwoodsman. At times she felt an almost unendurable craving for the ordinary luxuries of civilisation. The bathing appliances here – or rather, the lack of them – were often positive torture to her. She hated the food – continual coarse beef varied by stringy goats' flesh or game from the lagoon. She had come to loathe wild duck – when the men had time to shoot it. She could never bring herself to destroy harmless creatures, and was a rank coward over firearms. Talk of the simple life! Why, it was only since they had got Fo Wung that there had been any vegetables. And the climate – though the short winter had been pleasant enough as a whole – was abominable. The long summer heat, the flies and the mosquitoes! What had she not suffered the first summer after her marriage! And now the hot weather was coming again. That was not the root of the trouble, however – Bridget was honest enough to confess it. The root lay in herself – in her own instability of purpose, her mercurial temperament. She had been born with that temperament. All the O'Haras loved change – hungered after strong sensation. She was spoiling now for emotional excitement.

Well, the little human drama of the Blacks' camp had taken her out of herself for an hour or two. It had been so funny to see Oola stroking the lace frills of Lady Bridget's old petticoat and looking up at Wombo with frank coquetry as she mimicked the 'White Mary's' gestures and gait. Lady Bridget meant to stand by the savage lovers. She would not allow Colin to treat them badly when he came back.

Ninnis, the overseer, broke upon her restless meditations. He was a rough specimen, originally raised in Texas, who, after knocking about in his youth as a cow-boy in the two Americas, had come to Australia about fifteen years previously, had 'free-selected' disastrously, and, during the last five years, had been in McKeith's employ. He was devoted to his master, but he looked upon McKeith's marriage as a pernicious investment. His republican upbringing could not stomach the 'Ladyship,' and he persisted in calling Lady Bridget Mrs McKeith. He considered her flighty and extravagant in her ideas, and was always divided between unwilling fascination and grumpy disapproval. To-night he was in the latter mood and this incensed Lady Bridget.

'I've been writing up the log,' he began in a surly, aggressive tone, 'and I thought I'd better make a note of Wombo and that gin having come to the head-station, in case of there being trouble with the Blacks.'

'Why should there be trouble with the Blacks?' she asked, in a manner equally unconciliatory.

'Well, ye know – though, I daresay, it wouldn't seem of much consequence to you – Wombo's gone agen the laws of the tribe, and that's a serious matter. If they know he's skulking here under protection, they'll be spearing the cattle, and the Boss won't like that.'

'I'll explain to Mr McKeith,' said Lady Bridget haughtily.

'Well, I reckon it's best not to keep them on the head-station against the Boss's orders,' persisted Ninnis.

Lady Bridget set her little white teeth. 'Naturally, Mr McKeith's orders don't apply to *me* – as I had to tell Mrs Hensor.'

'Mrs Hensor knows the Boss better than most people,' said Ninnis, at which Lady Bridget flashed out.

'We need not discuss that question, Mr Ninnis.'

Ninnis' jaw stiffened underneath his shaggy goatee.

'Well, I guess you know your own business, Mrs McKeith, and it's up to you to square things with the Boss.'

Lady Bridget reared her small form and bent her head with great stateliness.

'But I'll just say, though,' went on Ninnis, 'that I hear Harris of the police is coming along. And what Harris doesn't think he knows about the heel of the law being kept on Blacks – and every other darned unit in the creation scheme' – muttered Ninnis in parenthesis – 'ain't entered in the Almighty's Log-book.'

Ninnis expectorated over the veranda railings – a habit of his that jarred on Lady Bridget.

'Well, what about Harris?'

'He's had his eye on Wombo and would be glad of an opportunity to best him – on account of a little affair about a colt Wombo rode for him at the last Tunumburra races – and lost the stakes – out of spite, Harris declares.'

'Oh, I know about that – and I told Mr Harris what I thought about his treatment of the Blacks. But he can't punish Wombo if I choose to have him here. I don't think Mr McKeith would bring Harris to Moongarr – he knows I can't bear him.'

'Well, I reckon that's up to you to square with the Boss,' repeated Ninnis surlily. 'I'm told Harris is on the look-out for desperate characters going along the Leura – these unionist organisers – dropping in at stations on pretence of getting rations and spying out the land, and calling on the men to join them. There was a boundary rider from Breeza Downs to-day – caught us up with the tailing mob and fetched back their new chum and Zack Duppo, leaving us awful short-handed – so that if Joe Casey doesn't fetch in the milkers so early to-morrow you'll know it's because I've had to send him out herding. They're doing their shearing early at Breeza Downs with shearers Windeatt has imported from the south, and he wants police protection for them and himself.'

Lady Bridget laughed.

'Harris and his two constables will have enough to do if they are to protect the district.'

'That's just what Windeatt has been clamouring about. Now the Government have sent up a military patrol, I believe. But they say it isn't strong enough, and all the able-bodied men on the Leura are enrolling as specials. No doubt, that's what been keeping the Boss. You may be sure if there's fighting to be done – black or white – he'll be in it.'

Lady Bridget angered Ninnis by her apparent indifference, and he bade her a cross good-night. Had it been anybody else she would have encouraged him to stay and talk. As it was, she resumed her lonely pacing, and did not go to her room till the whole station was abed.

When at last she went to sleep she dreamed again vividly of Willoughby Maule.

CHAPTER 13

———————●———————

McKeith returned, without warning, the following afternoon. He was not alone, but had spurred on in advance of the other two men he had brought with him. Lady Bridget, reading in her hammock at the upper end of the veranda, heard the sound of a horse approaching, and saw her husband appear above the hill from the Gully Crossing. She got to her feet, expecting that he would ride up to the veranda, calling 'Biddy – Biddy,' as he usually did after an absence. But instead, he pulled up suddenly, turned his horse in the direction of the Bachelors' Quarters, and passed from her line of vision.

She supposed, naturally, that someone at the Quarters had attracted his attention, then remembering that Ninnis and the white men were out with the cattle, wondered, as the minutes went by, who and what detained him.

Tommy Hensor, running up from the garden with his evening dole of vegetables, enlightened her.

'Boss come back, Ladyship. I can see him. He is up, talking to Mother.'

Lady Bridget was too proud a woman to feel petty jealousy, nor would it have occurred to her to be jealous of Mrs Hensor. Her sentiment of dislike towards that person was of quite another order. But she was just in the mood to resent neglect on the part of McKeith.

She went to the veranda railing, whence she had a view of the Bachelors' Quarters, and was able to see for herself that Tommy's report had been correct. She called to the child:

'Go at once, Tommy, and tell the master that *I* am waiting.'

Tommy flew off immediately on his small, sturdy legs, and Lady

Bridget watched the scene at the Bachelors' Quarters. McKeith had dismounted, and with one foot on the edge of the veranda, was facing Mrs Hensor, who looked fresh and comely in a clean blouse and bright-coloured skirt. The two seemed to have a good deal to say to each other, though Lady Bridget heard only the voices, not the words. Her Irish temper rose at the thought that Mrs Hensor might be giving him her version of the Wombo episode. She felt glad that the black-boy and his gin were comfortably sleeping off the effect of their wounds, and of the plentiful meals supplied them in the hide-house, and thus were not in evidence. When McKeith spoke, it was in a dictatorial, angry tone – that of the incensed master. Clearly, however, Mrs Hensor was not the object of his wrath. Lady Bridget saw little Tommy run excitedly up to deliver her message, and almost cried out to him to keep away from the horses' heels, to which he went perilously near. As things happened, the beast lashed out at him, and Tommy had a very narrow escape of being badly kicked. Lady Bridget heard Mrs Hensor shriek and saw her husband drag the child to the veranda and examine him anxiously, Mrs Hensor bending with him. Then McKeith lifted up Tommy and kissed and patted him almost as if he had been the boy's father. It always gave Bridget a queer little spasm of regret to see Colin's obvious affection for the little fellow. He was fond of children, specially so of this one. Lady Bridget knew, though he had never said so to her, that he was disappointed at there being no apparent prospect of her having a child.

And she – with her avidity for any new sort of sensation, although she scoffed at the joy of maternity – felt secretly inclined sometimes to gird at fate for having so far denied her this experience. She herself liked Tommy in her contradictory, whimsical fashion; but now, the fuss over, the boy – who clearly was not in the least hurt – made her very cross, and she became positively furious at seeing McKeith delay yet further to unstrap his valise and get out a toy he must have bought for Tommy in Tunumburra. Then, his grievance aparently coming back on him, he put the child abruptly aside, and leaving valise and horse at the Bachelors' Quarters, walked with determined steps and frowning visage down the track to the veranda. There, his wife was standing, very pale, very erect, her eyes glittering ominously.

McKeith was through the gate and up the flight of steps in three or four strides.

He seemed to sense the antagonism in her, and demanded at once, without waiting to give her any greeting.

'Biddy, what's this I'm hearing about Wombo and that gin?'

'I think you might have asked me before going to Mrs Hensor for information,' she answered with equal curtness.

He stared at her for a moment or two as if surprised; his face reddened, and his eyes, too, glittered.

'I don't know what you mean. I had to speak to Mrs Hensor about beds being wanted up there, and of course I asked her how things had been going on.'

'And did she tell you that she had been inhuman and insolent?'

'Inhuman . . . Insolent!'

'She spoke to me impudently. She defied my orders.'

'I am given to understand that she was carrying out mine,' said McKeith slowly. 'And if that's so, Mrs Hensor was in the right.'

'You put that woman before *me* – before your wife?'

'There's not another woman in the universe I'd put before my wife. But that's no reason for my giving in to her when she does what I know to be folly.'

'I see. You call an act of common humanity folly – doing what one could to relieve the agony of a fellow creature. I am glad that I differ from you – and from your servant. Mrs Hensor refused to help that poor gin who had a spear through her arm and was shrieking with pain.'

'Oh, you don't know black-gins as well as I do. They'll pretend they're dying in agony just to wheedle a drop of rum or a fig of tobacco out of a white man; and they'll take it quite as a matter of course when one of their men bashes their head in with a *nulla-nulla.*'

'I suppose you'll allow that a spear wound may hurt a little,' said Bridget. 'I believe that you yourself suffered from the effect of one – at least, you once told me so.'

And memory – so active these late days, brought suddenly back the vision of him as he had approached her that evening at Government House. What a great Viking he had looked! – in modern dress, of course, but bearing mark of battle in a slight drag of the left leg, only noticeable, she knew now, when he was shy and proud, and under, to him, difficult social conditions. But what a *man* she had felt him to be then, among the other men!

It seemed an outrage on her idealised image of him to hear him speaking in that dry, caustic manner.

'Ah, that's different. The Gulf natives have a nasty way of barbing and poisoning their spears. An ordinary spear-thrust is nothing to either black or white. Wombo could have pulled the thing out, and in a few hours the gin would have been all right again.'

'You think so – well in a few hours she was in a high fever. I took her temperature this morning when I re-bandaged the wound.'

McKeith laughed shortly.

'It wouldn't be surprising, if you had given her grog and tobacco and as much meat as she wanted. That what you did, eh?'

'Yes, it was. They were both starving.'

'Well, I wouldn't bank on your stock of medical knowledge, Biddy – not if I was down with fever or otherwise incapacitated. But that's not the point – which is that those blacks have been kept here against my express orders.'

'They've been kept here by *my* orders,' flamed Lady Bridget.

McKeith's jaw squared, and there showed in his eyes that ugly devil which many a black and white man had seen, but never his wife before.

'Look here, milady – there can be only one boss on this station. And now you'll excuse me if I act according to my own discretion.'

Without another word he walked up the veranda and down the few steps connecting it with the Old Humpey. She heard him go into his office, and presently the door of it slammed behind him. She knew that he was going to the culprits in the hide-house, and wondered what punishment he would mete unto them. Had he gone to the office for his gun? At this moment, anything seemed possible to Lady Bridget's heated temper and excited imagination.

She stood waiting, absorbed in her fears, so abstracted from her ordinary outside surroundings that she was unaware of the approach of two horsemen from the Gully Crossing. They did not stop at the garden gate, but made for the usual station entrance at the back. One of them, lingering behind the other, gazed earnestly at Lady Bridget's tense little figure and bent head, poised in a listening attitude and conveying to him the impression that something momentous had happened or was about to happen. And just then, appalling shrieks, from the rear of the home, justified the impression.

Lady Bridget ran through the sitting-room to the veranda behind, which again connected on either side the new house with the Old Humpey and kitchen and store-wing – the hide-house standing slightly apart at the end of the store building. The shrieks in male and female keys came from the hide-house and mingled with McKeith's strident tones fulminating in Blacks' lingo. The noise brought Mrs Hensor and Tommy down from the Bachelors' Quarters, and the Chinese cook, the Malay boy and Maggie the housemaid from the service department. The three verandas and garden plot made a kind of amphitheatre; and now, into the arena, came the actors in the little tragedy.

From the hide-house, McKeith dragged the prisoners, and through the gateway in the palings which made the fourth side of the enclosure. With one hand he clutched Wombo, with the other Oola, who in her lace-trimmed petticoat and flowered kimono was truly a tragi-comic spectacle.

McKeith carried his coiled stockwhip in the hand which held Wombo. It was plain, judging from the state of Wombo's new shirt, that he had given the black boy a thrashing; Oola was unscathed. Of course, Colin could not lift his hand to a woman, though he was a brute and the woman only a black-gin. Lady Bridget felt faintly glad at this.

She watched the scene, half fascinated, half disgusted, all her attention concentrated on these three figures. She had but a dim consciousness of two men riding round the store-wing and dismounting. One of the two remained in the background screened by the trails of native cucumber overhanging the veranda end. The other – a wiry, powerful figure in uniform, with a rubicund face, black bristling moustache and beard and prominent black eyes, reminding one of the eyes of a bull – walked forward and spoke with an air of official assurance.

'Can I be of any use to you, Mr McKeith, in dealing with that nigger? A bad character, as I've reason to know.'

'No, thank you, Harris. I can do my own dirty jobs,' said McKeith shortly.

He had released the pair and now stood grimly surveying them. Oola was crying and squealing; Wombo stood upright – a scowl of hate on his face. His whole nature seemed changed. A flogging will rouse the semi-civilised black's evil passions like nothing else. There was something of savage dignity in the defiant way in which he faced his former master.

'What for you been take-it stockwhip long-a me? *Ba'al* me bad black boy long-a you, Boss. What for me no have 'em gin belonging to me? Massa catch 'im *bujeri* White Mary like it gin belonging to him. What for no all same black fellow?'

McKeith cut short the argument – sound logic it seemed to Lady Biddy – by an imperious, silencing gesture, and a sudden unfurling of his stockwhip, which made a hissing sound as it writhed along the ground like a snake. The black boy sprang aside. McKeith pointed to the gidia scrub and issued a terse command in the native language.

'*Yan*' (go). '*Ba'al you woolla*' (don't talk any more). '*Yan.*'

Wombo turned appealingly to Lady Bridget.

'Lathychap!'

'*Yan,*' stormed McKeith again, and, as Lady Bridget made a movement of sympathetic response towards the black fellow, he added sternly: 'You'll oblige me by not interfering in this business. The Blacks know that what I say, I mean, and I'll have no more words with them.'

Bridget stood quite still, her attitude and expression all indignant protest, but she said nothing. Her face was turned full towards the man hidden by the creepers, who was watching her with intense interest, but she was unconscious of his gaze.

Wombo retreated slowly. Oola, cowed, whimpering, behind him. Then, she made an appeal to Lady Bridget, stretching out her unbandaged arm imploringly.

'White Mary – you *pidney* (understand). That fellow medsin man – husband belonging to me. Him come close-up long-a srub – throw 'im spear, *nulla-nulla* – plenty look out Wombo. *Ba'al*, Wombo got 'im spear – ba'al got 'im *nulla-nulla*. Suppose black fellow catch 'im Wombo – my word! that fellow *mumkull* (kill). Wombo – *mumkull* Oola – altogether *bong* (dead). *Yūcke! Yūcke!* Lathychap suppose Massa let Wombo sit down long-a head-station – two day, three day – black fellow get tired – up stick – no more look out. No catch 'im Wombo. Lathychap!' she pleaded, '*būjeri* you *pialla* (intercede with) Boss.'

Lady Bridget came down the steps from the veranda and went up to McKeith.

'Colin, what the gin says is true. Her tribe will kill them, and they have no weapons and no means of protection. Will you, as a favour to me, let them stay for a few days? At least, till her arm is healed and the danger past?'

McKeith hesitated perceptibly, then the consciousness of weakening resolve made him harden himself the more, made his speech rougher than it might have been.

'No, I can't, Biddy. I never break my word. They've *got* to go.'

He turned fiercely on Wombo, who stood sullen and defiant again, and from him to Oola, who crouched in the dust, sobbing pitifully and rubbing her damaged arm.

'Plenty me sick, Boss – close up *tumbledown*' (die), she wailed.

'Stop that! *Yan* – do you hear? *Yan – yan – burri – burri –*' (go quickly).

The whip lashed out again. It stung Wombo's bare leg, and flicked Oola's petticoat. The two ran screaming lustily towards the rocks and scrubby country at the head of the gully.

Lady Bridget uttered a shuddering exclamation and made an impetuous movement with arms partly outstretched as if to follow the pair. Then her arms dropped and she stood stock still.

There was a dead silence. In all the relations of husband and wife, never had there been a moment more crucial as affecting their ultimate future. They looked at each other unflinchingly, neither speaking. McKeith's lips were resolute, locked, his pugnacious jaw set like iron. Here was the stubborn determination of a fighting man, never to admit himself in the wrong. And his eyes seemed to have a steel curtain over them – which, however, had Bridget's spiritual intuition been awake to perceive it, softened for an instant, letting through a gleam of passionate appeal.

But Bridget's soul was steel-cased also. He saw only contempt, repulsion in her gaze. The larger issues narrowed to a conflict of two egoisms. It seemed to both as though, in the space of that last quarter of an hour, they had become mortal foes.

The police inspector broke in upon the tense silence. Here was another egoism to be reckoned with – malevolently officious.

'They'll be hiding in the gully, Mr McKeith. No fear of them taking to the outside bush with the tribe hanging round. I'll just round 'em up and drive 'em into the scrub and strike the fear of the Law into them. I'll do it now before I turn out my horse into the paddock.'

'No,' flamed Lady Bridget. 'You'll leave those unfortunate creatures alone – or – if you molest them – whether it's by my husband's permission or not – well – you'll find I'm a bad hater, Mr Harris.'

The police inspector flushed a deep red.

'Maybe I'm not such a bad hater either, my lady – but with my respects. . . .'

'That will do, Harris,' interposed McKeith. 'I told you that I'd do my own dirty jobs. There's no occasion for you to go against her ladyship's wishes.'

Harris touched his helmet to Lady Bridget and, leering with veiled enmity, replied:

'I'm never one to put myself up against the ladies, except where my duty comes first – and that's not the case – yet. But as I was saying, with my respects, my lady, Mr McKeith knows very well how to treat the blacks. He knows that you've got to keep your word to them, whether that means a plug of tobacco or a plug of cold iron.'

Lady Bridget drew back and looked at Harris for a second or two with an expression of the most withering haughtiness. Then, without a word she turned her back on him. The inspector infuriated, muttered in his throat. McKeith interposed sharply:

'Bridget, Harris is going to stay the night.'

'Ah! at the Bachelors' Quarters,' Lady Bridget smiled with distant calm. 'Of course, Mrs Hensor knows. I'm sorry I can't ask Mr Harris to dinner at the house this evening.'

Now, by the social canons of the Bush, the police inspector, being technically speaking of higher grade than the casual traveller, should have been accepted as a 'parlour visitor.' He would thus have occupied one of the bachelor spare rooms in the Old Humpey and would have joined the Boss and his wife at dinner. Harris had never before stayed the night at Moongarr, and he had confidently expected to be received with honour. Thus he regarded Lady Bridget's speech as an insult.

'Oh, I'm not one to force my company where it is not wanted,' he blustered. 'I'm quite content with a shake-down at the Quarters, though if I'd known I might have gone by the short cut with the Specials – it's rather late, however, to push on to Breeza Downs, where – though perhaps I say it as shouldn't – I'm sure of a welcome from Mr and Mrs Windeatt, being, so to speak – for law and order – the representative of His Majesty in the Leura district.'

Lady Bridget smiled with detached amusement, as she turned again and patted the head of an elderly kangaroo dog, which came up to her with its tongue out and a look of wistful enquiry in its bleared eyes, scenting plainly that something was amiss. 'Good dog, Veno,' she murmured.

Harris bridled.

'I'll bid you good evening then, my lady,' he said stiffly. 'No doubt,

Mr McKeith, you'll spare me half an hour in the office by and by. Just to concert our measures for the proper protection of the Pastoralists and the safeguarding of the woolsheds this shearing season.'

'Yes, yes, of course,' McKeith answered mechanically. The spunk had gone out of him, as Harris would have phrased it; and the Inspector, looking at Lady Bridget, guessed the reason.

'And what now about the gentleman from Leichardt's Town, Mr McKeith? Will I be taking him up with me to the Bachelor's Quarters? Or may be,' Harris added unpleasantly, 'her ladyship won't object to having *him* in the house.'

McKeith muttered angrily, 'Damn! I'd forgotten.'

It was not like him to lose himself during working hours in even a momentary fit of abstraction – except, indeed, when he was riding without immediate objective through the Bush. His eyes were still upon his wife's slight figure as she moved slowly towards the veranda, with the air of one who has no more concern with the business in hand. Her graceful aloofness, which he knew to be merely a social trick, stung him inexpressibly, the faint bow she had given Harris when he bade her good evening had seemed to include himself. It galled him that he did not seem fitted by nature or breeding to cope with this kind of situation. The half consciousness of inferiority put him still more at disadvantage with himself.

'Biddy, wait please,' he said dictatorially.

She paused at the steps, her hand on the railings, her eyes under their lowered lids ignoring him.

He went closer and spoke rapidly in a harsh undertone.

'I didn't tell you – though I rode ahead on purpose – I met a man at Tunumburra who said he knew you. He's out from England – been staying at Government House, and brought a letter from Sir Luke Tallant. I hope that at any rate you'll be civil to *him*.'

She flashed a quick glance at him, and her eyelids dropped again.

'But naturally. I'm not in the habit of being uncivil to – my friends.'

And just then – Mrs Hensor, who loved cheap fiction, said afterwards it was all like a scene out of a book – there appeared in the space between the two wings, a man who had strolled unobserved from one side, out of the background of creepers, and who advanced with quickened step to where the husband and wife stood.

CHAPTER 14

———————•———————

A striking individual. Tall – though not as tall or as massively built as Colin McKeith, firm boned and muscular, but with a sort of feline grace of movement. There was the unmistakable stamp of civilization, and, at the same time, an exotic suggestion of the East, of wild spaces, adventure, romance. Not in the least a Bushman, but wearing with ease and picturesqueness, a backwoods get-up. Clothes, extremely well cut; riding breeches and boots; soft shirt and falling collar with a silk tie of dull flame colour knotted at the sinewy throat, loose coat, Panama hat. So much for the figure. The face ugly, but distinguished, sallow-brown in colouring. Nose long, fine, with a slight twist below the bridge; cheeks and chin clean-shaven, an enormous dark moustache concealing the mouth. Hair black, slightly grizzled, and when he lifted his hat forming a thick lightly frosted crest above his forehead. Eyes black – peculiar eyes, sombre, restless, but with a gaze, steady and piercing when concentrated on a particular object, as, just now, it was concentrated on Lady Bridget.

The gaze seemed compelling. Lady Bridget suddenly lifting eyes that were instantly wide open, became aware of the man's presence. The effect of it upon her was so marked that McKeith, watching her face, felt a shock of surprise. The change in her was noticed by the Police Inspector, with malevolent curiosity. So also by Mrs Hensor, a little further away.

The new-comer saluted her with a low bow, his hat in one hand, the other extended.

'You haven't fogotten me, I hope, Lady Bridget, though I should think that I am the very last person in the world you would have expected to see in these parts.'

Lady Bridget had turned very white. She stared at him as if he had been a ghost, and at first seemed unable to speak. But her confusion lasted only a few seconds. Almost before he had finished his sentence she had pulled herself together. Her hand was in his, and she spoke in her old fluty voice and little grand manner, with the old slow, faintly whimsical smile on her lips and in her eyes. It came over McKeith that he had not of late been familiar with this aspect of her, and that she was exhibiting to this man the same strange charm of her girlhood which had been to him, in the full fervour of his devotion, so wonderful and worshipful, but of which – he knew it now – the Bush had to a great extent robbed her.

She laughed as she withdrew her hand from that of the newcomer. And standing on the steps, her head almost on a level with his, met his eyes with challenging directness.

'Really, Mr Maule, you shouldn't startle a nervous creature in that uncanny way – appearing like the unmentionable Personage or the angel if you prefer it, only with this difference, that we weren't speaking of you. I hadn't the most distant notion that you were on this side of the equator. If my husband had mentioned your name I should not have been so taken by surprise.'

'Were you really so surprised? I thought I *must* have sent my shadow on before me – because I've been thinking so tremendously of you these last few days, and of the prospect of seeing you again. I daresay you know,' he added, turning politely to McKeith – 'that I had the pleasure of meeting your wife when she was Lady Bridget O'Hara, one winter at Rome, with her cousins, Lord and Lady Gaverick. And later, we saw something of each other in London.'

'No, my husband doesn't know,' Bridget gave a reckless laugh, and her eyes challenged those of McKeith before he could answer. 'You see, Colin and I, when we married, came from opposite poles geographically, morally and mentally. He did not understand or care about my old environment any more than I understood – or cared about his. So we agreed to bury our respective pasts in oblivion. Don't you think it was a good plan?'

'Quite admirable. I admire your mutual courage in adopting it.'

'You think so! It has its drawbacks, though,' said McKeith dryly. 'I must apologise for having left you to announce yourself. The fact is, those Blacks put other things out of my head. They had to be taught they couldn't disobey orders without being punished for it.'

'Poor wretches! Yes! I know the popular idea of asserting British supremacy over coloured races, by the force of the whip. I have not always seen it answer; but then my experience has been with natives rather higher in the scale of evolution than the Australian aboriginal.'

'You believe in the power of kindness – as I do,' exclaimed Lady Bridget. 'My husband and I take different views on that subject. But we need not discuss them now. Come and have some tea, and tell me about the Tallants.'

Maule followed her to the door of the living room where she turned to give some orders to Maggie, the maid-servant, and to the Chinese cook. McKeith went off with Harris to see after the horses and have a talk with Ninnis at the stockyards. Thus, Maule was left alone for a few minutes to study and form hs own opinion as to Lady Bridget's setting. She was a woman who, whatever her surroundings, must always impress them with her personality. This bush parlour was original in its simplicity. Walls lined with unvarnished wood which was mellowing already to a soft golden brown. Boards bare, but for a few rugs and skins. A fine piece of tappa from the Solomons, of barbaric design in black and orange, made the centre of an arrangement of South Sea Island and aboriginal weapons. Divans heaped with cushions flanked the great fireplace. Two writing-tables occupied spaces between French windows – one the desk of a business-like roll-top escritoire; the other, the flap of a Chippendale bureau, with a Chippendale arm-chair before it. There were a few other pieces unmistakably English. In fact, Eliza Countess of Gaverick, in addition to a handsome present of plate, had sent her niece the furnishings of her old room at Castle Gaverick. A few pictures and etchings hung on the other walls – among them several wild seascapes – reminding one a little of Richard Doyle's exquisite water colours – in which green billows and foamy wave-crests took the shapes of sea-fairies. Also some weird tree studies – mostly gum and gidia, where gnarled limbs and bulbous protuberances turned into the faces of gnomes and the forms of strange monsters. Maule had no doubt that these were Lady Bridget's own. There was an upright grand piano – the alleged cause of Steadbolt's conversion to Unionism, and all about the place a litter of newspapers, books and work. The room was filled with flowers – sheaves of wattle and of the pale sandal-wood blossoms, as well as many sub-tropical blooms with which he was not familiar. Blending with, yet dominating the mixture of perfumes, a peculiar scent resembling incense, appealed to him; and this he did not at first trace to a log of sandal-wood smouldering on the open hearth more for effect than warmth, for the early spring evenings had scarcely a touch of chill. The French windows stood open to the veranda, a room in itself with its many squatters' chairs, hammocks and tables. Beyond, stretched the green expanse of plain, utterly lonely, the waters of the lagoon taking a reddish tinge where they reflected the lowering sun. It seemed an inconceivable environment to have been chosen by the Lady Bridget he had known in London, one of whose chief attractions to him had been that she represented a certain section of the aristocracy of Great Britain, decadent perhaps, but 'in the swim.'

She came now along the veranda from the Old Humpey with the light, rather hurried tread he remembered, talking rapidly when she joined him.

'I've been seeing about your room. I suppose you know enough now of the Never-Never to understand that we are quite primitive in our habits. You won't find a spring mattress – or water laid on – or any other convenience of civilisation.'

'May I remind you that I've roughed it pretty well in the Andes.'

'Yes, but you have had so many luxuries since then that you will have forgotten what roughing it feels like – just as I've forgotten now that I was ever anything but a barbarian – I see you shave still.'

'Yes – why?'

'Only that I discovered just now the white ants had eaten all the woodwork of the spare-room looking-glass. The thing crumbled in my hand and fell on the floor and was broken. A bad omen for your visit, isn't it?'

'I hope not. So you are superstitious as ever?'

'I haven't ceased to be a Celt – though I've become a barbarian. I'll borrow the overseer's looking glass for you.'

'Pray don't. I've got one of sorts in my razor case. Is dinner regarded in the Never-Never as a sacred ceremonial?'

'The men don't put on dress clothes, if that's what you mean. As for the repast, for a long time, as a rule, the menu was salt junk and pumpkin. We've improved on that a little since the Chinese cook and the Chinese gardener came back from the goldfields – there was another rush at Fig Tree Mount that fizzled out. To-night, you will have kangaroo-tail soup, and kid *en casserole*. If you make believe very hard you might possibly imagine it young venison. . . . Here, Kuppi!' The Malay boy brought in the tea-tray and she signed to him to put it on the table between the fire and the window.

'Tea,' she asked, 'or would you rather have whiskey and water? I can't offer you soda water because, till the drays come, we have nothing to run the seltzogene with. . . . Do you know that the Unionists cut our dray horses' throats? We're lucky to have whiskey in the store. They broke open the cases of spirits and stole a lot of things. . . . Vicissitudes of savage life, you see!'

She rattled on, scarcely pausing. She was seated on a divan, the tea before her – he in a squatter's chair with long arms, in which he sat silent, leaning forward, his hands on the chair-arms, his eyes fixed upon her. She avoided looking at him. Her small sun-browned hands fidgeted among the cups. If anything remained of her anger and emotion, she hid it under a ripple of absurd housewifely chatter, not waiting for him to answer.

'Well, is it to be tea or whiskey?'

'Tea, please,' and then at last she stopped and looked at him and could not turn her eyes away, or did not want to do so. His black orbs stared with a disquieting fixity – a sort of inhuman power – from out of his foreign-looking face. That stare was his chief weapon in the subjugation of women – they called it magnetic, and no doubt it was so. It increased the fascination of his ugly good looks.

The gaze of each one seemed to fuse in that of the other. Hers, at first coldly curious, tentative, caught light, warmth, intensity from the sombre fire of his. Suddenly he said:

'In God's name, Biddy, how did you come to marry that rough brute.'

'*Is* he a rough brute! It's very rude of you to say so. But do you know, just for a half minute to-day, I rather thought so myself. I don't pretend to agree with Colin's methods of treating the Blacks, though I'm told it's the only way to treat them – you know they did commit terrible atrocities up here. . . . Still to flog a black man, a wild, warlike, human creature, seems to me nearly as bad as shooting him. Do you know – the first thing I ever heard about Colin was that he had a great many notches on his gun, and that each one meant a wild black-fellow that he had shot dead.'

'And now he flogs tame ones,' Maule observed quietly. Her brilliant eyes searched his face for a sign of malevolent sarcasm, but not a muscle quivered. Her own eyes wavered under his steady look. She busied herself among the tea things.

'Sugar?'

'Please.'

But she paused, the tongs balanced in her delicate fingers.

'It is frightfully thrilling – life in the Bush.'

'What part of it? The shooting or the flogging?'

She burst out: 'You know I hated that. You know I was furious about the flogging. You know' – She pulled herself up.

'I know nothing – except that you must have changed enormously in a very short time to have been thrilled with anything but horror – by that sort of thing.'

'Yes, I have changed. But it isn't time that changes one. Time never counts with me. It's only feeling that counts. Oh, of course, I think it all horrible – about the Blacks up North. They're not allowed on this station – except one or two half civilised stock-boys – and this one fell in love and carried off his gin, and brought her here against my husband's orders.'

'Yes? And you had befriended them – I gathered that. But it doesn't explain *you*.'

She took up a piece of sugar with the tongs, holding it suspended as she spoke, jerkily.

'Why should I be explained? As for my finding life in the Bush thrilling. . . . I was dead sick of falsities when I left England, I wanted to be thrilled by something real.'

'And you found that – in your husband?'

'Yes; I did. He *is* real, at least. He is true to himself. So few men have the strength of their goodness or the courage of their badness, when it comes to a big test.'

'Oh! I grant you. Yes; I know that's what you're thinking. *I* wasn't true to myself in the big test. . . . But *you* were to blame for my having been false to the higher ideal.'

'*I!* Oh – what makes you –' But she thought better of the impetuous question that trembled on her lips, and went on in a different tone.

'What does that matter! I'm not saying anything about high ideals. What is high? . . . . What is low? . . . . You've just got to invoke truth and freedom – as far as your conception of them goes. . . . And there's a reason for Colin's hatred of the Blacks.'

'Ah! Is it permitted to ask the reason?'

'His family were all massacred by the natives – father, mother, sisters – all. Well, one admires a man steadfast in revenge – going straight for what he wants – and getting it – doing it – in love or in hate. Now I have answered your question.'

The gesture of her head seemed a defiance. She dropped the

sugar into his tea, and he took the cup from her hands, and slowly drank it without saying a word.

It was she who broke the silence.

'You provoke me. You make me say things I don't want to say. You always did.'

'Ah! Then marriage has not changed you so immensely, after all!'

She bit her lip and rose abruptly.

'Do you want any more tea? No. Then come to the veranda and tell me how it is that Luke Tallant has allowed you to exchange Government House for the Never-Never?'

He had followed her through the French window.

'I see you haven't heard the bad news.'

'No – what? We only get a mail once a week.'

'I thought McKeith would have broken the shock. He came on, he said, to do so. Poor Lady Tallant.'

'Rosamond! The operation?'

'She died under the anaesthetic. Sir Luke got the news by cable the day before I left Leichardt's Town. He wired at once for leave and has started for England by this time.'

'Oh? poor Rosamond! Poor, poor Rosamond!'

'Is she to be so greatly pitied! She has been saved much suffering!'

Then as Bridget went on murmuring, 'Oh, poor Rosamond, she did love life,' he added gently. 'Life can be very cruel. . . . I myself have had cause for gratitude to Death, the great Simplifier. If my wife had lived she must have been a hopeless invalid doomed to continual pain.'

Lady Bridget gave him a swift look of reproach.

'Oh, do you expect me to congratulate you?' she exclaimed bitterly. 'Yes,' she went on, 'perhaps, to *her* Death was merciful – but not to Rosamond. And Luke did care for his wife. He will be broken-hearted.'

She stood gazing out upon the plain, on which the mist was gathering. From across the gully sounded the cattle being driven home.

When she turned to him, her eyes were full of tears.

'I think I'll go now,' she said simply. 'Colin will show you your room. He's there – coming up from the lagoon.'

She went through a French window lower down the veranda into her bedroom, and Maule descended the steps into the garden and presently joined his host.

CHAPTER 15

———•———

A little later, McKeith having tubbed and changed his riding clothes, came to his wife's room. He looked very large and clean and fair, and the worst of his temper had worn off in a colloquy with Ninnis, and the imparting and receiving of local news. But his eyes were still gloomy, and his mouth sullenly determined. And he had remembered with remorse that he should have softened to Bridget the sudden news of her friend's death. The sight of her now – a small tragic figure with a white face and burning eyes, in a black dress into which she had changed, deepened his compunction.

'I am very sorry, Biddy.' He tried to put his arm round her shoulder, but she drew back.

'What are you sorry for, Colin – that Rosamond Tallant is dead, and that you forgot to tell me, and let me hear it from – Willoughby Maule?' She paused perceptibly before pronouncing the christian name, 'Or that you behaved like an inhuman monster to those wretched Blacks, and refused me the only thing I have asked you for a good time past?'

Her tone roused his rancour anew.

'I think we'll drop the subject of the Blacks; there is no earthly use in talking about them, I make it a rule never to threaten without performing, and I'd punish them again, just the same – or more severely – under similar circumstances.'

'Very well. You will do as you please, and I shall do as I please, too.'

'What do you mean?'

'Just what I say. I agree with you that there's no use in discussing things about which we hold such different opinions. Quite simply, I can't forgive you for this afternoon's work.'

'Biddy, you exaggerate things.'

'Perhaps. But I don't think so in this case. Let me go out, Colin. Dinner must be ready by now.'

'No. I've got something to ask you first. I want to know why you looked so upset – as if you were going to faint – when that man came up to you to-day?'

'Naturally, I was startled. I had no idea he was in Australia.'

'But why should that have affected you. One might have imagined he had been your lover. Was he ever your lover, Biddy? I must know.'

'And if he had been, do you think I should tell you,' she answered coldly.

McKeith's face turned a dark red. His eyes literally blazed.

'That's enough,' he said. 'I shall not ask you another question about him. I am answered already.'

He stood aside to let her pass out into the veranda, and she walked along to the sitting-room.

Dinner went off, however, more agreeably than might have been expected. Lady Bridget's manner was simple and to the guest charming. The black dress, the touch of pensiveness was in keeping with the shadow of tragedy. But she spoke in a natural way, and with tender regret of Lady Tallant – questioning Maule as to when he had last seen her, and learning from him how it had been at Rosamond's instigation that he had cabled proposing himself as a companion in Sir Luke's loneliness. It had been only a week after his arrival in Leichardt's Town that the blow had fallen.

'You know, Tallant and I always hit it off very well together,' he observed explanatorily, addressing McKeith. 'It was at their house that I used to meet Lady Bridget during the few months that I had the honour of her acquaintance in England.'

McKeith looked at his guest in a resentful but half puzzled way. A spasm of doubt shook him. Suppose he had been making a fool of himself – insulting his wife by unreasoning suspicions? A vague contempt in her courteous aloofness had stung him to the quick. And the other man's easy self assurance, the light interchange of conversation between them about things and people of which McKeith knew nothing – all gave the Australian a sense of bafflement – the feeling that these two were ruled by another social code, belonged to a different world, in which he had no part. He had been sitting at the head of his table, perfunctorily doing his duty as host, wounded in his self-esteem – almost the tenderest part of him, morose and miserable. Now he snatched at the idea that he had been mistaken, as if it were a life-buoy thrown him in deep waters. He began to talk, to assert himself, to prove himself cock of his own walk. And Maule suavely encouraged him to lay down the law on things Australian, while Lady Bridget withdrew into herself, baffling and enraging McKeith still more hopelessly. He did not seem now to know his wife! A catastrophe had happened. What? How? Why? . . . . Nothing was the same, or could be the same again.

It was a relief when dinner was over. The men pulled out their pipes in the veranda. Lady Bridget, just within the sitting room window, smoked a cigarette, her small form extended in a squatter's chair, listening to, but taking scarcely any part in the conversation. The two outside discussed local topics – McKeith's failure to trace the perpetrators of the outrage on his horses. Maule's impressions of Tunumburra – where he had met McKeith in the township hotel, and the two had apparently, in the usual Bush fashion, got on intimate terms – the rumours of an armed camp of Unionists, and the expected conflict between them and the sheep owners and free shearers at Breeza Downs, whither the Government specials were bound. Lady Bridget gleaned that Maule had placed himself under McKeith's directions.

'What are your immediate movements to be?' he asked his host. 'Remember, I am ready to fall in with any plans you may have for making me useful.'

McKeith did not answer at once. He took his pipe from his mouth, and knocked the ashes out of it against the arm of his chair, while he seemed to be considering the question. Then, as if he had formed a definite determination, he leaned forward and addressed his wife in a forcedly matter-of-fact tone.

'I don't suppose you know much about what has been going on, Biddy. The same boat that brought up the specials brought a hundred or more free labourers, and they're on their way up to the different sheep-stations along the river – a lot of them for Breeza Downs, where Windeatt has begun shearing. Windeatt is in a blue funk because of a report that a little army of Unionists, all mounted and armed, are camped that way and threatening to burn down his wool-shed and sack his store. They burned old Duppo's wool-shed last week.'

'He's a skinflint, and I'm sure he deserved it,' put in Lady Bridget indifferently.

McKeith checked a dry sarcasm. He became aware of Maule's eyes turning from one to the other.

'Well –' He got up and leaned his great frame against the lintel between Maule and Lady Bridget. 'The Pastoralist Executive at Tunumburra have asked us cattle-owners – who are more likely to be let alone than the sheep-men, to help in garrisoning the sheep-stations; and I've promised to ride over to Breeza Downs to-morrow and do my share in protecting the place. Harris and I are going together.'

Lady Bridget seemed more interested in blowing smoke-rings than in her husband's news.

'I may have to be away several days,' continued McKeith. 'Then there's the new bore we're sinking – the water is badly wanted – cattle are dying – I can't run any risk of the bore-plant being wrecked. The men who are working there must be sent off because we're short of rations – thanks to those murderous brutes keeping back the drays – and the muster has to be stopped for the same reason. I won't answer for when I can be back.' . . . As she made no answer, he asked sharply: 'Do you understand, Biddy?'

'Yes, of course. I have no doubt, Colin, that you'll find it all highly stimulating. And perhaps you will be able to shoot somebody with a clear conscience, which will be more stimulating still. Really Mr Maule, you are lucky to have come in for a civil war – I heard that in South America that was your particular interest. Do you carry civil wars about with you? Only, there's nothing very romantic in fighting for mere freedom of contract – it seems so obvious that people should be free to make or decline a contract. I wonder which side you would take.'

Her levity called forth an impatient ejaculation from McKeith.

'I'm afraid in my wars it's generally been what your husband would consider the wrong side,' said Maule with a laugh. 'I've usually fought with the rebels.'

'Then you'd better not go to Breeza Downs. You'd better stop and fight for me,' exclaimed Bridget.

'That's just what I was about to propose your friend should do,' said McKeith in hard deliberate tones. He looked straight at his wife – shoulders and jaws squared, eyes like flashing steel under the grim brows. The expression of his face gave Bridget a little sense of shock. She raised herself abruptly, and her eyes flashed pride and defiance too.

'How very considerate of you, Colin – if Mr Maule *likes* to be disposed of in that way. *He* is to be allowed freedom of contract I presume, though the shearers are not.'

'You needn't be afraid that I shall strike, Lady Bridget,' laughed Maule. 'It will suit my general principles to keep out of the scrimmage. I don't know anything about the rights and wrongs of your labour question, but I confess that, speaking broadly, my sympathies are usually rather with Labour than with Capital.'

'Capital!' echoed McKeith derisively. 'It's blithering irony to talk of us Leura squatters as representing capital. We're all playing a sort of battledore and shuttlecock game – tossed about between drought and plenty – boom and slump. A kick of the beam and one end is up and the other end down. There's Windeatt, who will be ruined if his wool-shed is destroyed and his shearing spoiled. No rain, and the banks would foreclose on most of us. Take myself. Two years ago the skies were all smiling on my fortunes. This last year, it's as if the hosts of heaven had a down on me.'

'The stars in their courses fought against Sisera,' murmured Lady Bridget.

'I'm Sisera, am I?' He gave her a fierce look and crossed to the veranda-railing, where he began cutting tobacco into the palm of his hand. 'Well, there is something in that. But the stars have never licked me yet. Sisera was a coward, or they wouldn't have *downed* him.'

'Ah, but there was Jael to be reckoned with,' put in Maule softly.

'Jael!' McKeith plugged his pipe energetically. 'The more fool Sisera for not giving Jael a wide berth. He should have gone his way and kept her out of his affairs.'

A hard little laugh rang from the depths of the squatter's chair. Maule got up and strolled into the sitting-room, where he seemed engrossed in the pictures on the wall. Just then Cudgee, the black boy, hailed McKeith from the foot of the steps.

'That fellow pollis man want'ing Massa. He sit down long–a Old Humpey.'

'All right.'

McKeith looked into the parlour. 'My wife will entertain you, Maule. I daresay you've got plenty to talk about. I'll see you later.'

Presently they heard him outside speaking to the Police Inspector. 'Come into the office, Harris, and have a smoke and a glass of grog.'

CHAPTER 16

Lady Bridget and Willoughby Maule were alone again. She got up from the long chair, and as she did so her cigarette case dropped from her lap. He picked it up and it lay on his open palm, the diamonds and rubies of her maiden initials glistening on the gold lid. They looked at each other across it.

'*I* gave you this,' he said, 'and you have kept it – used it?'

He seemed to gloat over the bauble.

Her fingers touched his hand as she took the case from him, and he gave a little shiver of pleasure.

'Let me have it; I want another cigarette.' She selected two and gave him one of them.

They moved to the divan near the fireplace, where some red embers remained of the log of sandalwood. Its perfume lingered faintly in the atmosphere.

'That's good,' he said. 'It's like you; the only thing in this god-forsaken desert that *is* like you.'

'Oh, you don't know me – now.'

'Don't I! Well, your husband has given me the chance of knowing you – better – and I warn you that I shall not scruple to avail myself of the opportunity.'

She shook her head dubiously. 'Give me a light.'

He stooped and lit his own cigarette, then, bending, held its tip to her. They both inhaled a few whiffs in silence. Presently, he said:

'I find it difficult to understand McKeith.'

'Don't try. You wouldn't succeed. I observe,' she added, 'that you must have become rather friendly at Tunumburra?'

'Oh, yes. I can generally get on with open-air men. Besides, I wanted him to like me. I wanted him to ask me here.'

'Well – and what do you think of it, now that you are here?'

'Great heavens! What do you imagine that I should think of it! The whole thing seems to me the most ghastly blunder – the most horrible anomaly. You – in these surroundings! Married to a man so entirely beneath you, and with whom you don't get on at all.'

'You have no right to say that.'

'The thing is obvious; though you tried to carry it off before dinner. Your manner to each other; the lack of courtesy and consideration in him; his leaving you. . . .'

'Stop,' she interrupted. 'There's one thing you *must* understand. I don't mind what you say about yourself – I want to hear that – but I can't allow you to criticise my husband.'

'I beg your pardon. It isn't easy in the conditions to preserve the social conventions. I will try to obey you. At any rate, you allow me to be frank about myself. . . . It was sweet of you to keep this – more than I could have dared hope for.'

He fingered tenderly the cigarette case on her lap.

'I suppose I ought to have sent it back to you. But I didn't want to. You see it was not like an engagement ring.'

'No, worse luck.'

'Why, worse luck?'

'The ring would have been the outward and visible sign of an inward and spiritual bond. If you had been really engaged to me – formally, officially engaged, you couldn't have thrown me over so easily.'

'I – throw you over! Is it quite fair to put it that way?'

'No, I admit that. Let us be honest with each other – this once.'

'This once – very well – but not at this moment. I daresay there will be time for a talk by and by.'

'I wait your pleasure.'

'There are some things I should like to understand,' she went on, '– about you – about me, it doesn't matter which. And, after all, I only want to know about you out of a sort of perverse curiosity.'

'That's so like you. You always managed to infuse a bitter drop into your sweetness. And you *could* be so adorably sweet. . . If only I could ever have felt sure of you.'

'Where would have been the use? We never could spend an hour together without hurting or annoying each other. It's a very good thing for us both that neither cared enough to make any real sacrifice for the other.'

'There you wrong me,' he exclaimed. 'I did care – I cared intensely. The touch of your hand – the very sweep of your dress thrilled every nerve in me. I never in all my life loved a woman as I loved you. That last day when you walked out of my rooms. . . .'

'Where I never ought to have gone. Fancy the properly brought-up English girl you used to hold up to me doing such a shocking thing as to visit you alone in your chambers! . . . Oh! Is that Colin back again?'

For Maule had started visibly at the sound of quick steps mounting to the veranda, and McKeith's towering figure appeared in the doorway, looking at them.

Lady Bridget turned her head, her cigarette in her hand, and glanced up at his face. What she saw in it might have made a less reckless or less innocent woman feel uneasy. She was sure that he must have heard that last speech of hers about visiting Maule in his chambers. Well, she didn't care. Besides Colin hadn't the smallest right to resent any action of hers before her marriage. . . She did not turn a hair. Maule admired her composure.

'*Bon sang ne peut mentir*,' he thought to himself, and wished they had been talking in French.

'You look as grim as the statue of the Commander,' said Lady Bridget. 'What is the matter?'

'Lady Bridget and I have been exchanging unconventional reminiscences,' put in Maule with forced lightness.

McKeith took no notice of either remark, but strode across the room to the roll-top escritoire, where he usually wrote his letters when in his wife's company. He extracted a bundle of papers from one of the pigeon holes.

'This is what I came for. Sorry to have interrupted your reminiscences,' and he went out again, passing along the back veranda.

Maule had got up and was standing at the fireplace. Lady Bridget rose too.

'I'm going to bed. We keep early hours in the Bush.'

'What! Already!' he exclaimed in dismay.

'I was up at six this morning. Well, I hope you won't be too uncomfortable with the white ants in the Old Humpey – they are perfectly harmless. Your room is next to the office, as I daresay you've discovered. And you'll find Colin there I suppose, with your friend the Police-Inspector.'

'Don't call that man Harris my friend. We've had one or two

scraps at each other already. He was pleased to take it for granted that I'm what he calls a "new chum," and didn't like my shewing him that I knew rather better than he does what police administration should be in out-of-the-way districts.'

Lady Bridget nodded. 'Then we're both under ban of the Law. I *detest* Harris. . . . Good-night.' And she flitted through the French window without giving him her hand.

The station seemed in a state of unquietude till late into the night. The lowing of the tailing-mob in the yards was more prolonged than usual, and horses were whinnying and answering each other down by the lagoon as though there were strangers about. Lady Bridget, lying awake and watching through her uncurtained windows the descent of the Southern Cross towards the horizon, and the westward travelling of a moon just out of its first quarter, could hear the men's voices on the veranda of the Old Humpey – that of Ninnis and the Police Inspector; Maule seemed to have retired to his own room.

McKeith was evidently busy upon preparations for his absence from the station. He must have been cleaning guns and pistols. There were two or three shots – which startled and kept her in a state of tension. At last she heard the interchange of good-nights, and the withdrawal of Ninnis and Harris to the Bachelors' Quarters. Finally, her husband came to his dressing-room – not along the front veranda, as would have been usual, but by the back one, through the bathroom. Even this deviation from habit seemed significant of his mood – he would not pass her window. He moved about for a time as if he were busy packing. Then came silence. She imagined him on the edge of the camp bed, so seldom used, smoking and ruminating.

Whiffs from his pipe came through the cracks of the door between the two rooms, and were an offence to her irritated nerves. She had grown accustomed to his tobacco, but, as a rule, he did not smoke the last thing at night. He had seemed to regard his wife's chamber as a tabernacle, enshrining that which he held most sacred, and would never enter it until he was cleansed from the grime and dust of the stockyard and cattle camp, and had laid aside the associations of his working day. That attitude had appealed to all that was idealistic in both their natures, and had kept green the memory of their honeymoon. It angered her that to-night, of all nights, he should disregard it.

In personal details, she was intensely fastidious, and at some trouble and cost had maintained in her intimate surroundings a daintiness almost unknown out-back. Her room was large, and much of its furnishing symptomatic of the woman of her class – the array of monogrammed, tortoise-shell backed brushes and silver and gold topped boxes and bottles, the embroidered coverlet of the bed, the flowered chintz and soft pink wall paper, the laced cambric garments and silk-frilled dressing gown hanging over a chair. When service lacked, and there was no one to wash and iron her cambric and fine linen, she contrived somehow that the supply should not fail, and brought upon herself some ill-natured ridicule in consequence. The wives of the Leura squatters thought her 'stuck-up' and apart from their kind. If they had known how much she wanted sometimes to throw herself into their lives – as she had thrown herself into the lives of her East-End socialistic friends! But the stations were few and far between, and the neighbours – such as they were – left her alone.

Letting her mind drift along side-tracks, she resented now there having come no suggestion from the Breeza Downs women that she should accompany her husband and share the benefits of police protection, or – which appealed to her far more – the excitement of what might be going on there. Of course, though, there was nothing for her to be nervous about here – she wished there might have been. Any touch of dramatic adventure would be welcome in the crude monotony of her life.

But the adventure promised to be of a more personal kind.

Suddenly, she jumped out of bed and softly slipped the bolt of the door into her husband's dressing room. She did it on a wild impulse. She felt that she could not bear him near her to-night. He should see that she was not his chattel. . . . But, perhaps, he did not want to come. . . . Well, so much the better. In any case, she wanted to show him that she did not want him. She wondered if he would venture. . . . She wondered if he did really care. . . .

He appeared in no hurry to test her capacity for forgiveness. . . . Or it might be that the minutes went slowly – laden as they were with momentous thought. She lay in a tumult of agitation, her heart beating painfully under the lawn of her nightgown. She had a sense of gasping wonderment. She felt, as Colin had felt, that something tremendous had happened – and with such bewildering suddenness – altering all the conditions between them.

Yet, through the pain and bewilderment, her whole being thrilled with an excitement that was almost intoxicating – like the effect of an insidious drug, or the fumes of heady wine. She knew it was the old craving for sensation, the fatal O'Hara temperament awake and clamouring. Try as she would – and she did try in a futile fashion – she could not shut off the impression of Willoughby Maule – the sombre ardour in his eyes, the note of suppressed passion in his voice. There was no doubt that this unexpected meeting had re-started vibrations, and that his influence was a force to be reckoned with still.

If Colin had acted differently – if he had not behaved so brutally to those poor blacks – if his manner to her had not been so hard and overbearing. And then his leaving her alone like that with Willoughby Maule! Of course, he was jealous. He had jumped at conclusions. What right had he to do so? What could he know? He must suspect her of horrible things. His questions had been insultingly dictatorial. Now, he wanted to shew her that he flung her off. He would not put out a finger to hold her to him. Had he not said something like that before their marriage! . . . It was abominable.

The whiffs of tobacco smoke came no more. He was moving about again. She heard him in the bathroom. After a minute or two he came to the door and tried to open it.

'Biddy,' he said. Then in a deep-toned eager whisper, 'Mate!'

She sat up in bed; she had the impulse to go and open the door, but some demon held her back. She lay down again on her pillow. . . . The bed had creaked. . . . He must have known that she was awake. . . . He waited a minute or two without speaking . . . knocked very softly. . . . She was silent. . . . Again she heard him moving about in his dressing-room, and, after a little while, she heard him go out, passing along the back veranda. He did not return. It was dawn before Bridget dropped into the heavy morning slumber, which follows a night of weeping.

BOOK III

From the Point of View of Colin McKeith and Others

CHAPTER 1

When Lady Bridget awoke, it was then near the hour at which they ordinarily breakfasted. Finding, when she had dressed, that all was silent in the next room, she looked in.

It was empty, the bed had not been slept in, but there were signs that McKeith had got into his riding clothes and that he had packed a valise.

Maule was waiting in the dining-room, and Maggie, the serving maid, gave a message from McKeith that he had had his breakfast at the Bachelors' Quarters with Mr Harris and that they were both going to start for Breeza Downs immediately.

Bridget made no pretence of breakfasting. She told Maule to forage for himself, and, after swallowing a cup of coffee, made the excuse of household business – to see if the Chinaman had put up his master's lunch – if the water-bags were filled – what were to be the proceedings of the day. She had a hope that McKeith might say something conciliatory to her before he left. The remembrance of that disregarded appeal – the word 'Mate' to which she had given no response, weighed, a guilty load, upon her heart.

But she was sore and angry – in no mood to make any advance or stoop to self-justification. He was outside the store, where Ninnis was weighing rations for Harris, and McKeith's and the Police Inspector's horses, ready saddled, with valises strapped on, were hitched to the paling.

Harris sulkily touched his helmet to Lady Bridget, but McKeith had his back to her and seemed wholly absorbed in some directions he was giving.

'You'll see to it, Ninnis, that six saddle-horses are kept ready to run up, in case the Pastoralist Executive sends along any message that's got to be carried down the river – there's that lot of colts Zack Duppo broke in, they'll do. And you can get in Alexander and Roxalana from the Bore pasture, in case the buggy should be wanted – and one or two of the old hacks that are spelling out there. Of course, her ladyship's horse mustn't be touched, and you'll see Mr Maule has a proper mount if he wants it – the gentleman who'll be here for a bit – a friend of her ladyship's from England – you understand. You'll keep on those new men for the tailing mob, though I'm not sure they mightn't be Unionists in disguise. Anyway, Moongarr Bill is a match for them. . . . And you'll just mind – the lot of you – that it's my orders to stockwhip blacks off the place, and that if any Unionist delegates show their faces through the sliprails they're not allowed to stop five minutes inside the paddock fence.'

'Right you are, Boss,' responded Ninnis, and there was a change of grouping, and McKeith strode out to the yard to look into some other matter, all without sending a glance to his wife.

Presently Moongarr Bill came up, chuckling mysteriously, 'Say, Boss, I believe there's one of them dashed organising chaps coming down now from the top sliprails.' And as he spoke, a man rode to the fence, harmless enough looking, of the ordinary bush type.

He was about to get off his horse in the assured manner of a bushman claiming the usual hospitality, but McKeith – big and grimly menacing – advanced and held up his hand.

'No, wait a bit. Don't unsaddle. I'd like first to know your business.'

'I'm an Organiser,' said the man defiantly, 'and I'm not ashamed of my job. Trades Unions are lawful combinations, and I've come to have a talk with your men. . . .' He ran on with professional volubiliity. 'My object in going round your district is to bring about a peaceful compromise between employers and employed – Do you see. . . . ?'

'Stop,' thundered McKeith. 'I'd have you understand that there's an organiser on this station already. *I'm* the Organiser here, and I'm not taking stock in Trades Unions at present.'

'But you'll let me have a talk with your men? No harm in that.'

'No, you don't,' said McKeith.

'Well, I can spell my horse an hour or two, can't I?'

'No, you can't. You'll ride off my station straight away.'

'I've been off tucker since yesterday,' said the man, who seemed a poor-spirited creature. 'Anyhow, Boss, you'll give me something to eat.'

'Yes, I'll do that.' The laws of bush hospitality may not be violated. Food must be given even to an enemy – provided he be white. McKeith called to the Chinaman to bring out beef and bread. A lump of salt junk and a hunk of bread were handed to the traveller.

'Now you be off, and eat that outside my paddock,' said McKeith. 'See those gum trees over there? You can go and organise the gum trees.'

The man scowled, and weakly threatened as he half turned his horse's head.

'Look here, Boss, you'll find yourself the worse for this.'

'Shall I. In what way, can you tell me?'

'You'll find that your grass is burned, I daresay.'

'I'm obliged to you for the hint. I'll take precautions, and I'll begin by shepherding you straight off my run,' said McKeith. 'Harris, if you're ready now, come along here.'

The Police Inspector stepped off the store veranda, where he had been standing, a majestic and interested onlooker. The Organiser – after all, a mere man of straw, crumpled under his baneful stare.

'You can't give me in charge – you've got no warrant – I've done nothing to be given in charge for.'

'Some of your people have, though, and here's a bit of information for any skunk among your cowardly lot,' said McKeith. 'I've offered one hundred pounds reward for the scoundrels who cut my horses' throats and robbed my drays on the road to Tunumburra. There's a chance for you, if you're mean enough to turn informer.'

'I know nothing about that,' said the Organiser.

'Eh? Well, if my grass is burned, I shall know who did it, and so will this Police Inspector. And I am a magistrate, and will have you arrested. Get on your horse, Harris, we'll start at once, and ride alongside this chap till he's over my boundaries.'

Harris unhitched his horse and mounted, but not sooner than McKeith was he in the saddle. Then McKeith looked at last towards the veranda where Bridget stood, white, defiant, with Maule at the French window of the dining-room just behind her.

McKeith took off his hat, made her a sweeping bow, which might have included his guest, turned his horse's head and rode in the direction of the sliprails, Harris and the sulky Organiser slightly at his rear.

Bridget never forgot that impression of him – the dogged slouch of his broad shoulders – the grim set of his head, the square, unyielding

look of his figure, as he sat his horse with the easy poise of a
bushman who is one with the animal under him – in this case, a
powerfully made, nasty tempered roan, one of Colin's best saddle-
horses – which seemed as dogged tempered as its master.

Maule showed tact in tacitly assuming the unexpected necessity for
McKeith's abrupt departure – also that he had already bidden good-
bye to his wife.

Lady Bridget made no comment upon her husband's scant
courtesy to his guest when she rejoined Maule after an hour or two
spent in housewifely business. They strolled about the garden,
smoked cigarettes in the veranda, she played and sang to him, and he
brought out his cornet, which he had carried in his valise, being
something of a performer on that instrument.

A demon of reckless gaiety seemed to have entered into Lady
Bridget. Watching McKeith disappear behind the gum trees, she had
said to herself: 'I can be determined, too. I have as strong a will as he
has. He did not choose to say one regretful word. He was too
stubborn to own himself in the wrong. He left me in what – if he
believed his suspicion to be true – must be a dangerous position for a
woman – only it shall not be dangerous to *me*. I know exactly how far
I am going – exactly the amount of excitement I shall get out of it all.
Neither Willoughby nor he deserve an iota of consideration. I shall
amuse myself. So! No more.... But he can't know that. He has
never thought about *me*. He has thought of nothing but his own
cross-grained pride and selfish egoism. No man of ordinary breeding
or *savoir-faire* would have gone off like that!'

She forgot in her condemnation of Colin to make allowance for the
primal nature of the man; for a certain kinship in him with the loftier
type of savage, whose woman must be his wholly, or else deliberately
relinquished to the successful rival, and into whose calculation the
subtleties of social jurisprudence would not naturally enter.

Nor did she remember at the moment that Maule had been
described by her own relatives as a person of neither birth nor
breeding – a fortune-hunter – not by any means a modern Bayard.
He at least was a man of the world, she thought, and would
appreciate the situation. He had lost that touch of unaccustomedness
– she hardly knew how to describe it – which had often irritated her
in their former relation. In their talk that day he seemed much more
at home than she was in the world she had once belonged to. He
spoke of 'personages' with the ease of familiar acquaintance.

Apparently, he had got into quite the right set – a rather political set, she gathered. He told her that he had been pressed to stand for a well-nursed Liberal Constituency, and implied that but for the catastrophe of his wife's death he would now be seated in Parliament, with a fair prospect in the future of place and distinction. Of course, it was the money which had done it, she told herself, though he had undoubted cleverness, she knew, and, as he pointed out, his experience in a particular South American republic – very much to the fore just now in European diplomacy – stood to his advantage. His marriage had given him opportunity. He alluded without bad taste to his dead wife's generosity. She had left him her entire fortune unfettered. He was now a rich man. He explained that she had had none but very distant relations and that, otherwise, charitable institutions would have benefited. She had been a very good woman, he said – a woman with whom nine hundred out of a thousand decent men would have been perfectly happy. He let it be inferred that he was the thousandth man. His eyes, not his lips, told her the reason why.

Their talk skimmed the surface of vital things – the new awakening in England; the threatenings of a socialistic upheaval; his individual aims and ideas – she recognised her own inspirations. He spoke of his political ambitions. Suddenly she said:

'I wonder why you made the break of coming out to Australia – why you did not stay in England and follow on your career?'

'There are bonds stronger than cart ropes which may drag a man by force from the path he has marked out for himself. Surely you must understand?'

'Really, Mr Maule.'

'Why will you be so formal!' he interrupted impetuously. 'It is absurd. Women nowadays always call men they know well by a *petit nom*.'

'Do I know you well! I often think I never knew you at all.'

'That is what Lady Tallant used to say to me, latterly, about you and myself – that we never really knew each other.'

'Oh, poor Rosamond! It makes me miserable to think of her. You became friends, then – latterly?'

'She was very nice to me when she came back from Leichardt's Land. And besides, she was anxious for me to come out to Luke and help him a bit. . . . She told me about your marriage. She knew I could settle to nothing – of course, the world in general thought it was because of that tragedy – my wife's death – and the child – you understand?'

Bridget nodded slowly.

'Lady Tallant knew the truth – that I was tormented by one ceaseless longing – after the impossible. I fancy she thought that if I could realise the impossibility, I might get over the longing. . . . But – Bridget, it's no use pretending – I did try to do my duty. I think I succeeded, to a certain extent, in making my wife happy – but there was always the same gnawing regret. . . .'

'You must put all that out of your head,' she interrupted curtly.

'I cannot. A man doesn't love a woman like you, and, because she is married to another man, put her out of his head – in two years or ten – or Eternity, for that matter.'

She laughed joylessly. 'Eternity!' she scoffed.

They were in the veranda after luncheon, she swinging slowly in the hammock, playing with a cigarette, he smoking likewise, scarcely attempting to suppress the stormy feeling in his face and voice. For her, the crude brown-grey landscape rose and fell with the motion of the hammock, and jarred with the exotic memories he evoked. She had been called back to the varied emotional interests of her girlhood, and realised, in a rush, how deadly dull was life in the arid wastes of the Never-Never. Nothing more exciting than to watch the great parched plain, with the dry heat-haze upon it, getting browner every day, and the shrinking lagoon and its ever widening border of mud. Nothing, when she turned her eyes to right and left, but ragged gum trees and black gidia forest. What a dead blank wilderness it was!

She gave a little gasp as if for breath. He seemed to read her thoughts.

'Do you remember Rome – and the Campagna, that first day we went to Albano? And our walk through the woods down to Lake Nei? It was then I first knew that I loved you.'

'Will – if you are going to stay here you mustn't talk like that. It's not playing the game.' She spoke pleadingly.

'Does your husband play the game?' Maule retorted. 'Is it playing the game to leave you here alone with me, when he must know – or at least, guess – how things have been between us? Do you think I didn't notice yesterday that he suspected me – suspected us both? I should have been a blind mole not to see by his face and manner how he felt. Upon my soul, he would have no defence – if. . . .'

She stopped him with a gesture.

'I must ask you again not to discuss my relations with my husband; they do not concern you.'

'Do they not!' And as she rose abruptly from the hammock, 'I beg your pardon,' he added humbly, 'I will do my best not to offend again.'

He got up too and stood, his back against the veranda railings.

'Lady Bridget, you mustn't be angry with me. I suppose I am a little off my balance, you must remember that this is – for me, a rather staggering experience.'

'Shall we go for a ride?' she asked suddenly. 'I don't suppose you have much idea of what a wild western station is like.'

'Oh, I'm fairly well acquainted with life on big pastures,' he answered lightly, taking her cue. 'You would be surprised, perhaps, at the list of my qualifications as an "out-back squatter." I'm a bit of a rancher – had one in the Argentine – a bit of a doctor – a bit of a policeman – I was in charge once of a constabulary force out in British Guiana. That's where I got a rise off Harris – a bit of a law breaker, too – in fact a bit of everything. Yes, I should enjoy a ride round here with you immensely.'

'Then do you mind looking for Mr Ninnis, the overseer, you know.'

'Yes, I know Ninnis. Had a yarn – as he'd say – with him last night while your husband was talking to Harris. Ninnis doesn't get on well with Harris – another point of sympathy. We're quite friends already. Ninnis and I – he's been in South America, too.'

'You'll find him somewhere about the Bachelors' Quarters, and I'll go and put on my habit,' she said.

Lady Bridget appeared as Maule and Ninnis were finishing saddling the horses. Ninnis had stayed near the head station, and was keeping a sharp look-out for bush fires, he said. Otherwise, there appeared to be no elements of disquiet. Lady Bridget noticed with surprise that Ninnis seemed to defer to Maule, which was not his usual attitude towards strangers. She attributed this to a community of experiences in South America, and also to Maule's undoubted knack of managing men.

CHAPTER 2

——————•——————

They rounded the lagoon and skirted the gidia scrub. Maule was on a Moongarr horse, Bridget rode a fiery little chestnut. Maule had already had opportunity to admire the famous O'Hara seat. They had hunted together once or twice on the Campagna, that winter when they had met in Rome. It was difficult to avoid retrospect, but Bridget seemed determined to keep it within conventional limits. They found plenty, however, to talk about in their immediate surroundings. Perhaps it was the effort to throw off the load on her heart that made Bridget gaily confiding. She drew humorous pictures of the comic shifts, the almost tragic hardships of life on the Leura – how she had been left servantless – until Ninnis had got up Maggie from the Lower Leura – when the Chinamen decamped during the gold rush. She described the chivalrous *sundowner* who had on one occasion helped her through a week's washing; and Zack Duppo the horsebreaker, whose Christmas pudding had been a culinary triumph, and the loyalty of faithful Wombo, who had done violence to all his savage instincts in acting as house-servant until the advent of the Malay boy Kuppi. She told of her first experience of a summer out West. The frying of eggs in the sun on a sheet of corrugated zinc, so intense was the heat. The terror of snakes, centipedes, scorpions. The plagues of flies and white ants. Then how, during the servantless period, in utter loneliness and Colin's enforced absence at the furthest out-station she had had an attack of dengue fever, and no woman within forty miles of her.

'And your husband allowed this? But where was that barmaid-looking person who seems to keep house here for stray gentlemen – and, who has the yellow-headed and blue-eyed little boy?'

Bridget's lip curled.

'Mrs Hensor had accepted a temporary situation at an hotel in Fig Tree Mount – the only time I've regretted her absence,' and the musical laugh seemed to Maule to have acquired a note of exceeding bitterness. 'Perhaps you don't know,' she went on, 'that Mrs Hensor is a sort of Helen of the Upper Leura – though unfortunately as yet no Paris has carried her off – I wish there was one bold enough to do it. She had to be asked to take a change of air because there was rivalry about her between the buyer of a Meat Preserving Establishment and the chief butcher at Tunumburra. Fair Helen scorned them both. Result: The two buyers bought beasts elsewhere and, as you would understand, on a cattle station, butchers may not be flouted. Though I daresay,' Lady Bridget added with a shrug, 'if I could have had the butchers in the house – I draw the line only at Harris – and had sung to them and played up generally, I might have scored even off Mrs Hensor. But they wouldn't come until after she had gone and there was no further danger of a duel taking place outside the Bachelors' Quarters.'

Maule took her cue again and laughed as if the matter were one to jest about. But as he looked round, his face did not suggest merriment. Nor for that matter did the landscape. They were riding at the edge of the immense sandy plain, patched with brown jaggled grass and parched brambles and prickly lignum vitae – nothing to break the barren monotony but clumps of stunted brigalow and gidia, a wind-mill marking the site of an empty well with the few hungry-looking cattle near it.

Now they dipped into a scrub of dismal gidia.

'This is the most depressing country I have ever ridden through,' he said.

'You don't know what a difference three inches of rain makes,' she answered. 'Then the grass is green, the creeks are running, and at this time the dead brambles are covered with white flowers. But it doesn't rain. There's the tragedy.'

'The tragedy is that you – you of all women should be wasting your youth and beauty in this wilderness. How long is it going to last?'

She shrugged again, and for an instant turned her face up towards the sky. 'You must ask the heavens?'

'Meaning, I presume, that like most of the Australian squatters, your husband hasn't capital enough at his back to stand up against continued drought?'

'Precisely.' She looked at him, with her puzzling smile.

'But you couldn't have understood his position when you married him?'

'No, I didn't – altogether. But I should really like to remind you that I am not in the witness box.'

'I think you owe me the truth!' he said, passionately.

'What do you call the truth?' she asked, reining in her horse and meeting his eyes straight.

But she had to turn hers away before he answered, and he as well as herself was conscious of the compelling effect his gaze had upon her.

'I could have made you marry me if I had been strong enough to persist,' he said.

'Cannot any man do what he is strong enough to do – if he wishes it enough to persist?'

'I should have put it this way. If I had thought less of you and more of myself. But after what you said that day, when you jeered so contemptuously at the kind of environment in which, *then*, I should have had to place my wife – what could I do – except withdraw? But you suffered, Bridget,' he went on vehemently. 'Not so much as I did – but still you suffered. You thought of me – I felt it, and you must have felt too, how continually I thought of you. I used to try and make you think of me – dream of me. And I succeeded. Isn't that true?'

'Yes, it is true,' she answered in a low voice.

'Only lately, since I have been in the district, it has seemed to me that the invisible wires have been set working afresh. Isn't that true also?'

'Yes, it is true,' she said again, as if forced to the acknowledgment.

'Then, can there be any question of the bond between us? You see, it's independent of time and space! for you *were* sorry – you *did* care. That's the truth you owe me. If after – after we parted in that dreadful way, I had gone back, had thrown up everything, had said to you, "Come with me *anywhere*, let us be all in all to each other – on the slopes of the Andes, on an island in the South Seas – you would have come?" '

'I always told you,' she said with her puzzling smile, 'that the slopes of the Andes appealed to me.'

'Peru would have been more picturesque than this, anyway. Is that all I can get out of you – that grudging admission? Well, never mind, I am satisfied. You have owned up to enough. I won't tease you now for more admissions.'

'I have admitted too much,' she said gloomily. 'The curse of the O'Hara's is upon me. Almost all of them have gambled with their lives, and most of them have lost.'

She gave her horse the rein as she spoke, and they cantered on over the plain. After that, she resolutely forbade sentiment.

Mr Ninnis was gratified by an invitation that evening to dine at the Home, and came down in his best dark suit and his most genial mood.

Bridget sang. She had not been singing much lately. Colin's gloom over the evil prospects of squatting on the Leura re-acted upon her spirits. And besides, the piano had been attacked by white ants, and the tuner had not been so far up the river for a long time. It was inspiring to learn that Maule added to his gifts that of getting a piano into tune. Ninnis promised to rummage among the tools for a key that would serve.

Ninnis had never admired Lady Bridget so much as he did this evening. Certainly he thought her more flighty and incomprehensible than ever, but he could not deny her fascination. It seemed quite natural to him that she should be in high spirits at seeing an old friend from England, who appeared to know all her people. Ninnis had taken immensely to Maule. Beside Maule knew parts of the world where Ninnis had been. It was curious to see the American-isms crop out. Ninnis considered Maule a person of parts and of practical experience. He said to himself that the Boss had done wisely in leaving Maule at the head-station while they were short-handed. Maule showed a great interest in Bush matters – said he wanted to learn all he could about the management of cattle – thought it not improbable that he might invest money in Leichardt's Land. Ninnis agreed to show him round, and Maule begged that he might be made useful – even offered to take a turn with the tailing-mob, so that Moongarr Bill and the other stockmen might be free to muster more cattle.

Nothing was heard of the Blacks during the next day or two, but one morning Ninnis discovered that an old gun, which the station hands and the black-boys were allowed to use on Sundays for shooting game in the lagoon, had disappeared in the night. Circumstantial evidence pointed to Wombo as the thief. Cudgee owned to having seen him skulking among the Gully rocks. A deserted gunya was found near a lonely, half-dry waterhole in the scrub, and there were rumours of a tribe of wild blacks having passed towards the outlying country in the Breeza Downs direction.

No news came, however, of either racial or labour warfare. McKeith sent not a word of his doings, and Harry the Blower was not due yet on his postal, fortnightly round.

McKeith had been gone a week, and the time of his absence seemed like that sinister lull which comes after the sudden shock of an earthquake and the tornado that follows upon it. Then, one day, something happened.

All the men except the Chinamen were out. Moongarr Bill, Ninnis, and the stockmen on the run, while Maule – a book and a sandwich in his pocket – had gone herding with Joey Case and one of the extra hands.

A sense of mutual embarrassment had that day driven them apart. He had been afraid of himself, and she too had felt afraid. During these seven days she had rushed recklessly on as though impelled by a fatality, never pausing to consider how near she might be to a precipice. Whenever possible, she had ridden out with Maule and Ninnis, or with Maule alone. She found relief from painful thoughts of Colin in the excitement and emotion with which Maule's society provided her. She went with him on several occasions behind the tailing-mob, though ordinarily, she could not endure being at close quarters with cattle. But it interested her to see Maule ride after and round up the wild ones that escaped; to watch his splendid horsemanship which had the flamboyant South-American touch – the suggestion of lariat and lasso and ornate equipment, the picturesque element lacking in the Bush – all harmonizing with his deep dark eyes and Southern type of good looks.

To-day, she had preferred to remain at home alone. She had been pulled up with a startled sense of shock. Last evening when they were walking together on the veranda he had begun again to make love to her, and in still more passionate earnest – had held her hands – had tried to kiss her. She had found herself giving way to the old romantic intoxication – then had wrenched herself from him only just before the meeting of lips.

At last, she had realized the strength of the glamour. She fought against it; nevertheless, in imagination gave herself up to it, as the opium-smoker or haschisch-eater gives himself up to the insidious *fantasia* of his drug.

Yes, Bridget thought it was like what she had read of the effects of some unholy drug – some uncanny form of hypnotism.

For she knew that she did not really love Maule – that her feeling for him was unwholesome.

There was poison in it acting upon her affection for and trust in her husband. Maule made subtle insinuations to McKeith's detriment, injected doubts that rankled. There were no definite charges, though he would hint sometimes at gossip he had heard in Tunumburra. But he would convey to her in half words, looks, and tones that he had reason to believe Colin unworthy of her – that her husband had led the life of an ordinary bushman, and had fully availed himself of such material pleasures as might have come to his hand. The veiled questions he asked about Mrs Hensor and her boy, brought back a startled remembrance of the scene outside the Fig Tree Mount Hotel and Steadbolt's vague accusation. She had almost forgotten it – had never seriously thought about it. Yet now she knew the midge-bite had festered.

Could it be that there was a chapter in Colin's life of which she knew nothing? Was it not too much to believe that he had always been faithful to his ideal of the camp fire? Ah! Maule would have jeered at that – would have been totally incapable of understanding the romance of that dream-drive – a dream in truth. But how beautiful, how sane, how uplifting it seemed, compared with the feverish haschisch dream in which she was now living. Restless under the obsession, she wandered up the gully and, as she sat among the rocks, wrestled with her black angel – and conquered. Clearly there was but one thing to do. She must send Maule away at once before Colin came back. As for Colin, that trouble must be faced separately. Maule must ride back to Tunumburra – he knew the track. Or, should he wish to explore the district further, Harry the Blower was due with the mail to-morrow, and could guide him to any station on the post-man's route which might appear to Maule desirable.

Bridget knew that Maule would leave the tailing-mob before the other men that afternoon, and would probably come to look for her here. So having arrived at her decision and wishing to put off the inevitable scene as long as possible, she set forth by another route for the head-station.

CHAPTER 3

———————•———————

But she had only gone a few steps, when out of the gidia scrub, came Oola the half-caste, her comely face bruised, her eyes wild with grief and terror, her head tied up in a blood-stained strip torn from Lady Bridget's lacy undergarment, the gaily-flowered kimono hanging in dirty shreds upon her brown bosom.

'White Mary! Lathy-chap!' she cried. 'Plenty poor feller Oola. Plenty quick me run. Me want 'em catch Lathy-chap before pollis-man come. That feller pollis-man take Wombo long-a gaol. Mithsis' – the gin implored. '*Bujeri* you! – Mithsis tell pollis-man Wombo plenty good blackfellow. No take Wombo long-a gaol.'

'What has Wombo been doing?' asked Lady Bridget. 'Did he steal the gun?'

'*Yowi* (yes). Wombo plenty frightened long-a ole husband belonging to me.' And Oola dropped and knocked her head upon the ground, wailing the ear-piercing death-wail of the Australian native women.

'Oola, you must stop howling!' said Bridget, alive to the seriousness of the situation. 'Has Wombo shot your husband with our gun?'

'*Yowi*, Mithsis. That feller husband altogether *bong*' (dead).

From Oola's broken revelations Bridget pieced the story. It appeared that the tribe had followed in hot pursuit of the fugitives, and, knowing his peril, Wombo had sneaked up to the head-station in the darkness, possessed himself of an effectual weapon, and fled away with the gun. The offended blacks had discovered the guilty pair on the outskirts of Breeza Downs, and Oola's husband, with a company of braves, had attacked their gunya. Then – to quote Oola – 'that feller husband throw spear at Wombo – hit Oola long-a *cobra* (head) with *nulla nulla*. Him close-up carry off Oola. My word! Wombo catch him *pho pho*. Plenty quick husband belonging to me *tumble down*.' And Oola wailed anew.

'Where's Wombo now?' Bridget asked.

'Blackfeller *yan* (run) along-a pollis-man. Pollis-man close-up black's camp. That feller Harris catch 'im Wombo – fetch um long-a Tunumburra gaol. Mine think it stop to-night Moongarr. Close-up station now.'

Lady Bridget at once saw through the affair. Here was Harris taking a legitimized revenge on Wombo, and doubtless also on herself. Clearly, he had been patrolling the Breeza Downs boundaries in search of Unionist incendiaries, and seizing Wombo instead, had acted promptly without waiting for a warrant or consulting McKeith. Wombo would be charged at the township with theft of the gun and murder of Oola's husband. To a certainty he would be hanged if the matter ran its ordinary course. That it should not do, Bridget declared within herself – if she could by any possibility prevent it.

The half-caste woman and the white lady went swiftly through the gidia scrub towards the head-station. At the gully crossing, Maule, on his way back from the tailing-mob, overtook them, and dismounting, walked with Lady Bridget to the house. She forgot then all the scene of last evening, told him the black's story, begged him to help her in the rescue of Wombo.

He reflected for a minute or two.

'We're up against Harris,' he said, 'and Harris has a grudge against all of us. But Harris feels some respect for my knowledge of constabulary law, which, I take it, is pretty much the same in most countries where there are white settlers and native races.'

She looked up at him, letting him feel that she was relying on his astuteness and his strength. He went on:

'Ninnis is mustering with Moongarr Bill and the others, a good way off, and they're camping out to-night. . . . That leaves only Joe Casey and the other extra hand. Ninnis put me in authority here. Somebody has got to take command, and it must be either you, Lady Bridget, or myself. Perhaps I'm the best qualified of the two. . . .'

She laughed shakily in assent.

'Anyway, I fancy that I know how to deal with this sort of affair better than you do,' he said. 'Will you let me manage it my own way?'

She nodded.

'I suppose I may assume that your husband left me in a position of some responsibility. And if I seem to be taking too much on myself – or, on the other hand, deferring too much to Harris, you'll trust me and not interfere?'

There was no time for discussion, had she wished to go against him. Oola was shrieking and pointing frantically to the track down from the upper slip rails, along which Harris and his prisoner were to be seen riding.

The Police Inspector, uniformed, burly, triumphant, exhaled the Majesty of the Law as he rode slightly in advance leading the black-boy. Now, as they pulled up at the fence, Wombo presented a sorry spectacle – a spear wound in his left shoulder, a spear graze on his leg, his wrists handcuffed and his feet tied to the stirrup-iron with cords so tight that they cut into his tough, black flesh.

Harris dismounted, tied Wombo's horse securely to the veranda post and then made his statement which coincided with Bridget's idea of what had happened. It was too late to push on to Tunumburra. He proposed to lock up his prisoner at Moongarr for the night. Could he have the hide-house?

Not long before, the Police Inspector had locked up a horse stealer, whom he had in charge, in the hide-house for a few hours while he took a meal.

To Bridget it seemed an irony that Wombo should be imprisoned in the very room he had so lately shared with his stolen gin.

She was quivering with indignant pity at sight of the sores on the black boy's legs made by the raw hide thongs, and Oola, who had crept up the off side of the black-boy's horse, was wailing anew. Maule checked with a look the angry protest on Lady Bridget's lip and answered the Police Sergeant in her stead.

'Why, certainly. I'm sure her Ladyship won't object. You'll let me see to that for you, Lady Bridget,' and, as she bowed her head, he addressed Harris again. 'Mr Ninnis and most of the others are camping out to-night on the run, and I seem to be the only responsible man in the place – of course you know that Mr McKeith asked me to stop and help look after things for Lady Bridget if necessary.' Then he complimented Harris genially upon his zeal. 'You've got your warrant, I suppose,' he asked incidentally.

The Police Sergeant looked a little uncomfortable.

'Well, fact is, I wouldn't waste time going back to Breeza Downs head-station for that. Mr McKeith's there and they had a bit of an alarm. Those Unionist skunks tried to fire the shed one night, but no particular damage was done, and they've dispersed. But Windeatt is in such a fright of their making another attempt on his head-station that he's pushing the imported shearers on with the shearing for all he's worth, and keeps any man he can get hold of on guard night and day round the house and sheds, while I and my lot have been doing a bit of riding after the Unionists. . . . Now, if you please, we'll have the key of the hide-house,' concluded Harris. 'I'd like to get my prisoner stowed away safe before I take an hour's spell myself. I'm pretty well knocked up, I can tell you. No sleep at all last night watching that nigger who was tied up to a gum tree, and I've been in the saddle all day.'

Maule proffered the usual refreshment with a deprecatory reference to Lady Bridget, who stood stonily apart. Then on pretext of getting the key of the hide-house, he had a few words with her in the office.

'I'm going to take care of this,' he said, as she gave him the key of the padlock which secured the hide-house door, and he forthwith fastened it to the ring of his watch-chain. 'Of course you want the black-boy to escape?'

'I shall let him out myself,' she answered.

'That would only make McKeith more angry. I have a better plan, in which you need not be implicated.'

'I would rather do it myself,' she said. 'I'm not afraid. If it had been possible, I would have cut those horrible thongs straight away and let the poor wretch get into the bush. He'll be safe at the head of the gully in the gidia scrub.'

'I promise you that he shall be safe in the gidia scrub before sunrise to-morrow. Trust me.'

She shook her head. 'But I can't take services from you, after. . . .' she began hastily and then stopped.

'You call that a service! Yes – to humanity, if you like. Oh, I know. After yesterday evening. *Now*, you blame me for being true to myself. . . . All that has got to be settled between us, Bridget – for good and all. I thought it out as I rode behind the tailing-mob to-day. But for the moment,' he fingered the key agitatedly, 'Bridget, you *must* let me do this thing for you. Don't refuse me that small privilege, even if you deny me all others.'

She wavered – yielded. 'Very well. You can manage it better than I could. So I will accept this last favour.'

'The first, not the last. What have I done but cause you pain? . . . If you knew the torture I have been going through. . . .' He checked himself. She was staring at him, half frightened, half fascinated.

'No, no. There must be an end.'

'Yes. There must be an end. Later on, we'll decide what the end is to be.'

He went out to the veranda carrying the key. Bridget did not follow him. She had no power either to resent or to compel him. She sat waiting. When, after about a quarter of an hour, he came back, she was still in the office as he had left her, seated by the rough table on which were the station log, the store book, and branding tallies.

He came in triumphantly, exhibiting the key.

'Harris wanted to take possession of this. It was lucky I had put it on my chain. However, he's satisfied that Wombo is securely locked up and an extra glass of grog and a hint that, as he hasn't provided himself with a warrant there's no obligation on him to stand over his prisoner with a loaded gun, eased his mind of responsibility. The man is in a beast of a temper though, he evidently expected to be entertained down here. I hope Mrs Hensor will give him a good dinner. He insists on sleeping in the little room off the store veranda where he says he can keep watch on the hide house. I suppose it's all right?'

Bridget nodded. 'I'll tell Maggie.' Maule asked for ointment with which to dress the black-boy's wounds and abrasions, and she gave it and left him.

The afternoon was drawing in. Then came the sound of the herded beasts being driven to the yard at sundown and, by-and-by, of Joe Casey's stockwhip as he got up the milkers. The shorthandedness and disturbance of Harris' arrival made everything late, and the goats which should have been penned by now, were busy nibbling at the passion vines on the garden fence. But all this made little impression on Bridget's preoccupied brain. She had the thought of that coming interview with Maule before her. Oola's continuous wailing was an affliction, and she gave the half-caste a blanket and some food and told her to camp on the further side of the hide house where, with eyes and ears glued by turns against the largest chink between the slabs, she might see and speak to the prisoner.

CHAPTER 4

———————•———————

Maule's and Lady Bridget's *tête-à-tête* dinner was an embarrassed meal, with Kuppi and Maggie hovering about the table. The man's eyes said more than his lips, and the woman sat, strained and silent, or else uttered forced commonplaces.

They were alone at last on the veranda, with night and the vast distances enfolding them. The air was close and hot, the sky banked with storm clouds, and, occasionally, there were flashes of sheet lightning and low growls of thunder. Before long the head-station was very quiet. Harris had inspected the hide-house and, having assured himself of the safety of his prisoner, had retired to the veranda room, making a great parade of keeping his door open, his gun loaded, and his clothes on, ready for any emergency. Joe Casey had gone to his hut, the Chinaman and the Malay boy to theirs, and Maggie, the woman servant, to her own tiny room wedged in between the new house and the kitchen wing.

But it was still early. At that hour, Maule laughingly reminded Lady Bridget, the dining world of London would scarcely have reached the dessert stage.

She would not waste time on banalities.

'I've been waiting to tell you something. My mind is quite made up. I can't go on like this any longer. You must go away to-morrow.'

'To-morrow!' he echoed in dismay.

'Yes. I've thought it out. You don't know the country, but the mailman will be here to-morrow, and he can show you the road.'

'You are very kind. . . . Why are you so anxious to get rid of me?'

'Surely you understand. You made me a scene yesterday. You'd go on making me scenes.'

'And you?'

She gave a hard little laugh. 'Oh! I – don't want to play any more.'

'You call it play! To me it's deadly earnest. I let you go once. I do not mean to let you go again.'

'But you are talking wildly. Don't you see that it is impossible we can be friends.'

'Oh! that I grant you. We must be everything to each other – or nothing.'

In spite of her cold peremptoriness he could see that she was deeply agitated. That fact gave him courage. His voice dropped to the tender persuasive note which had always affected her like a spell.

'My dear – my very dearest. . . . We made a great mistake once. Let us forget that. Death has opened the gate of freedom – for me, at least – and I can only feel remorseful thankfulness. We have again a chance of happiness. We will not throw it away a second time.'

'You seem to forget that if you are free *I* am married.'

'What a marriage? Call it a mad adventure.'

'That may be,' she said bitterly. 'But it doesn't alter the fact that I did care very much for my husband.' She brought out the last words with difficulty.

'*Did* care. You put it in the past tense. You don't care for him any longer. It would be astonishing if you did. One has only to see you together. . . . Oh, Biddy, it was so like you to rush off to the other side of the world, and ruin your life for the sake of some strange impracticable idea! I can follow it all. . . .'

'You are mistaken,' she put in.

'I think not. You married in a fit of revulsion against the conditions in which you were living – the hollow shams of an effete civilisation – that's the correct phrase, isn't it? And – well, perhaps there was another reason for the revulsion. . . . And you thought you had found the remedy for it all. Oh! I admit that he is very good looking, and, of course, he worshipped you – until he had you secure, and then he reverted to the ways of his kind. "Nature's gentlemen" usually do. . . .'

'Be silent, Will,' she exclaimed vehemently. 'You don't understand.'

'My dear, your very anger tells me that I do understand. Why! naturally your imagination was set on fire. The Bush was painted to you in its most glowing colours. No doubt, as you said, it's a Garden of Eden in good seasons. Wonderful vegetation, glorious liberty – no galling conventions – vast spaces – romance – and the will o' the wisp wealth of the Wild. Confess now . . . are not my guesses correct?'

'Yes – partly.' She spoke with reluctance. 'But I remember that *you* used to talk to me about the joys of the Wild,' she added with sharp irony.

'Oh, yes, I know it all. I've been there myself. And it's only when El Dorado proves a delusion that one begins to hanker – I did before I met you – for the advantages of civilised existence.'

'Well, you have secured those. Why not go and enjoy them as I'm asking you to do.'

'They have no value for me, unless I may share them with you. Bridget, I can give you everything now that you once asked for.'

'With your wife's money?'

He drew back sharply. 'Ah! You *can* hit a man!' and there was silence for a few minutes. Then he leaned closer to her, and his fingers touched the gold cigarette case which lay on the arm of the squatter's chair in which she was sitting. He went on in a changed manner.

'Poor Evelyn left her fortune to me, knowing the truth. She was a noble-souled woman. I was not worthy of her. But unworthy as I may have been, Bridget, I deserved better of my wife than your husband deserves of you. At least, I did not deceive her.'

'What do you mean? Colin did not deceive me. That, at all events, is not one of his faults towards me.'

'Has he told you, then, why he keeps on his station that insolent woman and her yellow-haired blue-eyed boy?'

Bridget started visibly. He saw that his shaft had struck the mark. But she answered calmly:

'I don't know what you want to imply. I thought you knew that Mrs Hensor's husband was killed on one of Colin's expeditions, and that he looked after her and her boy on that account.'

'Oh, yes, I've heard that story. But it seemed common gossip at Tunumburra that there was another – less creditable – explanation.'

She turned fiercely upon him. 'You have no right to make such an abominable accusation.'

'I only mention what I heard. I went about a good deal there in bar saloons, and to men's gatherings. Naturally, I was interested in the district where, by the way, McKeith does not appear to be over popular. Of course, I attached no great importance to the gossip then. It only made me wonder. Oddly enough, to-day when I was out with the tailing mob, one of the men repeated it – I need not say that I stopped him. He said he'd had it as a fact from a man who was a long time in your husband's employ – a man called Steadbolt.'

Again the scene in front of Fig Tree Mount Hotel flashed before Lady Bridget, and Demon Doubt rose up clothed now in more material substance. Her voice shook as she answered, though she tried to be loyal:

'Steadbolt was discharged from my husband's employment. He is another of Mrs Hensor's rejected suitors. That speaks for itself.'

'Strange that Mrs Hensor should reject so many suitors without apparent reason,' said Maule.

Bridget did not seem able to bear any more. Her head drooped upon her hands, her shoulders heaved convulsively.

'I don't know what to do – I am alone. It's an insult to talk to me in this way.'

'I want to protect you from insult – I want to take you out of these miserable conditions – and there's only one way to do that,' he pleaded.

He took her hands in his and kissed them passionately. 'Oh, I love you. There's nothing in the world I would not do to make you my wife. Why should you hesitate? It breaks my heart to see you unappreciated, neglected, living the sort of rough life that might suit a labourer's daughter, but which is sacrilege for Lady Bridget O'Hara. A man had no right to condemn a beautiful, refined woman like you to such a fate.... Well there' – as she murmured incoherently, 'I'll not say any more about that since it hurts you. You see, I respect your wishes. I'll even go away at once, if you command it, and leave you to form your own judgment. I will stay in Leichardt's Town – in Sydney – anywhere – until you have decided for yourself – as I know you must do – how impossible it is for you to remain here. Then I will meet you wherever you please, and we will go to Europe together – bury ourselves abroad – wait in any part of the world you may choose, until the divorce proceedings are over, and we are free to marry. You need not be afraid of scandal, the thing can be kept out of the English papers. It's so far away that nobody will remember you were married to an Australian. Besides, anything of that sort is so easily got over nowadays. My darling, why do you look at me with those tragic eyes? It is not like the old Biddy to be a slave to Mrs Grundy.'

She had been listening, sitting rigid in her chair, her hands still in his, looking at him in a strange fixed manner, almost like a person in the first stage of hypnotism. Now she snatched her hands away and gave a sobbing cry.

'Oh, I'm not the old Biddy. I never can be again.'

'Dear love – believe me, when I promise you that you shall never have cause for regret.'

He would have taken her into his arms, but she drew herself back.

'Will, you don't understand. And I don't understand myself, I can't see things clearly. It's all been so sudden – Colin going away – you – everything. . . . I want to be alone. I want to find myself.'

He moved aside with a slight inclination of his head as if to let her pass. 'I told you that I would do anything you wish.'

'You mean that – really? Then I wish you to go away at once. You said you would leave me to decide for myself. I take you at your word, and I shall write to you, by-and-by. Promise me that you will go.'

'I have no choice. Your will is law to me. But understand, dearest – I am only waiting.'

'It's good of you not to want to worry and argue. . . . Don't you understand? I couldn't bear you to be here when Colin comes back. You must go to Tunumburra to-morrow.'

'Go to Tunumburra to-morrow?' he repeated blankly.

'It's on the way to Leuraville, and you can take the steamer from there. I will write to you in Leichardt's Town. Oh, it's quite simple. The mailman will be here early. You can leave a letter saying that you are recalled.'

'I understand.' Her definite planning gave him hope that she had already made up her mind, and that she would join him in Leuraville or Leichardt's Town. After all, that might be best. 'But I shall see you again. The mailman is not here yet. I have still a few hours respite.'

She made no answer at first. Then 'Good-night,' she said abruptly, and flitted like a small white ghost along the dim veranda.

'Lady Bridget!' His voice stopped her. It shook a little, but the manner was conventional, and she gained confidence from that and turned irresolutely.

'Lady Bridget. While we've been talking about ourselves, we've forgotten that unfortunate black-boy. I only want to tell you, that you may depend on your wishes being carried out. I shall go to my room and watch my opportunity. Trust me, that's all – in everything.'

'Thank you,' she answered simply. 'I do trust you.'

She came back a few steps, and he met her in the middle of the

veranda. In one of her swift transitions of mood a humorous element
in the situation seemed to appeal to her, and she said with a laugh:
'It's comical, isn't it?' The two tragedies, black and white – we two
here – those two out there!'

Just then the black curtain of cloud, that had been rising slowly
and obscuring the stars, was torn by a strong flash of chain lightning.
It threw up her face in startling clearness and he saw, in strange
blend with the conflicting emotions upon it, the wraith of her old
whimsical smile.

He did not answer her laugh. In truth, the man's nature was stirred
to a more deep-reaching extent perhaps than ever in his life before. It
may have been the flash of lightning recalling a momentary flash of
illumination that had once shone upon his own soul.

That had been when he was kneeling by the bedside of his dying
wife, and her last words had revealed to him a magnanimity of
devotion for which he had been wholly unprepared. He had thought
her merely amiable and stupid – except in her love for him – and his
sentiments towards her had been a mixture of boredom, and the
tolerant consideration due to the bestower of substantial benefits.
Nevertheless, she had awakened, during a spasm of remorseful self-
abasement, some nobler quality latent in the man.

And now – as that flash of lightning illuminated Bridget's face and
made him keenly sensitive to the charm of her personality – her
wayward fascination, her inconsistencies, her weakness, her temperamental craving for dramatic contrast, her reckless toying with
emotion – by a curious law of paradox, there came back upon
Willoughby Maule that scene with his dying wife, and he had again
the flashing perception of something sacred, unexplainable, to which
his own nature could not reach.

It sobered him. He had had the impulse to snatch her to his breast,
to seal the half-compact with a lover's kiss, so passionate that the
memory of it must for ever bind her to him.

But the impulse was past. They stood perfectly silent, stiff, in the
interval – it seemed a very long one – between the lightning flash,
and the distant reverberation of thunder which followed it.

Then he said mechanically, like one walking out of a dream?
'There's going to be a storm. Are you frightened?'

'No,' she answered. 'I'm never frightened of storms!' – and added,
'besides, Colin would be so glad of rain.'

Before he could reply, she had glided away again and he was alone.

He thought it strange that she should be thinking of her husband and his material interests just then.

CHAPTER 5

───────────●───────────

It must have been a little while after midnight when Bridget was awakened by more thunder and lightning and a confused tornado of sound. She had been dreaming that Harris was throwing her from the gully cliffs on to the boulders in its bed – only it seemed to her bewildered senses that the boulders rose towards her instead of her descending to meet them. Next she discovered that rain was pattering on the zinc roof, and that the violent concussions she felt beneath her must be due to the horns of goats knocking up against the boards of her bedroom. Ah! she thought, the men had forgotten to pen the goats, and they were sheltering from the rain in the open space under the floor of the house. There could be no more sleep for her that night, unless they were dislodged.

She waited through the din until there came a lull in the storm, then got up and put on her shoes and a waterproof coat over her nightdress. It was not the first time by any means that, when sleeping alone, she had been obliged to rise and drive away stray animals that had been inadvertently allowed means of entrance.

She went out to the back veranda, which was connected by steps with the verandas of the other two wings. The moon was full and shed occasional pale gleams through the scudding clouds. The close heat had given place to a chill wind and the rain came down intermittently but in no volume – it could not make much difference to the parched earth. There was not a light visible anywhere. The goats were still making a noise under the house.

Lady Bridget got a stick from a heap of sandal-wood boughs stacked against the veranda, and passing to the front, where the piles supporting the house were higher, proceeded to belabour an elderly nanny, who, with her mate, was now nibbling twigs of the creepers.

But she was surprised to see only two or three goats, she had thought there must be many more. The animals were refractory, and her beatings of no avail. Now, suddenly, she was seized with a fit of nervous shivering and realised that she felt physically ill. It was of no use for her to try and drive off the goats. She sank down on the veranda steps of the Old Humpey, and afterwards thought she must have fainted.

The sound of Maule's approaching footsteps and his alarmed ejaculation seemed to bring her to herself. He appeared to have come round the back of the Old Humpey. He was horrified at the sight of her convulsive shivering.

'You mustn't stop here,' he exclaimed. 'I was afraid the goats would disturb you, and I've been getting them out as quietly as I could. Most of them are shut up in their fold.'

She saw that he was almost fully dressed. With an effort she controlled her terror, and asked:

'You've not been asleep.'

'Oh! off and on. I've been keeping my eye on Harris' room,' he pointed across the yard to the kitchen and store-building opposite – at the end of which Harris had installed himself – to the squat outline of the slab and back hide house. 'My ear, too,' he went on, 'for Harris' slumbers are neither silent nor peaceful. When he's not snoring, he groans and stirs, and the worst of it is that he's got his door wide open on to the veranda and his bed right across the window that looks straight at the door of the hide house. I thought I'd take advantage of the thunder, but it was no good. He was awake and looking out. Now he has lain down again, and as soon as I hear him snoring I shall try once more.'

A fresh fit of shivering seized Bridget.

'This won't do,' he said, and went hurriedly into his own room, which opened a few doors down on to the veranda, and coming back with an opossum rug on his arm and a glass of brandy and water in his hand, he made her drink the spirits and wrapped the rug round her. Presently the shivering ceased.

A moon-gleam between two clouds closing on each other showed her his eyes glowing with sombre passion. She saw that he was holding himself under stern restraint. Though where they were, the veranda running between the end of the Old Humpey and the new house, made a kind of passage so that they were in shadow, there was a possibility of watchful eyes discovering their whereabouts.

'Will you go back to your room, and I'll get rid of these goats,' he said, trying to speak in a matter-of-fact way. 'I suppose there isn't a yard where I could put them, nearer than their own by the lagoon.'

'I don't think so,' she answered dully, and without stirring from where she crouched upon the steps. When he urged her anew to go back to bed, she answered petulantly:

'Oh, do let me be. I like the wind and the rain – they're soothing. And I couldn't sleep now until I know that Wombo is safe in the scrub.'

He made no further protest, but set to work shepherding the goats. She watched him drive them out of the gate till his dark form and the piebald shapes he was driving before him were lost in the night. She knew that it would take some little time to pen them all securely in their fold. But the night was young yet.

From shivering, the fire of the brandy and the warmth of the fur rug had turned her temperature to fever heat. She felt keenly excited; the blood in her veins seemed boiling, and the occasional raindrops and moist wind were pleasant on her face. She had gone to the end of the veranda and stood there with long withes of the native cucumber vine that grew over the Old Humpey swaying around her in the breeze. There was not a light in the place. Even moon and stars were now veiled. Her brain raced round desperate and futile schemes for eluding the vigilance of the Police Inspector. She wished now that she had thought of asking him to dinner and putting opium into his coffee – that was the sort of thing they did in novels. She did not know that a less developed brain than her own was working at this moment to the same end, on an inspiration from the bush *Debil-debil*, or such savage divinity as watches over the loves of the Blacks.

She saw what at first she had thought part of the shadow of a neighbouring gum tree cast on the strip of grass that ran at the back of the Old Humpey. But the lesser shadow moved, halted, and the greater shadow was stationary and grew denser as the moon sailed again across a clear patch of sky.

Then Bridget realised that the moving shadow was the half-caste Oola, shrouded in the dark blue blanket she had given her, and that the gin had halted at the casement window of Maule's bedroom. Now, Oola, with her hands on the sill, curved her lithe body, drew her bare feet to the window ledge and dropped within.

Bridget ran along the grass to the window, and from there watched Oola move about the room and in the almost darkness fumble among the objects on the dressing-table. Then Bridget could hear the little click of the tongue and the guttural note of exultation a black tracker gives when he comes upon a trail. Bridget drew aside against the wall, so that Oola, again springing over the window sill, did not observe her. But Bridget saw the watch and chain with the iron key attached to it which the gin had stolen, and seized Oola's arm as the dark form crouched upon the grass again. The gin uttered a smothered shriek. Bridget took the watch from her hand, detached the key from the chain, and slipped watch and chain into the pocket of her coat, while Oola, clutching Lady Bridget's knees, pleaded chokily:

'Mithsis – you gib me key – no make im noise. No tell pollis-man me let out Wombo. My word! plenty quick he *yan* long-a scrub. *Ba-al* pollis-man catch Wombo. Mithsis – *bujeri* White Mary! You gib it key to Oola.'

The key was in Oola's hand. '*Ba-al* me tell,' whispered Bridget. 'you go quick.'

She, too, bent her body and followed Oola, who sped like a hunted hare round the corner of the Old Humpey. Now she wriggled in the shadow of the yard railings. Now she crept stealthily past Harris' window – and – oh! *Debil – debil* be praised! the Police sergeant's stertorous snoring was clearly audible.

Blessed, likewise, be the retiring moon and the sweeping clouds! Lady Bridget, every nerve a-quiver and the rushing blood throbbing in her temples, also crept noiselessly beneath the window in the wake of Oola, crawling like Oola, but more to the back of the hide-house into the shelter of its drooping bark eaves.

Bending cautiously round the slabs, she watched, as the gin, with a swift wriggling motion like that of a snake, drew herself along the sunken earth floor beneath the eaves and then, softly raising herself to the level of the padlock, put in the key. There was a muffled grating of iron under the gin's hand, as the padlock unclosed and the hasp dropped, then a creak of the door on its hinges, while it opened and shut behind the undulating shape in the aperture. Then a low throaty ejaculation – the black's call of warning. And now with a quickness incredible, the wriggling movement of two blanket-shrouded serpentine shapes round the hide-house – in and out among the grass tussocks and the low herbage, now hidden for a moment by friendly gum shadows in the dimness, now dark moving blurrs upon the lesser darkness, and now altogether invisible. . . .

Lady Bridget knew that in five minutes, once they could be upright again, the fugitives would have reached the gully, and after that the gidia scrub. Then security from the terrors of a white man's gaol would be almost assured to them.

Lady Bridget waited – waited, it seemed to her an eternity, in reality it was barely over the five minutes she had mentally given the two blacks for their escape. That five minutes had been full of alarms, and she could feel her heart thumping, so tense was the strain. She had to consider the possibility of Harris being awakened; also, of Maule's return and an attempt on his part to free the hide-house prisoner. Also there was the danger of the clouds breaking before she had done her work.

She heard a movement of the sleeper in his bed below the open window opposite. Harris might have been aroused, and perhaps have stirred without awakening. . . . But the snoring had ceased. . . . She did not think, however, that he could be fully awake. . . . Presently the snoring recommenced.

She crept very slowly along the earthen floor, drawing her hands along the slabs as she went. A splinter from one of them ran into her finger – but that did not matter. Now she touched the door, which lay back towards her, for the blacks had not waited to close it. She pushed it very softly, holding her breath at the creak of the hinge and listening intently for the recurrent snore which sounded through the window only three paces from her.

At last the thing was done – the padlock fastened, the key turned in the lock, and now in her pocket. She dropped flat on the earth, her cloak drawn lightly between her knees, and wriggled snake-like, as Oola had done past Harris' windows, then pushed herself on hands and knees along the ground, squeezing her body against the palings of the yard, till she reached the Old Humpey on the opposite side. Once round that corner, she got on to her feet, feeling sick and giddy but intensely relieved. She leaned against the gum tree which had protected Oola, and now realised that it had been raining in a driving gust and that she was wet to the skin.

The bleating of a kid, which had been left under the house and had found its way into the yard, startled her anew. She thought that she heard sounds in the wing near the hide-house – steps on the veranda. Was Harris stirring? Had he discovered the flight of his prisoner?

She waited again till all was quiet. By this time, there was a watery radiance just overhead. She looked towards the lagoon, but there was no sign of Maule. She felt the shivering begin again, though her head seemed burning, and she could hardly think collectedly. Her chief idea was to get back to bed.

But she was able to reason to herself that Maule must somehow be informed of the escape. She did not think he could have got back yet to the spot where he had left her. Or he might come straight to his room and miss the key and his watch. In any case, these must be restored to the place from which Oola had taken them.

She lifted herself to the window-sill as Oola had done, and in a moment was inside the room. It had been an easy enough business, only that in clutching the window frame, the jagged end of the splinter she had run into her hand caught and tore her flesh. The room was of course empty.

She lifted a candle – which, with matches, stood on the dressing table – and put back the watch and chain, and the key now separate from them. That fact would show Maule that it had been tampered with. But she must find some more exact means of conveying what had happened. Premature action on his part might give the alarm. Her brain worked in flashes. She had vivid ideas, which in her fevered state she could not hold properly. She must write to Maule. A notebook that he must have taken from his pocket lay on the table also. She tore out a leaf – paused – She must write so that only he would understand. An accident might happen to the paper.

There must be no definite statement to implicate him or herself. Some words in French occurred to her. She wrote them down and continued the note in that language. At the close she begged him to act so that there should be no ground for suspicion – reminded him of his promise to go away on the morrow – said she would write to him at the Post Office at Leuraville. She did not sign the sheet, but folded it across – addressed it to Maule and laid it under the watch on the table.

A fresh spasm of shivering seized her. Suddenly she remembered the opossum rug she had left. She opened the door leading from Maule's room into the veranda, and went out. She stood bewilderedly, looking across the faint-lit yard to the dim veranda of the kitchen wing opposite, as she fought against the sick faintness that threatened to overcome her. Then she walked along the veranda to the place where she had parted from Maule. The rug was lying there, and she threw it round her, and waited on the steps with chattering teeth and shaking limbs.

In a minute or two, he joined her. She saw by the fitful moonbeams that he was wet and muddy – truly in a worse plight than herself. She could hardly speak for the rigor. Seeing her condition, he took her up in his arms, and carried her along the veranda towards her own room. The clasp of his arms, the warmth of his body, even through his wet clothing helped her to steady herself. She continued to tell him of the great achievement.

'Wombo has escaped – I saw Oola taking the key out of your room. Harris was asleep – snoring. She let Wombo out, and I locked the door of the hide-house again afterwards, and put the key back in your room. It's all right – nothing can be found out till the morning. They're safe in the scrub by now.'

'Well, I'm thankful for that at any rate,' he answered. 'But at this moment I cannot think of anything or anyone but you. My dearest – I'm so afraid of your being ill – what can I do?'

'Nothing. I have sal volatile in my room – stuff to take for a cold. I only want to get off my wet things and go to bed – I can sleep now. Don't be frightened about me.'

She staggered when he put her gently down inside her own door, but recovered herself courageously, lighted her candles, laughed at her own disordered appearance, bade him go at once and look after himself.

He kissed her hand reluctantly.

'Till to-morrow.'

She looked at him alarmedly. 'Will! But you have promised me. You are going away to-morrow.'

He did not reply. His eyes were roving round the chamber, dimly lighted by the two candles. He was observing the feminine details – the untidinesses so characteristic of her; the daintinesses, equally characteristic – all in such odd contrast with inevitable bush roughnesses. He noticed the silver and ivory on the dressing-table; the large silver-framed photographs – an autographed one of the Queen of Wartenburg – Molly Gaverick and Rosamond Tallant in Court veil and feathers, Joan Gildea at her type-writer – the confusion of books, the embroidered coverlet on the large bed, the bush-made couch at its foot upholstered in rose-patterned chintz on which she had seated herself.

'You have *got* to go,' she urged. '*Whatever* happens, you are leaving here with the mailman to-morrow. . . . Promise – on your word of honour – that *nothing* shall hinder you.'

'Of course, I shall keep my promise, though it breaks my heart to leave you like this. But I know – I feel that the parting will not be for long. . . . Yes. . . .' as she slowly shook her head and a strange fateful look shadowed the feverish brightness of her eyes. 'I *couldn't* leave you if I didn't feel certain of that.'

'Oh, I'm tired out. I'm tired – dead tired –' Her face was ghastly, her lips like burning coals. 'I can't argue any more. And now it's good-night – good-bye.'

'Not good-bye. At least there will be time to-morrow for that.'

'You *must* go – Good-night.'

He left her, but waited in the veranda, reassuring himself by the sound of movements on the other side of the closed door. When all was silent, and the candles extinguished, he went back to his own room.

He saw on the dressing-table his watch and chain with the key detached beside them – a confirmnation of the truth of what Lady Bridget had told him. But she had forgotten to tell him of the note she had left also, and, naturally, he did not look for it. Had he known and looked he would have discovered that the note was gone.

CHAPTER 6

———————•———————

Lady Bridget always looked back upon the next few days as a confused nightmare. She awoke in the grip of fever – that malarial kind which is common in Australia – tried to get up as usual, but fell back upon her bed, faint and dizzy. Her brows ached. She had alternations of burning heat and icy coldness. There came active periods in the dull lethargy which is often a phase of fever, and from which she only roused herself at the spur of some urgent call on her faculties. One of these was Willoughby Maule's anxious message of enquiry conveyed by Maggie, to which she had the presence of mind to return the answer that she had caught cold, and was staying in bed for the present, but would no doubt be quite well shortly. Also that she was sorry not to bid him good-bye, but begged that he would not think of postponing his departure.

She heard as in a dream the sound of the mailman's arrival, and presently, of the saddling of horses in the yard, and then the *clop-clop* of their feet as they were ridden past her end of the house to the Gully crossing. There were two horses. So Maule had left the head-station with Harry the Blower, as she had bidden him do. She was conscious of relief.

She realised in bewildered fashion, that Maule was gone out of her life at Moongarr, and connected the sound of his horses' departing feet with the thud of Sir Luke Tallant's hall door, when he had left her at the first interview which had led to their final quarrel.

From that effort of memory she sank again into mental coma. Maggie took it to be natural sleep, and laid the mailbag just brought by Harry the Blower, on her mistress' bed to await her awakening. Much later in the day, on the return of Mr Ninnis and the other men from their cattle-muster, finding the bag still untouched, Maggie broke the seals at her mistress' dazed order, and having sorted out Lady Bridget's letters, carried away the bag for Ninnis to take his own mail.

But Lady Bridget paid no heed to her letters, and thus it happened that for the time being, she was quite unaware of an event which was of great importance to her.

She had been scarcely even distantly conscious of the hue and cry, and general excitement at the head-station, when it was discovered that the prisoner had escaped. Harris had his own suspicions – it might be said, his certainties, but the man's crafty nature bade him keep his accusations for an opportunity when he ran less risk of being worsted. He meant to wait until McKeith's return. Meanwhile what he had not been prepared for was Willoughby Maule's departure with the mailman before he himself came back from an unsuccessful hunt after the fugitives. That move had lain outside his calculations. He had gleaned enough from Mrs Hensor, as well as from his own observation, to feel sure that Maule and Lady Bridget were in love with each other, and he had never supposed that they would part so abruptly.

The head-station was very shorthanded in the absence of Ninnis and the stockmen, and Harris had been obliged to go out by himself on the man-hunt. He did not know the country at the head of the gully, where he concluded that Wombo was hiding, and lost himself in the gidia scrub. Thus, he was in a very disagreeable temper, when he at last arrived at the Bachelors' Quarters.

To Lady Bridget the day passed, and all the seemingly distant noises of it, like a phantasmagoria of vision, sound, impressions – the echoes of station activity; the Chinamen's pidgin English as they weeded the front garden; Tommy Hensor's voice when he brought the cook a nestful of eggs some vagrant hen had laid in the grass-tussocks, the men going forth with the tailing-mob – and at intervals the scorching recollection of that hinted scandal concerning Colin and Mrs Hensor of which Maule had told her. . . . Horrible . . . unbelievable . . . and yet. . . .

Then, after a long while, with lucid breaks in the dreamy stupor, she heard the roar of Ninnis' incoming mob of wild cattle from the range. She could even wonder whether he had been able to muster that herd of five hundred or so for the sale-yards. She knew that her husband was counting upon the sale of these beasts – probably at £6 a head – to enable him to fight the drought, by a speedy sinking of artesian bores. She felt herself reasoning quite collectedly on this subject, until the roar of beasts turned into the roar of the mighty Atlantic, breaking against the cliffs below Castle Gaverick. . . . She saw the green waves – real as the heaving backs of the cattle – alive, leaping. . . . And she herself seemed tossed on their crest . . . she saw and felt the cool embrace of the wave-fairies she had once tried to paint for Joan Gildea's book. . . . Oh! she had never fully appreciated the strength of that now inappeasable longing for the Celtic home, the Celtic traditions which had been born in her. She had never known how much she loved Castle Gaverick . . . how much she loathed the muggy heat, the flies and the mosquitoes now brought by last night's rain, the fierce glare beating upon the veranda, the sun-motes dancing on the boards. . . .

The appearance late that evening of Mrs Hensor, who having heard the mistress was ill, had come down partly from curiosity, partly from genuine humanity to see what might be amiss, was the next thing that roused Lady Bridget from her fever-lethargy.

'Maggie told me you'd been out in the rain last night, and had caught cold, and I thought Mr McKeith would wish me to ask if I could do anything,' Mrs Hensor said.

Lady Bridget sat up in bed, for the moment her most haughty self.

'Thank you; but there's no occasion for you to trouble, Mrs Hensor. I would have sent for you if I had required your services.'

'And I'm not aware that I was engaged to give them,' snorted Mrs Hensor. 'It was out of consideration for Mr McKeith that I came. I've got quite enough to do at the Quarters, and I'm really glad not to have to trouble myself down here – what with Mr Ninnis wanting extra cooking, and Mr Harris in such a rage over Wombo's getting away – I'm wondering if *you* heard anything last night, of that, Lady Bridget? And Harris is put out, too, over Mr Maule going off with Harry the Blower, while he was hunting for the black-boy. However,' Mrs Hensor concluded, 'the master will be here to-morrow to see into the rights of things.'

'How do you know that the master will be here to-morrow?' asked Bridget sharply.

'Harry the Blower brought me a letter from Mr McKeith,' replied Mrs Hensor with malign triumph. 'I suppose he thought you'd be too busy doing things with Mr Maule to bother over the station affairs, and that Mr Ninnis might be out on the run – and so he wrote to tell me what he wanted done as he often used to before.'

Lady Bridget closed her eyes, and leaned back against the pillows trying hard to control the muscles of her face, and not to betray her mortification. Moreover, she was certain that Mrs Hensor had stated the exact truth.

'I should prefer to be alone,' she said, feeling the woman's eyes upon her.

'Then I'll go, as you don't want me,' returned Mrs Hensor. 'But if I was you, Lady Bridget, I'd take a dose of laudanum, and get myself into a perspiration, for I believe it's a touch of dengue fever you've got the matter with you.'

A touch of dengue in tropical Australia may be serious or the reverse – sharp and short and critical, or tedious and less dangerous. Lady Bridget's case was the sharp, short kind demanding prompt treatment. When McKeith came home the following day, he found her delirious, and incapable of recognizing him.

Worn out as was the strong man's frame – not only with wild jealousy and tortured love, but with sleepless nights of patrol work, days in the shearing-shed, sharp fighting with a second conflagration – fortunately put out before much damage had been done – and a final dispersion of Unionist forces, Colin never for one instant relaxed his watch by Bridget's bedside.

All night he tended her, fighting the fever as he had fought the fire at Breeza Downs, plying her with continued fomentations, dosing her with quinine, laudanum and the various medicines he had found efficacious. For never was a better doctor for malarial fever than Colin McKeith – he had had so much experience of it. When towards morning she fell into a profuse sweating, and he had to change and wring out the blankets in which he had wrapped her, he knew that the fever danger was past.

She awoke at mid-day from a deep, health-restoring sleep, so weak however, that her bones felt like water and her face looked as white as the pillow case. But her brain was clear.

She saw that there was no one else in the room, which was still in great disorder. The blankets, hot and heavy, were almost unbearable, but she had not strength to fling them off. It felt frightfully warm for the time of year and the air that came in through the open French window seemed to be blowing from an oven. The sky, as she glimpsed it from her bed between the veranda eaves and the railings, looked curiously dark and had a lurid tinge.

Lifting herself slightly, she became aware that Colin was in the

veranda with his back to her, looking out over the plain. The set of
his figure as he bent forward, with his hands on the railings and his
eyes apparently strained towards the horizon, reminded her of the
determined hunch of his square shoulders and the dogged droop of
his head when he had ridden away with Harris and the Organizer.

She called faintly, 'Colin.'

He turned round instantly and came to the bed. She stared up at
him, frightened at the look in his face. . . . Something dreadful must
have happened. She was too weak to go over coherently in her mind
the sequence of events and feelings. She only sensed a menacing
spectre, monstrous, terrifying. She could not realise her own share in
the catastrophe she felt was impending. She could not believe that
Colin could change so much in less than ten days. Everything had
come about with such incredible swiftness. His face looked haggard,
ravaged. The cheeks seemed to have fallen in. The features were
rigid as if cut out of metal. The whites of his eyes between the
reddened lids were very blood-shot and the eyes themselves seemed
balls of blue fire. There was not a shade of kindliness in them, only
the gleam of a fixed purpose which no entreaties would alter.

She could imagine that he might have looked like that, when, as a
boy he had beheld the mutilated bodies of his father, mother, sisters,
stretched stark, after the blacks had done their hideous work.

And it was true that he did feel now somewhat as that boy had felt,
for again to his tortured imagination that which he held dearest
seemed to be lying foully murdered before his eyes. She, his love,
had been ravished from him, and he could only regard her as dead to
him for ever more.

'Colin,' she gasped. 'What is the matter?'

The muscles of his face relaxed, it seemed automatically, as if
there were no soul behind. He laughed a dry ironic laugh. 'Never
mind. You mustn't speak.'

He felt her pulse, examined her as a doctor might have done – all
without a word, and straightened the blankets and pillows.

'You must have food,' he said, and went out. She heard him calling
Maggie. After a few minutes he came back with a tumbler of beaten
egg and milk, to which he had added brandy, and told her she must
drink it.

Her hand was too weak to hold the tumbler. He put one arm
under the pillow, raised her head and held the glass to her lips until
she had drunk every drop of the mixture. All this with no show of

tenderness or one unnecessary word. She needed the nourishment and stimulant, and after them felt better.

'I remember.... I must have been ill.... What was the matter with me?'

'Dengue,' he answered shortly.

'I was out in the rain.... I got a chill.... I remember.'

'Oh, you were out in the rain! ... I should have thought you could have done what you wanted without that.' The bitterness of his tone was gall-like. And again the ironic laugh.

She winced and drew her head aside. He took away his arm instantly from behind the pillow and straightened himself, looking down on her, still with that dreadful light in his eyes. She could not bear it, and turned her head away from him.

'Don't look at me.... I'm going to get up.'

'No, I think you'll stay where you are.' His voice broke slightly but hardened again. 'I won't talk to you. I won't let you speak a word yet ... that will come afterwards.'

'But I don't understand.'

'Better not now. I'll tell you this. You're through the fever. It won't come back if you do as I tell you – You understand something about dengue. You'll stop here till you're stronger. You've got to take the brandy, eggs and milk till you feel sick of it. To-day you'll have slops. I've told Maggie about preparing your food, if the fever comes back – it won't if you keep quiet – but if it does – hot bottles – blankets – laudanum – I've mixed the doses – until you get into a sweat. Remember that. And you'll have someone in your room to-night.'

'In my room – *You?* What do you mean?'

'It won't be me – I'm going away.'

'Going away – what is it?'

She noticed that he turned and looked at the sky.

'Why is it so dark – and the heat so stifling?' she asked.

'These damned Unionists have fired the only good pasture left on Moongarr. It's been burning since two o'clock this morning. I sent the men out. Now I'm going myself – to save what I can.'

He left the room abruptly. In a minute or two she heard him outside calling 'Cudgee ... Harris' – and then giving the order to saddle up. She got out of bed and tottered to the window. She could see now the wide range of the disaster. The lurid haze was spreading. The horizon shrinking, and the air was hotter than ever. The fire seemed still a long way off, but there was nothing to stop the flames if once they reached the great plain. The course of the river, here at best a mere string of shallow waterholes, was quite dry. The rain of the other night had been too insignificant and local to do any good. The brown mud-strip round the lagoon below, was not perceptibly diminished. She knew that the narrow water channels flowing from their one working artesian bore, must soon be licked up by the flames. And the Bore in process of construction, was at a standstill for want of workmen.

Bridget gazed out despairingly towards the shrinking horizon and upon the parched plain with the rugged clumps of dun coloured gum trees scattered upon it – the near ones looking like trees of painted tin, sun-blistered. The swarms of flies, mosquitoes in the veranda offended her. She disliked the cattle dogs mooching round with hanging jaws and slavering tongues. The ferocious chuckle of a great grey king-fisher – the bird which white people called the laughing jackass – perched on the branch of a gum tree beside the fence, made her shudder, because the bird's soulless cachinnation seemed an echo of Colin's laugh.

Ah! that was the bush, undivested of romance – hard, brutal, vindictive, in spite of the mocking verdure of her honeymoon spring. . . . And Colin was a part of the Bush. He resembled it. He too could be strong and sweet and tender as the great blossoming white cedar down by the lagoon, as rills of running water making the plain green – when his desires were satisfied. And he could be brutal and vindictive likewise, when anyone dared to thwart his will and defy his prejudices.

She staggered about the room, feminine instinct prompting her to freshen her appearance, to change her soiled, crumpled nightdress, to throw a piece of lace over her dishevelled head, to pull up the linen sheets which had been rolled clumsily to the foot of the bed, so that the blankets could be wrapped round her. But she sank again presently, exhausted, on her pillows.

In a short time McKeith came back, booted and spurred, and stood as before looking at her with forbidding sternness.

'You'd better have stopped quiet. I've told Mrs Hensor to come down and look after you. She knows what to do.'

Bridget cried out passionately: 'I won't have that woman in my room. How dare you tell her to come near me.'

'Dare! That seems a queer way to put it. However, you can order her out if you don't want her. There's Maggie – and I'm sending Ninnis back to-night.'

'When are you coming home?'

'I can't say. I've got things to do – and to think about.'

His words and his manner seemed to convey a sinister meaning.

'I see – you are angry about the black-boy. If you want to know I will tell you exactly what happened.'

He laughed again and his laugh sounded to her insulting.

'Oh, I know what has happened. You needn't tell me. I had some conversation with Harris this morning. I know *everything*; and now I've got to settle in my own mind how things are to go on.'

She went very white and repeated dully: 'How – things – are to go on?'

'Between you and me. You don't imagine, do you, that they can go on the same?'

'No,' she retorted with spirit, 'certainly they can't go on the same.'

Maggie had come along the veranda and was at the French window.

'Mr Harris says he's ready, sir, and the horses. . . .'

'All right.' McKeith went out of the door, but turned and paused as if he were going to speak to his wife. But he thought better of it and walked rapidly away – perhaps because she avoided his look.

She supposed that he was infuriated with her because of her part in Wombo's escape, and she thought his anger unjust. No doubt, too, he suspected Maule's connivance, and she knew that he was furiously jealous of Maule. But surely he would understand that she must have sent Maule away. What more can a wife do in the case of an over-insistent lover? And how should a husband expect an explanation when he had literally thrown her into her lover's arms, or at least had left her defenceless against his solicitations! Had he treated her differently after the Wombo episode in the beginning, she might have told him the truth about her former relations with Willoughby Maule.

As things had been, it was rather for Maule than for Colin that she found excuse.

She was bitterly hurt and offended against her husband. Oh, yes. He was right. They could never again be the same to each other. If he had come back penitent, pleading for forgiveness, overwhelmed with contrition at her dismissal of Maule, she might then perhaps have explained everything and they might have become reconciled.

But now, his vile temper, his insupportable manner, his dominant egoism made any attempt of conciliation on her part impossible. She had a temper too – she told herself, and her anger was righteous. And she also had an egoism that wouldn't allow itself to be trampled on. She had rights – of birth, of breeding, to say nothing of her rights of wifehood and womanhood for which she must insist upon respect. If he would not bend to her, even to show her ordinary consideration and courtesy, then she would not lower her pride one iota before him.

Thoughts of this kind went through her mind as she lay smarting under the burning sense of outrage, until the reappearance of Mrs Hensor. Then, the new effort she made in sending away the woman exhausted brain and body and left her with scarcely the power to think – certainly not to reason.

CHAPTER 7

───────●───────

But Lady Bridget did not know what had followed upon her husband's home-coming. She had not been in a condition to realize how all night through he had tended her, putting aside every other consideration, giving no heed to the affairs of the station, refusing to see the Police Inspector who had sent in an urgent message soon after his arrival.

Only when turning for a moment to the veranda and noticing the red glare in the sky, had he been startled out of his absorption in his wife's illness. In ordinary circumstances, he would have been on his horse in a twinkling and riding as for life to fight the worst foe a squatter has to face in times of drought. He knew that if the fire spread, it might mean his ruin. As it was, he rushed up to the Quarters to rouse Ninnis and send him with Moongarr Bill and all available hands to do what he could in arresting the flames. But he himself dared not leave Bridget till the fever was down, and the crisis past. That could not be till she had awakened from the deep sleep into which she had fallen.

With the sight of her in that sleep, however, the pull on his forces slackened, though he was still too strung-up to think of snatching even an hour's sleep for himself. He watched, alternately, the Bush fire and Bridget's face, thinking his own dour thoughts the while. Every now and then, he would creep on tip-toe to the veranda railings and gaze out upon the lurid smoke which it seemed to him was thickening over the horizon. When the sun was risen he washed and dressed and went up to the Bachelors' Quarters where Mrs Hensor was already about and gave him tea and food, which he badly needed. From her he learned a considerable amount of what had been going on at Moongarr. From the Police Inspector, a little later, he learned a good deal more.

Harris' manner was portentous; he asked for a private interview in the office, saying that he had stayed on purpose to see the Boss, because his tale was impossible to write. Then he told his own version of the capture and locking up of Wombo, taking blame on himself for having left the key of the hide-house in Maule's possession.

'But you see, Boss, he twitted me a bit about not having a warrant, and there's no doubt, wherever he's learned it, that the chap has got the whole constabulary lay-out at his finger ends – besides having the ear of the Governor and the Executive down in Leichardt's Town. He's got money too, no end of it. They were saying in Tunumburra that his wife left him a quarter of a million.'

'Go on – that's nothing to do with us,' put in McKeith gruffly.

'He's an old friend of her Ladyship's, I understand,' sniggered Harris.

'What the devil has that got to do with Wombo?' said McKeith furiously.

Harris drew in his feelers.

'I wouldn't swear that it had, Mr McKeith, and I wouldn't swear that it hadn't. All I know is, that Mr Maule had the key of the hide-house in his bedroom that night, and, being a close friend of her Ladyship's, he was no doubt aware that she didn't relish the notion of Wombo's being had up for theft and murder – I'm not saying who it was let out Wombo. It's a mystery I don't take upon myself to fathom – I'll leave that to you.'

'There's one easy solution of the mystery that doesn't seem to have occurred to you,' said McKeith. 'The gin Oola could easily have stolen the key – they're cunning as the devil – half-castes – and as treacherous – I know them – I've had my own good reasons for not letting one of them inside the fence of my head-station.'

'That may be – I can only say what I know, and you can form your own opinion.'

'Say what you know then – I'm waiting to hear. But be quick about it, man, I've no time to waste this morning.'

Harris began his tale – how he had watched at the window of his little room, till after midnight, his gun ready, his eyes glued on the padlocked door opposite; how overcome with drowsiness against which he had vainly struggled – 'for a man that's been pretty near two days and nights in the saddle may be excused if his eyes begin blinking,' Harris put it. He had dropped dead asleep – he confessed it – at his post. Then, how on awakening suddenly, for no apparent reason, all seeming quiet around, he had got up as he was, half dressed and in his boots – had stepped across to the hide-house, had found the padlock intact and, hearing no sound, had concluded the black-boy was inside safe asleep. How then, with a relieved mind, he had been going back to his stretcher, when the noise of a goat bleating had set him on the look-out from his veranda. How, presently, looking at the veranda opposite, he had seen the door of Mr Maule's bedroom open, and a woman come out, how she had stood a few moments facing him, with the moonlight straight on her, so that there was no possibility of his making a mistake. Harris paused. McKeith glared at the man, who, had he been quick at psychological interpretations, would have read an awful apprehension underlying the ill-restrained fury in the other's face. The question came in hoarse jerks.

'What – Who – Who was it you saw –?'

'It was the Lady Bridget, Boss. . . . I –'

Before he could proceed, a strong arm struck out and McKeith's hand clutched at the Police Inspector's neck.

'You hound! You contemptible skunk! Take back that lie, or I'll throttle it in your throat.'

Harris was of powerful build also, and, moreover knew some tricks of defence and assault. He freed himself by a dexterous duck of his head, and a sharp shake of his body, and stepped backward so that the office table was between him and his antagonist.

His face was scarlet, his bull's eyes protruded from their full sockets. But he was wary, and not anxious to provoke the devil in McKeith.

'Wait a bit,' he said thickly. 'If you'll keep your hands off me, and let me finish what I was going to say, I'll show you the proof that I'm not telling you lies – though you're mistaking my meaning in regard to her Ladyship. . . .'

'Leave her Ladyship out of it, will you,' McKeith snarled, his teeth showing between his tense lips.

'I would do that willingly, Boss, for there's no disrespect intended I can assure you. Only it means that this Wombo. business will have to be reported, and if you can help me to the right evidence – well, so much the pleasanter for all parties,' returned the Police Inspector craftily.

McKeith made a slight assenting movement of his head, but said nothing. His brows puckered, and he stiffened himself as he listened, strung to the quick, while Harris continued.

'Well – I did see – that lady,' – the volcanic gleam from McKeith's eyes stopped him from pronouncing Lady Bridget's name. 'I saw her come out of that room,' he jerked his thumb along the veranda. 'The moon was right on her just then. I saw her give a shiver – she'd been out in the wet. Then she walked up the veranda to where there's the covered bit joining on to the Old Humpey, and I noticed her sit down on the steps –'

'Stop,' broke in McKeith. 'If you were on the veranda over there, you couldn't have seen as far as the steps.'

'Right you are, Boss. But I wasn't waiting on the veranda. When the lady turned her back, I moved into the yard, and I was standing by that flower-bush' – Again he jerked his thumb, this time to the centre bed, and a young bohinia shrub covered with pink blossoms – 'If you try yourself from there, you'll find you can look slick through to the front garden. That's where I saw Maule step out of – I guessed he'd come round by the back of the Old Humpey. I guessed too, he thought she oughtn't to be sitting out there in the damp – She was shivering again – she'd put a rug that was lying on the steps round her. He just picked her up in his arms, and carried her right along, and when I stepped across I saw him take her into one of those rooms at the end of the front veranda. . . .'

A muffled growl, something like the sound a hunted beast might make when the dogs had got to touch of him, came from McKeith. Again he stiffened himself; his lips hard pressed; his eyes on Harris' face. The Police Inspector avoided his gaze; but he too was watchful.

'You see I was thinking of my prisoner, and wondering if there could be anything afoot about him. So as I knew there was nobody – then – in Mr Maule's room, I went back and looked in. I wanted to make sure, if I could, where the key of the hide-house might be. There was a candle left alight, and I saw the key right enough on the chest of drawers beside Maule's watch and chain. It never came into my mind then, that anybody could have used it. I noticed a bit of folded paper under the watch. That's it, Mr McKeith. There's the proof that I am not lying about what I saw.'

Harris had taken out of his breast pocket, a piece of newspaper in which was wrapped the leaf torn out of Maule's notebook, folded and addressed. He opened it out, and laid it on the office table in front of

McKeith, keeping his own stubby finger on one corner of the sheet.

Still McKeith maintained his difficult self-restraint.

'So you stole – a private communication that had been left in another person's room, and was intended for his eyes alone?'

'Come now, Boss. You know well enough that a constabulary officer who's up against tricks to release a prisoner has got to keep his eyes peeled, and mustn't let any clue to mischief escape him. How was I to know that there wasn't some plot to cheat the law? – How do I know that there wasn't? That's why I'm showing you the paper. I'm not a French scholar – I suppose that's French – and as I suppose you are, I'll ask you to translate what's written there.'

McKeith pushed aside the man's finger, and taking up the paper carried it to the window, where he stood with his back to Harris, spelling out Lady Bridget's hurriedly written sentences.

He seemed a long time in getting at the sense of what he read. As a matter of fact, he had only a limited acquaintance with any modern languages except his own. He had picked up some colloquial German, and once when laid up in hospital, had set himself to read Balzac's *Père Goriot* with the aid of a dictionary. Thus he had acquired a fairly extensive if somewhat archaic vocabulary. But Lady Bridget's veiled intimation of Wombo's escape couched in up-to-date and highly idiomatic French which would have been perfectly intelligible to Willoughby Maule, conveyed little to him beyond the fact of a secret understanding between his wife and a man whom he knew had once been her lover. That idea drove every other into the background of his thoughts. He did not care in the least how Wombo had escaped. It seemed clear to him that Oola had stolen the key after Harris had gone back to his room, while Maule and his wife were together – together in Lady Bridget's own chamber. The blood surged to his brain, and his temples throbbed as though they would burst. In the madness of his jealousy, the words of the paper, combined with Harris' revelations were damnatory confirmation of his wife's guilt. He felt now that he had foreseen what would happen, from the moment that he had surprised the look on Lady Bridget's face, when Maule had unexpectedly appeared before her. She had given herself away then. And, a little sooner, rather than a little later – as might have been the case had he not left them together – the inevitable had come to pass.

Yes, through the agony of that conviction now brought home to him, a dogged resolve formed itself in his mind – the determination not to betray himself or her. It beat upon him with insistent force. Though his goddess must be dethroned from her shrine in his heart, she should not be cast down for a vulgar brute like Harris to gloat over her shame. . . .

'Well, Boss,' the Police Inspector asked with affected nonchalance that bordered on insolence. 'Can you make anything that's satisfactory to you out of that?'

McKeith turned, Harris thought he was going to leap upon him in a fit of blind fury, and started up from hs seat by the office table. McKeith's eyes blazed, his taut sinews quivered; his face was now quite pallid, and the hand in which he held the piece of paper was clenched so tight that the veins stood out like thick cords, and the knuckles were perfectly bloodless.

But suddenly the pitch on his nerves was eased. His eyelids dropped, and when he lifted them, the eyes were quiet and intently observant.

He moved into his usual office chair.

'Sit down again, won't you, Harris?' he said, and Harris resumed his former place.

'What were you asking?' McKeith continued. 'Satisfactory to me – is it? Yes, perfectly satisfactory, thank you. . . . I'm only amused – as you see . . . to find that I was quite right in my suspicions.' And he laughed in what Harris thought a very odd way.

'Eh? I don't take your meaning.' Harris' manner was distinctly objectionable.

McKeith gave him a sharp look, and his teeth went over his under lip. Then, to the man's evident surprise, he laughed again, throwing his head back so that the muscles of his throat showed under his beard, working, as it were, automatically. It really seemed as if the man's mechanical merriment were no part of himself. He was, in fact, gaining time to propound an explanation which he did not believe in the least, but which happened to be almost the exact truth.

He answered with an air of ironic indifference.

'Well, you know, I wouldn't go in for the detective line, if I were you, Harris. You aren't subtle enough for it. You jump too quickly at conclusions which have nothing to do with the main point. In fact, you're a fool, Harris – a damned fool.'

Harris' puzzled expression turned to one of extreme indignation.

'Seems to me, Mr McKeith, that it's you who are – well, damned queer about this affair. I'm sure I don't know what you've got to laugh at. But if you've found out who let the black-boy out of the hide-house, I'd be glad to know, that's all.'

McKeith ceased from his mirthless laughing and his sarcastic bluff. He leaned forward, facing Harris with his hands on the paper which he had laid on the table before him. He picked up the other's last words.

'Yes, that *is* all. It's the only part of this note which concerns you. Well, I can tell you that it was the half-caste woman, as I thought, who let Wombo out of the hide-house. She stole the key from Mr Maule's room when *he* was asleep, and let Wombo out when *you* were asleep – a longer time perhaps than you imagined, Harris. The black-boy made for the scrub, and I suppose they were in too great a hurry to think of shutting the door. Oola sneaked back – they've got the cunning of whites and blacks put together, those half-castes – and no doubt she guessed there'd be a hue and cry directly the door was found open. So she locked it again – and brought the key to her ladyship.'

McKeith seemed to force the last words from between his teeth.

'Well, that's quite simple, isn't it?'

'Now, I shouldn't call it as simple as you make out, Boss. It appears mighty odd to me that the gin should have worried round after her ladyship when she might have sneaked back with the key to the place she took it from. And then there's all the rest – the putting the key back and fitting in times and all that. . . . Seems to me a bit too much of the Box and Cox trick – a sort of jig-saw puzzle, d'you see.'

Manifestly, Harris was endeavouring to square probabilities. McKeith still held himself in.

'I've given you the facts. You can figure out your details for yourself. I've my own business to attend to, and I must be off on it.'

He got up, and folding Lady Bridget's note, deliberately put it in his breast pocket. Harris stretched forth a restraining hand.

'Boss, I say – that's important – for my report, you know.'

McKeith's temper burst out.

'Damn your report. I'm a magistrate, and I've taken your report, and the blacks are in the scrub and you can go and find them for yourself if you choose. You have no warrant, remember. No, I'm not going to be bothered any more about that black-boy. What. . . . Not I – with a fire raging on my run, and not enough hands to put it out.'

'But her ladyship. . . .' spluttered Harris.

'Listen here you. . . .' McKeith's face and attitude were menacing. 'I came back to find her ladyship down with dengue as bad as could be. It was on her that night, and if she had to be carried to her room in a fit of shaking, what business is that of yours? Understand me, Harris. Don't you go mixing up my wife's name with this beastly black-boy affair, or you'll have to reckon with me – and I can tell you, you won't relish that reckoning.'

'There was no offence meant. I only wanted to do my duty,' protested the Police Inspector, cringing after the way of bullies.

'You'll find opportunity enough for doing that if you ride back to Breeza Downs and lend the Specials your valuable assistance in protecting the sheep-owners against the Unionists. And I might remind you, as I reminded that damned Organiser who's fired my run, that there's a hundred pounds reward still waiting for anybody who catches the men that robbed my drays and killed my horses.'

McKeith paused a moment before going out by the further door of the office which looked out on the plain.

'I'll leave you now to run up your horse and make your own arrangements. As soon as I can, I shall start to help in getting the bush fire under. You can arrest that Organiser if you are keen on arresting somebody. Send in when you're saddled up, and if I'm ready we'll ride to the turn-off track together.'

McKeith went back to his wife's room. She was still sleeping. Then it was that spasms of mortal agony began literally to rend the man. He left her side and seated himself on the bed in his dressing-room. He sat with his arms folded across his chest. His shoulders heaved. Deep dry sobs shook his huge frame. He would not let a groan escape from between his clenched teeth, but there was blood on his lower lip where he had bitten it in the effort to control himself. Presently, he heard a sound in the next room – a half moan – a name spoken. No, it would not be his name that she would utter first on her return to consciousness.

The man got up; stretched his long, lean frame, shuddering as if it had been on the rack. He drew two deep breaths, braced himself, wiped the blood from his lip, put on the stony mask which Bridget saw when she opened her eyes and found him looking down at her.

CHAPTER 8

———————•———————

NEXT morning, Lady Bridget was better and her mind clearer. There had been no return of fever, and, though the physical weakness was great and her temperature – had she taken it – would have been found a good deal below normal, her fierce determination not to remain helpless any longer gave her strength to get up and dress. She was not able, however, to do anything but lie in a half-alive condition in the hammock at the end of the veranda. All night the fire had blazed, but more fitfully, and this morning the lurid glare had died down. Only a murky haze, faintly red here and there, spread over the north-eastern sky. Small, isolated smoke-clouds rose above the stretches of forest, and an irregular-shaped tract of charred grass at the edge of the plain showed how far the flames had encroached upon it before they had been got under. One might well conceive with what almost superhuman exertions the beaters had at length accomplished their task. A large number of cattle had been driven by the fire on to the pasture beyond the home paddock – a pasture that had so far been carefully nursed in view of possible later necessity.

Bridget was bushwoman enough to comprehend the crippling effect upon McKeith's resources of this calamity, had she allowed her mind to dwell upon that aspect of affairs. But her mind was incapable just now of dealing with practical issues. She felt utterly weak, utterly lonely. Although she was glad Maule had gone, she missed his sympathetic companionship to an extent that she could hardly have thought possible.

As the hammock swayed gently at the slight touch of her fingers on its rope edge, her imagination drifted dangerously and her senses yielded to the old drugging fascination. He seemed as close to her as had been his bodily shape a few days previously. She was conscious of the pull of his will upon the invisible cords by which he held her. If it were an unholy spell, it was, now, at least, in her desolation, a consoling one. He loved her; he wanted her. She knew that he was passionately eager to devote his life to her. He would wait expectantly until she wrote. With a few strokes of her pen she might end her irksome captivity in this wall-less prison of desert plain – this wilderness of gum and gidia.

As she lay there in the hammock, a child's clumpy boots pattered along the garden path and Tommy Hensor came up the steps with a big cabbage leaf gathered in his hand. He opened it out when he reached the veranda and displayed three Brazilian cherries, the first fruits of a plant growing in the Chinaman's garden.

'La——ship . . . La——shp! I got these myself. I made Fo Wung give 'em me for you.'

At any other time the child's offering would have been received, at any rate, graciously. Now Tommy shrank away, startled by the look on Lady Bridget's face and the forbidding gesture with which she warned him off.

'Go away! . . . Go away! . . .' she cried. 'I don't want you.'

Tommy's common, freckled little face crumpled up and his blue eyes filled with tears. He dropped the cabbage leaf and the cherished Brazilian cherries and ran down the steps again, blubbering piteously.

Lady Bridget got up as soon as the child had clicked the garden gate behind him. She was ashamed of the spasm of revulsion that had seized her. She wanted to cast away from her the dreadful thought his appearance had suddenly evoked. She picked up the cabbage leaf with the fruit and flung them over the railings into a flower bed, where the butcher-birds and the bower-birds quarrelled over them, and the big, grey bird in the gum tree on the other side of the fence cachinnated in derisive chorus to Bridget's burst of hysterical laughter.

A little later Maggie came out from the bedroom with some letters in her hand.

'I've laid holt on your mail, Ladyship, turning out your room. I expect you forgot all about it.'

Yes, she had forgotten, absolutely; it seemed years since Harry the Blower had passed by and Willoughby Maule had departed. She languidly inspected the envelopes. Nothing among them of any importance – except one.

It was a blue telegraph-service envelope, and had been forwarded on by the postman from Crocodile Creek, the nearest telegraph station. In the last fifteen months they had brought the bush railway a good deal further up the river, and Crocodile Creek was the present terminus. Thus the road journey was now considerably shorter than when Colin McKeith had brought his bride home.

Lady Bridget read the several lines of the cabled message over two or three times before the real bearings of it became clear to her fever-weakened intelligence.

At last she grasped the startling fact that the cablegram was from her cousin, Lord Gaverick, and that it had been despatched from London about seven days previously. This was what it said.

> '*Eliza Gaverick died twentieth leaves you Castle and fifty thousand difficulties executors your presence urgently desired wire if can come, Gaverick*'

Lady Bridget let the blue form drop on her lap. She stared out over the brown plain and the herds of lean beasts all shadowy in the smoky mist over the horizon, then round, along the wilderness of gidia scrub, with its charred patches afar off, from which there still rose thin spirals of smoke.

Destiny had spoken. Here was the order of release. There was no gaoler to keep the prison doors locked any longer – except – except – No, if she wished to break her bonds, Colin would never gainsay her.

Late that night the men came back from fighting the fire which they had now practically put out. Even in the moonlight they looked deplorable objects, grimed, covered with dust and ashes, their skins and clothes scorched by the fierce heat.

They seemed drunk with fatigue, and could scarcely sit their horses. When they dismounted they could hardly stand.

Their feeble *coo-ees* at the sliprails brought out Ninnis, who had been sent home in the afternoon and had been taking some well-earned repose so as to be ready for the next shift – happily not required. He and the few hands left to look after the head-station and the tailing-mob held the men's horses when their riders literally tumbled off them. Ninnis made McKeith take a strong pull of whiskey and supported him along to the Old Humpey. For Colin had had strength to say that Lady Bridget must on no account be disturbed. Ninnis led him to the room lately occupied by Willoughby

Maule, and was surprised at his employer's vehement refusal to remain in it.

'I'll not stop here. . . . No, I won't go to my dressing-room. In God's name, just let me stretch myself on the bunk in the Office and go to sleep.'

He threw himself on a bush-carpentered settle, with mattress and pillows covered in Turkey-red, which was used sometimes at mustering times when there was an overplus of visitors. There he lay like a log for close on twelve hours.

By and by, Lady Bridget, at once longing and reluctant, came softly in to see how he fared.

A storm of pity, anger, tenderness, repulsion – the whole range of feeling, it seemed, between love and hate – swept over her as she looked at the great gauntform stretched there. Colin was still in riding clothes and booted and spurred. His moleskins were black with smoke and charcoal; his flannel shirt, open at the neck, showed red scratches and scorch-marks on the exposed chest and was torn over the arms, where were more excoriations of the flesh. And the ravaged face! How hard it was. How relentless, even in the utter abandonment of bodily exhaustion! The skin was caked with black dust and sweat. The darkened thatch of yellow hair was dank and wet. The fair beard, usually so trim, was singed in places, matted, and had bits of cinder and burnt leaves sticking to it.

A revolting spectacle, offending Lady Bridget's fine, physical sensibilities, but a *man* – *the* Man. She could not understand that tornado of emotion which now made her being seem a very battleground, for all the primal passions. She turned away with a sense of nausea, and then turned to him again with a kind of passionate longing to take him in her arms – brutal as she thought him, and unworthy of the affection she had once felt for him – felt still alas! – and all the romance she had once woven about him. . . . She saw that a fly was hovering over the excoriated arm and drew the ragged sleeve over its bareness. Then she noticed the mosquito net reefed up on a hoop above the bunk, and managed to get the curtain down so that he should be protected from the assaults of insects. But as she touched him in doing this, he stirred and muttered wrathfully in his sleep, as though he were conscious of her tenderness and would have none of it; she fled away and came to him no more.

She had been racking her brain since receiving the cablegram as to what answer she should return to it.

After that pitiable sight of her husband, Bridget moved restlessly about the house, with intervals of lassitude in the hammock, for she still felt weak and ill. But quinine was keeping the fever down, and she resolved that her husband should not again be required to nurse her. She did not go into the Office any more, but busied herself in a defiant fashion upon little cares for his comfort when he awoke. He should see that she did not neglect her house-wifely duties – at least while she remained there to perform them. The qualification was significant of her mood.

Thus, she gave orders that the veranda of the Old Humpey should be kept free from disturbing footsteps, and saw that the bathroom was in order, and a change of clothing set ready for him when he should awake. Also that there should be a meal prepared.

He did not wake till the afternoon. She heard him go straight in to take his bath, and hastened to have the dining room table spread. But she saw him go out of the bathroom – all fresh and more like himself – and cross the yard on his way to the Bachelors' Quarters, making it clear to her that he wished to avoid the part of the house she occupied. Bridget went back to the front veranda in a cold fury, pierced by stabs of mental pain. She watched him from the end of the veranda go into the living room of the Quarters, and thought bitterly that he would ask Mrs Hensor for the food he required. No doubt too, he would obtain from Mrs Hensor, information as to how she herself had been getting on during his absence, and Mrs Hensor would give him a garbled report of her own dismissal from the sick room. . . . How dared he – oh! how *dared* he treat her, Lady Bridget, his wife, with such cruel negligence, such marked insult!

It did not occur to her that he might wish to see Ninnis, who, when at the station, was usually about this time, in his office at the back of the Bachelors' Quarters.

After a time, she heard Colin's voice again in the yard, and his step on the Old Humpey veranda. He came now by the covered passage on to that of the New House, and advanced towards her.

He only came, she told herself, because it would have seemed too strange had he continued to ignore her existence.

And he was conscious of her resentment. By a curious affinity, his own spirit thrilled to the unquenchable spirit in her. Qualities in himself responded to like qualities in her. He admired her pride and pluck. Yet the two egoisms reared against each other, seemed to him – could he have put the thought into shape – like combatants with lances drawn ready to strike.

He believed that it was love which gave her strength – love, not for him, but for that other man whose influence he was now convinced had always been paramount, and who with renewed propinquity had resumed his domination.

Certain phrases in that letter he had read long ago on Joan Gildea's veranda, and which had been haunting him ever since Willoughby Maule's re-appearance, struck his heart with the searing effect of lightning. He felt, at the first sight of her there on the veranda, before she turned full to him, a passionate yearning to take her in his arms, and cover her poor little wasted face with kisses – to call her 'Mate'; to remind her of that wonderful marriage night under the stars. But when he saw the proud aloofness of her look, his longing changed to a dull fury, which he could only keep in check by rigorous steeling of his will against any softening impulse.

So his face was hard as a rock, his voice rasping in its restraint, when he came near and spoke to her.

'You have not had any more fever?'

'No.'

He put two or three questions to her about her health – whether she had taken the medicine he had left for her, and so on, to which she returned almost monosyllabic replies, sufficiently satisfactory in the information they gave him.

'That's all right then,' he said coldly. 'I thought it would be, though I didn't at all like leaving you in such a condition.'

'Really! But it doesn't seem as if you had felt any violent anxiety about me since you came back. I heard you go to the bathroom a long time ago, and I saw you going up to the Quarters.'

He did not appear to notice the latter implication.

'I had to sleep,' he said curtly. 'I was dead beat.'

'Yes, I saw that,' she answered.

'A-ah!' The deep intake of breath made a hissing sound, and he flushed a brick red. 'You came and looked at me?'

'I went into the Office.'

'I didn't want you to see me. You must have loathed the sight of me. I was a disgusting object.'

She said nothing.

If he had glanced at her he would have seen a piteous flicker of tenderness pass over her face – a sudden wet gleam in her eyes. And had he yielded then to his first impulse, things might have gone very differently between them. But he kept himself stiffened. He would not lift his eyes, when she gave him a furtive glance. The expression of his half averted face was positively sinister as he added with a sneering little laugh.

'One can't look as if one had come out of a bandbox after fighting a bush fire.'

She exclaimed, 'Oh! what does it matter?'

He utterly mistook the meaning of her exclamation.

'You are quite right,' he retorted. 'When it comes to the end of everything, what does *anything* matter!'

For several moments there was dead silence. She felt as if he had wilfully stabbed her. He on his side had again the confused sense of two antagonists, feinting with their weapons to gain time before the critical encounter.

'Well?' He swung himself savagely round upon her. 'That's true, isn't it? The end *has* come. . . . You're sick of the whole show – dead sick – of the Bush – of everything? – Aren't you? Answer me straight, Bridget.'

'Yes, I am,' she replied recklessly. 'I hate the Bush – I – I hate everything.'

'Everything! Well, that settles it!' he said slowly.

Again there was silence, and then he said:

'You know I wouldn't want to keep you – especially now,' – he did not add the words that were on his lips 'now that bad times are coming on me,' – and she read a different application in the 'now.' 'I – I'd be glad for you to quit. It's as you please – maybe the sooner the better. I'll make everything as easy as I can for you.'

'You are very – considerate. . . .' The sarcasm broke in her throat.

She moved abruptly, and stood gazing out over the plain till the hysterical, choking sensation left her. Her back was to him. He could not see her face; nor could she see the dumb agony in his.

Presently she walked to a shelf-table on the veranda set against the wall; and from the litter of papers and work upon it, took up the cablegram she had lately received.

'I wanted to show you this,' she said stonily, and handed him the blue paper.

There was something significant in the way he steadied it upon the veranda railing, and stooped with his head down to pore over it.

The blow was at first almost staggering. It was as though the high gods had shot down a bolt from heaven, shattering his world, and leaving him alone in Chaos. They had taken him at his word – had registered on the instant his impious declaration. It *was* the end of everything. She was to quit.... He had said, the sooner the better.... Well – he wasn't going to let even the high gods get a rise out of him.

He laughed. By one of those strange links of association, which at moments of unexpected crisis bring back things impersonal, unconnected, the sound of his own laugh recalled the rattle of earth, upon the dry outside of a sheet of bark in which, during one of their boundary rides at Breeza Downs lately, they had wrapped for burial the body of a shepherd found dead in the bush. Both sounds seemed to him as of something dead – something outside humanity.

He handed her back the telegram, speaking still as if he were far-off – on the other side of a grave, but quite collectedly and as though in the long silence he had been weighing the question.

'It seems to me that this has come to you in the nick of time, to solve difficulties.'

'Yes,' she assented dully.

'You've got no choice but to go as your cousin says. There's money depending on it.'

'Money! ... Oh, money!' she cried wildly.

'Money is apt to stick on to lawyers' fingers when they're left to the handling of it.... This is a matter of business, and business can't be put on one side – especially, when there's as large a sum as fifty thousand pounds in the proposition. I guess from this that you're wanted.'

'Yes,' she said again. She was thinking to herself, 'That's his Scotch carefulness about money; he wouldn't consider anything in comparison with that.'

'You had better take the northern route,' he went on. 'There ought to be an E. and A. boat due at Leuraville pretty soon – I'll look it out.... Perhaps you'd like to make the start to-morrow?'

'To-morrow – oh yes, to-morrow – just whenever suits you.'

'I couldn't take you down myself. There are things – serious matters I've got to see to on the station. And besides, you'll allow it's best for me not to go with you. Ninnis could drive you to Crocodile Creek, and put you into the train; and Halliwell will look after you at Leuraville, and see you on board the steamer.'

'Oh, I wonder that you can spare Ninnis,' she returned bitterly. 'I suppose you'd want Moongarr Bill still more on the run. But there's

Joe Casey – I daresay somebody else can milk the cows, and get up wood and water. Or there's Cudgee – I don't mind who goes with me. . . . I can drive myself.'

'My God! do you imagine I'd put a black-boy – or anyone but my own trusted overseer in charge of you! What are you thinking of to talk like that?'

He took a few steps along the veranda, moving with uncertain gait; then stopped and leaned heavily against the wall. In a few seconds he had recovered himself, and came back to her, speaking quietly.

'I will think out things and arrange it all. You'll be perfectly safe with Ninnis, I think it would be better for you to sleep one night at old Duppo's place. There's fresh horses for the buggy there – I've got Alexander and Roxalana in the paddock now – they're the best. . . .'

Oh, how could he bear that those horses, of the dream-drive, should take her away from him! He went on in the same matter-of-fact manner. 'I expect the answer to the cablegram will get as quickly as if Harry the Blower took it, if you send it from Crocodile Creek yourself. And there's your packing – there's not much time, but you won't want to take a lot of things. Anything you cared about could go afterwards.'

'Go afterwards – What do you mean? I want to take nothing – nothing except a few clothes.'

'Ah well – it doesn't matter – As you said – nothing matters – now. . . . Well, I'll go and see Ninnis, and settle about to-morrow. . . . Then there's money. . . .' he stopped at the edge of the steps leading down to the Old Humpey, looking back at her – 'what you'll need for the passage – and afterwards – I know what you'll be thinking; but I can arrange for it with the Bank manager at Leuraville.'

A mocking demon rose in her.

'Please don't let yourself be inconvenienced. I only want the bare passage money. And directly I get to England I will pay you back.'

His hands dropped to his sides as if she had shot him. His face was terrible. At that moment, she could have bitten her tongue out.

'I don't think – you need have said that, Bridget,' and he went slowly down the steps, and out of her sight like a man who has received a mortal hurt.

CHAPTER 9

If purgatory could hold worse torture than life held on that last evening Lady Bridget spent at Moongarr, then neither she nor her husband would have been required to do any long expiation there. It would be difficult to say which of the two suffered the most. Probably McKeith, because he was the strongest. Equally, he showed it the least when the breaking moment had passed. Yet both husband and wife seemed to have covered their faces, hearts and souls with unrevealing masks. No, it was worse than that. Each was entirely aware of the mental and spiritual barrier, which made it absolutely impossible for them to approach each other in the sense of reality. A barrier infinitely more forbidding than any material one of stone or iron. Because it was living, poisoned, venomous as the fang of some monstrous deadly serpent. To come within its influence meant the death of love.

There was not much more of the day to get through. Husband and wife both got through it in a fever of activity over details that seemed scarcely to matter. He busied himself with Ninnis – first explaining to the overseer as briefly as he could, the necessity for Lady Bridget's voyage to England – a necessity that appealed to Ninnis' practical mind, particularly in the present financial emergency. It surprised him a little that McKeith should not himself see his wife off; but he also recognised practical reasons against that natural concession to sentiment. On the whole, it rather pleased him to find his employer ignoring sentiment, and he fully appreciated the confidence reposed in himself.

The two men went over questions connected with the journey, overhauling the buggy so that springs, bars and bolts might be in order, seeing that the horses were in good condition, sending on

Cudgee that very hour, with a second pair in relay for the long stage of the morrow, when over fifty miles must be covered. There would be another pair at old Duppo's, and, after a day and night of comparative rest, Alexander and Roxalana would be fresh for the last long stage of the journey. They calculated that under these provisions the railway terminus at Crocodile Creek, might be reached on the eve of the third day. And there were many instructions, and much careful arranging for Lady Bridget's comfort during the journey.

Then there were letters to write, business calculations, a further overdraft to be applied for to the Bank, pending the cattle sales. . . . Would there be saleable cattle enough to meet demands and expenses of sinking fresh artesian bores – now that the fire had destroyed all the best grass on the run?

McKeith found no consolation in the prospect of his wife's riches. That only added gall to his bitterness, new fuel to his stubborn pride, new strength to the wall between them.

He sat brooding in his office, when the business letters were written – to the Bank-manager; to Captain Halliwell, the Police-magistrate at Leuraville; to the Manager of the Eastern and Australian Steam Navigation Depot, Leuraville, enclosing a draft to pay the passage; to the Captain of the boat advertised for that trip, who happened to be an acquaintance of his – all recommending Lady Bridget to the different people's care – all anticipating and arranging against every possible drawback to her comfort on the voyage – all carefully stating the object of her trip to England – business connected with the death of a near relative. Then, after the ghastly pretence of dinner – during which appearances were kept up unnecessarily before Maggie and the Malay boy, by a forced discussion of matter-of-fact details – looking out the exact time of the putting in of the next E. and A. boat at Leuraville – all of which he had already done, and pointing out to Bridget that she could catch it, with a day to spare.

There was food for the journey too, to be thought of, and other things to talk about. As soon as the meal was ended, McKeith went back to the office, and Bridget saw or heard no more of him that night. He did not come even to his dressing-room. She concluded that he was 'camping' on the bunk in the office, and when her own packing was done, she lay in wakeful misery till dawn brought a troubled doze.

Her packing was no great business – clothes for the voyage, and a

big furred cloak for warmth, when she should arrive in England in
the depth of winter – that was all.

Everything else – her papers, knicknacks, personal belongings –
she left just as they were. Colin might do as he liked about them. She
felt reckless and quite hard.

Only one among those personal possessions moved her to
despairing tears. It was a shrivelled section of bark chopped from a
gum tree, warped almost into a tube.

She placed this carefully in the deepest drawer of her wardrobe.
Would Colin ever find it there – and would he understand? All the
time, through these preparations, strangely enough she did not think
of any possible future in connection with Willoughby Maule. The
events of the past few days seemed to have driven him outside her
immediate horizon.

When she came out in the morning dressed for her journey, she
found her husband in the veranda waiting to strap up and carry out
her baggage. Scarcely a word passed between them; they did not even
breakfast together. He said he had been up early, and had had his
breakfast already, but he watched her trying to eat while he moved
about collecting things for her journey, and he poured out the coffee,
and begged her to drink it. While he was there, Chen Sing brought in
the basket of food he must have ordered for the buggy, and there was
Fo Wung too, the gardener, with fresh lettuce and water-cress, and
a supply of cool, green cabbage leaves in which he had packed a few
early flat-stone peaches, and some Brazilian cherries.

Lady Bridget thanked them with the ghost of her old sweetness,
and they promised to have the garden 'velly good – *tai yat* number
one' and to 'make plenty nice dishes,' for the Boss during her
absence.

While they stood at the French window, McKeith filled flasks with
wine and spirits, and packed quinine and different medicines he had
prepared in case of her needing them. Then after shewing her the
different bottles, he took the supply out to Ninnis to be put in the
buggy.

Everything was ready now – the buggy packed, the hood unslung
so that it could be put up and down in protection against sun or rain
– this last alas! an improbable eventuality. Alexander and Roxalana
were champing their bits. Ninnis in a new cabbage-tree hat and clean
puggaree, wearing the light coat he only put on when in the society of
ladies he wished to honour, was standing by the front wheels

examining the lash of his driving-whip. McKeith had given him his last directions. There was nothing now to wait for. McKeith went slowly up the steps of the back veranda, and in at the French window of the sitting room, where Bridget had been watching, waiting. At his appearance, she went back into the room. She stood quite still, small, shadowy, the little bit of her face which showed between the folds of her motor veil, where it was tied down under her chin – very pale, and the eyes within their red, narrowed lids, dry and bright.

'Are you ready, Bridget?' he asked.

'Yes.'

He came close, and took a little bag she was holding out of her hands, carried it to the back veranda, and told one of the Chinamen to give it to Mr Ninnis – all, it seemed to her, to evade farewells. She called him back in a hard voice.

'Colin – I've left my keys,' – pointing to a sealed and addressed envelope on her own writing-table. 'There are a few things of value – some you have given me – in the drawers.'

'I will take care of them,' he answered hoarsely.

They stood fronting each other, and their eyes both smarting, agonised, stared at each other out of the pale drawn faces.

'Colin,' she said; and held out her hands. 'Aren't you going to say good-bye?'

He took her hands; his burning look met hers for an instant and dropped. There was always the poisonous wall which their soul's vision might not pierce – through which their yearning lips might not touch. For an instant too, the hardness of his face was broken by a spasm of emotion. The grip of his hands on hers was like that of a steel vice; she winced at the pain of it. He dropped her hands suddenly, and moved back a step.

'Good-bye – Bridget.'

'Is that all you have to say? All?'

He stuttered, helplessly. 'I – I – can't. . . . There's nothing to say.'

'Nothing! You let me go – like this – without one word of apology – of regret. I think that, at least, you owe me – courtesy.'

Her tone lashed him. He seemed to be struggling with his tongue-tied speech. When words came they rushed out in fierce jerks. 'I'll say this – though where's the good of talking. . . . What does it amount to anyway, when you're down on the bedrock, and there's nothing left but to give up the whole show and start fresh as best you can? I'll say this – I've never pretended to fine manners – I leave them – to others. I'm just a rough bushman, no better and no worse. Apology! – that's my apology – As for regret. My God! isn't it all one huge regret? No, I won't say that. . . . Because there are some things I *can't* regret – for myself. For you, I do regret them. I was an insane ass ever to imagine that I and my way of living could ever fit in with a woman brought up like you. The incompatibilities were bound to come out – incompatibilities of temper, education, breeding – outlook on things – they were bound to separate us sooner or later, I'm glad that it's sooner, because that gives you a chance of getting back into your old conditions before you've grown different in yourself – dried up – soured – maybe lost your health, roughing it through bad times in the bush. . . . As it is, you'll get out all right – Never fear that I won't see you get out all right.'

'And you?' she put in.

'Me! I don't count – I don't care. . . . A man's not like a woman. I've always been a fighter. And I've never been *downed* in my life. I'm not going to be *downed* this time. I shall make good – some time – somehow. I'm not the sort of small potato that drops to the bottom of the bag in the big shake-up.'

She winced visibly. He read distaste in her slight gesture, in the expression of her eyes. It was true that the man's pugnacious egoism – a lower side of him asserting itself just then – had always jarred upon her finer taste. He recognised this subconsciously, and his self-esteem revolted at it.

'You needn't be afraid,' he exclaimed harshly. 'If I wanted to hold to my rights, and keep you here with me – what has happened would prevent me – I've got too much pride to hang on to the skirts of a rich wife. But you won't be harmed. . . . I don't know yet, but I believe there's a way by which you can win through straight and square – no smirch that you need mind – And if there is – whatever the way of it is, I'll do my best to bring you out all right.'

'You are generous.' Her eyes flashed but her voice was coldly bitter. 'May I ask what you propose to do?'

'There's no use. . . .' he said heavily. 'I told you talking was no good – now. I've got my own ideas. . . .'

'Then, if that's how you feel, the sooner I go the better pleased you will be,' she returned hysterically. 'Oh, I'm ready to go.'

He moved to the steps, not answering at once. Then he said:

'The buggy is waiting, will you come?'

He went down the steps in front of her, but stopped at the bottom to help her, for her foot had stumbled on the edge of the veranda. His strong arm upheld her until she was on the gravel. The touch of his fingers on her arm, brought home the incredible horror of it all – the suddenness, the brutality. She pulled her veil hastily over her face to hide the gush of tears. She could not speak for the choking lump in her throat. He released her at once and strode on. Not another word passed between them. Ninnis greeted her with gruff cordiality – began a sort of speech about the cause of her departure – condolence and congratulations stupidly mixed. McKeith impatiently cut him short.

'All right, Ninnis. Get up. And mind, the horses are fresh. They'll want a bit of driving at the start.'

He helped Bridget to her seat, tucked the brown linen coverlet round her knees. In doing so, he bent his head – she thought he had dropped something. Then through the thin linen of the covering, and her light summer garments, she felt the pressure of his burning lips – as though they were touching her flesh.

She bent forward. Their eyes met in a wild look. Just for a second. The horses plunged under Ninnis' hands on the reins. McKeith sprang back.

'Wo——oh! Gee on then!' Ninnis called out. 'Good-bye, Boss. You can trust me to look well after her ladyship. . . . Be back again as soon as I can.'

And if Colin spoke, the sound did not carry to his wife's ears. Her last impression of him as the buggy swayed and rattled down the hill was again the dogged droop of his great shoulders.

It was too late now. She felt that the Furies were pursuing her. Ah, but the end had come – come with such hideous misconception – every word spoken – and there had been so few in comparison with the immensity of the occasion – a hopeless blunder. It had been the tussle of two opposing temperaments, it was was like the rasping steel of a cross-cut saw against the hard, heavy grain of an iron-bark gum log. Then the extraordinary involvements of circumstance. Each incident, big and little, dovetailing and hastening the onward sweep of catastrophe. It seemed as though Fate had cunningly engineered the forces on every plane so that there should be no escape for her victims. Like almost all the tragedies of ordinary human life, this one had been too swift in its action to allow of suitable dialogue or setting.

CHAPTER 10

From Joan Gildea to Colin McKeith.
Written about a year later.

MY DEAR COLIN,

I find it impossible to recognise my old friend in the hard,
business-like communication you sent me from Leichardt's Town.
I almost wish that you had allowed the lawyer you consulted to put
the case before me instead; it would have seemed less unfitting,
and I could have answered it better. But I quite appreciate your
objection to taking the lawyer into your confidence as regards the
personal matters you mention to me. It would be cruelly unjust – I
think quite unpardonable in you to bring forward the name of
Mr Willoughby Maule in connection with Bridget. Not that *he*
would mind that. I honestly believe that he would snatch gladly at
any means for inducing Bridget to marry him. Whether she would
do so, if you were to carry through this amazing scheme of yours,
it's impossible for me to say. At present she certainly prefers to
keep him at a distance. He has never been to Castle Gaverick. And
except for a few visits on business to London that is where she has
lived since she came over here.

Your letter followed me to Jamaica where I've been reporting on
the usual lines for *The Imperialist*, but, of course I couldn't answer
it until I had talked it over with Bridget and, as you desired, had
obtained her views on the matter. It was a shock to her to realise
that your reason for never writing to her and for refusing to let her
write to you, was lest that might affect the legality of these
proceedings, which I understand you have contemplated from the
beginning of your quarrel. Bridget is too proud to show you how

deeply she is wounded by your letter. All she has to say is, that if you really wish to take this action, she will not oppose it.

But Colin, do you really wish it? I refuse to believe that you seriously contemplate divorcing your wife. You must know that you have not the accepted grounds for doing so. As for the law you quote which allows divorce in cases of two years' so-called desertion, I can only say that I consider it a blot on Leichardt's Land legislation. Divorce should be for one cause only – the cause to which Our Lord gave a qualified approval; and Bridget has never been unfaithful – in act or desire, to her husband. I would maintain this in spite of the most damning testimony, and you must in your heart believe it also. Besides, your testimony is ridiculously inadequate.

I am glad, however, that you have at last made your accusations in detail – in order, as you say – that I – and Bridget, incidentally, I suppose – should fully understand why you are adopting this attitude towards her. I'm glad too, that you do not mean to make any use of the evidence against her and are prepared to take all the blame for the unhappy state of affairs between you! I write sarcastically. Why, it would be monstrous if you had any other intention! Oh, how I hate this pedantic roundabout way of writing! I feel inclined to tear up these sheets – I've torn up two already. Really, you've made it so difficult for me to treat you naturally. If I could talk to you, I'd make you understand in five minutes – but I can't – so there!

Naturally, I had heard of your bringing Mr Willoughby Maule to the station, and when I learned what followed, naturally also, I concluded that you had discovered his identity with that of the man Bridget had once cared for. I blame myself horribly. But for my carelessness you would never have read that letter of Biddy's – she knows all about it now – and your insane jealousy would not have jumped to conclusions – at any rate so quickly. And perhaps if I had not bound you to secrecy you'd have had the matter out with her, which would probably have saved all this trouble. Anyhow, I can't imagine that you would have left her alone with him as you did – and with bad feeling between you – at the mercy of her own reckless impulses and that of Willoughby Maule's ardent love-making. She doesn't pretend that it wasn't ardent, or that he did not do his best to get her to run away with him – or that the old infatuation did not come back to a slight extent – Is it surprising after your conduct? No wonder she compared his devotion favourably, with yours. Colin, your leaving her in such conditions wasn't the act of a *man*, of a gentleman. I speak strongly, but I can't help it. I know your stubborn pride and obstinacy, but you were wrong, you have disappointed me – oh! how bitterly you have disappointed me!

Then there was that business about the blacks. What a fool you were – and how brutally self-opinionated! I don't wonder Bridget thought you an inhuman monster.

Now I have said my worst, and you must take it as it is meant – and forgive me.

As for the true story of that night's adventures, out of which your Police Inspector seems to have made such abominable capital – I used to think Police Inspectors were generally gentlemen – but they don't seem to be, out on the Leura – I've got all the details from Biddy. A tragi-comic business – so truly of the Bush, Bushy! I could laugh over it, if it weren't for its serious consequences. Of course, Biddy got up to turn out the goats which were butting with their horns under the floor of her bedroom. I've often got up myself in the old days at Bungroopim, when stray calves got into the garden, or the cockatoo disturbed our slumbers. Do you remember Polly? and how she would keep shouting out on a moonlight night 'The top of the mornin' to ye' – because we'd forgotten to put her blanket over the cage – I believe there were several occasions when you and I met in midnight dishabille and helped each other to restore tranquillity. If anyone was to blame for Biddy's adventure, it was your wood-and-water joey – or your Chinamen – or whoever's business it may have been to see that the goats were properly penned.

Naturally, Mr Maule, when he was disturbed too, came and did the turning out for Bridget and shepherded the creatures to the fold.

Then meanwhile, she saw the black-gin sneaking in at Mr Maule's back window to steal the key; and *would* it have been philanthropic, impulsive Biddy, if she hadn't helped in the work of rescue, and sent the two sinners, with a 'Bless you, my children!' off into the scrub? It was like Biddy too, to go and put the key back in Mr Maule's bedroom and to scribble that ridiculous note in French so that he shouldn't go blundering to the hide-house and hurry up the pursuit.

I told Bridget how the Inspector had watched her go out of Mr Maule's room, and had grabbed the note afterwards, and shown it to you. She had forgotten altogether about that note – supposed that, of course, it had reached its proper destination. She couldn't remember either exactly what she had written – except that she wanted to word it so that if there should be any accident, nobody – except Mr Maule, for of course, they'd determined on the release before that – should understand to what it referred. So she didn't mention any name – she believes she dashed off some words he had quoted to her about Love triumphant, and securing happiness and freedom by flight. And then she put in something referring to a scene they'd had that day in which he had begged her to fly with him, and she had made him promise to leave next morning, pacifying him by a counter promise to write.

She told me about her fever and ague – you don't need proof of that after the state in which you found her – and how Mr Maule carried her to her room and left her there after a few minutes. She doesn't remember anything after that, until she came out of the fever and saw you – with the face and manner I can well imagine – standing by her bedside.

I am sure that Bridget began to 'find herself' then, and that the way in which she left Moongarr was one of those shocks which make a woman touch reality. It may be only for that once in her life, but she can never be the same again. You have put your brand on your wife, Colin – that is quite plain to me. She has changed inwardly more than outwardly.

But she is extremely reticent about her feelings towards you. That in itself is so unlike the old Bridget, and I have no right to put forward my own ideas and opinions – they may be quite wrong. Really, the news of Eliza Lady Gaverick's death, and of Bridget's change of fortune, coming just at that moment, is the sort of dramatic happening, which I – as a dabbler in fiction – maintain, is more common in real life than in novels. I am certain that if I had set out to build up the tangled third act of a problem play on those lines, I couldn't have done it better. All the same, I'm very sorry that this change of fortune didn't come off earlier or later, for I am well aware of how you will jib at it.

Well, I can tell you, on her own authority, that Bridget never wrote to Mr Maule as she had promised. She had no communication with him from the time he left the station until they met on the

E. and A. boat. He joined her, as you know, at the next port above Leuraville. It was rather canny of him to go there – yet I don't see how, in the circumstances, he could have loafed round Leuraville without making talk – though I think it was a great pity he didn't. Of course he had his own means of communication with the township, and knew she was on board. No one was more surprised than she at his appearance on deck next morning. I don't think, however, that she saw much of him on the voyage. She said that she got a recurrence of the malarial fever off the northern coast and had to keep her cabin pretty well till they reached Colombo. Then she asked him to leave the steamer and take a P. and O. boat that happened to be in harbour – and this he did do.

I am bound to say that Willoughby Maule must have improved greatly since the time when young Lady Gaverick decided he was a 'bounder.' I daresay marriage did him good. I believe that his wife was a very charming woman. Or, it may be that the possession of a quarter of a million works a radical change in people's characters. Or, again, it may be that he is more deeply devoted to Biddy than I, for one, ever suspected. There is no doubt that given the regrettable position, his behaviour in regard to her now is commendable.

But Bridget doesn't love him – never has loved him. I state that fact on no authority whatsoever except my own intuition. Also I am honestly of opinion she has cared for you more than she has cared for any man. You don't deserve it, and I may be wrong. But, nevertheless, it is my conviction. Make of it what you please. I have been, I candidly own it, surprised to see what discretion and good feeling she has shown through all this Gaverick will business. There has been a good deal of disagreeable friction in the matter. Lord Gaverick has not come off so well as he expected. He has got the house in Upper Brook Street, which suits young Lady Gaverick, and about fifteen hundred a year – considerably less than Bridget. The trouble is that Eliza Gaverick left a large legacy to her doctor – the latest one – and there was a talk about bringing forward the plea of undue influence. That, however, has fallen to the ground – mainly through Biddy's persuasion. I believe it is Bridget's intention to make over Castle Gaverick to her cousin, but this is not given out and of course she may change her mind.

And now, Colin, I think I have said everything I have to say. The main point to you is, no doubt, the answer to your question. As I said at the beginning of this letter, Bridget will not oppose any course you choose to take in order to secure your release from her – that is the exact way she worded it. But I cannot believe that, in face of all the rest I have told you, you will go on with this desertion – divorce business – at least without making yourself absolutely certain that you both desire to be free of each other. Remember, there has been no explanation between you and Biddy – no chance of touch between the true selves of both of you. Can you not come to England to see her? Or should she go out to you. I think it possible she might consent to do so, but have never broached the idea and cannot say. Yes, of course I understand that this might invalidate the legal position. But as only two years are necessary to prove the desertion – even if you should decide together that it is best to part – isn't it worth while to wait two years more in order to make quite sure? No doubt, you will say that I am shewing the proverbial ignorance of women in legal questions. But I can't help feeling that there must be some way in which it could be arranged. I do beseech you, Colin, not to act hastily.

You say that if this divorce took place, Bridget's reputation would not suffer, and that she could marry again without a stain upon her character as they say of wrongfully accused prisoners who are discharged. But again – is that the question?

I know nothing of your present circumstances – health, outlook on life – anything. Bridget once hinted to me that you might have your own reasons for desiring your freedom. She would give no grounds for the suspicion that there is any other woman in your life. I do not think anything would make me credit such a thing and I put that notion entirely out of court. I do not know – as your letter was dated from Leichardt's Town – whether you still live at Moongarr. It is possible you may have sold the place. I hear of severe droughts in parts of Leichardt's Land, but have no information about the Leura district. Now that Sir Luke Tallant has exchanged to Hong Kong, Bridget hasn't any touch with Leichardt's Land, and I have very few correspondents there.

Write to me – not a stilted, legal kind of letter like the last. Tell me about yourself – your feelings, your conditions. We are old friends – friends long before Bridget came either into my life or yours. You can trust me. If you do not want me to repeat to Bridget anything you may tell me, I will faithfully observe your wishes. But I can't bear that you, whom I should have thought so well of – have felt so much about – should be making a mess of your life, and that I should not put out a hand to prevent it.

                                        Always your friend,
                                                    JOAN GILDEA.

CHAPTER 11

It was a long time before Mrs Gildea received an answer to her letter. She had begun to despair of ever getting another line from Colin McKeith, when at last he wrote from Moongarr, six months later.

MY DEAR JOAN,

Your letter has made me think. I could not write before for reasons that you'll gather as you go along. I shall do as you ask and tell you everything as straightly and plainly as I can. I feel it is best that you should know exactly the sort of conditions I'm under and what a woman would have had to put up with if she had been with me – what she would have to put up with if she were going to be with me. Then you can judge whether or not I'm right in the decision I have come to as the result of my thinkings. You can tell my wife as much as you please – of the details, I mean. Perhaps, you had better soften them to her, for you know as well as I do – or better – that her impulsive, quixotic disposition might lead her into worse mistakes than it has done already. Of course, she'll have to know my decision. I am sure that if she allows her reason play, she will agree it is the only possible one.

I'm not going to talk about what happened before she went away, or about that evidence – or anything else in that immediate connection. I was mad, and I expect I believed a lot more than was true. I don't believe – I don't think I ever did really believe – what I suppose you would call 'the worst.' But that doesn't seem to me of such great matter. It's the spirit, not the letter that counts. The foundation must have been rotten, or there never would have been a question of believing one way or the other – because we should have *understood*. Explanations would not have been needed between true mates. Only we were not true mates – that's the whole point. There was too great a radical difference between us. It might have been a deal better if she *had* gone off with that man.

But to come now to the practical part of the situation. You know enough about Australian ups and downs to realise that a cattle or sheep owner out West, may be potentially wealthy one season and on the fair road to beggary the next. It will be different when times change and we take to sinking artesian bores on the same principle as when Joseph stored up grain in the fat years in Egypt against the lean ones that were coming. That's what I meant to do and ought to have done at any cost. But – well I just didn't.

The thing is that if I could have looked ahead, perhaps even six months, I might not have thought it acting on the square to a woman to get her to marry me. If I could have looked a year ahead, I wouldn't have had any doubt on the subject.

But you see I justified it to myself. One thousand square miles of country – fine grazing land most of it, so long as the creeks kept running – and no more than eleven thousand head of stock upon it, seemed, with decent luck, a safe enough proposition, though you'll remember I was a bit doubtful that day on your veranda at Emu Point, when we talked about my marrying. The truth was that directly I saw Bridget, she carried me clean off my head – and that's the long and short of it.

Besides, I'd been down south a good while, then, figuring about in the Legislative Assembly and swaggering on my prospects. I'd left Ninnis to oversee up here, and Ninnis didn't know the Leura like some of the old hands, who told me afterwards they'd seen the big drought coming as long back as that.

I remember one old chap on the river, when he was sold up by the Bank in the last bad times, and his wife had died of it all, saying to me, 'The Leura isn't the place for a woman.' And he was right. Well, I saw that I was straight up against it that spring when we had had a poor summer and a dry winter, and the Unionists started trouble cutting my horses' throats, and burning woolsheds and firing the only good grass on my run that I could rely upon. I didn't say much about it, but I have no doubt that it made me bad-tempered and less pleasant to live with. . . . That was just before the time Biddy went away. Afterwards, the sales I'd counted on turned out badly – cattle too poor for want of grass to stand the droving and the worst luck in the sale-yards I'd ever known.

First thing I did was to reduce the staff and bar everything but bare necessaries – I sent off the Chinamen and every spare hand. Ninnis and I and the stockman – a first-rate chap, Moongarr Bill – worked the run – just the three of us. You can guess how we managed it. A Malay boy did cooky for the head-station.

After Christmas I left Ninnis and Bill to look after the place. I had to go to Leichardt's Town. I had been thinking things out about Biddy all that time – you know I'm too much of the Scotchy to make hasty determinations. Well, I had that Parliament Bill, allowing divorce after two years desertion in my head, from the day Biddy left me. It seemed the best way out – for her. I had heard about that fellow going Home in the same boat with her, and never guessed but that it was a concerted plan between them. That note Harris showed me made me think it was so. I don't think this now – after what you told me.

But what did rub itself into me then was that I ought to let her marry him as soon as she decently could. I couldn't see the matter any other way – I don't now. He has lots of money – though a man who would buy happiness with another woman out of the money his wife had left him – well, that's a matter of opinion. Besides, she has got the fortune the old lady left her and can be independent of him if she chooses. There's nothing to prevent her living any kind of life that pleases her – except me, and I'm ready and willing to clear out of the show. One thing I'm sorry for now, and that is having torn up the draft she sent to pay me back her passage money, and putting the bits in an envelope and posting them to her without a word. I suppose it should have been done through a lawyer, with all the proper palaver. Perhaps she didn't tell you about that. I somehow fancy she didn't. But I know that it would have hurt her – I knew that when I did it. And perhaps that is why I did it. You are right. I haven't acted the part of a gentleman all through this miserable business. But what could you expect?

For you see, my father worked his own way up, and my grandfather was a crofter – and *I* haven't got the blood of Irish kings, on the other side, behind me.

Now I'm being nasty, as you used to say in the old Bungroopim days when I wouldn't play. *You* were my Ideal, in those days, Joan – before you went and got married. I've been an unlucky devil all round.

Well there! I had to try and arrange things for an overdraft with the Bank in Leichardt's Town, but I went down chiefly to consult lawyers about the divorce question, so that it should be done with as little publicity and unpleasantness as possible. It appeared that it could be done all right – as I wrote you. What would have been the good of my havering in that letter over my own feelings and the bad times I had struck? It never was my habit to whine over what couldn't be helped.

Luck was up against me down there too. I got pitched off a buckjumper at a horse-dealers', Bungroopim way. I had been 'blowing,' Australian fashion, that I could handle that colt if nobody else was able to. The end of it was that the buckjumper got home, not me. I was laid up in hospital for close on two months, with a broken leg and complications. The complications were that old spear wound, which inflamed, and they found that a splinter from the jagged tip had been left in. Blood-poisoning was the next thing; and when I came out of that hospital I was more like the used up bit of soap you'll see by the *coolibah*[1] outside a shepherd's hut on ration-bringing day, than anything else I can think of.

As soon as I could sit a horse again I went to work at Moongarr. I had found things there at a pretty pass. Not a drop of rain had fallen up to now on the station for nearly nine months. *You* know what that means on the top of two dry seasons. As soon as I was fit, we rode over the run inspecting – I and Ninnis and Moongarr Bill. There's a lot of riding over one thousand square miles, and we didn't get our inspection done quickly. Day after day we travelled through desolation – grass withered to chips, creeks and waterholes all but empty, cattle staggering like drunken men, only it was for *want* of drink. The trees were dying in the wooded country; and in the plains the earth was crumbling and shrinking, and great cracks like crevasses were gaping in the black soil where there used to be beautiful green grass and flowers in spring.

The lagoon was practically dried up, and the little drain of water left was undrinkable because of the dead beasts that had got bogged and dropped dead in it. They were short of water at the head-station, and we had to fetch it in from a waterhole several miles off that we fenced round and used for drinking – so long as it lasted. When we were mustering the other side of the run, it came

---

[1] *Coolibah* – a basin made from the scooped out excrescence of a tree.

to our camping at a sandy creek where we could dig in the sand and get just enough for horses and men. The water of the Bore I'd made, was a bit brackish, but it kept the grass alive round about and was all the cattle had to depend on. You can think of the job it was shifting the beasts over there from other parts of the run which was what we tried to do, so long as they were fit for it.

We were selling what we could while there was still life left in the herd, but the cattle were too far gone for droving. We managed to collect a hundred or so – sent them in trucks from Crocodile Creek Terminus, for boiling down and netted about thirty shillings a head on them. That was all. I guess that – by this time, out of my eleven thousand head with No. 666 brand on them I'd muster from four to five hundred. The mistake I made was in not selling out for what I could get at the beginning of the Drought. But it was the long time in Leichardt's Town that had me there.

It was bad luck all through from first to last. Mustering those beasts for boiling down started that old spear wound afresh. Until it got well again, there was nothing for it but to sit tight and wait.

Moongarr Bill left to make a prospecting trip on my old tracks up the Bight – took Cudgee and the black-boy with him. He had an idea that he'd strike a place where we'd seen the colour of gold on our last expedition, but weren't able then to investigate it. I've never been bitten by the gold fever like some fellows, and I daresay that I've missed chances. But I thought cattle were a safer investment, and I've seen too much misery and destruction come from following that gold will o' the wisp, for me to have been tempted to run after it.

Old Ninnis was the next to leave, I made him take the offer of a job that he had. When it came to drawing water five miles for the head-station, and keeping it in an iron tank sunk in the ground, with a manhole and padlocked cover for fear of its being got at, the fewer there were of us the better. Now the station is being run by the Boss and the Malay boy, who is a sharp little chap, and more use in the circumstances than any white man. We've killed the calves we were trying to *poddy*[1]. And the dogs – except one cattle dog – Veno – Biddy would remember her; how she used to lollop about the front veranda outside her room. Now, what the deuce made me write that! – Well, the dog goes with me in the cart when

[1] *Poddy* – to bring up by hand.

I fetch water, and takes her drink with the horses at the hole.

I'm getting used to the life – making jobs in the daytime to keep myself from feeling the place a worse hell than it really is. There's always the water to be fetched and the two horses and the dog to be taken for their big drink. If you could see me hoarding the precious stuff – washing my face in the morning in a soup plate, and what's left kept for night for the dog. When I want a bath I ride ten miles to the bore. Then there's saddlery to mend, and dry-cleaning the place and pipes between whiles – more of them than is good for me. Stores are low, but I've still got enough of tobacco. I daresay it's a mercy there's no whiskey – nothing but a bottle or two of brandy in case of snake-bites – or I might have taken to it.

Thank God I've got a pretty strong will, and I've never done as I see so many chaps do, find forgetfulness in drink – but there's no saying what a man may come to. It's the nights that are the worst. I'm glad to get up at dawn and see to the beasts. And there's that infernal watching of the sky – looking out all the time for clouds that don't come – or if they do, end in nothing. You know that brassy glare of the sun rising that means always scorching dry heat? Think of it a hundred times worse than you've ever seen it! The country as far as you can look is like the floor of an enormous oven, with the sky, red and white-hot for a roof, and all the life there is, being slowly baked inside. The birds are getting scarce, and it seems too much trouble for those that are about to lift their voices. Except for a fiend of a laughing-jackass in a gum tree close by the veranda that drives me mad with his devilish chuckling.

Well, how do you think now, that her ladyship would have stood up against these sort of conditions? Many a time, walking up and down the veranda when I couldn't sleep, I've thanked my stars that there was no woman hanging on to me any more. Most of the men on the river have sent away their women – stockmen's wives and all. There was one here at the Bachelors' Quarters, but I packed her off before I went to Leichardt's Town.

I'm just waiting on to get Moongarr Bill's report of the country up north – how it stands the drought, and what the chances are for pushing out. As for the gold find – well, I'm not banking on that. As soon as I hear – or if I don't hear in the course of the next two or three weeks – I shall pull up stakes, and burn all my personal belongings, except what a pair of saddle bags will carry.

Before long, I'm going to begin packing Biddy's things. They'll be shipped off to her all right.

When the divorce business is over, I shall make new tracks, and you won't hear of me unless I come out on top. I've got a queer feeling inside me that I shall win through yet.

Well, I'm finished; and it's about time. I've run my pen over a good many sheets, and it has been a kind of relief – I began writing this about three weeks ago. Harry the Blower – that's the mailman – comes only once a month now, and not on time at that.

I suppose the drought will break sooner or later, and when it breaks, the Bank is certain to send up and take possession of what's left. So I'm a ruined man, any way.

Good-bye, Joan, old friend. I've written to the lawyer, and Biddy will be served with the papers soon after this reaches you. I'm not sending her any message. If she doesn't understand, there's no use in words – but *you* know this. She's been the one woman in the universe for me – and there will never be another.

He signed his name at the end of the letter; and that was all.

CHAPTER 12

Harry the Blower came up with his mails a day or two later. Among the letters he brought, there were three at least of special importance to Colin McKeith.

One was from the late Attorney General of Leichardt's Land, in whose following he had been while sitting in the Legislative Assembly, and whom he had consulted in reference to the Divorce petition. This gentleman informed Colin that proceedings were already begun in the case of McKeith versus McKeith, and that notification of the pending suit had been sent to Lady Bridget at Castle Gaverick, in the province of Connaught, Ireland.

The second letter was from the Manager of the Bank of Leichardt's Land, regretfully conveying the decision of the Board that, failing immediate repayment of the loan, the mortgage on Moongarr station must be foreclosed and that in due course a representative of the Bank would arrive to take over the property.

The third letter was from Moongarr Bill, dated from the furthest Bush township at the foot of the Great Bight, which had formed the base of Colin's last exploring expedition. A mere outpost of civilisation it was – that very one which he had described at the dinner party at Government House where he had first met Lady Bridget O'Hara. Apparently, in Moongarr Bill's estimation, its only reason for existence lay in the fact that it had an office under the jurisdiction of the Warden of Goldfields, for the proclamation of new goldfields, and the obtaining of Miner's Rights.

Moongarr Bill's epistolary style was bald in its directness.

Dear Sir – he began: –
The biggest mistake we ever made in our lives was not following

up the streak of colour you spotted in that gully running down from Bardo Range to Pelican River. If we had stopped, and done a bit of stripping for alluvial, for certain, we should have found heavy, shotty gold, with only a few feet of stripping. But I've done better than that – got on the lead – dead on the gutter. To my belief, that gully is the top dressing of a dried up underground watercourse. It's a pocket chock full of gold.

You see, it's like this:

Here followed technical details given in local gold-digger's phraseology which would only be intelligible to a backwoods prospector or a Leichardt's Land mining expert. McKeith read all the details carefully, turning the page over and back again in order to read it once more. There was no doubt – making due allowance for Moongarr Bill's exaggerative optimism – that the find was a genuine one.

The writer resumed:

'I've pegged off a twenty men's ground, this – being outside the area of a proclaimed goldfield – our reward as joint discoverers. The ground joins on to your old pegs; and the wonder to me is that nobody has ever struck the place. However, that's not so queer as you might think, for there has been very little talk of gold up here – in fact the P.M. does Warden's work. Besides, the drought has kept squatters from pushing out, and it's too far off for the casual prospector. Luckily, the drought has driven the Blacks away too, further into the ranges; and I haven't seen any Myalls this trip like the ones that went for us last time. It's a pity Hensor pegged out then. He'd have come in for a slice of luck now – we three being the only persons in the world – until I lodged my information at the Warden's office this morning – who had ever raised the colour in this district or had any suspicion of a show. I reckon though that if the find turns out as I think, you'll be making things up to little Tommy.

I'm to have my Miners' Right all properly filled up to-morrow, and shall make tracks back to the gully at once, so as to leave no chance of the claim being jumped. I've named it "McKeith's Find" so your name won't be forgotten. I don't count on a big rush at first – all the better for you – but I shall be surprised if we are not entitled at the end of four months to our Government reward of

£500, as there are pretty sure to be two hundred miners at work by that time.

I'm writing to Ninnis – though I don't know if he has done his job yet – telling him to lose no time in getting here; and you won't want telling to do the same. I reckon that whether the drought has broken by this time or not, it will pay you better to start for here than to wait at the station until there are calves coming on to brand and muster. Ninnis will be in with us all right, and it would be a fine thing if you came up together. He's a first-rate man, and has had a lot of experience in the Californian goldfields. Poor luck, however, or he wouldn't have come over to free-select on the Leura.

It took me a good three weeks to get as far as the Pelican Creek, and I couldn't have done it in the time if there had been Blacks about. Knowing the lay of the country too, made it easier than it was before for us. Cudgee has turned out a smarter boy than Wombo was. No fear of Myalls with their infernal jagged spears being round without his sniffing them. One of the horses died from eating poison-bush. Don't go in for camping at a bend in Pelican Creek, between it and a brigalow scrub, first day you sight Bardo Range going up the Creek, where there's a pocket full of good grass one side of a broken slate ridge – *it's no good*. But I wouldn't swop the other horses for any of Windeatt's famous breed. There's some things it would be well for you and Ninnis to bring, and a box of surveyor's compasses would come in handy.

Here followed half a page on practical matters,, and then the letter ended.

McKeith pondered long over Moongarr Bill's letter, as he sat in the veranda smoking and watching a little cloud on the horizon, and wondering whether rain was coming at last. . . . If Moongarr Bill was right, the gold-find would mean a fresh start for him in his baulked career. At any rate, it behoved him to take advantage of the chance and to go forth on the new adventure without unnecessary delay. But the savour was gone for him from adventure – the salt out of life. The stroke of luck – if it were one – had come too late.

And now the Great Drought had broken at last.

Next evening there came up a terrific thunderstorm, and a hurricane such as had not visited the district for years. It broke in the direction of the gidia scrub, and razed many trees. It passed over the head-station and travelled at a furious rate along the plain. Hailstones fell, as large as a pigeon's egg, and stripped off such leafage as the drought had left. Thunder volleyed and lightning blazed. Part of the roof of the Old Humpey was torn off. The hide-house was practically blown away. The great white cedar by the lagoon was struck by lightning, and lay, a chaos of dry branches and splintered limbs, one side of the trunk standing up jagged and charred where it had been riven in two.

Upon the hurricane followed a steady deluge. For a night and a day, the heavens were opened, and poured waterspouts as though the pent rain of nine months were being discharged. The river 'came down' from the heads and filled the gully with a roaring flood. The lagoon was again almost level with its banks. The dry water-course on the plain sparkled in the distance, like a mirage – only that it was no mirage. No one who has not seen the extraordinary rapidity with which a dry river out West can be changed into a flooded one, could credit the swiftness of the transformation.

Then the heavens closed once more. The sun shone out pitilessly bright, and the surface earth looked, after a few hours, almost as dry as before. But the life-giving fluid had penetrated deep into the soil; the rivers and creeks were running; green grass was already springing up for the beasts to feed upon. The land was saved. Alas too late to save the ruined squatters. There were so few of their beasts left.

Nevertheless, the rain brought new life and energy to the humans. Kuppi, the Malay boy fetched buckets of water from the replenished lagoon, and scoured and scrubbed with great alacrity. He came timidly to his master, and asked if he might not wash out with boiling water the closed parlour and Lady Bridget's unused bedroom. He was afraid that the white ants might have got into them.

McKeith's face frightened Kuppi. So did the imprecation which his innocent request evoked. He was bidden to go and keep himself in his own quarters, and not show his face again that day at the New House.

Since Lady Bridget's departure, McKeith had slept, eaten and worked in the Old Humpey, his original dwelling.

But Kuppi did not know that the white ants had not been given a chance to work destruction upon 'the Ladyship's' properties. Regularly every day, McKeith himself tended those sacred chambers. Bridget's rooms were just as she had left them.

He had done nothing yet towards dismantling that part of the New House in which she had chiefly lived. He had put off the task day after day. But since receiving Moongarr Bill's letter, and now that the drought had broken, and the Man in Possession a prospect as certain as that there would come another thunderstorm, he knew that he must begin his preparations to quit Moongarr.

To do this meant depriving himself of the miserable comfort he found during wakeful nights and the first hour of dawn – the time he usually chose for sweeping and cleaning his wife's rooms – of roaming, ghost-like, through the New House where every object spoke to him of her. In the day time, he shrank from mounting the steps which connected the verandas, but in the evenings, he would often come and stroll along the veranda, and sit in the squatter's chair she had liked, or in the hammock where she had swung, and smoke his pipe and brood upon the irrevocable past. And then he would suddenly rush off in frantic haste to do some hard, physical work, feeling that he must go mad if he sat still any longer.

To-day however, after Kuppi had fled to the kitchen, he went into his old dressing room and stood looking at the camp bed, and thought of the day of Bridget's fever when Harris had given him her note to Maule, and he had sat here huddled on the edge of the bed wrestling dumbly with his agony. The association had been too painful, and in his daily tendance he had somewhat neglected this room and had usually entered the other by the French window from the veranda. Thus, he saw now that a bloated tarantula had established itself in one corner, between wall and ceiling, and an uncanny looking white lizard scuttered across the boards, and disappeared under a piece of furniture, leaving its tail behind. A phenomenon of natural history at which, he remembered now, Bridget had often wondered.

He opened the door of communication – where on that memorable night, he had knocked and received no answer – and passed through it treading softly as though he were visiting a death chamber. And indeed, to him, it was truly a death chamber in which the bed, all covered over with a white sheet, might have been a bier, and the pillows put lengthwise down it, the shrouded form of one dearly loved and lost. He gazed about, staring at the familiar pieces of furniture, out of wide red eyes, smarting with unshed tears. In her looking glass, he seemed to see the ghost-reflection of her small pale face with its old whimsical charm. The shadowy eyes under the untidy mass of red-brown hair, in which the curls and tendrils stood out as if endowed with a magnetic life of their own; the sensitive lips; the little pointed chin; and, in the eyes and on the lips, that gently mocking, alluring smile.

There were a few poems that Colin had taught himself to say by heart, and which he would recite to himself often when he was alone in the Bush. *The Ancient Mariner* was one, and there were some of Rudyard Kipling's and he loved *The Idylls of the King* – in especial *Guinivere*. Three lines of that poem leaped to his memory at this moment.

> *'Thy shadow still would glide from room to room*
> *And I should evermore be vext with thee*
> *In hanging robe and vacant ornament.'*

He went to the wardrobe where her dresses hung as she had left them, only that daily, he had shaken them, cared for them so that no hot climate pest should injure them. And in so doing, he had been overwhelmingly conscious of the peculiar, personal fragrance, her garments had always exhaled – an experience in which rapture and anguish blended.

How he had loved her! ... God! how he had loved her! ... And yet, latterly, how he had got to take his supreme possession of her as a matter of course; had allowed the joy of it to be blunted by depression and irritability over sordid station worries. He remembered with piercing remorse how often he had neglected the trivial courtesies to which he knew she attached importance. How he had been prone to sullen fits of moodiness; had been rough, even brutal, as in that episode of the Blacks. ... Brutal to her – this dainty lady, his fairy princess! ... And now he had lost her. She was gone back to her own world and to her own kin.

If only he had yielded to her then about the Blacks! If he had curbed his anger, shown sympathy with the two wild children of Nature who were better than himself, in this at least that they had known how to love and cling to each other in spite of the blows of fate! He had horse-whipped Wombo for loving Oola, and swift retribution had come upon himself. ... That he should have lost Bridget because of the loves of Wombo and Oola! It was an irony – as if God were laughing at him. He set his teeth and laughed – the mirthless laugh which had startled Harris. ... Well, whether it were automatic or planned retribution on the part of the High Powers, the trouble could be evened up and done with. 'I was a damned fool,' he said to himself; 'and I've been taught my lesson too late for me to benefit by it. Except this way – I'm not going to be *downed* for ever. I'll go through my particular piece of hell, on this darned old earth if I must, and then I'll wipe the slate and come out on top of something else that isn't love. There's possibilities enough along the Big Bight to satisfy most men's ambition. And it's not much odds any way, so long as *she* isn't seriously hurt.'

With that summing up of the matter, he seemed to gain stoic energy. Now he went back to his dressing room, and pulled out to the veranda a couple of worn portmanteaux. Into these he put a variety of personal belongings. Among them, pictures from the walls, and old photographs in frames that had been on the dressing table. It was significant that none of these were portraits of his wife. The portmanteaux he dragged along the veranda to the side of the steps leading down to the front garden. Then, instead of returning to Lady Bridget's room, he attacked an escritoire in the parlour in which he had kept family and private papers, and which flanked her Chippendale bureau. He brought out another collection – note-books, papers, bundles of letters dating much further back than his occupation of Moongarr – salvage from the wreck of his old home. His mother's workbox; his father's *Shakespeare*; the family Bible – a piteous catalogue. He looked long at the book and the photographs. These last were portraits of his father, his mother and his sisters, who had all been massacred by the Blacks, when he was a boy. He separated all such relics from the general lot, placing them, and also two or three packets of papers upon a shelf-table in the veranda – it was that table where Lady Bridget had laid the cablegram from Lord Gaverick, which she had shown him the day before she had left Moongarr. Now it seemed to him an altar of sacred memories. He brought various other small things out of the parlour – things he had not the heart to destroy – all belonging to his youth – and placed them there. As he looked at them, a sudden thought seemed to strike him, and a wave of emotion passed over his face, softening its hardness for an instant. But the grimness came back. He made a quick movement back to Lady Bridget's room; and when, after a minute or two, he came out again, he was carrying a curious object which he had taken out of the deep drawer beneath her hanging wardrobe. It was a dry piece of gum-tree bark, shrivelled and curled up at the sides, so that the two edges almost met. At first he put it on the heap that he had turned out of the portmanteaux for destruction. His grim thought had been to top with this strange memorial of his marriage-night, the funeral pyre he had intended to build. But again the spasm of emotion contorted his features. His shoulders shook, and a dry choking sound came from his lips. He took up the piece of bark too, and laid it with the daguerreotypes on the table.

He seemed afraid to give himself time to think, but went from room to room here and in the Old Humpey, dragging one thing after another out on to the veranda. Some of the heavier articles he had to hoist over the steps connecting the two verandas, and then to drag them down the other steps into the front garden, where they strewed the gravel round the centre bed.

In spring and summer, when the Chinamen had been there to water and Lady Bridget to superintend the planting and pruning, this bed had always been gay with flowers, banking a tall shrub of scented verbena the perfume of which she had been particularly fond of. Now there were weeds – most of them withered – instead of flowers. The verbena bush had long been dead, and the dry leaves and branches, beaten down by the late storm, made a bed of kindling.

Never was there garden so desolate – the young ornamental trees and shrubs all dead; the creepers dead also; even the hardy passion vines upon the fence, mere leafless, fruitless withes of withered stems.

McKeith paused after lugging down two squatters' chairs – the first house carpentering he had done for his wife after their arrival at the head-station, and in which, he had resolved, no future owner of Moongarr should ever sit. That was the thought fiercely possessing him. Rough chairs and tables and such-like that had been there always, might remain. But no sacrilegious hands should touch things made for her, or with which she had been closely associated. They should be burned out here in the deserted front garden, where not even Kuppi – the only other occupant of the head-station – would witness his preparations. He himself would lay and kindle the funeral pyre, and to-night, when there would be only the stars to see him, he would light the first holocaust.

He stood considering. Sweat dropped from his forehead. His gaunt frame was trembling after his effort, which had been heavy, and he leaned against one of the tarred piles supporting the veranda to rest. But only for a few minutes. Then, his feverish activity recommenced. He piled up the wooden furniture on the bed of withered verbena branches, filled the interstices with dead leaves that he collected from the garden, laid the smaller things – books, papers, pictures – where they would asssist the conflagration, and did not stop until the pyre had reached to the level of the veranda railing. He reflected grimly that there was a chance of sparks setting fire to the house itself, and calculated the extent of the gravel between, deciding that if he was there to watch there would be no danger.

All the time, the old kangaroo dog, Veno had been nosing round him, sniffing at the objects lying round, then looking up at him with bleared, wistful eyes, and evidently unable to understand these strange proceedings. Once or twice, he had roughly pushed the dog away, but, when he had finished the work and seated himself from sheer fatigue on the veranda steps, Veno came and squatted beside him, the dog's head upon his knee. He filled his pipe and smoked ruminatively; the exertion had had one good effect; it had dulled the fierceness of his pain.

As he sat there – a faint breeze that had risen with the approach of sunset, cooling his heated body – he thought again about Moongarr Bill's letter. He looked at the great pyre in front, and caught the gleam of the lagoon below through the bare branches of the trees – the little ripple on its surface, the freshening green at its marge. Then he gazed out over the vast plain towards the horizon. From his low position on the steps, the middle distance was hidden from him. Through the reddish tinge cast by the lowering sun, he could discern, far off likewise, the unmistakable signs of new-springing grass and the course of the river, for so long non-existent. From the gully he heard the sound of rushing water. It had been a roaring torrent just after the storm, and he knew that a flood must have come down from the heads.

Yes, the Drought had broken. The plain would soon be green again. Flowers would spring up as they had done for Bridget's bridal home-coming. If the rain had fallen a few months sooner the station might have been saved.

And even now, with the remnant of three or four hundred cattle, provided there were no crippling debt, no spectre of the Man in Possession, he might still hang on, and in time retrieve his losses, lie low, sink artesian wells, make the station secure for the future.

He had been so fond of the place. He had taken up the run with such high hopes; had so slaved to increase his herd, to make improvements on the head-station. He had looked upon this as the nucleus of his fortune; the pivot on which his career as one of the Empire-builders would revolve. . . . And now. . . .

Well, some clever speculator no doubt would buy it at a low price during the Slump, stock it with more cattle, work it up during a good season or two, and, when cattle stations boomed once more, sell it at an immense profit. That was what he himself would have done had he been a speculator in similar conditions. Even still, he could do it with a small amount of capital to supply a sop for the Bank. . . . Now that the Drought had broken they would be more likely to let him go on. . . . He thought of the £3,000 Sir Luke Tallant had made him put into settlement on his marriage. He had not wanted to do that at the time; his Scotch caution had revolted against the tying up of his resources, and his instinct was justified. If only he had command of that money now! It was his own; his wife was rich; that was the one benefit he could have taken from her. . . . But it was impossible to broach the question.

Suddenly the dog stirred uneasily, sniffed the air and leaped to the gravel walk where it stood giving short, uncertain barks, as though aware of something happening outside for which it could not account.

McKeith lifted his head, bent in the absorption of his thought, and looked about for the disturber of Veno's placidity. But Kuppi was nowhere in sight, nor was there sign of other intruder. Where he sat, the garden fence, overgrown with withered passion vines, bounded his vision, and had anybody ridden or driven up the hill through the lower sliprails, he would not have seen them, probably would not have heard them. For there were no longer dogs, black boys, Chinamen or station hands to voice intimation of a new arrival. All the old sounds of evening activity were hushed. No mustering-mob being driven to the stockyard; no running up of milkers or horses for the morrow; no goats to be penned – they had been killed off long ago; no beasts grazing or calling – no audible life at all except that of the birds, who, since the rain, had found their notes again and were telling each other vociferously that it was time to go to bed. Indeed, the silence and solitariness of the once busy head-station had enticed many of the shyer kinds of birds from the lagoon and the forest. Listening, as he now was, intently, McKeith could hear the gurgling *Coo–roo–roo* of the swamp pheasant, which is always found near water – and likewise rare sound – the silvery ring of the bell-bird rejoicing in the fresh-filled lagoon.

But Veno was still uneasy, and Colin got up on to the veranda. He stood there, listening all the while, strained expectancy in his eyes as if he too were vaguely conscious of something outside happening. . . .

And now he did hear something that made him go white as with uncanny dread. It was a footstep that he heard on the veranda of the Old Humpey – very light, a soft tapping of high heels and the accompanying swish of drapery – a ghostly rustle – 'a ghostly footfall echoing.'. . . For surely in this place it could have no human reality.

It approached along the passage between the two buildings, halted for a few seconds, and then mounted to the front veranda.

The man was standing with his back to the Old Humpey. He would not turn. A superstitious fear fell upon him and made his knees shake and his tall, lean frame tremble. . . . He *dared* not turn his head and look lest he should see that which would tell him Bridget was dead.

But the dead do not speak in syllables that an ordinary human ear can hear. And Colin heard his own name spoken in accents piercingly clear and sweet.

'Colin.'

To him, though, it was as a ghost-voice. He stood transfixed. And just then the dog bounded past him. It had flown up the steps barking loudly. That could be no immaterial form upon which the creature flung itself, pawing, nosing, licking with the wildest demonstrations of joy.

He heard the well-remembered tones:

'Quiet Veno. . . . Good dog. . . . Lie down Veno – Lie down.'

The dog seemed to understand that this was not a moment for effusiveness. Without another sound, it crouched upon its haunches gazing up at the new-comer.

Then Colin turned. Bridget was standing not a yard from him. A slender figure in a grey silk cloak, with bare head – she had flung back her grey sun-bonnet and shrouding gauze veil. . . . He saw the face he knew – the small, pale face; the shadowy eyes, wide and bright with an ecstatic determination, yet in them a certain feminine timorousness; the little pointed chin poked slightly forward; the red-brown hair – all untidy curls and tendrils, each hair seeming to have a life and magnetism of its own. It was just as he had so often pictured her in dreams of sleep and waking.

He gazed at her like one who beholds a vision from another world. And then a great sob burst from him – the pitiful sob of a strong man who is beaten, broken with emotion. The whole being of the man seemed to collapse. He staggered forward, and such a change came over the gaunt, hard face, that Bridget saw it through a rain of tears which fell down her cheeks.

'Oh, Colin – Won't you speak to me?'

'Biddy!' He went close to her and gripped her two wrists, holding her before him while his hungry eyes seemed to be devouring her.

'It's you – it's really you. You're not dead, are you?'

'Dead! Oh no – no. . . . I've come home.'

'Home!' He laughed.

'Oh don't – don't,' she cried. 'Don't laugh like that.'

'Home!' he repeated, grimly. 'Look round you. A nice sort of home. Eh?'

'I don't care. It's the only real home I've ever had.'

'But look – look!'

She followed his eyes to the great pyre in the garden, with the dead leaves, and the pieces of furniture, the squatters' chairs, the little tables he and she had covered together, the hammock that he had cut down leaving the ropes dangling – many other things that she recognised also. Then her gaze came back to the veranda. To the open portmanteaux; the different objects still strewing the ground; and then to the shelf-table against the wall near the hammock, and, there, to his most cherished possessions. She knew at once his mother's work-box, the shabby *Shakespeare* – the portraits, and, on top of all, the piece of gum-tree bark.

She snatched her wrists from his grasp, darted to the shelf, seized the shrivelled piece of bark, and pressed it against her bosom as though it had been a living thing.

'Oh, you *couldn't* burn this! . . . You were going to burn it with the rest – but you *couldn't* – any more than you could have burned your mother's things. . . . I thought of it all the way – I knew that if you could burn this, too, there would be no hope for me any more. I *prayed* that you might not burn it.'

'But how – how did you know I was going to burn the things?' he stammered bewilderedly.

'I saw it all – I saw you – just like this, on the veranda – so thin and hard and miserable – and so proud, yet – and stubborn – I saw it all – saw the bonfire ready – And I saw this piece of bark – And then something made you stop and you put it with your mother's things instead. You remembered – Oh! Mate, you *did* understand? You *did* remember – that first night by the camp fire – and we two – just we two' – she broke off sobbing.

'You saw – you saw –' he kept saying. 'But how – how did you know? Tell me, Mate.'

'I saw it all in a dream – at Castle Gaverick. Three times I dreamed the same dream; and I felt, inside me, that it was a prophetic warning. We're like that, you know, we Irish Celts. And you – though you're a Scotchman – you used to laugh at such things! But they're true; they're true – I've had glints of second sight before. Joan Gildea understood. When I told her, she believed it was a warning God had sent me, and she said I must go to you – go at once lest it should be too late. She wanted to come with me, but it would have been difficult for her to leave her work, and I didn't want her – I wanted to come to you all on my own.'

'And then? – then?' he asked breathlessly.

'Oh, then I left Castle Gaverick at once, and, in London, I took my passage – there was an E. and A. boat just going to start. Of course I knew the route. I got out of the steamer at Leuraville, and came straight on by train – I didn't wait anywhere. I thought I'd get out at Crocodile Creek and pay somebody to drive me up here. But you've got the railway brought nearer, and when I got out at Kangaroo Flat there was a most extraordinary thing – Then, I knew why the voice inside had been urging me on so quickly.'

'An extraordinary thing –? What was it?' he said in the same breathless, broken way.

'It was Mr Ninnis. He was there, standing on the platform just off his droving trip – he was going to take the next train to Leuraville. If I had stayed there as Captain Halliwell wanted me to, I should have missed him. He'd got a letter from Moongarr Bill – Oh, I know all about that. But it doesn't matter – it doesn't matter in the least. You can go if you like and find the gold – I'll stop at Joan Gildea's cottage in Leichardt's Town and wait for you – I don't care about *anything* if you'll only let me be your Mate again. But Colin –' she rushed on, for he could not speak, and the sight of a great man struggling with his tears is one that a woman who loves him can scarcely bear to see. And yet the sight made Bridget happy for all its pain – 'Colin, when I first saw Ninnis, do you know what I thought –? That you had sent him to meet me. That you, too, had been warned in a dream?'

'No, I wish I had been – My God, I wish I had been.'

'What would you have done, Colin?'

'I'd have been there myself,' he said simply. 'It would have been me, not Ninnis, that you saw at Kangaroo Flat Station.'

She held out her arms. The roll of bark dropped on the boards of the veranda. In a moment he was pressing her fiercely to his breast, and his lips were on hers.

And in that kiss, by the divine alchemy of true wedded love, all the past pride and bitterness were transmuted into a great abiding Peace.